Romantic Suspense

Danger. Passion. Drama.

Dangerous Christmas Investigation
Virginia Vaughan

Colorado Christmas Survival
Cate Nolan

MILLS & BOON

DANGEROUS CHRISTMAS INVESTIGATION
© 2024 by Virgina Vaughan
Philippine Copyright 2024
Australian Copyright 2024
New Zealand Copyright 2024

First Published 2024
First Australian Paperback Edition 2024
ISBN 978 1 038 93557 1

COLORADO CHRISTMAS SURVIVAL
© 2024 by Mary Curry
Philippine Copyright 2024
Australian Copyright 2024
New Zealand Copyright 2024

First Published 2024
First Australian Paperback Edition 2024
ISBN 978 1 038 93557 1

MIX
Paper | Supporting
responsible forestry
FSC® C001695

Published by
Harlequin Mills & Boon
An imprint of Harlequin Enterprises (Australia) Pty Limited
(ABN 47 001 180 918), a subsidiary of HarperCollins
Publishers Australia Pty Limited
(ABN 36 009 913 517)
Level 19, 201 Elizabeth Street
SYDNEY NSW 2000 AUSTRALIA

Cover art used by arrangement with Harlequin Books S.A.. All rights reserved.

Printed and bound in Australia by McPherson's Printing Group

Dangerous Christmas Investigation

Virgina Vaughan

MILLS & BOON

Virginia Vaughan is a born-and-raised Mississippi girl. She is blessed to come from a large Southern family, and her fondest memories include listening to stories recounted around the dinner table. She was a lover of books from a young age, devouring tales of romance, danger and love. She soon started writing them herself. You can connect with Virginia through her website, virginiavaughanonline.com, or through the publisher.

Books by Virginia Vaughan

Love Inspired Suspense

Lone Star Defenders

Dangerous Christmas Investigation

Cowboy Protectors

Kidnapped in Texas
Texas Ranch Target
Dangerous Texas Hideout
Texas Ranch Cold Case

Cowboy Lawmen

Texas Twin Abduction
Texas Holiday Hideout
Texas Target Standoff
Texas Baby Cover-Up
Texas Killer Connection
Texas Buried Secrets

Visit the Author Profile page at millsandboon.com.au for more titles.

And I will restore to you the years that the locust
hath eaten, the cankerworm, and the caterpiller,
and the palmerworm, my great army
which I sent among you.
—*Joel* 2:25

To Carter. Your adventurous spirit inspires me to try new things. You always have a smile on your face and laughter in your heart. Your kind and loving spirit makes me so proud of the person you are becoming.

Chapter One

Deputy Sabrina Reagan hummed along to a Christmas song playing on the radio as she waited at the stoplight to make a left-hand turn into the shopping center parking lot. A chill had settled in the December air and, for the first time in years, she was looking forward to the approaching holiday. Christmas decorations had sprung up everywhere she looked. The light poles that lined the streets had been adorned with flags reading Merry Christmas or Happy Holidays at each intersection, the radio station played Christmas songs on a loop and a twenty-foot Christmas tree had been erected in court square of their little Texas town. She'd promised her son, Robby, that they would go to the lighting ceremony this weekend and she was looking forward to seeing the smile on his little face at all the lights and wonder of the season. It had been a long time since she'd looked forward to Christmas but this year, finally, she was, and Robby had a lot to do with it.

A horn honked behind her and she realized she had the turn arrow. She waved to the offended driver then made her left turn. She'd been lost in thought about Christmas again. This was the first year that Robby was really old enough to understand what was happening—as much as a four-year-old could understand. She glanced in her rearview mirror and adjusted it to see him sleeping in his car seat on the back seat. The Christmas party at his preschool had worn him out. When she'd picked him up, he'd run to her with pictures he'd drawn, crafts he'd made and a secret present for her inside a paper sack that he'd forbidden her to peek at.

She thought of her brother, Robby's namesake, and how much he would have loved seeing his nephew's eyes sparkle at all the Christmas lights. She was determined to make this Christmas a good one. They were due. Her brother's death five years ago had shattered her peace and turned Sabrina's life upside down. She was finally, slowly climbing out of a spiral of grief and her little boy had been the one to give her the will to want to live again.

She pulled into a parking space in front of the grocery store and glanced at Robby's face as he slept. Despite his name, it wasn't her brother's face she saw reflected in the features and mop of dark hair.

Jake.

She'd clung to Robby as her lifeline after her brother's death and discovering her pregnancy, but it had been Robby's father that she had pushed away in her grief.

She cut the engine and sighed.

Yes, she'd pushed Jake away, but he'd been the one to leave town. He hadn't fought hard enough or stuck around long enough to even discover he'd had a son. And he'd never responded to the letter she'd mailed to him letting him know about the birth of their little boy.

Why then did her heart still break at the idea of never seeing him again?

She shoved those thoughts aside and turned her attention back to the present. Her mother had always told her not to wake a sleeping child but she'd neglected to place a grocery order and there wasn't enough food at her house to feed the little guy tonight. She had to wake him and make a grocery run. From experience, she knew he would be cranky. He was worn out from his long, busy day.

She climbed out of the vehicle and had barely closed her own door before a man appeared from behind a parked car and pressed her against her SUV. He produced a knife and stuck it at her throat, digging it into her skin.

All of her police training meant nothing in the moment. Sabrina's heart raced and her knees threatened to buckle at the fear that pulsed through her. She stared into her attacker's face. He was young but there was a coldness behind his gray eyes. He could end her life with one move and she sensed no hesitation from him.

She gulped down several heavy breaths then dared a glance at her baby. She could only see the top of his head but he seemed to be still sleeping soundly and her fear morphed into anger. If this was a carjacking, he could have it but he wouldn't leave here with her child inside.

"Mr. Creed says you've been sticking your nose where it doesn't belong." The man's sneer was only accentuated by his hot, sticky breath.

Creed. So this wasn't a carjacking but that didn't make this assailant any less dangerous.

"Who are you?"

"I'm here to deliver a message. Back off unless you want us coming after someone you love."

Her instinct was to fight back but fear paralyzed her as she followed his gaze to the back seat. Her cheeks burned with anger and her body tensed. She couldn't allow anything to happen to her son.

He must have felt her fight reflex kick in because he released her and was gone, disappearing behind another row of cars before Sabrina could even catch her breath.

Her gun was still at her side in its holster but she hadn't even had time to try to reach for it. At least he hadn't taken it from her. That was brave. He'd known he had the upper hand threatening her son.

She crawled back into her SUV and locked the doors. Her hands were shaking with a mixture of fear and rage boiling through her veins. She gripped the steering wheel, trying to calm down enough to think straight.

Creed had threatened her son.

Paul Creed was a drug dealer who'd gotten too big for his britches and fancied himself some kind of drug kingpin. Sabrina had targeted him right away when she'd started working Narcotics at the Mercy County Sheriff's Office. She blamed Creed for her brother's overdose and, while many longed to make detective or move up to Homicide, Sabrina was happy to remain where she was. She wasn't going anywhere until Paul Creed was behind bars once and for all.

She started the SUV and sped away and didn't stop until she was out of the shopping center parking lot. She hit the speed dial on her cell phone and waited until her supervisor, Commander Kent Morgan, picked up.

She gave him a quick rundown of the incident.

"Are you or Robby hurt?"

She liked that that was his main concern. He was only ten years or so older than her with a wife and a kid on the way but he'd become a fatherly figure to her and tough but caring supervisor. "No, we're both fine. I'm shaken but Robby slept through it all."

"Good. I'll call over to the security office at the plaza and get copies of the security tapes. Maybe we can identify this assailant."

She hoped so. She would enjoy putting a little fear into this kid the way he had her, though she doubted he would roll over and admit to being ordered to threaten her by Paul Creed. Creed had a way of keeping his employees loyal.

"Have you heard from Max?" Max Harris, a DEA agent who'd gone undercover in Creed's group, had vanished from town several weeks ago. At first, she'd worried that Creed had discovered his identity and harmed him, but a call from his DEA supervisor had let them know that he was safe and would be returning soon. He hadn't given a reason for Max's absence but she'd been glad for some kind of update. She and Max had committed to working together to find evidence to identify Creed's supplier and end his organization. He was usually the one to give her a heads-up when she'd been targeted but his absence meant she hadn't been privy to this attack. She didn't like the feeling of being ambushed and was ready for Max to return and keep her up to date on what was happening in Creed's organization. Plus, she was curious to know what had caused him to leave so abruptly.

"I haven't seen him yet but I received a call saying he was back in town and would meet me here at the sheriff's office in an hour."

That was a relief. "I'll be there too. First, I need to drop Robby off at my mother's."

"That's a good idea. Stay safe."

She ended the call, glad to hear Max had finally returned. She was ready to have Paul Creed behind bars and she couldn't make that happen without him.

She ran through a fast food drive-through and ordered Robby chicken nuggets and fries, then turned the car toward her mother's house. It wasn't the nutritious meal he should have had but it would have to do for tonight.

Twenty minutes later, she pulled up to her mother's house, parked then unbuckled her son from his car seat. Her mother met her at the front door.

"Sabrina, I didn't know you were coming by tonight."

"Neither did I," she explained. She went inside and set Robby down in front of the television. She gave him his nuggets and fries, turned on his favorite cartoon, and he was a happy kid. Sabrina pulled her mother into the kitchen and recounted what had happened. "Can I leave Robby here for a couple of hours? I need to go meet Kent at the sheriff's office."

"Of course you can. I'm supposed to meet Bob at ten tonight. Do you think you'll be back before then?"

"10:00 p.m.?" Her mother's new boyfriend, Bob Crawford, kept odd hours. "I should be back before that but why so late?"

She shrugged. "He has meetings all evening but he wants us to drive to that new resort in Houston for the weekend. I can cancel if you need me to keep Robby longer," she offered.

Her mother liked this new beau and Sabrina didn't want to do anything to hamper her burgeoning relationship. Besides, she would feel better having Robby with her and ensuring his safety for herself. "Don't cancel. Enjoy the weekend. I'll be back for Robby in plenty of time before you leave."

"Okay, but be careful. I don't like how you keep placing yourself in danger this way, Sabrina."

Her mother worried about her and that was understandable but she of all people knew the reason why Sabrina was so committed to bringing Paul Creed's organization down. Sabrina had lost a brother but her mother had lost a son.

"I know you worry, Mom, but I have to do this."

"I wish you'd become a teacher or an accountant or something safe like that."

She chuckled that her mom thought teaching was a safe profession but didn't say so. Instead, she pulled her into a hug. "I'll be okay. I'm just heading to the sheriff's office to meet up with Kent and an informant. I'll only be an hour or two."

She kissed Robby's cheek and told him to mind his grandma before she ran out the door and turned her SUV toward the sheriff's office.

The parking lot wasn't full, as the day shift had left and only a skeleton crew worked the evening shift at the office while the remaining deputies were out on patrol. She parked then headed into the office, waving at her fellow deputies Mike Tyner and Drake Shaw. The evening dispatcher, Allison

Meeks, was in a small room in the corner. Sabrina waved to her as she passed by and Allison returned her wave.

"Have you seen Kent?" she asked Drake and Mike.

"I think he's in the break room," Drake told her. "I saw him head back that way a while ago."

She hurried back there and found Kent pounding on the vending machine. A pack of peanut M&M's fell to the bottom and he bent down and fished it out. He tore into it and popped one into his mouth as he looked at her.

"Are you okay?"

She took a deep breath. "I will be. I think I was more angry than frightened especially since Robby was there with me."

"I get that."

"Where's Max? Have you seen him?"

He nodded. "He came in the back entrance a few minutes ago. He was using my office to make a call."

"I think I'll go see him and tell him what happened. He's going to be furious but I'm so glad he's back."

It wasn't unusual for informants to enter through the back entrance to avoid being seen by everyone inside the sheriff's office. Of course, she trusted her coworkers but it never hurt to be cautious. Max's work with the DEA had to remain a secret in order to protect his undercover identity.

She walked down the back hallway and spotted a tall figure coming out of Kent's office. She recognized the broad shoulders and the dark hair. "Max!"

He turned and his mouth twitched, a tic she had never seen in Max before. She'd only seen it from…

Sabrina's heart stopped cold.

This man was not Max.

It was Jake. Max's twin and her ex.

"Jake! What are you doing here?"

Shock rattled through him at her recognition. He grabbed

her arm and pulled her into the office, closing the door behind him.

"Sabrina, how did you know it was me?" he asked before immediately waving away the question. She'd always been one of the few people that could tell him and Max apart. Even their own father couldn't but that could have been caused by either the excessive drinking or the apathy about his sons' lives. Their mother had been the only one before she died, then Sabrina. To everyone else, he and his brother had been identical.

He should have known he wouldn't be able to fool Sabrina but he honestly hadn't even expected to see her. He'd forgotten how beautiful she was. Her shoulder-length dark hair was pulled into a bun at the nape of her neck and her green eyes were wide with surprise. He glanced at the uniform she wore complete with badge on her shirt and gun at her hip. She was a deputy. Max had failed to mention that or that she was his liaison to the Mercy County Sheriff's Office. That would have been nice to know. His brother had spoken about his undercover work in Mercy and many of the details but Jake wasn't surprised he hadn't mentioned Sabrina to him. They didn't speak of her often, not after the way things had ended between her and Jake five years earlier.

He'd fallen in love with this dark-haired beauty but her brother's death had sent her spiraling into grief. Try as he might, he hadn't been able to pull her out of it. It had broken his heart not to be able to help her through it. She'd pushed him away so many times he'd felt he had no choice but to leave her to her grief. He'd regretted it every day since.

She folded her arms and glared at him. "What are you doing here, Jake? And where is Max?" Realization dawned on her. "Are you trying to fool people into believing you're Max?"

He was, but he certainly hadn't been expecting to be called

out on it. "Why not? There aren't many people who can tell us apart."

"I did."

"Well sure, you can, but who else could?"

"Why are you doing this? Where is Max? Why isn't he here?"

He saw her look of anticipation and knew the news he had to tell her was going to be difficult. He did his best to keep his own emotions in check but it wasn't easy. Apparently, she and Max had grown close during their investigation into Paul Creed.

He pulled out a chair for her. "Maybe you should sit down."

Her eyes widened and the annoyance on her face turned to worry, but she took the seat. "What's wrong? Where is Max?"

He took a deep breath, then just spilled it. "Max and I met up a few weeks ago. I'd gotten some intel from an informant about movement by a drug cartel that I thought he might want to know. We met halfway and I gave him what I had. We hadn't seen one another in a while so we spent a few hours catching up. We were driving to a diner when the car slid on some ice and went off the road. I woke up in the hospital with a concussion, a broken wrist—" he held up a cast on his left arm as proof "—and some cuts and bruises but otherwise I was fine. Max, on the other hand, wasn't. He'd sustained major head injuries and was brain-dead. His DEA supervisor, Carl Price, was called in and was there at the hospital with me waiting for the end. We talked a good bit about Max and about the mission. That's when we came up with this plan. I wanted a way to honor my brother's legacy and finishing his last assignment was a way I could do that. We're both law enforcement. I've been with San Antonio PD for four years and this isn't the first time I've worked undercover. Carl got the okay from his higher-ups then filled me in on the basics of the case and the major players and I figured I could bluff my way through the rest."

She shook her head. "This can't be real. How was this even authorized?"

"That should tell you how important it is to them to find Creed's supplier that they gave us the okay. I have to at least try for Max."

Tears had filled her eyes as he recounted the story and now a few slipped down her cheek. She put her hands over her face. He hadn't realized how close she and Max had been and that surprised him. Max knew how much Jake had loved her and how hard it had been for him to leave her. He'd also known how futile it would have been to stay.

Jake was glad to see she'd finally been able to move past her grief and pull her life together but the last thing he'd expected was for her to take a job at the sheriff's office.

She wiped her face with her hand. "Poor Max. He was a good man."

"Yes, he was." Jake hadn't yet properly dealt with his feelings. There hadn't been time because he'd been dealing with preparing to step into his place. He took a chance and reached for her hands. At first, she accepted his touch but then she slowly pulled them away.

"Sabrina, I know you want to get this guy Paul Creed as much as I do. Do you want this investigation to implode because Max died?"

She shook her head. "I want Creed in jail."

"I can do this. Max's boss told me all about his investigation into Creed. I know you have your reason for wanting to bring him down." While he was surprised that she'd joined the sheriff's office, he wasn't surprised she'd chosen the narcotics division. He didn't mention her brother. He didn't need to. "I have a reason as well. I can do this but I need you to be on my side. Can you do that?"

She stood and paced the floor. "Does Kent know about this?"

"No. He didn't even flinch when he saw me. Only Max's DEA supervisor and now you know."

"You're asking me to lie to my entire team."

"Isn't that what undercover work is about? I'm only asking you not to out me as Jake. Let me honor my brother."

He thought for a moment she was going to refuse but, after wrestling with it for several moments, she finally nodded. "I'm only going along with this because I don't want Max's investigation to have been in vain but I'm worried, Jake. I don't know if you can pull this off."

"I can," he assured her. He wanted to see confidence in her green eyes but all he saw was doubt in them. About him. About if he could complete this mission and take down a notorious drug dealer.

He had to do it. He owed it to his brother's memory to finish what he'd started.

He owed it to her too.

Jake still had a difficult time believing that he was sitting in a room with Sabrina Reagan. She looked good. The last time he'd seen her, she'd been an emotional wreck with grief after her brother's death. She'd been angry and bitter and nothing he could do or say had made it better. He'd wanted to be with her, to give her comfort during such a difficult time, but she'd pushed him away.

The way he'd left her still broke his heart. It had felt brutal to leave town while she was still struggling but there hadn't been much he could have done for her. They'd planned to leave town together and he'd already had a job lined up in Dallas but it hadn't been a good fit for him. She was supposed to have come with him. That had been the plan. Only her brother's death had changed everything.

He was glad to have her on his side again but things still felt awkward between them.

"Sabrina, do we need to talk about how things ended with us?"

She stiffened at his suggestion and her chin jutted out. "Not at all. That was a long time ago, Jake. That's all in the past."

He nodded and breathed a sigh of relief. "I'm glad to hear that." He pulled out a chair and motioned for her to sit down again. He took the opposite chair. "Why don't you give me a rundown of the case you and Max were trying to build against Creed."

"I thought you said Max's boss filled you in."

"He did but I know how undercover work flows. I'm sure there's stuff Max hadn't gotten around to reporting yet. I figured you would be the closest to him in that respect. I'm also interested in how you became his liaison."

"I joined the sheriff's office after my brother died. As you know, my father was in law enforcement and so was his father. It's a family tradition. I guess they always hoped that Robby would join the force but he never wanted that, even before the drugs took him. After his overdose, I asked to work Narcotics. As long as those drugs are on the street, other people's family members are in danger."

"How did the DEA get involved?"

"Your brother was investigating a smuggling ring that he believed was supplying local drug dealers. He was trying to connect Paul Creed to this ring. That was his primary mission. He wanted to find out who was supplying him with drugs then follow that back to the supplier. He believed it was someone working out of this part of Texas. He discovered I had been targeting members of Creed's group and had arrested many of them so his boss reached out to the sheriff. They informed us that he was going to be working undercover in town. The plan was that I would be his contact and whatever information he gathered, I would send to his boss at the DEA. Imagine my surprise when I learned Max was the undercover agent on the case. It was unsettling."

"I imagine it was."

She stared at him then looked away. "So what is your plan, Jake?"

"I step into Max's life. I'm confident no one will know the difference."

"How will you explain having been gone for so long?"

"I was in a car accident." He held up his arm, which held a cast from hand to elbow. "I have the broken bone to prove it. Plus, Max's boss had his medical records sealed then created fake ones to show he was in a coma but ultimately came through it. He also adjusted the official police report of the crash to remove any mention of me or that Max was killed. Anyone who checks it out will find out just what we want them to know—that Max was injured in a car wreck and was hospitalized for three weeks before being released. If there's something I don't know or can't figure out, I figure I'll blame it on memory loss from the accident."

She nodded in a gesture he hoped meant she thought it was a decent plan. It wasn't perfect but it was all he had and he really believed he could make it work.

She glanced at her watch then stood. "I should go. I need to prep for an early morning surprise visit to Dale Lowrey's apartment with his parole officer. I feel certain we'll find some drugs and that will give me a reason to bring him in and question him about Creed."

The name sounded familiar but Jake couldn't place it. "Is that one of Creed's crew?"

She shot him a concerned look. "Yes. Dale's been working for Creed practically since middle school. He's been busted multiple times for selling drugs downtown and just got out of prison early for good behavior on a four-year stint for robbery six months ago. I've been keeping a close eye on him. I'm hoping I can convince him to turn on Creed. If he doesn't, he'll have to go back to jail and finish out his time for breaking his parole if we find drugs in his place."

He stopped himself before he warned her to be careful dealing with Lowrey. She was a trained deputy and didn't need him second-guessing her. Yet he was surprised at how easily the worry came to him where she was concerned.

"I hope you find the evidence you need."

"Thank you. I'm sure he's moving drugs for Creed again. Hopefully, an early morning raid will find it. My mom will be out of town so I'll have to find someone to take Robby to school but I'll work it out."

"Robby?" That had been her brother's name but he was dead so she couldn't be referring to him.

She stopped herself and her eyes widened. She gulped. "My son. He's four years old."

That news hit him like a ton of bricks. Sabrina was a mom. He took a moment to catch his breath before responding. "I'm sorry. I didn't know. Max never mentioned it. I didn't even know you'd gotten married." He'd thought he'd prepared himself for every sting but that was one he hadn't anticipated.

"I'm not married. Robby's father…" Confusion clouded her face and she seemed to struggle for words then finally gave a loud sigh. "It's too complicated to go into right now. I really should go. Give me your phone."

He pulled his cell from his pocket and handed it to her. "Why?"

She quickly entered a phone number and contact information into it. "Max and I used the code name Tiffany Matthews in case anyone looked through his contact list. The cover was that she's an old girlfriend that he still occasionally saw. I even have a social media account set up for her in case anyone goes looking. If you need to reach me, call me at that number." He took his phone back as she grabbed her purse and walked to the door. She stopped and turned to him. "Stay safe, Jake."

He nodded and repeated the phrase back to her. "Stay safe, Sabrina."

He waited until after she'd disappeared up the hallway then slipped out the back entrance and to his car. He hadn't come to town to reconnect with Sabrina Reagan but it had been good to see her again and know that she was doing better. Why hadn't his brother mentioned they were working together? He grimaced. He knew why. Max understood how difficult it had been for Jake to walk away from the only woman he'd ever loved.

And all those old protective feelings about her had resurfaced once he was around her. Only she wasn't that same devastated woman he'd left behind. She'd pulled herself together, started a career and a family, and looked to be strong and determined in her mission. But he'd seen a hint of the kind person he'd once known when she'd worried about his safety and the funny Sabrina in her Tiffany Matthews cover. That had been the name that had once adorned her fake ID in high school and he imagined Tiffany's social media page would have old photos of her and Jake together.

He shook off those nostalgic memories. He couldn't allow Sabrina's presence to affect his mission. He was in town to bring down a drug dealer, not rekindle a long-ago romance.

Chapter Two

Max's cell phone had been damaged in the accident so Jake had cloned it. He had multiple messages from a cell phone number that he didn't recognize but assumed it was Creed's number based on the messages.

Where are you?

Why haven't you responded?

You'd better be dead.

That last one had hurt when Jake had read it.

Now that he was back in town, he needed to make contact and reestablish Max as a member of Creed's team.

He'd stopped by the sheriff's office first after arriving in Mercy County. Now he turned his rental car toward the small apartment complex where his brother had leased an apartment. He parked then grabbed his bag and walked up to Max's door. He unlocked it then walked inside and shed his bag and jacket, momentarily overwhelmed by his brother's presence. This might have been his undercover home but it still had his feeling to it. Although there were no photographs of family or friends, necessary to keep them safe, the big-screen TV, oversize couch and sports memorabilia decorated the room. A circular table and chairs sat to the side near the small kitchen. The coffeemaker on the counter appeared to be the most used appliance given the multiple mugs sitting beside it. Jake opened the refrigerator. It was empty except for a twelve-pack case of soda with a few cans missing. Apparently, his brother had eaten out a lot based on the lack of groceries in his apartment.

A swell of grief pulsed through him. Jake slammed shut the refrigerator and shoved those emotions as far back as he could. He'd been fighting them ever since he'd decided to take on this mission. He couldn't grieve his brother and be his brother at the same time.

A knock on the door grabbed his attention. He tensed and reached for the gun in the holster at his side. He glanced through the peephole and saw two men standing outside. He spotted guns beneath their jackets. Creed's men. Had to be.

He slipped the gun back into its holster. This was the risk he'd agreed to take upon assuming his brother's identity. Max would know these guys.

He opened the door and tried his best to look unflustered. He nodded at them. "How's it going, fellas?"

He didn't recognize either man from their photos but that didn't mean anything. He knew the lower men in the organization came and went. Sabrina might recognize them. He should have asked her about those members she was targeting.

The bigger of the two did the speaking. "Creed wants to see you."

Jake leaned against the door. "How did he know I was back?"

"He's had someone watching your apartment. Wanted us to bring you in if you showed your face here again. We were driving by and saw the lights on."

He nodded and took a deep breath. *Here we go.* "Let me

get my coat." He left the door open as he reached for his jacket and slid it on. These men hadn't blinked at seeing him so they believed he was Max, only he had no idea how well they'd known his brother. They weren't the ones he needed to be concerned about.

He followed them downstairs then slid into the back seat of their car and watched as they headed to the edge of town toward the old industrial area then stopped in front of an old abandoned warehouse. A tall chain-link fence with a privacy liner hid the building but it was opened from inside so they could drive through. On the other side of the fence, he spotted cars in all forms of disrepair. Obviously a chop shop. It seemed drugs weren't Creed's only business. Once they arrived, the two men escorted Jake through the building and up a set of stairs to an office on a second floor.

He tensed as they opened the door and, for the first time, had second thoughts about this. Too late now. He was here and was about to find out if his ruse could fool anyone. He steadied his breath, then stepped into the room. A man stood at the window and turned to him. Jake recognized him from his photographs. Paul Creed. The leader of this drug ring and the man his brother had fought to bring to justice.

Jake's pulse kicked up a notch and he felt sweat beading on his forehead as Creed stared at him. This was the moment of truth. Was he going to have to fight his way out of here? His hand itched to reach for his gun but he resisted. He couldn't make the first move and jeopardize his undercover identity.

Finally, Creed spoke. "Take a seat," he said, motioning to a chair sitting in front of a desk.

Jake pulled it up and sat down.

"We've all been wondering where you've been." He motioned to the cast on Jake's arm. "Looks like you've had some trouble the last few weeks."

Jake held up his arm then nodded. "You could say that. I was in a car accident. My car slid off the road and rammed a tree. I woke in the hospital bed and learned I'd been in a medically induced coma for several weeks to treat some brain swelling. Ultimately, I made it out alive with a concussion, a broken wrist and some cuts and bruises."

"How terrible. I wish you'd let someone know. I would have sent flowers."

"I appreciate that but, like I said, I was out of it for several weeks and once I did wake up, my phone was smashed in the wreck. I lost all of my numbers so I had no way to contact anyone. I headed back to town as soon as I was able."

Creed stood then slid into the big chair behind the desk. The shape of his shoulders was less tense, which implied that he believed Jake's story. He started to relax a bit himself.

"For a while there we were wondering if you'd skipped town. Some of the men even wondered if perhaps you vanished so suddenly because you were a cop." Max had mentioned one of Creed's lieutenants—Jacoby—didn't trust him and looked for any opportunity to undermine him to Creed.

He shook his head. "It wasn't my intention to be gone so long. I'd planned to spend the weekend with a lady friend of mine out of town but I never made it. If you're still not convinced, I'd be happy to email you a copy of the accident report or my hospital bill as proof."

Creed chuckled and Jake knew he believed the story. "I'm glad you're better, my friend. I would appreciate if you could send me a copy of that accident report though."

That request didn't bother Jake since he was sure Creed was only being thorough. He could see by the way he'd relaxed that he'd bought every word and didn't doubt Jake was who he said he was and what had happened. He'd believed that no one would be able to tell him from Max and it seemed he was right. And, if anyone noticed any differences, he could also use the excuse of the wreck and head trauma to explain it away.

"I'll have Joe and Tony drive you back to your apartment

to rest for the night then we'll start back to work bright and early tomorrow."

"I've had weeks of rest. I'm ready to start now. Before I left, we were preparing for a big shipment coming in about a month. Did I miss that?"

"No, we had to push taking control of the product back a few weeks thanks to some local law-enforcement issues. The sheriff's office staked out the river dock where we were supposed to make the trade-off."

"How did they know you were doing it there?"

"We don't know. That's when some people began to suspect you, Max."

Had his brother known the location and passed it on to Sabrina? He didn't know and he wasn't going to risk giving away that he didn't know either unless he was forced to. "Obviously, it wasn't me. I planned on being here for it. Now I can be. What can I do to help?"

"I've got Jacoby already procuring trucks. I was able to put off my supplier for a few weeks but he won't be happy if we have another issue. And these aren't the type of men you want to make angry. Our biggest problem is a local Mercy County deputy who has been targeting my men. Deputy Reagan. She's been a complication."

Jake was surprised he knew Sabrina by name. A part of him was proud that she'd made such a headache for Creed and his men. The other side of him was horrified that she'd made herself such a target.

She'd always been stubborn and determined. It had been one of the things he'd most admired about her and that was before she'd made it her job to bring down Creed. Her brother's death had sent her on a mission.

He had to remind himself that she was a well-trained officer of the law and it wasn't fair of him to keep thinking of her as someone in need of rescue. She was determined to get Creed and it wasn't right of him to try to stop her.

Besides, he was glad to have someone on his side who knew the truth about him. Hiding his identity wasn't that big of a deal for him. He'd worked undercover multiple times before. But having someone he didn't have to hide from was comforting.

Creed's cell phone rang and he pulled it from his pocket then glanced at the screen. "I need to deal with this."

Creed stood and walked out as he answered the call. He left Jake alone in the office. Did he normally do that? It felt like a trap that Jake could easily walk into. However, he couldn't allow this opportunity to pass.

Either this was a test of his loyalty or Creed trusted Max completely.

He prayed it was the second one.

Once Creed was out of the room, Jake made his way around the desk and tapped on his computer. If the names of his suppliers were in there, he needed to find them. Maybe he could end this charade before it really got started.

He pulled a flash drive from his pocket, slid it into the drive on Creed's computer then started the process of copying it. It would be easier to search through once he was somewhere safe and alone. He watched the door, praying that Creed didn't return before the copy was done.

He heard Creed's voice as he headed back so Jake pulled the flash drive from the laptop and closed it.

Creed entered the room and motioned to Jake to follow him. He led the way back down the staircase and toward a waiting car. "I'm glad to have you back, Max." He opened the back car door. "But I've got meetings tonight that were already scheduled. I'll meet you back here in the morning and we'll discuss our next steps in getting our shipments ready."

Max climbed back into the back of the car and Creed closed the door.

He fingered the flash drive in his pocket and hoped that Creed hadn't had cameras set up in the room. He didn't breathe easy again until the car pulled into his apartment complex parking lot and stopped close to his building.

"Do we need to pick you up tomorrow?" Tony, the driver, asked.

He shook his head. "No. I have a rental car."

He got out and slammed the door then walked up to his apartment. Once he was alone and the door was locked, he pulled out the flash drive. This might be all the ammunition he needed to bring down Creed and his supplier. He dug his laptop from his bag then inserted the flash drive. The screen filled with a bunch of indecipherable gibberish.

Encrypted.

He rubbed his face. Of course it wouldn't be that easy.

He pulled out his cell phone and called Sabrina's number. She didn't answer so he left a voicemail, hoping she checked her messages soon. "We need to meet," he told her.

He wasn't entirely sure that he'd read Creed right. It had seemed too easy to step into Max's role and his instincts were on high alert. Either Max had been really good at gaining Creed's trust or else Creed was giving him a long leash to strangle himself with.

He ordered take-out then settled in front of the TV and did his best to drown out the silence of the empty apartment. He didn't like it. It gave him too much time to think about his brother and how he would never see him again. They hadn't been good at staying in touch throughout the years since they'd both chosen to focus on their respective careers, Max's with the DEA and Jake's as a detective with the San Antonio PD.

Finally, he couldn't take the silence any longer. He grabbed his keys and headed toward the sheriff's office, hoping that Sabrina had gotten his message. He took the long way, driving at times fast and erratic and at other times slow and cautiously, making certain that no one was following behind him.

He pulled into the back parking lot and parked. However,

before he got out, he spotted another car across the street. It was sitting with its lights off and someone crouched behind the steering wheel.

He closed the door and watched it. Something about the car seemed out of place and it raised the hairs on the back of his neck.

The back door to the sheriff's office opened and Sabrina exited and walked to her car. He watched her as she climbed in, started the engine and pulled away. As she turned out of the parking lot, the mysterious car started its engine and followed her.

Jake's gut clenched. He'd been right about that car. He started his rental then pulled out behind the trailing car. Like the car he was following, he kept his lights off and operated under the cover of dark. He had a bad feeling about this. Was this what Creed had meant when he'd talked about taking care of the problem?

He hit the redial button on his cell phone and hoped Sabrina answered this time.

She did after several rings. "Hello?"

"Sabrina, it's Jake. I'm behind you but there's another car following you too."

"I don't see it."

"It's driving without lights and keeping its distance but I'm sure he's following you. I watched him as he got behind you when you left the parking lot. It's possible he's trying to follow you to your home to figure out where you live or he might be waiting for a moment to run you off the road."

"I don't care for either of those scenarios."

"I'll keep following him but I wouldn't recommend going home."

"Don't worry. I won't. I'm calling for backup. But you need to be careful too, Jake. You don't want to be seen helping me."

If it came down to it, he knew he would choose to help her and burn his undercover mission but he didn't think that would happen. He was in a nondescript rental car and no one in Creed's organization had seen him driving it. Plus, thanks to daylight savings time and few roadside lights, it was already pitch-dark out. He would act if he had to and hope the darkness covered his identity but that was a last resort.

He listened as she used the radio to call for assistance. He recognized the road they were on. A mile or so up the road, it became more barren with fewer lights and businesses. At least, it used to be that way when he was growing up here. If he was right, that was where this car and its sketchy occupant would make its move.

He was right. They made the curve and suddenly the car turned its lights on and sped up, pulling up beside Sabrina's vehicle. Jake sped up too. He had to do his best to keep this driver from running her off the road while also maintaining his cover.

Sabrina sped up too but the sedan kept up with her and tried to force her off the road. Jake didn't know what his plan was. If he wanted her to wreck or pull over so he could abduct her. Either way, he couldn't allow it.

He was just about to hit the gas and slide into the other lane to engage with the car when sirens and flashing lights overtook him as two patrol cars roared up behind him. They came alongside the car and forced them to pull over to the shoulder.

Jake slowed down then moved to the other lane and passed them, noting not only a driver but a passenger he hadn't noticed earlier. He breathed a sigh of relief that the deputies would handle the situation and detain them at least long enough for Sabrina to get home safely.

A mile or so up the road as the streetlights resumed, Sabrina's vehicle pulled to the shoulder and stopped. Jake did the same then hopped out and hurried to check on her. She let the window down and he leaned in. Her hands were clenched on the steering wheel and she looked shaken but at least she was alive.

"Are you okay?"

She nodded but kept her hands clenched on the steering wheel. "That was too close."

"You shouldn't go home. They might try to find you at your house."

She nodded again. "I'll go to my mom's place. She has Robby there."

"I'll follow behind you to make sure you make it there safely and aren't followed."

He thought for a moment that she might protest that and insist that she didn't need his help but she finally gave him a nod. "Okay. Thank you. If you hadn't been here, I don't know what would have happened."

"You would have handled it on your own, but I'm glad I was there and saw them."

"Why were you at the sheriff's office?"

He reached into his pocket and pulled out the flash drive. "I took this from Creed's laptop but it's encrypted. I was hoping someone from your office could break it."

She nodded then took it from him. "I'll give it to Jana Carter tomorrow. She's our IT guru."

He climbed back into his car after giving the area a quick scan. The road here was flat and he could see in several directions pretty far. No one was around to follow them. He was going to make sure she made it safely home but he also didn't want his cover blown.

He followed behind as she drove to a subdivision on the outskirts of town. The last time he'd seen her, her family had lived closer to town but things had obviously changed. Her mother had moved and Sabrina now had a son.

He drew a deep breath as that last one affected him again. So many changes.

She pulled into a driveway and he parked on the curb and got out. "Nice place," he told her.

"My mom moved here after my dad died last year. Few people know it so it's a safe place for her and Robby."

Robby. Her son. "You named him after your brother. That's nice."

She nodded. "Having him was the only thing that kept me going. I knew I had to figure out a way to keep living for my son's sake."

He was glad she'd found a reason. When he'd left her, she'd been in a very dark place that he hadn't been able to reach. She'd needed a reason to live and it hadn't been him or the future he'd wanted for them together.

But knowing that she'd found someone else, someone who could reach her, who could give her a reason to go on, bothered him at a level he didn't want to admit. He didn't like that someone else had been able to give her what he couldn't.

Only, she hadn't mentioned a husband. Complicated is what she'd called it. Divorce? Widowed? She still had the same name. Perhaps Robby's father had been nothing more than a moment of passion. He didn't care for any of those options.

He paused and did the math. Robby was four years old. Five years since he'd left her. Could it be...?

He dismissed that notion. She would never have kept something like that from him.

Sabrina walked to the front door and produced a key and unlocked the door. She stepped inside. The house seemed quiet but he spotted the light from a television off to the right in what appeared to be the living room.

"Mom?"

A woman poked her head from the kitchen. He recognized her as Beverly Reagan, Sabrina's mother. She was a few years older and grayer but hadn't changed much as far as he could tell. "In the kitchen," she called out.

They stepped into the living room and he spotted a child curled up on the sofa. He was cute with dark hair and dimples, features he definitely thought he recognized. Sabrina reached down and pulled him to her, taking him into her arms. He gave her a hug then locked blue eyes with Jake, eyes so much like his and Max's that it caught his breath.

"Who's he, Momma?" the boy asked in a sweet high-pitched voice.

Sabrina glanced back at Jake then placed him back down. "This is my friend. Go in the bedroom and play, Robby. We'll be going home in a bit."

The little boy hurried to do as he was told.

Sabrina opened her mouth to say something but her mother chose that moment to walk in from the kitchen. "Max, it's good to see you again."

Sabrina looked like she started to correct her mother then changed her mind. She pulled out her cell phone then plugged it into the charger on the counter. She was avoiding his eyes and the conversation they were going to have to have.

He took the hint and extended his hand. "It's good to see you again too, Beverly." He wondered if Max had spent time with Sabrina and her family enough for her mother to remember him from when they were kids. That wasn't his business. He and Sabrina had had a professional relationship but they had once all been friends when the three of them attended school together.

"Coffee?" Mrs. Reagan asked.

"It's late, Mom. I don't think Max wants—"

"I'd love some," he interrupted. "I probably won't sleep anyway but coffee doesn't really keep me up." He suddenly had something that would definitely prevent him from sleeping.

Mrs. Reagan stepped back into the kitchen, poured coffee into a mug then handed it to him. He sipped it. "It's good. Thank you."

"I'm glad you finally made it back to town. My daughter has been very worried about you. You shouldn't have stayed away so long without letting her know. I'd begun to wonder if you'd left her the same way that no-good brother of yours did."

Sabrina's eyes widened and she shot him an *I'm sorry* look. It wasn't necessary. He wasn't proud of the way he'd left her and they hadn't really discussed it.

He held up his hand to assure her he wasn't going to reveal himself to her mother. "I shouldn't have stayed away for so long. I've already given my explanation and apologies to Sabrina."

"It's okay, Mom. Max didn't abandon us. He was in a car accident." She motioned toward the cast on his arm. "He's back now and we're still working on bringing down Paul Creed."

Beverly waved her hand at Sabrina to stop. "I don't like to hear about what you're doing, Sabrina, but I'm glad you have Max to watch out for you. Besides, Robby's been asking about his uncle Max."

Sabrina spit out her coffee. "Mom!" Her face reddened.

Uncle Max. Confirmation for what he already suspected.

He looked at Sabrina, who was staring past him. He turned. Her little boy stood in the doorway of the kitchen clutching a stuffed animal. "I'm ready to go home, Momma."

Sabrina rushed to him and scooped him up into her arms. "Honey, we're going home in a bit." She headed down the hall to the playroom.

Jake dropped his coffee mug onto the table then walked back into the living room. Photographs of Sabrina and the boy were shown prominently. He saw the resemblance clearly now. The same nose. Blue eyes and dark hair he and his brother shared. No denying it.

And Max had known. They'd spent hours together and his brother hadn't mentioned Sabrina had had his child.

Why didn't you tell me, Max?

"Jake."

He turned. Sabrina stood in the hallway entrance. He couldn't look at her knowing what she'd kept from him.

"Let me explain."

He put up his hand to stop her. "I don't want to hear it." He beelined for the door. Suddenly, the air was sparse and he needed to get out of there before more truths tumbled on him.

He'd already lost so much that he was struggling to keep control of his emotions. He couldn't handle this on top of it.

He forwent the sidewalk and stepped through the grass to get to his car parked at the curb. Sabrina was right behind him.

She grabbed his arm in an attempt to stop him. "Jake, please. Let me explain."

He couldn't hold it back any longer. He jerked his arm away and spun on her. "Explain what? That you lied to me? That you kept something this important from me?"

She lowered her head. "I'm sorry."

"Did Max know?" She hesitated to answer. "Did he?"

Finally, she nodded. "Yes, he knew. He figured it out. He wanted to tell you but I begged him to let me be the one."

"But you didn't."

"I didn't know how to tell you." A tear slipped down her face. He checked the urge to wipe it away and comfort her. That was messed up. He was the wronged one, not her.

"You know how bad it was for me when my brother died. I was distraught. I didn't want to go on. I didn't know how to move forward. You had already left town when I discovered I was pregnant. Knowing that I had this child growing inside me was the only thing that kept me going. Robby brought me back to life."

"You still kept it from me. I had a right to know I had a son."

"I could barely function for myself and Robby, much less think about you. I was suddenly a single mom with a baby. I was overwhelmed and scared out of my mind. I know I should have told you but I was fighting so hard to get back to a normal, stable life."

His anger turned to agony that he hadn't been there for her. "I would have helped you, Sabrina. I would have done anything to help you."

"I know." Now the tears did flow. "I wasn't in a place to want your help. I'm sorry for how I treated you, Jake, and I'm sorry for keeping this from you. I did try to reach out to you a couple of years ago. I wrote you a letter telling you all about Robby, but I never heard back from you so I assumed you got it and decided you didn't want to be a part of his life."

"I never received any letter."

"I realize that now. The last I'd heard, when you left town, you were joining the Dallas police department. That's where I sent it."

He'd left Dallas soon after his arrival and gone to San Antonio. And his undercover work had caused him to avoid social media or anything that might give up his identity. That could explain why she hadn't been able to locate him.

"When Max showed up in town and found out about Robby, he insisted there was no way you received that letter and decided not to see Robby. That's when I realized you must not have gotten it. He told me then where you were and said to contact you again. He said if I didn't, he would. I was working up my nerve when he suddenly vanished."

That stung to know that his brother had kept this from him. He should have come out and told him the truth despite Sabrina's request. He'd had a right to know.

He pulled open the car door. "I have to go."

"Jake." He stopped and looked back at her. "I truly am sorry."

He climbed into the car and started the engine. He couldn't look at her. She'd kept something so big and fundamental from him.

As he drove away, he couldn't turn his mind from the little boy with the wide grin and blue eyes.

He was a father.

Chapter Three

Well, that had not gone the way she'd hoped.

Sabrina wiped the tears from her face as she watched the car disappear around the corner. The pain and anger in Jake's face, the look of betrayal, had rocked her. She'd never meant for any of this to happen.

She marched back into the house and confronted her mother. "Why would you say that?"

Her mother's eyes widened in an innocent expression. "What did I say? Max knows about Robby. We spoke about it the last time he was here. He loves that little boy."

"No, Mother, you don't understand. That wasn't Max. That was Jake pretending to be Max."

Her mom's brows crunched. "Why would he pretend to be his brother?"

"Because Max was killed in a car wreck a few weeks ago. He was working undercover in Paul Creed's organization. Jake came to town to finish that but he has to pretend to be Max in order to do it." She sighed. "I shouldn't have even told you that. It could compromise his cover."

Realization dawned on her mom's face and she slid into a chair. "You mean, I just told Jake Harris that he's Robby's father? Oh, honey, I'm sorry. I didn't mean—"

Sabrina fell into a chair, defeated. "No, it's not your fault, Mom. I should have told him a long time ago, then this wouldn't have happened. I should have been honest with him. Besides, I'm pretty sure he'd figured it out before your slip-up."

"After the way he left you, I can understand your not wanting to share Robby with him."

"I've been angry at Jake for a long time but the truth is that I pushed him away, Mom. You know how I was. I was inconsolable after Robby's death. I don't blame Jake for leaving. There was nothing he could do for me. I wish I'd responded better but I didn't."

"You can't blame someone for how they grieve."

"I know but I was just so angry. I didn't even want Jake around me. I didn't want to continue living. Now I know how my actions then hurt everyone. I robbed Jake of being a father and I robbed my son of having a father. I tried to apologize to him but he wouldn't listen to me."

Her mom reached her hand across the table and placed her hand over Sabrina's. "Give him some time, honey. He'll come around."

She was grateful for her mother's support and prayed she was right. She couldn't really blame her. Sabrina was the one who'd kept the truth from Jake. She was the one to blame for his anger.

She quickly changed the subject to something more pleasing. "Have you packed for your weekend getaway with Bob?"

Her mom's face brightened at the mention of her trip. "I haven't even started packing. I can't decide what to bring and, you know me, I'd pack my entire closet if I could."

Sabrina stood and motioned to her. "Come on. I'll help you choose a few outfits before I leave."

They spent the next hour rummaging through the closet picking out things to pack until her mom's suitcase was ready to go. Her mother gushed with the heady excitement of new love. Sabrina was happy for her but realized she'd hadn't felt that feeling in a long time. Not since her early days with Jake. Back when her brother and father were alive and anything in life seemed possible.

She glanced at the clock. It was late and she still had that early shift. "We should head home." She pulled her mom into a hug. "Have a fun trip and tell Bob I said hello."

She walked down the hall to the second bedroom that had been designated as a playroom and where Robby slept whenever he stayed over. She opened the door and peered inside. He'd fallen asleep on the floor. She wasn't surprised given the lateness of the hour. She pushed his hair back and gave him a kiss on the forehead before carrying him out to the SUV and loading him into the car seat. He didn't even rouse as she buckled him up. She'd never known such love as she had for this little boy. She hadn't believed it was possible to feel anything again after her brother died but little Robby had opened up her heart and helped her heal from her pain. It had been a long hard road, but she'd finally come out on the other side.

She owed Jake the truth. He hadn't deserved to find out he was a father that way. Max had been right to press her to contact him and now she wished she'd had the courage to do so earlier.

She hoped Jake could forgive her. Her mother was right. Robby needed his father. She prayed he wouldn't hold her sins against their child.

Jake had been driving aimlessly, trying to figure a way to wrap his brain around this new knowledge. He was a father. Had been a father for years and Sabrina hadn't told him.

He gripped the steering wheel tighter as worry wove its way through him. He didn't have a great role model when it came to fathers. His and Max's was a major alcoholic who'd finally drunk himself to death a few years after he and his brother had left town. They'd returned briefly to close up the house and scatter their dad's ashes.

Sabrina had been his rock during that difficult time. He'd done his best to keep his emotions in check. He and Max had both suffered at their father's hands and his feelings about his dad were convoluted but he had been their father. Sabrina had seen past Jake's flippant attitude to the real grief. She'd been there for him but he hadn't done the same for her when it mattered the most.

Now she'd lied to him in the worst possible way.

He turned the car toward the industrial side of town back toward the factory Creed worked out of. He needed to get back into his undercover persona and the mission. He would think about Sabrina and Robby once this was all said and done.

The parking lot was crowded and when he entered, so was the factory floor which surprised him. A crowd of men were standing around in a circle and someone from the center was speaking. Jake couldn't see the man or hear his words over the rumble of the group.

Suddenly, the crowd broke up and Paul Creed stepped out. He spotted Jake and looked surprised. "You're back."

"Yeah, I am. What's going on here?" These men hadn't been here when he'd left.

Creed motioned him to follow him up to his office.

Once they were inside, Jake looked at him. "What's up? It's kinda late to have a meeting, isn't it?"

"It's not actually. I've got men about to bring product into several nightclubs in the area. They're picking up. The real parties don't get started until close to midnight."

Jake nodded then mentally kicked himself for that slip-up. Max would have known that. Had he blown it?

"Since you're here, you should know I got word from my supplier earlier tonight. They're unhappy with the fact that Deputy Reagan keeps interfering. They want her taken care of as soon as possible."

He felt his jaw clench. He was targeting Sabrina? "I think you mentioned that earlier."

"I'm officially placing a hit on the deputy. She won't be bothering us anymore. I just told several of my men to take care of her tonight."

For once, he was glad he'd trained himself to keep his emotions in check. He wanted to scream and take this man down until he rescinded that hit. But he had to think about getting to Sabrina first.

"Are they going to hit her at her house?"

He nodded. "They're heading there now. And I've given them instructions not to leave any witnesses."

His hands began to sweat. He needed a reason to get out of here and warn her about the impending strike. They knew where she was and they were coming after her and Robby.

They were targeting his family.

"Why don't you call it off and let me see to it?" he suggested. That would the easiest thing for him. Convince Creed to call off the hit and let him take care of her.

"No, I have another assignment for you, Max. I'll fill you in tomorrow. I'm still making plans."

"I can help with those plans, Paul."

Creed looked at Jake for a split second too long in his opinion before refusing his help. "I'll let you know when I need you."

Jake could see it in his face. He didn't trust him completely. Whatever trust Max had built with him had evaporated during the time he'd been away. He was still questioning him. Or maybe it was because he somehow sensed that Jake wasn't Max.

He could wonder about that later. For now, he needed to warn Sabrina that her life was in danger.

He waited until he was on the road to call her cell phone. It rang and rang and then clicked over to voicemail. He left a message to call him back and that Creed had placed a price on her head.

He tried her cell phone again and then again and was about to give up and call into the sheriff's office when someone answered.

"Hello?"

"Sabrina, it's Jake. Finally."

"This isn't Sabrina. It's her mother. Jake, I'm so—"

"No time for apologies, Bev. I need to talk to Sabrina."

"She's not here. She and Robby went home. I guess she forgot she'd put her phone on the charger here in my kitchen because she left it."

So he had no way to contact her. "Does she have another cell phone or a landline at her house? Any other way I can get in touch with her?"

"No. I was going to leave it. I figured she would come by and get it tomorrow morning. I'm getting ready to leave on a trip or else I would take it to her. Is everything okay?"

"Definitely not. I need her address now. Where does she live?"

She must have heard the urgency in his voice because she rattled off the address and he quickly keyed it into his GPS.

"She's in danger, isn't she?"

"Yes, she is but I'm on my way to her and Robby."

"What can I do?"

"Call the sheriff's office and tell them she's in trouble. They need to send a team to her house."

"Okay, I will. Take care of them, Jake."

"I will." He ended the call. He'd already turned the car toward the directions the GPS indicated. He knew that part of town and it would take him fifteen minutes to get there. He had no idea where Creed's men were or when they'd left.

He didn't breathe until he turned on her street. As he neared her house, he scoured the street for something or someone out of place. He found it. A car several houses down with four men inside. They were watching the house on the corner. The house's Christmas lights were lit up and the tree in the window shone. Sabrina was standing in the driveway next to her car getting Robby out of his car seat.

Jake pulled to the curb behind another parked vehicle and cut the engine. He saw activity in the car and knew they were getting ready to strike. If he had to burn his cover, he would do so, but he hoped it wouldn't come to that. He slipped a baseball cap over his head then got out and darted across the neighbor's lawn in the dark of night toward her house. As he reached her driveway, he heard the car down the street rev its engine.

They were coming.

Sabrina spotted him as she pulled Robby from the car and into her arms. "Jake, what on earth?"

"Get inside the house now." He pressed them and she ran without question toward the front door. She quickly unlocked it and hurried inside. He shut the door.

"What's happening?"

"Men with guns." He reached for his own weapon, then peeked out the front window and saw the car speed up to the front of the house then squeal to a stop. Two men with guns leaned out and started firing.

"Get down!" he shouted as the clatter of gunfire hit the house and burst through the walls and windows. Robby screamed and started crying as Sabrina covered him with her body. The Christmas tree hit the floor and she darted into the kitchen carrying Robby in her arms.

Jake scrambled to follow them as another round of bullets kept coming. He pressed them both toward the back of the house and crouched behind the kitchen island. Jake still had a clear view of the front window. The car was still there and the men were now getting out and approaching the house.

Robby cried and Sabrina did her best to comfort him and keep him quiet.

"Why is this happening?" she demanded.

"Creed put a hit out on you. His suppliers want you out of the picture."

She clutched Robby and he could see that news shook her. It had shaken him too. But now, more than her life was at risk.

She reached into her pocket then her face fell even further. "I don't have my phone to call for help. You?"

He'd left his in the car in the rush to get out. "It's been done. Your mom is calling in the cavalry." He saw her surprise. "You left your phone at her house. She's the one who told me where you lived."

She rubbed Robby's hair and did her best to soothe him but he could see fear in her face.

"What are they doing?"

"Getting out of the car. They're approaching the house. Do you have a safe room or any other way out of the house?"

She shook her head. "The backyard is gated. We'd have to climb over it and my neighbor has a big, mean dog."

So they were trapped.

He heard boots on the driveway and knew they were close. Armed men were about to break down the front door and kill his child and the woman he'd once wanted to marry and build a life with. And he wouldn't be spared either. Creed had ordered no witnesses. That included him.

He rubbed the back of his neck as the truth settled in.

They were in trouble.

Sabrina pushed over the kitchen table then settled Robby behind it. He was whimpering but had stopped wailing. She grabbed her weapon then took up a spot beside him. "We only need to hold on until my department arrives."

He admired her bravado and wished he had more time to observe it. She wasn't going down without a fight.

Sirens in the distance were a welcome sound. The gunmen heard them approaching and ran back to their vehicle.

They sped off as the first cruisers from the sheriff's office surrounded the house.

A wave of gratitude washed through him. *Thank You, God.* "The cavalry is here," he told her.

Sabrina put away her weapon then retrieved Robby from behind the table and rocked him on her hip. "It's okay, baby. We're okay now." She rubbed the back of his head then looked at Jake. "Let me go out first. We don't want anyone mistaking you for one of the shooters."

He agreed and let them go first. Not everyone in the sheriff's office knew who he was. In fact, most people didn't. That was the point. That everyone thought he was one of Creed's men. Only he didn't need that trouble today.

Kent hurried over to them and touched her arm. "Are you okay?"

She nodded but continued to clutch Robby. "Yes, we're fine thanks to him."

Kent shook Jake's hand. "Glad to have you back, Max. Thank you for looking out for them. Now, does someone want to tell me what happened?"

They waited until a paramedic had Robby in the back of an ambulance checking him over before he and Sabrina addressed Kent. "Creed told me that his suppliers wanted Sabrina dead. I tried to call her to warn her but she'd left her phone at her mother's. When I arrived, I spotted the car down the road loaded with men and guns. I knew I had to get them to safety."

She touched his arm, sending a spark through him. "You saved our lives," she said, glancing up at him with appreciation in her gaze. "I can't thank you enough."

The anger he'd felt for her earlier that evening had faded in the wake of her and Robby nearly being killed. "You can thank me by backing off of this investigation into Creed."

She pulled her hand away as if he'd pinched her. "You know I can't do that."

Irritation flooded him. She had a child to think about. It wasn't right that she was placing him in danger too with her recklessness. "Sabrina, you have to think about your safety. Creed has put a price on your head. Every lowlife thug in his crew will be gunning for you. It isn't only your life you're placing in danger. It's Robby's too. No witnesses. That was his order."

That point seemed to reach her. She bit her lower lip the way he'd seen her do when she was trying to think things through. "You're right. I can't put Robby's life in danger that way."

He breathed a sigh of relief. "Good. Then you'll back off the investigation?"

"No. But I will leave Robby with my mom. I hate to ask her to cancel her plans but she will for this. The house is still technically listed under the previous owner's name and few people know she's moved. He'll be safe there."

"I have to agree with Max," Kent interjected. "You have no idea who could be after you now."

"That's always been true, hasn't it? I've already been targeted twice before the hit. I'll stay close to the station but I'm not backing down. I won't let Paul Creed send me into hiding."

Jake shared a concerned look with Kent but he gave in to her. "Okay, but you'll be careful and you won't make a move without letting me know," Kent instructed her. "You're never to go anywhere alone either. You need backup."

Jake could see she didn't like that one detail but she nodded. "Fine. I won't go anywhere alone."

"Good. I'll also double patrols on your mom's neighborhood to keep an eye out for suspicious behavior. In the meantime, we've got a team canvassing this neighborhood for witnesses or video of the car and the men. I've also got roadblocks set up. We'll find the men who did this."

What they would find were dangerous men to be sure, but men looking to score a hefty payday. Jake hoped they would roll over on Creed for giving the kill order but first they had to capture them.

He glanced around at all the deputies and crime scene techs on the scene. In addition, a crowd of nosy neighbors had circled around the lawn despite the late hour. And once the TV news crews arrived, all this might be on television.

He was exposed out here. His identity in danger. He didn't know if the men who'd shot at the house had recognized him or not but he needed to keep his undercover identity in check in case he hadn't been compromised.

"I need to get out of here," he whispered to Sabrina.

She nodded then looked toward the ambulance where Robby was clutching his toy bear. He'd finally stopped crying but hadn't settled completely from all the chaos of what had just happened. "I should get him to my mother's." She glanced at her car. It was littered with bullet holes as was the house. Glass scattered on the ground and her Christmas tree was protruding through the front window.

His car parked down the street was still drivable. "I'll take you both over there."

But they needed to go before more people arrived who might decide to follow them. Since the moment he'd seen her again, his protective instincts had kicked in. And learning that he had a son had only intensified that desire. He might be angry with her and confused about his feelings about Robby but one emotion was pushing its way to the forefront of his consciousness.

He would do whatever it took to keep his family safe.

Chapter Four

Sabrina's heart finally stopped racing with fear and adrenaline as Jake turned onto her mother's street. Cold anger replaced it. Anger that Creed had sent men to her house. Around her son. She clutched Robby as Jake drove. She didn't even have a car seat so Jake was being extra careful while also watching his rearview mirror and checking for a tail.

Thankfully, her mom had a car seat in her vehicle that Sabrina could use until she could replace hers. She would also have to replace her car or get a rental until she could. She didn't know the extent of the damage to her house but, from what she'd seen, it would be extensive. She'd worked hard to purchase a home for her and Robby and it hadn't been easy on a single mom's salary. It broke her heart that it was now unlivable. Another thing Creed had taken from her.

Jake pulled into the driveway and parked. "Want me to carry him for you?"

Robby had finally settled down on the drive and fallen asleep on her shoulder. She wanted to keep him with her but her own adrenaline rush was fading and her energy zapped. She nodded so he climbed out, circled the car then lifted

Robby from her lap. Robby didn't rouse as he moved his head to Jake's shoulder instead.

She climbed out of the car and headed inside. The door opened before she arrived and her mother stood in the door-way, hand on her heart and tears welling up in her eyes. "You're both okay. God is good."

Sabrina's instinct wanted to refute her mother about God's goodness but she was just too tired tonight. Her faith had taken a hit when her brother died. Then Jake had left her. Her father's death last year had done little to make her believe any different. But she had been turning the bend again, realizing what a gift she had in Robby. What kind of a good God al-lowed so many terrible things to happen to one family? She didn't know but blaming God wasn't the answer. She hugged her mother. "We're okay, Mom."

Her mother released her then touched the back of Robby's head. She also touched Jake's arm. "Thank you for protect-ing them."

Sabrina led Jake down the hallway to the bedroom. Jake placed him on the bed then gently removed his coat, hat and boots before pulling the blanket over him. Sabrina watched as he stroked Robby's hair. His shoulders shook for a moment, then he took a deep breath and stood to face her. She recog-nized the firm line of his mouth as he fought for control and the what-might-have-happened fear that flashed through his eyes. He'd nearly lost something he hadn't even known he'd had earlier in the day.

He closed the door to the bedroom but didn't move from the hallway. He reached out to touch her cheek, sending chills through her. "I can't even think about what nearly happened tonight." His voice was choked, still full of emotion.

"I know. I'm glad you arrived when you did."

"When I couldn't reach you on your cell, I was worried I wouldn't make it in time." He looked back at the bedroom door and sighed. "I just found him. I can't imagine losing him now."

He leaned close and she sensed he wanted to hold her. Falling into his arms would be so easy and feel so good, yet she hesitated. That comfort would only be fleeting. Once the fear of the night became a memory, he would remember how angry he was at her for keeping Robby from him. She couldn't put herself out there only to be hurt again.

She stepped away from him and headed for the kitchen where her mom and Bob were sitting at the table. Jake followed her and, when she saw them, her mother jumped to her feet. She pulled the cell phone Sabrina had left charging from the cord and handed it to her. "Please keep this with you, Sabrina. I think tonight has proven that you never know when someone might need to reach you."

Sabrina placed it on the counter then took a coffee mug from the cabinet and poured herself a cup. It was late but there was little chance of her getting much sleep tonight after this attack.

Jake took the coffeepot from her and poured himself a cup too.

Bob motioned to the TV that was silently playing news clips. "I was just watching coverage about the police presence in your neighborhood, Sabrina. They said a neighbor noticed a suspicious vehicle and called it in and that the sheriff's office was still looking for the suspects."

She thanked him but she didn't want to hear the details. She knew who had attacked her home tonight. Her department would collect evidence and gather witness statements, but they would have a difficult time linking this attack back to Creed.

He'd taken her brother from her. Now he'd taken her home too.

She pushed the coffee away and stood, suddenly not wishing to relive this terrible night. "I should try to get some sleep. I've got that early morning meeting."

Her mother gaped. "You're not going to work tomorrow after what nearly happened tonight, are you?"

"Of course I am. I can't let Creed put me on the sidelines."

Her mother jumped to her feet. "Sabrina, why do you keep putting yourself at risk this way? You have Robby to think about."

She wasn't backing down. She couldn't allow Paul Creed to win. "I am thinking about Robby. I can't allow him to grow up in a world with drugs on every street corner. Creed is a blight on this area's good name and I won't rest until we bring him down."

Jake touched her arm. "Are you sure you're up for that? I'm sure it can wait a day or two?"

She glared at him as she pulled her arm away. They'd already had this discussion back at her house. She wasn't going into hiding. "I won't let Creed win. I won't let him stop me from doing my job. Robby will be fine here where he's safe while I do what I have to do."

"Of course I'll keep him safe," her mother assured her. "But it's not him I'm worried about, Sabrina. It's you. I've already lost a son. I can't risk losing a daughter too."

Bob reached for her mother's hand and held it then stood and pulled her into a hug. "Your mother knows how dedicated you are to your work, Sabrina, but you can't blame her for being fearful after tonight. Don't worry. I'll be around tomorrow and the next few days to make sure they're both safe. I'll even bring doughnuts when I come back in the morning. I know Robby likes the ones with sprinkles."

"Thank you, Bob. I appreciate it." She didn't particularly care for her mom's new boyfriend but was grateful he would be another eye to watch her son. She couldn't put her finger on what it was that rubbed her the wrong way, but she thought it was probably just jealousy that her mom was moving forward when Sabrina still seemed to be stuck in the past. Besides, it had only been a year since her dad had died and it felt disloyal to him to like this new man in her mom's life.

She walked down the hall to the extra bedroom. She had some clothes and toiletries here for when she and Robby stayed over. She gathered them into a bag. She had a spare uniform in her locker at the sheriff's office but she would have to go by her house tomorrow to see what else she could salvage. The sheriff's office had cots near the jail for officers to utilize. It wouldn't grant her the comfort of home, but it was a safe option now that her house was a crime scene.

Jake followed her, his broad shoulders filling the doorway. "Are you sure this is a good idea? Creed nearly killed you tonight."

She turned and looked at him. Why did everyone insist she step back and let Creed win? "I won't let him get away with this, Jake. If I give up now, he wins."

His mouth twitched with worry. "I don't like it but I can't stop you. Promise me that you'll be careful."

"I will. I won't be alone. Besides, I can assure you that Kent will be all over me to take extra precautions after tonight." Deputy-involved shootings were treated with caution. Sabrina hadn't had time to do anything but pull her gun but she'd been a target of a drive-by shooting. Kent was protective of his deputies but he was a professional. He would appreciate her commitment to her work, but he would also admire her determination not to become a victim. At least, she hoped that was how he would react once he'd had time to think about it. He had the authority to place her on desk duty, which would be infuriating.

She was also worried about Jake. He'd risked his cover once he'd discovered the plan to attack her at home. "What will you do about Creed? Is it safe for you to return?"

"I kept my head down and my face covered so I don't think the shooters saw me and I did my best to stay clear of the news outlets. I am glad to hear that Kent put out a statement that a neighbor called in seeing a suspicious vehicle. I was worried Creed might be suspicious I'd tipped off the police given the timing, but my cover should be intact."

She hoped that was the case. She was still counting on him to help her bring down Creed and his supplier.

"Do you need a ride to the sheriff's office?"

"No. I'll call Kent and ask him to send a deputy to pick me up."

"I'll call and check on you tomorrow." He slipped her cell phone into her hand. "You left this again."

She smiled and took it. She'd left it on the counter in her haste to assert herself.

"Good night," he told her.

"Good night, Jake."

He turned and walked away and the room seemed emptier without him. She glanced out of the window, watching him as he climbed into his car and sped away.

She was grateful to him for what he'd done tonight. She'd come far too close to losing her life and Robby's life.

Creed was dangerous and she was going to have to be on her high guard from now on.

Jake's mind was still awhirl as he headed back to the apartment, parked and got out. He was still shaking inside from the night's events. Sabrina and Robby were safe now but knowing how close they'd been to danger had rocked him. Now that his mind had time to process all that had happened, he could admit the gut punch that had come with the idea of losing them.

He didn't even know Robby. Didn't know how to be a father. But he wanted the chance to figure it out. If Creed's men had succeeded tonight, Jake's regrets would have followed him for the rest of his life.

He unlocked the apartment door then headed inside. He'd

only been back in town for a few hours but those hours had changed him. He'd thought losing his twin had turned his world upside down, but discovering he was a father and nearly losing his child all in the scope of one night was too much.

And Sabrina.

He'd thwarted two attacks against her today. What would losing her again, this time for good, do to him? He didn't want to find out.

Her mission against Creed was going to be the death of her.

Jake opened the nightstand drawer beside the bed and pulled out the Bible he'd seen there earlier when he was unpacking. It had to belong to his brother. He opened it and thumbed through the pages. Max had marked up passages and made notes in the margins. Jake had been surprised to learn from Max's boss, Carl, that his brother had rediscovered his faith and was a regular member of a Bible study group when he wasn't working a job.

Jake liked that. He hadn't thought about God in years but their mom had raised them in church and the congregation they'd attended had been good to both Max and Jake after their mom died.

And, tonight, his first thought at hearing they were in danger was to call out to God for help.

A knock on the front door grabbed his attention. He slid the Bible back into the drawer and closed it, then reached for his gun as he moved across the living room floor. He glanced through the peephole, surprised by who he saw standing on the other side.

He opened the door and Creed blew past him, rubbing his hands anxiously. The man looked to be on the edge and when a notoriously dangerous drug dealer was upset, it couldn't be good. "Where have you been, Max?" he demanded. "I came by earlier and you weren't here. Where were you?"

Oh you know, just thwarting your plan to murder my ex-girlfriend and my son.

"I was just out driving around. What's the matter?"

Creed looked as if he were bordering on full-blown panic.

"My men failed to take out the deputy. They shot up her house but she managed to escape unharmed. The police were tipped off by a neighbor. I'm surprised you haven't seen it. It's been all over the local news."

"I haven't watched the news."

"My supplier is not going to be happy, Max. He wanted this done." Creed was wringing his hands and looked to be close to full-blown panic. Whoever this supplier was, he had to be one scary guy to instill fear in Paul Creed.

Jake tried to remain calm. He didn't know if Creed coming to see him was normal behavior or not since he still had no idea how much Creed had trusted Max, but he tried to play it cool. "So we'll go see this guy, your supplier, and explain. I'll go with you. He can't kill us both, right?"

"Don't be so sure." The look in Creed's face when he locked eyes with Jake showed fear.

He rubbed the back of his neck and tried to come up with another plan. "Look, this guy needs you to move his drugs. He needs you as much as you need him. Right? We'll just explain that this deputy got lucky. It won't happen again." And, suddenly, he had an idea. "What if we make an anonymous tip to the police and have these fellas that botched the hit picked up? The cops will blame them for the attempted murder and we'll blame them to the supplier for messing up the job."

Creed thought about it for a moment then shook his head. "No. They'll tie me back to the hit. They'll definitely turn on me if they believe I gave them up. I can't take that risk. That Deputy Reagan has to die. It's the only way I can save myself." He walked to the door and reached for the handle but stopped before he opened it. As he turned to say something, Jake expected a thanks for listening or something along those lines. Instead, Creed's face turned hard as he glared at Jake.

"The next time I call you, you'd better answer if you know what's good for you."

He opened the door and walked off, leaving the door standing open.

Jake walked to it, watched Creed climb into his car and drive away, then closed it.

He leaned against the door and let out a deep breath.

Sabrina and Robby might be safe at the moment, but the threat wasn't over for them. Creed was even more determined than ever to kill her. Worse than that, there was some unknown figurehead supplying Creed drugs and demanding he take Sabrina's life. Even taking down Creed wasn't enough any longer. He had to find this supplier's identity to end the threat against her once and for all.

Mike Johnson was the county parole supervisor. Sabrina met up with him the next morning at the Lockwood Apartment complex Dale Lowrey had listed as his address when he'd been released from prison six months earlier. He'd been arrested along with another known associate of Creed's so she knew he was involved in the organization before he went to prison on drugs charges. Now Sabrina had received a tip that Lowrey was once again involved in the sale and distribution of drugs for Creed so she arranged to meet up with Mike to perform a search.

She'd borrowed her mom's car for the meeting until she could arrange a rental car. She parked then got out, stretching and working out the kinks from sleeping on a cot the night before. She shook hands with Mike, who was waiting for her. "Have you seen him?"

"Not yet. I parked around the corner so he wouldn't see me while I waited for you."

That was smart. If he'd been seen that gave Lowrey time to dispose of any drugs he might have in his possession. Since he was on parole, they didn't need a warrant or probable cause to search his apartment.

Johnson knocked and Lowrey quickly came to the door.

Johnson officially identified himself despite Lowrey knowing him from their monthly meetings, and Sabrina flashed her badge as well and identified herself. "We're here to perform a search," Johnson told him. "Please step back."

Lowrey didn't look happy but he didn't protest either. He knew he had no choice in the matter as part of his parole. Surprise visits were a part of his life until he was officially released from corrections custody.

They entered the small apartment and Sabrina spotted a woman and a small child in the kitchen. "Who are they?" she asked.

"My wife and daughter," Lowrey told her.

She stepped into the kitchen and identified herself. "We're going to perform a search of your apartment, Mrs. Lowrey. Are you aware of any illegal substances in the dwelling?"

She glanced at her husband then shook her head. The little girl clutched at her leg and the woman picked her up.

"Please have a seat." She turned to Lowrey. "I'm going to ask you and your family to remain in the kitchen while Mr. Johnson and I conduct the search."

"Why don't you start in the bedroom," Johnson suggested. "I'll start in here then move to the living room."

Sabrina nodded then walked to the bedroom. She clicked on the overhead light and glanced around then opened the dresser drawers and began searching. She went over the entire room and the smaller bedroom across the hall too before moving to the bathroom. She found no drugs, no large sums of cash or any drug paraphernalia. She was beginning to wonder if her tip wasn't reliable. Lowrey seemed to be keeping his nose clean.

"Found something," Johnson called to her.

She stepped into the kitchen where Johnson held up a small

plastic baggie filled with pills. "I found it in the daughter's shoe by the front door. Imagine if she'd taken it to school with her."

Suddenly, Lowrey's wife grabbed the shoe, leaped to her feet and whacked her husband with it. "What were you thinking bringing drugs in here?" she screamed as the little girl began to cry.

Johnson grabbed her and pulled her away before she could hit her husband again. "That's enough," he told her.

"It's not mine," Lowrey insisted. "I was only holding it for someone."

She'd heard that excuse before. In fact, during her time in Narcotics, she'd probably heard all the excuses. It was always someone else's fault.

"Stand up," Sabrina told him. "I'm placing you under arrest."

She drove Lowrey down to the sheriff's office and officially booked him. Then she placed him into an interview room. She let him sweat for a while hoping that he had time to think about what going back to prison would be like and hoped he would be willing to help her bring Creed's organization down in exchange for some leniency.

Once they were ready, Johnson joined Sabrina in the interview and informed Lowrey that he was going back to prison for violating his parole by having drugs in his possession. The man was nervous and kept rubbing his leg. She took that as a good indicator that he might be willing to answer her questions in exchange for a deal that kept him out of prison.

However, once she started asking him questions, Lowrey clammed up and refused to help them. She pressed him but could see the fear in his face. He was more frightened of Creed than he was of returning to prison.

"Think about your daughter," Sabrina said. She knew he'd been working during his time in prison to get straight and get back to his family but it seemed he wasn't able to keep up the straight and narrow life. "Do you want to go back to prison and not see your daughter?"

He glared at her for bringing up his child but still shook his head. "I can't help you."

Johnson stood. "That's enough. You'll go in front of a judge tomorrow at which time your parole will be revoked and you'll be returned to prison to finish out the remainder of your sentence. Your daughter will be in middle school before you see her again, Lowrey."

She walked out with Johnson, who shook his head. "I'm sorry. I really thought he might crack."

She'd thought so too. "I was hopeful but he's too afraid of Creed to talk."

That was the same brick wall she'd been hitting ever since deciding to focus on Creed. Even her own brother had been frightened of him so she understood the danger of asking these men to defy Creed, but she wasn't going to bring him down without help.

"I'll keep working on him," Johnson told her. "Maybe a night in jail will change his mind."

She thanked him but she wasn't holding her breath. She was familiar with Creed's tactics and they were intimidating.

She spotted his wife clutching the little girl sitting in the waiting area. As she signed out, the desk clerk spotted her watching them.

"They came in with Lowrey. It's his wife and daughter. She's wanting information about him."

"I know. Unfortunately, they were there when we arrested him. Let them know Mr. Johnson, his parole officer, will be out to speak with them soon."

She hated the look of disappointment and anger on the young woman's face. Another little girl would grow up without her father around and Creed was ultimately the one behind it. None of his men seemed willing to turn on him.

Her only hope now was depending on Max—Jake—to bring him down.

Chapter Five

Sabrina headed back for her desk and was writing up her report about Lowrey's arrest when Kent stuck his head out of his office and called for her.

She hit submit on the report then walked into his office.

He was already sitting back behind his desk when she entered. "I wanted to let you know we've identified the man who attacked you in the grocery store parking lot. His name is Lucas Davis. He has multiple arrests for drugs, assault and robbery."

She glanced through the file he handed her and shuddered at the image of the man who'd put a knife to her throat and threatened her son. "Do we have an address on him?"

He nodded. "I've already sent two deputies to the address on record but he wasn't there. I've put out a warrant for his arrest."

"Does he have any connections to Creed?"

"Nothing solid although they have known associates. Maybe he'll spill who hired him once we get him into custody."

She handed the file back to him. "I hope so."

"We're also still processing witness statements and forensics from your house but, so far, several neighbors recalled seeing a strange vehicle with several men inside. We're hoping to find video footage from security cameras to try to identify them."

She nodded. It wasn't good news. It had been dark so identifying them would be difficult but she knew Kent and the rest of her team would do their best. Jake could confirm that Creed had given the order but without knowing the shooters' identities his testimony would be worthless. "Can I go over there or is it still a crime scene? I'd like to pick up some clothes and toys for Robby."

He nodded. "I can have a deputy follow you over there and keep an eye out while you gather what you need. Then, it's probably best that you go to your mom's house and stay there."

"What do you mean?"

"I spoke with Sheriff Thompson about the attacks yesterday. She thinks it's a good idea that you take some time off and let the department handle the investigation."

Sabrina's heart sank. This was what she hadn't wanted to happen. "Why?"

"There were three separate attacks against you yesterday, Sabrina. We know from Max that Creed has placed a hit on you. It's too dangerous for you to continue to walk around like nothing happened. The sheriff thinks so and I agree with her."

Sabrina leaned across the desk. "Don't you get it, Kent? If you take me off the investigation, Creed wins."

"No, he doesn't. Max is still undercover plus this department will continue investigating. I'm adding Drake to the case. And this isn't forever. It's just until we know you're safe."

"I didn't join the sheriff's office to be safe. I joined for justice."

"I know. I'm sorry it has to be this way." He picked up the phone and called for a patrol deputy to escort her to her house. When he arrived, Sabrina, still seething, stood and headed for the door.

"I'll keep you updated on the investigations," he assured her.

She thanked him then walked out of his office. Down the hall, Sheriff Thompson's door stood open. Sabrina thought briefly about marching in there and demanding she change her mind but their sheriff couldn't be bullied. She was usually tough but fair. She'd made a decision and wouldn't be swayed. In fact, she might even call Sabrina reckless in her desire to find justice for her brother.

Sabrina walked to her desk, grabbed her keys and gun then walked to the car. She watched her mirrors as she drove but only the deputy appeared to be following her.

Her heart broke when she pulled to the curb at her home. The Christmas lights were still hanging from the eave but the front windows had been boarded up and her SUV was gone from the driveway. Crime scene tape cordoned off the lawn and driveway but Deputy Parkman removed it enough for her to pass through.

She choked back emotions as she walked through her destroyed home. This used to be her safe haven. Now she was sure they would never feel safe here again. She quickly gathered some clothes for both her and Robby. She didn't need to worry about the uniforms now but she still collected them, hopeful that Sheriff Thompson would change her mind.

Deputy Parkman kept watch as she worked then helped her load her mother's car with the items. "I'll follow you and make sure you don't have a tail," he said.

She thanked him then headed for her mom's house, taking her own safety precautions. They turned out to be unneeded since the only person following her was Deputy Parkman.

Her cell phone rang as she drove and she recognized the number.

"How are you this morning?" Jake asked once she answered.

"Not great," she admitted.

"Did something happen during your parole search?"

"We found drugs, but Lowrey is too scared of Creed to talk. Now Sheriff Thompson wants me to take some time off until this threat with Creed is over. She's basically sidelining me." She sounded like a petulant child who hadn't gotten her way but she couldn't help her frustration. The sheriff's decree was unfair. "Promise me you won't keep me in the dark, Jake, with what's going on with Creed."

He shouldn't agree to it and it wasn't right of her to put him on the spot since technically he was liaising with the sheriff's office and not just her, but she didn't want to get completely pushed out. Jake was her only connection left.

"I won't," he promised. "Creed came by my apartment last night. He was wild-eyed and acting strange. He said his supplier wasn't happy that the hit against you failed."

"I'm sorry to disappoint him."

Jake chuckled. "Me too. He didn't seem to suspect that I was involved though. I haven't seen him yet today. I'm heading over to the factory now."

"I'm glad he doesn't suspect you, Jake. I was worried he might." At least he was still able to investigate and gather evidence against Creed.

"I'm hoping I can convince him to call off the hit on you and let me handle it. If he thinks I'm targeting you, maybe no one else will."

It was a good plan. She hoped Jake could convince him. It might take the target off her back and then Sheriff Thompson would surely allow her to get back to work. "Let me know how that goes."

"I will. In fact, I was hoping I could come by later and spend some time with Robby."

She should have expected that request but it caught her off guard. Of course he would want to get to know his son and she didn't want to stand in the way of them having a relationship. "That should be fine. We'll see you then."

She ended the call surprised by the swell of emotion that overtook her. She'd known she would have to share Robby. It was the right thing to do and she certainly owed it to Jake, but the thought of sharing her son with him was scary.

She took a deep breath. She was just going to have to get used to it. Jake was a part of Robby's life now.

She parked then waved as Parkman drove off. She carried the belongings she'd gathered into the house. Her mother wasn't in sight but she passed by the playroom and saw Robby sleeping on the bed. That explained why the house was so quiet. Naptime. She dumped the stuff she was carrying onto the bed in the spare room. This would be their home for a while now and, while it wasn't his bed or his toys, at least Robby had a safe place that he was familiar with to stay. It could have been much worse.

She heard a noise and walked back into the living room only to find her mother dragging a crate across the floor.

"What are you doing?" Sabrina asked her.

"It's the Christmas decorations. I wasn't going to put up any since Bob and I had planned a getaway for Christmas but now that you and Robby are here, I thought I should. At least for his sake."

It was just like her mother to be so selfless and think of others. It was one of the things Sabrina admired most about her mom.

She grabbed ahold of the other end of the crate and picked it up. "I'll help you."

"Don't you have to get back to work?"

"No, I don't have to worry about that at the moment." She quickly explained Sheriff Thompson's order, then helped her mom lug the remaining totes from the storage room to the living room.

It didn't take long with both of them working to put up the tree and decorate it. They stood back and admired it.

"There's still some room on the bottom limbs for Robby to add his own ornaments."

Sabrina hugged her mom. "You're the best. Thank you for letting us stay here. I don't know what we would do without you."

"I'm sure Kent would have put you in a safe house. At least, this way, I still get to see you and Robby. Are you sure you're safe here?"

"As safe as anywhere else. No one knows where you live and since this house isn't even in your name, that helps." Sabrina's father had purchased this house from a friend of his. He'd signed the deed over but the official paperwork had never been changed. She'd pressured her mom to take care of that but, to her knowledge, she hadn't yet. "Kent also promised to increase patrols in the area but I wouldn't want to put you in danger though so if you'd rather we leave…"

"No, no, no. I was only concerned about your safety. I'm happy to have you both here. Honestly, it gets to be so quiet around here."

Sabrina understood the sentiment. Her childhood home had been full of laughter and silliness with her brother always pulling pranks and showing off. She hadn't realized back then how special her family was. Now both her dad and Robby were gone. Sabrina didn't have to deal with the quiet with an active four-year-old running around but she understood about loneliness and recognized it in her mother.

"So you and Bob seem to be getting along well. You must like him."

Her mother's face lit up with a smile. "He's wonderful. And he loves to have a good time. We go out to eat and travel and see the sights. I have fun with him."

"I'm glad to see you getting out again."

"Me too." She reached over and placed her hand on top of Sabrina's. "I'd like to see the same thing for you, sweetheart."

She shook her head, shaking away the thought. Romance

was the last thing on her mind. "I've got so much going on, Mom. I don't have time to date. I have to worry about my cases and Creed, plus Robby."

"I wasn't thinking about signing you up for a dating site. You and Jake used to be quite the item. It's obvious he still cares for you, Sabrina."

She took a sip of her hot chocolate then set it down. She'd given a lot of thought to her and Jake and decided it could never work out between them no matter how much they'd once cared for each other. "That's in the past, Mom. I'll always care about Jake and he is Robby's father so, in that sense, I suppose he'll always be a part of my life. But it's also because of Robby that I know nothing romantic will ever happen between us again. You saw how angry he was when he found out I kept the truth from him. I can never make that up to him. Never."

"Yes, I remember. But I also remember how worried he was when he learned Creed had sent men to kill you."

She waved that concern away. Any decent human being would have been worried when they learned of a hit against someone, and Jake was a good person. Plus, he knew she had Robby with her. His concern might have just as easily featured his newly discovered son.

Her mom reached across a tin of ornaments and pushed a strand of hair back from Sabrina's face. "Honey, it's time you forgive yourself for not being able to help your brother. It's time for you to move on. It's time for us both to get on with our lives. What you and Jake had five years ago made you happy. I would love to see that for you again. I'm only saying not to push him away because you're afraid. Sometimes, taking a risk is worth it. Promise me that you'll think about it?"

"I will."

They'd both suffered so much after her brother's death that, for a while, she wasn't certain her mother would ever smile again. Bob Crawford had brought that back to her mom and, whatever her feelings for him, he'd brought her mom back to life again.

She stared up at the twinkling lights on the tree and wondered if she could ever feel that way again. If she did, one thing was for certain. It wouldn't be with Jake Harris. He would never be able to see past her mistake enough to forgive her for it.

Jake headed for the industrial part of town, noticing that the roads were pretty barren. This part of town had become nearly uninhabitable as more businesses shut down and moved away. It made the perfect location for Creed to conduct his business. No nosy neighbors watching what he was doing.

Jake pulled up to the gate and waved at the two men who stood guard. They opened the gate and let him through. He parked in the lot and walked inside. Creed was on the factory floor having words with one of his foremen. Jake didn't know his name so he avoided joining the conversation. He walked past them to the break room and poured himself a cup of coffee.

Suddenly, a man appeared beside him, staring him down. Him, Jake recognized. Mick Jacoby, Creed's second in command and the source of the rumors that Max might have been a federal agent.

"What are you looking at, Mick?" Jake demanded. Max wouldn't kowtow to him so Jake couldn't either.

"I'd heard you were back." He glanced at the cast on Jake's arm. "Car accident, huh?"

"That's right. I understand you had your own thoughts about what happened to me."

"Still do. I don't trust you, Max. I never have."

So he'd been suspicious of Max from the start. Nothing Jake could do or say would change that, but at least he still seemed to believe Jake was Max. "Well, I'm back now and I'm taking point on setting up a new drop-off for the next shipment."

"I've already handled that. I've got the trucks ready and waiting."

"Where's the drop-off?"

Jacoby scoffed. "Like I would tell you so you could pass it on to the cops. Besides, from what I understand, Creed's supplier won't make a move until that deputy is out the way permanently."

He walked off, leaving Jake with a conundrum. He couldn't uncover Creed's supplier until the drugs were handed off and, apparently, that wasn't going to happen until Sabrina was dead.

That meant their only chance of ending this was the flash drive he'd copied from Creed's laptop. He'd forgotten to ask Sabrina about it when he'd spoken to her but it had been less than a day since he'd given it to her. He didn't know Jana Carter, the sheriff department's IT person, but he hoped she was good at her job.

The information on that flash drive might be the only thing that could keep Sabrina alive.

"Mom, you've gone overboard again," Sabrina said as she pulled another inflatable from the crate of Christmas decorations that littered the driveway. She'd already unveiled an eight-foot snowman and now her mom had added an inflatable Santa Claus. They'd moved from decorating the inside of the house to the outside. "Your front yard is just not that big."

Her mom chuckled. "I know but I couldn't resist. Robby will love it."

She couldn't argue with that. He would love it. Something about this Christmas had changed for them and it had everything to do with Robby. Her little boy had brought such joy and happiness into their lives and driven out the sorrow and grief that had plagued Sabrina for so many years.

"I want Robby to understand that Christmas isn't about Santa. It's about the birth of Jesus."

"Will you relax," her mom told her. "I also bought a manger scene."

"There won't be room to walk on the lawn if you add all three."

She smiled. "I know. The manger scene goes on the roof."

She must have seen Sabrina's surprise because she laughed. "Don't worry. I don't expect you to climb up there. I asked Bob to come over to help. He got called away to handle some issue at his job site."

Something about her calling on her new boyfriend to save the day ruffled Sabrina's ego. "I can do it, Mom."

"Honey, let Bob get on the roof. You're supposed to be laying low, remember."

"I don't think Creed's men are going to spot me just because I climbed onto the roof to put up Christmas decorations."

"Why take the risk?"

She walked into the garage and dug through the storage room until she found the manger scene. She dragged it, the inflatables and a crate of Christmas lights into the yard and began putting them up. A half hour later, Bob arrived. Her mother greeted him with a kiss and a mug of hot coffee. Sabrina couldn't help but see the glow in her mother's face as she talked with Bob. Her mom was falling for him hard and it was good to see her happy again. Sabrina didn't wish her mother unhappiness but this relationship with Bob had happened so suddenly and now he was all she could talk about. Sabrina didn't know if it was jealousy or a dislike of seeing her mother with someone besides her dad, but something about the man rubbed her the wrong way.

She pushed away those thoughts. She had to stop seeing suspicion in everything. She'd even done a background check on Bob Crawford and he'd checked out. No criminal history

to speak of and he was active in the church and local chari-
ties. Plus, she'd never seen him be anything but attentive and
affectionate toward her mother.

Bob Crawford wasn't the bad guy and Sabrina needed to
stop being so cynical. She needed to get over her dislike before she ruined her relationship with her mother the way she'd
ruined her relationship with Jake.

As she worked, Robby, who had awakened from his nap,
ran around the lawn laughing and giggling at the inflatables.
She carried the ladder from the garage to get busy hanging the
house lights. She should have done this earlier in the month
but her mother hadn't planned on being home for Christmas
and Sabrina had been so preoccupied with Creed and worrying about Max's sudden disappearance that she'd let time slip
by her. She'd promised herself that Robby would get all her
attention this year and this would be his best Christmas yet
and she'd already gone back on that promise without meaning to. She needed to be more intentional for her child's sake.
She supposed that issue had solved itself now that she'd been
ordered to take some time off.

A car pulled to the curb and Jake got out. He walked up
the driveway, shook Bob's hand and spoke to her mother before walking over to where she was untangling the lights. He
stopped before he reached her to kneel down to Robby and
say something to him that had the little boy giggling even
more and showing off the Christmas inflatables, pulling Jake
by the hand to follow him.

Her heart ached at the scene. Father and son enjoying a
happy Christmas moment. Tears pressed against her eyes as
she realized how much Jake had missed and it was because
of her that he had. She'd robbed him and Robby of that special time that they could never get back. How could he ever
forgive her for that?

He played with Robby a few more minutes but the moment

she stepped up onto the ladder, he rushed over to her. "Do you want some help with that?"

"I can handle it. I've strung lights before." She'd hung her own house lights with no help. A lot of good that had done her.

He put his hands on the ladder. "I don't mind, Sabrina."

"I appreciate it but I'd much rather see you with Robby. It was nice."

He looked back at Robby and a smile filled his face. "I liked it too. He's so excited about Christmas."

"Yes, he is, and I want to make this his best one yet."

"I want that too."

She reached to string a line of lights and reached a bit too far, causing the ladder to wobble. Jake steadied it but Sabrina lost her balance, falling backward. She screamed but Jake caught her before she hit the ground.

"I've got you," he said.

As she stared up into his blue eyes, she was stunned at the way her pulse raced and the electricity between them. From the look on his face, he felt it too.

Her mother and Bob came running, breaking the spell over them. "Sabrina, are you all right? I told you not to climb up that ladder."

Jake set her down and she tried to shake off the headiness from being in his arms. "I'm fine," she insisted. "I just tumbled. It was dumb. I should have moved the ladder."

"Honey, you're bleeding."

She lifted her arm and saw a gash on her forearm. She hadn't even felt it but it was bleeding badly.

"I'll get a towel," her mother said then dashed inside.

Jake took her arm and held it up. "Keep the wound up so it won't bleed as much. You must have clipped it on the ladder."

"I didn't even feel it," she said, her face warming as she realized she was too busy falling into his lovely blue eyes.

"That looks deep. You might need stitches," Bob stated.

Jake agreed. "I'll drive you to the emergency room."

Robby, seeing the commotion, came running up to her. "Mommy, are you hurt?"

"I'm okay, baby. Just cut myself. I'm going to go see the doctor to take care of it while you stay here with Grandma and Bob and finish the decorating."

He seemed okay with that once he knew she wasn't seriously injured.

"I'll finish hanging these," Bob offered but Jake stopped him.

"I can do it when I get back. I don't mind."

They argued for a few minutes over who would finish the light hanging until her mother returned with a towel and pressed it against her arm.

"I don't care who hangs them but someone needs to take my daughter to the hospital."

That seemed to bring Jake to his senses. "I'm driving her."

"Good, then Bob can finish the lights. Make sure she's safe."

"I will," he promised her.

Sabrina walked to the car with Jake's hand at her back. She was thankful he was there and for the comfort he provided. She still wasn't feeling much pain but the bleeding was still heavy and she could see for herself that stitches might be needed.

He made the drive to the hospital in record time and parked near the entrance to the emergency room. As he helped her from the car, she realized she was feeling a bit lightheaded, probably from the blood loss.

"I'm right here. Lean on me," he said and, for once, she didn't argue.

They walked inside and Jake planted her into a seat then walked to the counter and registered her to be seen.

"You don't have to stay," she told him as he slipped into the chair beside her. "I appreciate the ride but you don't have to stay."

"I'd prefer it if you don't mind."

She shook her head then stared off. She would have never believed that something as simple as talking to Jake Harris would be difficult, but she couldn't seem to find the words to speak to him. She wasn't looking for a fight but she also wasn't interested in discussing why she'd been so affected by his arms around her either.

It was getting harder and harder to make believe that he didn't still have an effect on her. That her knees didn't go weak at his touch or his smile send her spiraling like a silly schoolgirl on her first crush.

Jake Harris was not a crush. He'd been her first love. Her first everything until she'd pushed him away. She'd deprived him of knowing he had a son and that was something unforgivable. No use in losing her heart to him when he would never reciprocate. She'd missed her chance at happiness when she'd allowed grief to send her to a dark place.

She had no right to fall for him again.

The towel she'd pressed against her wound had bled through. Thankfully, the emergency room wasn't busy and they were able to send her to a curtained-off area quickly.

Jake paced as the nurse cleaned her wound then announced she would need stitches. "How did you manage to do this?" she asked Sabrina.

"I was hanging Christmas lights and fell. I guess I cut it on the ladder."

The nurse quickly stitched up the gash then arranged for her release. "My supervisor will have to come in and check on you and give the okay to release you. Once he does that, you'll be free to go."

There was little to do except sit back and wait for that to happen. She watched Jake standing by the curtain, peering out periodically to keep an eye out. She appreciated his being with her and doing what he could to keep her safe, but she realized he'd come to the house to see Robby, not to help her. "I'm sorry I'm taking away your time with Robby."

"It's okay. I'm sure he'll feel better knowing that his mom is okay."

He was probably right. After the attack at the house last night, she was surprised Robby hadn't clung to her leg or cried when she left. The trauma had to have affected him. He was one tough little kid.

Jake peered through the curtain again only, this time, his shoulders tensed.

"What is it?" Sabrina demanded, sitting up.

"I can see the outside entrance from here. Two of Creed's men just showed up."

She tensed too and hopped off the gurney, pulling on her jacket, and glanced over his shoulder. Sure enough, two men had entered the area and were glancing around.

"I don't recognize them. Are you sure they work for Creed?"

He nodded. "Definitely. I saw them last night at the factory."

"Do you think they're searching for me? How would they know I was here?"

He rubbed the back of his neck. "I'm not sure but we should get out of here before they see us."

She agreed. Waiting around would do them no good and they didn't want a confrontation with these men in the hospital. It still bugged her though that they were here. It couldn't be a coincidence, could it?

"I should call Kent and alert him." She reached into her pocket for her cell phone but it wasn't there. She clearly remembered sliding it into her back pocket earlier in the day. It must have dropped out when she'd fallen from the ladder. "I don't have my phone. Let me use yours."

He started to reach into his pocket to retrieve it, but

stopped. "We should go now. They're rounding the check-in desk."

Sabrina peeked out from behind the curtain and realized he was right. These men were in search mode and she and Jake were sitting ducks.

They slipped through the curtain and down the hallway to an emergency door that opened directly to the back area of the hospital which housed the labs and diagnostic equipment. Only employees were generally back here. Patients were usually escorted. Thankfully, she knew her way through the hospital, having run emergency drills last year as part of a crisis readiness response with the county and state law enforcement agencies.

She led him through the hallways until they were deep inside the building. There was a back door through the cafeteria's kitchen that led outside and that was where she was headed. They needed to get away from these men before they were seen, then call Kent to send backup.

Jake's heavy breathing and footfalls pressed her forward. They weren't running yet but they moved quickly through the building toward their destination. Her eyes scanned her surroundings and the people they passed, on alert for any evidence of their being discovered.

She heard rattling as she darted through a doorway and turned to see the two men appear at the end of the hallway. Only a locked set of doors kept them from approaching but she could see their faces through the glass inserts. They'd found them.

"This way." Jake pushed her through the doorway into the kitchen area.

She felt him pressing her to go faster and she darted around the personnel and equipment toward the back door. She burst through it into the cold night air but didn't slow down.

"Keep going," Jake insisted.

Her pace didn't slow as she ran across the parking lot.

Jake's car was parked on the other side of the medical center building but it was too dangerous to try to reach it with these men on their trail. She darted across the street to a grassy area with an embankment instead where Jake grabbed her arm and pulled her to the ground, taking cover behind the hill. Her heart was pounding and they were both out of breath but she was glad for the respite. She peeked over a hill at the door they'd just run through, watching and waiting to see if they'd been followed.

Sabrina's breath was visible on the air and the chill of the night rolled over her. She rubbed her arms, gasping when she hit the area with the newly treated gash. "That was close," she said but she spotted a worried expression on Jake's face. "Do you think we lost them?"

He let out a breath which she could see hanging in the air. He shook his head and she followed his gaze. The doors opened again and the two men exited the building and scanned the area, guns in hand. The duo locked eyes on their position then rushed their way.

He pulled his gun from its holster. "Did you bring your weapon?"

She shook her head. She hadn't brought anything—purse, ID, cell phone—when she'd left the house. Of course, she hadn't planned on needing any of that stuff when she was putting up Christmas decorations. Now she regretted that decision.

Shots rang out. They were firing and it was two guns against one. Getting into a gunfight now wasn't the smart move unless they were cornered.

"Let's get out of here," Jake said. "Try to make it to the shopping center across the way."

She couldn't agree more. They had to find a way to lose these armed gunmen before they caught up to them. The shopping center in the distance was a good idea. Even Creed's men wouldn't dare open fire around so many people...she hoped. It should provide them with cover and a place to hide and call for help.

But, first, they had to make it there alive.

Chapter Six

Sabrina didn't let up as they darted across a median and down a hill. Jake turned to glance behind them. Their pursuers were still there, doing their best to catch up before Jake and Sabrina made it to safety.

If she'd had her gun on her they might be able to stop and engage them but he couldn't take them both on alone. Getting to safety was their best chance of survival.

They reached the parking lot of the shopping center. Thankfully, it was lit up with Christmas lights and bustling with shoppers. Sabrina darted through the crowd and took cover in a vestibule that had a sign pointing to the restrooms so he followed her. They pressed themselves against the wall and crouched down, trying not to attract attention.

"Give me your cell phone," she instructed. He handed it over and she dialed a number. "I'll have Kent send a car and a patrol team to flush these guys out."

It was a good idea. Patrol officers could apprehend or at least distract the assailants while Sabrina and Jake got away. He was hoping too to keep his identity hidden.

If that still even mattered.

"They're on the way," Sabrina told him.

She fidgeted with her arm and panic filled him. He moved closer to her to examine her wound. "Were you hit?"

"No, it's just sore where the stitches are." She looked at him and her brows creased with worry. "Are you hurt?"

He shook his head. "No."

"Then what's the matter?"

He started to protest that nothing was wrong but she cut him off before he could speak.

"I know you, Jake. I've always been able to tell when something was bugging you. Now, what's wrong?"

He couldn't help a smile at the truth in her statement. She had always been able to read his emotions like a book. "It's probably nothing but those men might have seen me."

"Sure, they saw us both."

"I mean, they might have seen my face, Sabrina. If they know who I am then my cover might have just been blown."

"Oh." He saw the consequence of that settle on her face. "But you don't know if they did."

He shook his head. "I don't know for certain. I can't be sure how good of a look they even got of me."

She reached for his hand. "Then we'll worry about that later. For now, we're safe." Sirens sounded and patrol lights lit up the night as two sheriff's office cruisers pulled up to the curb. "Here's our ride."

Sabrina got back on the phone and coordinated with the patrol officers to clear out an area so that she and Jake could jump to a vehicle without being seen. "Take us to the station," she ordered the deputy behind the wheel once they were safely inside the patrol cruiser.

By the time they arrived at the sheriff's office, Kent was waiting in his office along with Sheriff Deena Thompson. It was the first time he'd met her so he reached to shake her hand and she reciprocated.

"Are you all right?" Kent asked Sabrina first thing.

She nodded. "I'm fine." She motioned to stitches on her

arm. "I cut myself while I was putting up Christmas lights and Max offered to drive me to the emergency room. That's when Creed's men arrived. We had to leave his car behind at the hospital."

Kent nodded then picked up the phone. "I'll have someone go retrieve it." He made the call and Jake handed over his keys to the deputy who arrived to go get the car from the hospital parking lot.

Once they were gone, Sabrina turned to Kent and the sheriff. "Those men might have blown his cover."

"How certain are you?" Sheriff Thompson asked Jake.

He rubbed the back of his neck and sighed. "I'm not sure at all if you want to know the truth. I saw them from behind the curtain at the hospital and they might have seen me from behind but we were running and hiding so they might not have gotten a good look at my face. Even if they did, I can't be sure they know who I am."

"What do you want to do?" Kent asked.

"I should at least find out."

Sabrina's mouth fell open. "What are you talking about? You can't go back there. Creed will know you're working undercover."

Jake understood her concern but how could he walk away from this investigation if there was a possibility that his identity hadn't been compromised? He owed it to his brother to at least make sure before he gave up. And he still needed to keep her safe.

Sabrina looked at Sheriff Thompson. "You can't let him go back in there. It's too dangerous."

Sheriff Thompson glanced at her then at Jake. "It's not my place to tell him what he can and can't do. Technically, this isn't our investigation. It's the DEA's. Maybe you should call your supervisor and talk to him about what you should do."

That was a good idea and he might do that. Carl would probably advise him not to risk it, but Jake wasn't willing to give up so easily. If his cover was still intact, he wasn't walking away from completing the mission his brother had started. Besides, with the target on Sabrina, flushing out Creed's supplier was now all the more important. If he could do that from the inside then it was the better option.

He glanced at Sabrina. He understood her concern but he'd given her the courtesy of knowing what was best for her. He hoped she would do the same.

"My real concern is how Creed's men knew you were there," Kent stated.

Sabrina shrugged. "I have no idea. I find it hard to believe they followed us from my mom's place. I made sure I wasn't followed there when I left my house this afternoon."

Unfortunately, Jake had an idea of who might have tipped them off. "I had a run-in today with Mick Jacoby. He doesn't trust me. It's possible he had someone following me and that I led them there." He found it difficult to believe he hadn't noticed a tail, but it wasn't impossible that was what had happened. If that was the case then his cover had surely been compromised. Going back in was a risk but it was one he had to take.

Kent glanced at Sheriff Thompson then back at Jake. "Whether or not you go back in is your call."

Jake made a decision. "I'll go back to the apartment and phone Carl and talk it over with him before I decide anything."

Sabrina folded her arms and he could see she wasn't happy with his decision. He didn't want to anger her but he couldn't just walk away. He owed it to Max and he owed it to her. As long as she was in danger, he had to do everything he could to stop Creed.

Sabrina was quiet on the drive back to her mom's house, which was fine with Jake. He was glad to have his car returned but he was extra careful to take precautions and check his mirrors for a tail as he drove. He still found it hard to believe that he could have missed one following him to Sabrina's house, but he had no other way of explaining how they'd tracked her to the hospital. They made it to the house without being seen. He stopped at the curb, noticing the lights were up and on. Bob must have finished hanging them as he and Sabrina were running for their lives. Through the front window, he spotted Beverly, Bob and Robby in the living room.

She saw it too. "What's going to happen to Robby if you get killed, Jake? You just found out you have a son and you want to take this big risk? Why would you do that?"

"You didn't like being told to back off the investigation, did you?"

Her face reddened at that admonishment.

"Creed is dangerous, Sabrina. He's placed a target on your back. As long as he's out there, I can't leave."

She reached for his hand. "Please just think about this, Jake. I know you want to bring Creed down. So do I. But think about your son. He needs his father." She leaned over and kissed his cheek, then hopped out and ran inside.

He made sure she was in before he drove off. He headed back to the apartment then had second thoughts. If his cover was blown, Creed's men would be waiting for him there. He had a lot to think about and he wasn't sure what to do. He wished there was a way to know whether or not his cover had been compromised before he placed himself in Creed's path. Confusion had set in. He'd come to town with only one mission—to finish Max's undercover job. Now everything had gotten so muddled.

He parked at the apartment building and scanned the lot and buildings. He didn't see anything out of place but his instincts were on alert. Something was wrong. He started the car and peeled out instead. He headed down the road, unsure of what to do next. He could return to the sheriff's office and admit the operation was over or he could risk his life to find out if his cover had been blown.

He turned back around. What he'd told Sabrina was right.

He had to take the risk. He parked then headed up to the apartment and approached the door. He was still watching but if someone was out there, they were doing a good job of hiding themselves.

He unlocked the door and pushed it open.

Suddenly, his neighbor's door opened and someone grabbed him from behind, shoving him into the apartment. Another figure ran at him with a baseball bat and slammed it against his head before he could reach for his gun.

Jake slid to the floor as agonizing pain ripped through him and darkness filled the edges of his vision. One of the men grabbed his arm and flipped him over and he saw it was the same two assailants who'd chased them from the hospital.

"Mr. Creed said to bring you in," one of them stated, and Jake was helpless to fight back as unconsciousness pulled him under.

Jake's first realization as he regained consciousness was that he was no longer at his apartment. He opened his eyes, pain ripping through his head at the light. He moaned in pain then jerked when he tried to raise his hand to shield his eyes. Both hands were tied to a chair. He pulled at his feet. They were bound too.

He glanced up and spotted one of the men who'd attacked him.

"You're awake. Good."

"Why am I here?" He figured he knew the reason but he needed to continue with his cover until he knew for certain it had been blown. "Why did Creed send you after me?"

"I just follow orders. We'll know soon enough. He's on his way here."

As he finished speaking, the door slid open. Jake braced himself, only it wasn't Creed who entered. It was the other one of the duo who'd overpowered him.

"Where's Creed?" number one asked his partner.

"On his way." He cracked his knuckles. "But, first, let's have some fun and tenderize this guy for him."

He punched Jake, sending him and the chair to the floor. Jake was riddled with pain at the punch and the sting of his back, arm and head as he hit the floor. The two men pulled him back up for more beatings. They weren't done with him yet.

Suddenly, someone shouted and the men calmed then moved aside. Creed stepped forward with several other men, including Mick Jacoby with a smug look, standing behind him. He folded his arms as he stared at Jake. "How long did you think you could fool us? You're playing both sides."

"I don't know what Jacoby said to you—"

"This isn't about what he said or didn't say, Max. You were seen by Ethan and Dax here helping that Deputy Reagan escape the hospital. You're helping her which can only mean that you aren't who you say you are. Are you working undercover?"

So Creed's men had seen him at the hospital and recognized him. That explained the abduction and beating. Creed thought he'd been betrayed. He had been, but if Jake could convince him otherwise then the case could still be salvaged.

And he had just the idea.

"It's not true," he told Creed. "I'm not working undercover and I'm not helping Deputy Reagan."

Jacoby stepped forward. "My men saw you with their own eyes. Are you calling them liars?"

Ethan and Dax nodded. "Yeah, we saw you," one of them—he didn't know which—said.

He looked at Creed. "You don't understand. I have a twin brother—Jake. He and Deputy Reagan were an item back in the day. High school sweethearts. I'd heard he was back in town to see her. It must have been him your guys saw."

"They said it was you," Jacoby insisted, running at Jake and punching him in the face.

Jake tasted blood but didn't give in to the pain. "We're identical twins. They probably wouldn't have been able to tell the difference between him and me."

Creed chuckled and turned to his men. "Identical twins. Sure, Max. You're really going to try to play the twin angle. How dumb do you think I am?"

He wasn't dumb but it helped that Jake wasn't lying about being a twin and could even prove his claim. "We both played ball for Mercy High School and we were good. There's a display at the high school with our picture, standing side by side on the basketball court. That will prove to you that I'm telling the truth about being a twin."

Jacoby looked ready to pounce on him again, but Creed stopped him. He appeared intrigued. "What's your brother's name?"

"Jake—Jake Harris. He's a detective with the San Antonio Police Department. The department can also confirm his existence."

"You have a twin brother who's a cop?"

"Yes, I do. We went our separate ways after college. He chose law enforcement and I chose another direction. He was always the good guy and I was the one who didn't like to follow the rules." That part wasn't true. Max had been the more determined one of the two of them. Jake had found a place in San Antonio PD while Max was always taking risks and working his way up the ladder. Working undercover had been a natural fit for him because he was charismatic and fearless while Jake had always been the more cautious one...at least until now.

"If you don't believe me, go to the high school and look at the display. I know it's still there because I saw it a few days ago. Go see that then come back and call me a liar again." He was daring them to do his bidding but he had to put up the bravado in order to sell his story. These men wouldn't easily be fooled but, this time, his story might sound reasonable.

Max had bragged about their photos still being displayed when they'd met up.

Creed considered it for a moment then nodded. He motioned to Ethan and Dax, who cut Jake's binds then forced him to stand.

"You're not actually believing his story, are you?" Jacoby asked Creed.

"We're all going together to verify your story," Creed told Jake. "That way, if I don't believe it, we won't have to drive far to dump your body."

They led him outside to the car then shoved him into the back seat and pushed him into the middle. Ethan sat on one side while Dax took the other. Jacoby didn't look happy as he climbed into the driver's seat but Creed, who took shotgun, didn't seem to care.

Jake took advantage of having access to his hands to touch his jaw where he'd been hit more than once. The physical pain stung, sure, but he was thinking what would happen if they didn't believe this story. If he couldn't talk his way out of this mess, these men would kill him. He didn't want to die but, more than that, he didn't want to abandon Sabrina. He'd give anything for one more chance to see her. He wasn't ready to die today.

They reached the high school and Dax used a crowbar to pry open the front door. Ethan grabbed Jake's arm and walked him down a long hallway to a display case near the front office, following behind Creed and Jacoby.

Even in the dark hallway, the trophy case was backlit and the honors and displays were visible. Creed bent over and looked hard at the photo of Jake and Max front and center on the basketball team. Their team had won the championship that year. Another photo of just Max and Jake showed them at homecoming. Sabrina was on Jake's arm in that photo and their names were listed which only served to further prove his story about he and Sabrina being high school sweethearts.

He glanced at the photo and the smiles on both their faces. He'd known even then how much he'd loved her. He hadn't even been able to imagine a life without her. And it had been just as empty and lonely without her as his teenaged self could have ever imagined.

Creed straightened. "I'll be. Even side by side, I can't tell the difference. It's creepy."

It wasn't the first time he'd heard that sentiment. He usually didn't care for it but he wouldn't argue about it today. "So then you believe me?"

Creed thought for a moment and looked at the photos again before finally nodding. "I guess I do. Your story checks out. You do have an identical twin brother named Jake Harris. The only question that remains is whether or not he's in town." He took out his cell phone and dialed information. "San Antonio Police Department and please connect me."

Jake waited as the call went through and Creed asked for him by name. Several moments passed before he ended the call and slid the phone back into his pocket.

"What did they say?" Jake asked him, praying for good news.

"That Detective Jake Harris was out of town on personal business."

Good. One of the DEA's demands for Jake taking over the investigation was that his chief had had to sign off on the assignment too. Thankfully, he'd agreed and promised to run cover for Jake's absence. It seemed that had paid off now. "Now do you believe me?"

Creed again thought for a moment before nodding. "Let him go."

The goon squad released him and Jake rubbed his jaw, still stinging from the beating.

Only Creed wasn't done. "The fact that your brother is in town and helping Deputy Reagan puts him in the line of fire.

You realize that, don't you? If he gets in the way of our target on Deputy Reagan, it could get him killed."

Jake nodded, understanding Creed's meaning, but he had to keep up pretenses. "Like I said, we aren't that close. If he's in town to see her then he won't hesitate to step in to protect her." He meant those words even if Creed took them to mean something different.

"Let's go."

They walked away, leaving Jake standing at the display case and on the hook to find his own way back. That was fine with him. He was just glad to see them walking away from him instead of walking him to some ditch to execute him. He'd managed to talk his way out of this one but he doubted Creed would trust him after this even if he did believe the story. There were too many suspicions around him now to let him back into the trusted circle. The case was compromised but not completely dead yet. He just needed to find the information about Creed's supplier sooner rather than later.

He stared at the high school photos in the case and all those memories came rushing back to him. Him and Max. Him and Sabrina. The three of them had been nearly inseparable and he'd never imagined a time when neither one of them weren't in his life. Now Max was dead and he'd lived years without Sabrina. Not one day had felt right to him either without her by his side. Leaving her had been the biggest mistake he could have made and he was determined to do whatever it took to make it up to her and Robby, even if it meant stepping into the line of fire to protect her.

He walked outside and headed down the road. It was a long, cold walk back to his apartment building but what else could he do? He didn't have his cell phone and pay phones were nonexistent these days. He rubbed his arms to warm them up, wishing Ethan and Dax hadn't waited until he'd shed his jacket to attack.

Headlights lit the dark street heading his way. He shielded

his eyes but was glad to see it. Maybe he could flag down the car for a ride or, at least, use the driver's cell phone.

Instead of slowing, the car sped up, darting toward him. Jake jumped out of the way but the car swerved, hitting him and sending him reeling. As he slammed against the pavement, the car skidded to a stop, the door opened and someone got out.

Jake tried to push himself up but the figure approaching put his boot on Jake's back and pushed him back down.

"Creed may have believed your story, but I still don't trust you," Jacoby told Jake as he pulled his gun. "And I'm determined to find out the truth."

Chapter Seven

Sabrina cooked up a pan of scrambled eggs and sausage then loaded it onto a plate and placed it in front of Robby. He dug into the meal but his attention was mostly on the kids' show playing on the television on the kitchen counter.

Usually, they would be heading out to preschool at this time of the morning but with the holiday season and the risks to her life, Sabrina was glad they had nowhere to go today. She pushed Robby's hair from his face. Maybe a break from her job and spending the day with him wasn't the worst thing in the world.

But her mind wasn't far away from Jake either and worrying about what he was going to do. She prayed he wouldn't try to go back to Creed's. It was just too dangerous and he wasn't ready to lose him. She glanced at Robby again. Jake had a son to think about now. He couldn't take unnecessary risks.

She picked up her cell phone and called him. The phone rang several times before sending the call to voicemail. "Hey, it's me. I'm wondering what you decided. Call me back."

She kept herself busy and tried to phone Jake several more times with no response. That worried her. If he'd gone back in with Creed and his cover was fine, he might not be able to answer her or call her back. She couldn't even think about the other alternative.

Finally, her phone rang and she scrambled to answer it, but it wasn't Jake. "Kent, hi."

"I wanted to let you know that I checked in with Jana about the flash drive. She's still working on breaking through the encryption. I'm asking Agent Price if the DEA's technical team can assist."

She sighed. It looked like that flash drive might be a dead end unless Jana could find a way to break it. Asking for help was the smart move. With Jake's cover blown, she'd been hoping that might identify Creed's supplier. "Thanks for the update. Hey, Kent, have you heard from Max?"

"No, I haven't. I take it you haven't either?"

"No. When I left him last night, he was still trying to decide what to do. I was hoping he would call me this morning."

"I'm sure he'll check in soon. Another reason I was calling is that the court clerk phoned. She's missing some paperwork on the Dale Lowrey case and the judge wants you to give him an account of the search of Lowrey's apartment. He's claiming Johnson planted those drugs."

She shook her head. "That didn't happen. Mike Johnson is too honest to do something like that."

"Well, the judge is expecting you at the courthouse in an hour. I'm sending Deputy Parkman to pick you up and take you. I don't want you driving around alone."

She ended the call then changed into her uniform. Thankfully, her mom was home to watch Robby since judges didn't care about babysitting issues.

She tried phoning Jake again as she waited for Deputy Parkman to arrive. Still no answer. Now she was starting to get worried. This wasn't like him.

Parkman arrived and Sabrina dashed out and got into the passenger seat. "Thanks for the ride, Tim."

"No problem. Commander Morgan instructed me to make

sure you weren't left alone. I'm to remain with you at the courthouse then drive you back home."

"After I see the judge, before you drive me home, I have one more stop to make. I need to go by and check on a friend."

He nodded then drove her to the courthouse. She was glad to have Deputy Parkman watching her back, but she was still on alert herself as she entered the courthouse. She went in front of the judge and explained what had happened in the Lowrey case, including the anonymous tip she'd received and her estimation of Johnson's character. She hadn't been in the room when he'd found the drugs but she had worked with him previously and known him to be an honest and forthright man. It wasn't uncommon for prisoners to accuse law enforcement of planting evidence and, given Lowrey's drug history and known association with Creed, Sabrina had no doubt that the drugs had belonged to him.

The judge agreed with her assessment and revoked Lowrey's parole, sending him back to prison to complete his sentence. Sabrina watched as his wife and daughter cried then hugged him before he was removed from the courtroom to return to jail. He'd made a decision to do something that would take him away from his family so it was difficult for her to feel sorry for him.

However, it made Sabrina wonder if Jake had also made a decision that might have taken him away from her and Robby.

She climbed back into the car with Deputy Parkman then gave him the address of Max's apartment complex where Jake had been staying. They pulled into the parking lot and she immediately spotted Jake's rental in a parking spot. Her heart skipped a beat at seeing it. If his car was here, why wasn't he answering his phone or responding to her calls?

Deputy Parkman parked and they got out and walked up to the apartment. She knocked but heard no movement from inside. The door was locked so they walked down to the manager's office and had them open the door. Sabrina's mind was whirling with what they might find. Was he lying unconscious or dead inside? It was the only thing that explained why he hadn't returned her calls.

The manager opened the door and Deputy Parkman stepped inside first. Sabrina held her breath as she glanced around. Jake wasn't there. Parkman checked the bedroom and bathroom then shook his head.

"He's not here."

"When was the last time you've seen Mr. Harris?" she asked the manager.

"I don't usually. I live on the other side of the complex. He pays his rent online and hasn't had any maintenance issues since moving in."

"I don't see any evidence of a struggle," Parkman noted and she couldn't argue. Jake was just gone.

"Lock this place back up," she told the manager then walked outside to the car.

"Where to now?" Parkman asked her. "Home?"

"No." She couldn't shake the idea that something terrible had happened to Jake. He'd been out of contact with her for too long. "Take me back to the sheriff's office. I need to speak with Kent."

They drove back to the sheriff's office and Sabrina immediately marched into Kent's office. "I'm worried about Max. I haven't heard from him since last night."

Kent leaned back in his chair. "Was he supposed to check in with you?"

"No. We didn't have anything planned to check in but he's been in touch with me often since he's been back in town. Now it's radio silence. He's not answering his phone, he's not returning my calls and Deputy Parkman and I went by his apartment and he's not there either even though his car is sitting in its parking space. I'm worried, Kent. He might have tried to go back to Creed's factory and been taken."

"Max has always been able to take care of himself," Kent

reminded her. "Plus, he knew the danger when he accepted this assignment."

She bit her lip. She didn't like keeping this secret from him. He still didn't know Max wasn't Max, and she wasn't sure if she needed to tell him now that he wasn't checking in.

"That's just it, Kent. I don't know that he can." She'd seen Max's capabilities and never worried about him, but she wasn't falling in love with Max Harris either. She'd seen Jake stand up to Creed and his men and step in to protect her, but she had no idea how he would do in a pinch or how well he could think on his feet. She trusted him but she wasn't sure she trusted him not to get himself killed. He was determined to finish the investigation for Max's sake and also to keep her safe.

Kent stood. "Look, he disappeared once before. He doesn't work for us so technically we have no control over his comings and goings. Sure, we made an agreement to give him backup if needed and in exchange, he would provide us with information, but we can't jump to conclusions without proof. If he needed help, he would have reached out. We don't know anything is wrong yet. It hasn't even been a day."

She'd zeroed in on his words though and they'd bit at her. "You think he might have just left town?"

He shrugged. "It happened before, then he showed back up after weeks with little to no explanation. I know you want Creed brought down and, I agree, Max is our best chance of that happening but we don't control him. He's free to leave whenever he wants. Last night, he wasn't sure whether or not his cover had been blown. It's possible he decided it was and just left."

She tried her best not to let Kent see how his words had impacted her, but his reminder was like a gut punch. She turned and left his office. Now she was worried, but not about Jake's safety, because Kent was right without even realizing it. Jake had left her before. He'd walked out of her life five years ago and she had no assurances that he wouldn't do so again. The thought of that nearly doubled her over. She found a quiet corner and sat down, putting her hands over her face. She tried to breathe and push away her doubts about Jake. He might leave her, and she couldn't blame him, but he'd expressed an interest in getting to know Robby. He wouldn't leave his son. Not on purpose.

She pulled out her cell phone and tried his number again. No answer. Panic rose in her. Something was wrong. She felt it in her gut.

She walked back to her desk and dug through her notes until she located the name and number for Max's supervisor, Carl Price. She should run this through Kent first but even he didn't know about Jake. Aside from her, only one other person knew the truth about him and he might have the answers she sought.

She walked outside for privacy then dialed the number for Agent Price of the DEA. When he answered, she introduced herself.

"I'm Deputy Sabrina Reagan of the Mercy County Sheriff's Office."

"Deputy Reagan, what can I do for you?"

"I'm calling about Agent Max Harris." She sighed, realizing there was no point in beating around the bush. "I'm calling about Jake."

"Jake?" He sounded stunned at the name. "I'm not sure who—"

"I knew it was him and not Max the moment I saw him but, don't worry, I'm the only one who knows."

He breathed a sigh of relief. "What about him? Why are you calling?"

"I think he might be missing. I haven't heard from him in hours and that's not like him. I'm worried that his cover might have been compromised."

"That is worrisome. How long has it been since he's checked in?"

"I haven't heard from him since last night. I was wondering… I mean, you haven't heard from him, have you? He hasn't let you know that he's abandoning the mission and going back to San Antonio?"

"No, I haven't heard a word from him. I confess, I've been waiting on a check-in myself."

"How long does he need to be missing before I start searching for him officially?"

"Let me make some calls and see if I can hear anything. I'll call you back."

She walked back into the squad room. She wouldn't rest until she heard something back from him. The fact that Price hadn't heard from him either didn't ease her mind. She was even more certain that something had happened to him.

Allison, the dispatcher walked past her desk and Sabrina heard her speak with Kent. "We have a reported break-in at the high school from last night. I sent patrols but they're asking for someone from investigations. Who should I give it to?"

Sabrina glanced around, realizing that all the desks were empty. Everyone else was out on calls. She hurried into Kent's office. "I'll go," Sabrina stated. Anything to get her mind off Jake and wondering why he hadn't returned her calls.

Break-ins were often also tied to drug crimes so it was a natural thing for her to cross over into burglary work. However, she didn't know what could be happening at the high school unless someone had left drugs in their locker.

Kent shook his head. "You're not supposed to be out in the field. Sheriff's orders, remember?"

"I'll be surrounded by deputies the entire time," she reminded him. "I'll be safe. Plus, everyone else is tied up with another case."

He rubbed his chin, considering it then gave the okay. "Make sure Parkman goes with you."

It was a compromise she was willing to accept.

Deputy Parkman drove her to the high school. Once there, she found the responding deputies were still on the scene. "What do we have?" she asked the lead one.

"The front entrance doors were broken in and we have footprints leading down the main hallway. They lead right to the front office but it doesn't look like the office was broken into. Those doors are still locked and it doesn't appear that anything was taken that we can see. I've contacted the principal who is on his way down here to confirm that."

She walked inside and spotted the multiple shoe prints that lined the main hallway. This was more than one person. And the prints were different sizes and marks. She counted at least three distinct ones. As the lead deputy had stated, they went straight to the office then stopped and turned back. Odd that they didn't seem to pass by anything of value. A few more steps into the office and they could have gotten computers, laptops, cameras and other valuable equipment.

A deputy approached her leading another man. "This is Principal Jackson. This is Deputy Reagan," he said, making introductions.

Sabrina shook his hand. "Thanks for coming down. If you could check the office or look for anything that might be missing that would be great."

"We have cameras set up around the office. I can get the video footage."

"Thanks. That sounds great." Cameras had made her job a lot easier in some ways. She hoped this would be one of those times.

He nodded then unlocked the office and started looking around.

As she walked around, Sabrina noticed the glass trophy case. She looked inside, startled to see a photo of Jake and

Max on the basketball team along with one of her and Jake and Max and a date on homecoming. She smiled at the memory. Simpler times.

The principal returned with his cell phone out. "Nothing appears to be missing. In fact, I looked through the video feed and it doesn't look like they even entered the office."

"Kids?" she asked.

"No. Adult men." He handed over his cell phone and she pressed play on the already cued-up video.

A group of four men, two in the front and two following behind, walked into view but like the principal stated, they stopped at the office doors. They turned to look instead at the glass trophy case.

She zoomed in on the faces and gasped at the recognition. It was Jake and he looked beaten and bruised. She recognized one of the other men too as Paul Creed.

But why would they come here to look at a trophy case?

That's when she realized. Jake must have shown them the images of him and his brother. Something had happened and he'd needed to prove he was a twin. Had they discovered he wasn't Max after all?

Her mind spun at what must have happened.

She pulled the lead deputy aside. "I want you to start a search of the school grounds and let me know if you find anyone." She didn't know what they'd done with Jake after they'd left. Had he convinced them or had they killed him and dumped his body?

She phoned Kent and updated him on seeing Jake on the video. "Creed definitely has him and he looked to be injured. We need to find him."

It was enough to convince him. "Don't worry. We will find him."

She hurried outside and joined in the search. She tried his phone again but it was still going straight to voicemail.

"Where are you, Jake?" she whispered to the wind. "And are you safe?"

She wasn't letting Kent send her back home again until she knew the truth.

Jake pulled at the ropes tying his hands and feet. He was tied up and lying on the dirt floor of a place he recognized. The old sawmill in Harper Woods. He and his brother and Sabrina had spent time in these woods as kids as had many of the other kids they'd known. This old sawmill had been the optimal place for parties and hanging out.

Now it was his prison.

He glared up at one of the men standing watch over him. He couldn't remember if that was Ethan or Dax. It didn't matter. Both of them were just pawns in this sick game.

"Why am I here?" Jake demanded. "Creed said he believed me."

Obviously something had gone wrong between the time Creed had let him go and Jacoby had grabbed him.

"Creed might believe you but Jacoby doesn't. He's keeping you out of the way until he can figure out what you're up to."

"I'm not up to anything," Jake insisted.

He'd known Jacoby didn't trust him but he hadn't expected this. He'd talked his way out of Creed's distrust but Jacoby hadn't been convinced.

He didn't know exactly how long he'd been here but, as he watched the sun set through the windows of the sawmill, he knew it had been at least a day. Sabrina must be going out of her mind with worry. He hoped he could get back to her soon.

He heard tires outside. His captor heard it too and got up and glanced out the window then moved to open the door.

Jake hurried to sit up. He'd been trying to wiggle or break his binds all day but Ethan or Dax, whoever he was, had been checking them periodically.

The doors swung open and Jacoby walked in with the

other half of the duo and Creed following behind him. "How is he?" Jacoby demanded.

"Still locked up tight," Ethan told him.

They moved toward Jake so he went on the offensive. "What is this? What's going on?"

Creed paced in front of him like a caged animal. "I trusted you. That's what's going on here. I let you into my operation and all the while you were spying on me."

"That's not true. I told you my brother—"

Creed stopped him. "I know, I know. It was your twin. Here's the thing."

Creed motioned to Jacoby, who pulled out his laptop and opened it up. A video was already keyed up. Jake swallowed hard when he saw it security feed from the hospital.

"Notice anything?" Jacoby asked him but didn't wait for an answer. He pointed to the screen. "It's clear to see that the man who helped the deputy escape from the hospital is wearing the same exact clothes as you."

Jake cringed at that video. He hadn't had time to change clothes and hadn't thought any more about it. Obviously, Jacoby had. Jake glanced at Creed. He seemed to believe it too.

"But wait, there's more," Creed said. "The night you showed back up in town, I wanted to believe your story but I had to be sure after the rumors so I sent someone to that city where you had your accident. I had someone go to the hospital and start asking questions. He cozied up to one of the aides and started asking about a car wreck. She remembered it. Said it was two brothers, twins. They were both cops. She also remembered that someone from the DEA was there. And that one of the brothers never left the hospital. He died from his injuries."

Jake did his best to conceal his shock. Creed had done his homework and, although HIPPA laws should have prevented anyone from talking, there were always slip-ups. Especially when someone dies and it's covered up. People notice.

He'd hoped they'd been far enough away from where the accident had happened that that kind of information wouldn't make it back to anyone here in town, but he should have known Creed was smart and careful. After the mix-up with him being seen with Sabrina, he'd hoped he'd talked his way out of being discovered but he'd only been fooling himself.

"Only one of those brothers made it out of that wreck alive," Creed continued. "Now, I don't know if you're Max or if you're really his brother or not, but I now know that, whoever you are, you're a cop who has infiltrated my operation. That's something I can't overlook."

Jake pulled at the ropes again and knew he was in trouble. Sabrina had been right about him not following up. He probably should have laid low after nearly being discovered before but he'd refused to leave her. He'd wanted this investigation over and done with and Creed and his supplier behind bars so he could build a future with Sabrina and Robby.

"Creed—"

He cut him off again. "I don't want to hear any more of your lies." He turned to his men. "Take him out to the woods and take care of him. Then head over to Deputy Reagan's house and take care of her too. I'm tired of these games. I've got business to see to." Creed turned and walked out.

One of the goons walked over and pulled out a knife. Jake tensed, thinking he was about to get stabbed but he used it to cut Jake's binds on his feet. However, they left his hands bound together. Each one of them grabbed him by the arm and pulled him to his feet. They took him and walked him outside to a car. Jake spotted Creed climbing into an SUV with some other men then driving away. Ethan opened the trunk to another car and Dax shoved Jake inside as Jacoby watched. They slammed the trunk, closing him in. Moments later, they climbed inside and started the car.

As Jake listened to the hum of the tires on the pavement, he knew he had to think of something or else he was going to die tonight. He wasn't ready to say goodbye to Sabrina and he wanted the opportunity to see his son grow up and become a man. He'd just discovered he was a father. He wasn't ready to end that now. He had to do something.

He searched the trunk and found a sharp piece of metal, which he used to cut at the ropes around his wrist. It took a few minutes but it sliced through the rope and also through his arm. He grimaced but couldn't do anything about that at the moment although he ripped off a piece of his shirt to use as a makeshift bandage.

His pulse shot up as the car stopped and the engine shut off. They were here, wherever here was, to the place they meant to kill him. If he didn't make it through the next few moments, he would lose everything and Sabrina might not ever know what had happened to him.

Would she wonder if he'd left her again? That would almost be worse than her believing he'd been killed. He never wanted to hurt her that way ever again.

As he grabbed the metal and braced himself for the fight of his life, he heard footsteps approaching. When the trunk opened, he acted, kicking the hood up so that it slammed against Ethan's head. He stumbled backward while Jake jumped from the trunk and tackled Dax, knocking him to the ground too. Before they could get back up, he darted into the woods. He heard shouting but kept running, taking safety in the camouflage of the trees.

He didn't know where he was but he was determined to get back to Sabrina and Robby no matter what.

The two men must have quickly recovered because gunshots fired at Jake as he ran. He had no idea where he was or how he was going to get away but his only thought was to get back to his family.

He'd known coming into this that it would be dangerous but he hadn't been thinking about Sabrina when he'd agreed to it. He'd only been trying to honor his brother by finishing this investigation. Now there was the real possibility that he might die because of it.

He pushed through branches and overgrown weeds. The gunfire ceased but he didn't realize it until he stopped and listened, realizing they were no longer shooting at him. They wouldn't just let him go though. They would be coming searching for him to end his life.

Lord, please let me get back to Sabrina. Help me through this.

He ran again. Darkness covered everything. The only light was from the moon above but he couldn't let that stop him. These men were dangerous and would be coming after him. He had to find a way to safety before that happened.

He stopped and crouched behind a tree to catch his breath and listen. He heard nothing except the sounds of chirping and humming of the night woods. No footsteps or rustling of leaves. Good. Maybe they'd gone another direction and weren't on his tail.

Then another sound caught his ear. Something else. He sat and listened until he realized what it was. Traffic.

He headed toward it, praying it remained. He must be close to the highway and hopefully he could flag down a car to help him. He ran and finally pushed out of the brush and onto the side of a road.

Headlights headed his way. Remembering how Jacoby had run him down, he hesitated only a moment. He had no choice but to take the risk. He darted up an embankment and into the road, waving his arms to flag down the car.

It slowed then stopped in the middle of the road and the driver rolled down the passenger window. Jake stumbled backward for a moment, wary of it being one of Creed's men but he couldn't think that way or he would never find help.

"Your car break down?" the man asked him.

"I was attacked," he replied. "I need to get to town to the sheriff's office. Can you take me there or call them for me?"

The driver's face registered shock then his eyes looked Jake up and down, his gaze focusing on the bloody bandage on his arm, the cast on his other arm, and the cuts and bruises on his face. He nodded and unlocked the door. "Get in. I'll drive you to town."

Jake thanked him then climbed into the passenger seat. As the man drove away, Jake leaned against the seat and sighed. He'd made it. He'd lived through being abducted by Creed's men.

He was going to see Sabrina and Robby again.

Chapter Eight

Sabrina went to the ladies' room and splashed her face with water.

The terror of seeing Jake beaten and bruised and being led around by Creed and his men had confirmed her worst fears. Jake's life was in danger. But it wasn't that truth that had sent her hiding out. It was the doubts about him that she'd allowed to creep into her mind. That Jake had left her again just as he had five years earlier.

She had done her best to push them away but they'd managed to keep popping up and breaking her heart. She should never have doubted him.

She composed herself, then walked back into the squad room. Kent, along with Sheriff Thompson and Deputy Josh Knight, who was the head of the department's SWAT team, were going over scenarios for rescuing Jake. Thanks to Max, they knew the location of Creed's base, the old factory on the industrial area of town, but they had no confirmation that Jake was being kept there. They couldn't breach the factory until they knew for certain where Creed was holding him.

Lord, please keep him safe until we can find him.

She surprised herself with that silent cry for help. God

hadn't been there for her when her brother and her dad had died. Why would He help her now?

Kent turned to look at her, regret shining in his face that he hadn't trusted her earlier intuition that something had happened to Jake. He motioned her over to join in on the planning. It was already late in the evening but the office hadn't slowed. They were already hours behind that video and each moment that they didn't find Jake was another hour of uncertainty.

"I'm putting together a team to survey the factory," Josh was telling them. "Once we have confirmation that Agent Harris is there, we'll wait for the signal to breach the factory." Josh was a former Navy SEAL and had built the department's SWAT team from scratch. He was currently focusing on training duties since being injured in a confrontation with a suspect but he was the most experienced tactically that the Mercy County Sheriff's Office had.

Sheriff Thompson looked over his suggestions then gave her okay. "Let's be careful on this. I've been in touch with Agent Price at the DEA and he's offered assistance in case we need it."

"They're not going to help?" Sabrina asked her.

She shook her head. "Agents understand going in undercover that they risk being captured. They're trained to think on their feet and take risks. The agency is still concerned about preserving the operation and discovering Paul Creed's supplier. He plays a much bigger role in the drug trade around the state and country."

"So they're just willing to sacrifice one agent in order to preserve their operation?" Sabrina couldn't imagine working for an agency that wouldn't intervene to rescue one of its agents when they were in trouble.

Sheriff Thompson must have seen her horror. She took Sabrina's arm. "The DEA is a big agency with a lot of red tape. I believe Agent Price cares about Max and will do what he can for him. In the meantime, we'll do what we can do."

"Thank you, Sheriff."

The sheriff turned back to Kent and Josh. "Keep me updated. I'll be in my office."

Suddenly, Allison rushed into the room. "Commander, we just received a call in dispatch about Agent Harris."

A buzz of excitement filled the room but Sabrina's heart fell and fear gripped her. "What was it?" she asked, fearful of the answer to the question even as she asked it.

Allison's face spread into a grin. "A motorist just picked him up on the side of the road. He'd been beaten and nearly killed but he's alive, Sabrina. He's alive."

Sabrina jumped into her embrace and Allison hugged her back. She could hardly contain herself. "Where is he now?"

"The driver is bringing him in. I sent a cruiser to intercept them. Apparently, he stumbled out of the woods near the old sawmill."

She breathed in a sigh of relief and fought back tears. He was alive. *Thank You, Lord, for bringing him home again.* Maybe God was listening after all.

She watched the door and listened to the radio, her leg bouncing nervously until she spotted the cruiser pulling into the station. She ran to the door and saw a car behind it. The passenger door opened and she spotted Jake lean over and say something to the driver before shaking his hand. Then he got out.

She ran to him, circling the car. Even from a distance, the outside lights illuminated blood on his face and clothes and he looked like he'd been through the wringer.

He saw her too. "Sabrina."

She pressed herself against him and his arms circled hers, pulling her in tightly. A swell of emotion threatened to overtake her but she finally managed to speak. "Don't you ever leave me again," she told him.

He leaned back and looked at her, smiling, then grimaced at the pain of the action. "Never again. That's a promise."

That was a promise she would make certain he would never break.

Jake leaned against Sabrina as she helped him inside. He'd been so frightened that he wouldn't see her again. Now he was here, safe, with her by his side.

"Call for an ambulance," Sabrina called out as they entered the station.

"No," Jake insisted. "I don't need to go to the hospital. I'm fine."

She touched his busted lip, causing him to grimace. "I can see you're not. You need to be seen by a doctor."

She wasn't wrong, but still he protested. "I took a beating, that's for sure, but I'm not seriously injured." He would have been if he hadn't fled. He'd been only moments away from getting a bullet to the back of his head. But he hadn't been shot. He touched her face. He was safe now.

She must have seen the determination in his face because she nodded. "Fine, but you need to sit and at least have a paramedic look you over." He started to protest again but she cut him off sternly. "I insist on that or I call for the ambulance."

He knew that look of determination in her eyes. It had been a long time since he'd been on the other end of it. He smiled at the memory. She'd always been a fierce protector of those she cared about. "Okay," he finally agreed.

She nodded to a woman who picked up the phone and called for a paramedic. Sabrina led him into a conference room. A couch sat on one end and she gently helped him down into it. His ribs ached as he lowered himself. He didn't think they were broken, bruised maybe, but not broken, yet she still shot him a glare of agitation.

"I'm fine," he assured her again. "I will be fine."

The door pushed open and the sheriff entered followed by Kent.

"I'm glad to see you're safe," Sheriff Thompson said.

"Thank you."

"Can you tell us what happened?"

"After I left you all the other night, I went back to my apartment. Two of Creed's men were there waiting for me. They knocked me out and tied me up."

"So they did recognize you from the hospital," Sheriff Thompson stated.

Jake nodded. "Yes, they did. I thought I had talked my way out of it. Creed seemed to believe me for a moment but then one of his men who never trusted me much obtained the video feeds from the hospital and they realized I was wearing the same clothes as the man at the hospital. I hadn't even had time to change."

"What about the break-in at the high school? How did that play into it?"

Jake glanced at Sabrina. She gave him a slight shake of her head confirming she hadn't told them about him taking over his brother's identity. They still believed he was Max and it was too complicated to explain at the moment. "It was a ploy. I tried to convince them it was my twin brother they'd seen at the hospital helping Sabrina. We went to the school so that I could show them our high school pictures proving that I had an identical twin."

They seemed to accept that explanation which was good because he wasn't up for a full-blown interrogation. His head was pounding and his ribs ached, making it difficult to breathe, much less talk.

Sheriff Thompson turned to Kent. "Let's get an arrest warrant for Paul Creed."

Jake also gave them the names of Mick Jacoby along with Ethan and Dax. "I don't know their last names but they're the ones who abducted me and kept me tied up."

Sheriff Thompson nodded and Kent strode away to make it happen. "We're already working on a plan to breach the factory. If we can't get Creed on drug charges, at least we'll be able to imprison him for kidnapping and attempted murder."

That would still leave Creed's supplier at large but it would have to be enough for now and hopefully that would alleviate the threat against Sabrina if Creed and his men were in custody. And, who knows, one of them might even crack and name the supplier. That was the best case scenario. "Thank you, Sheriff."

"My pleasure. You should give your boss a call too. He needs to know you're safe."

She walked out and left them alone and he turned to Sabrina. "You called Agent Price?"

"You've been missing for almost thirty hours, Jake. When I couldn't get in touch with you, I was hoping he'd heard from you."

So she'd thought he might have left her. He probably deserved that.

"I should call him and let him know you're safe."

She got up and pulled out her cell phone. He was glad to hand that task over to her as the pain in his rib cage intensified.

He hated that she ever thought for a moment that he would have left her. He would spend the rest of his life making certain she never doubted him again.

"I'm glad to hear he's safe," Agent Price said through the phone after Sabrina had let him know Jake had returned. She hated to phone him so late, it was nearly midnight, but knew he would want to be informed. "I hope he doesn't have any plans to confront Creed again."

She shuddered at the thought. "I'm planning on keeping him away from Creed."

"Good. Take care of him," Price told her. "I'll check in on him soon."

Sabrina ended the call then stared into the conference room at Jake. Price had encouraged her to take care of him and that was exactly what she planned to do. Her fears about losing him when he'd vanished had proven to her how much she'd started to care for him again. She'd pushed him away five years ago and now she knew how much she regretted that decision.

Kent exited his office and called her name. "Can I talk with you for a moment?" He closed the door behind her as she entered then motioned for her to sit down as he circled back around to his chair. He looked tired and worn out from lack of sleep just as they all were.

Instead of sitting, he folded his arms and stared at her, giving her the feeling of suddenly being called out by the principal.

"Is something wrong, Kent?"

"You haven't exactly been acting like a coworker where Max is concerned. When he went missing, you were upset and panicked. Now that he's back..." he hesitated before continuing "...well, it's obvious your relationship is something more than just professional. When were you going to tell me that you and Max have been seeing one another?"

Her face warmed at being called out for her unprofessional behavior. She couldn't dispute his observations because he wasn't wrong. She and Jake were much more than deputy and DEA agent. Somewhere along the way since he'd returned to town, their relationship had turned. "It's not what you think."

"Isn't it? You practically flung yourself into his arms the moment you saw him. Look, Sabrina, I don't begrudge you happiness. In fact, I've never seen you like this, but you have to know it breaks every protocol we have."

"I know."

"How long has this been going on?"

She stared at him and knew that, as long as she was coming clean, it was time he knew the real truth. "Years ago, I dated Max's brother, Jake. We were high school sweethearts planning a future together. At least, we were until my brother died. I didn't handle my grief so well and I pushed Jake away. It was only after he left town that I discovered I was pregnant with Robby."

Kent rubbed a hand through his hair then sat down.

"I sent Jake a letter telling him about Robby but I never heard back so I assumed the worst about him but when Max arrived back in town to start this undercover operation, he figured it out and knew his brother hadn't gotten that letter. He wanted me to tell Jake the truth but I never could get up the courage."

"Okay, that still doesn't explain how you and Max—"

"Max died three weeks ago in a car crash. That's why he vanished so suddenly. He drove out to meet up with his brother and he was killed."

Confusion clouded his face. "I don't understand. How—"

"I guess I forgot to mention that Jake and Max were twins. Identical twins."

Understanding dawned on his face and he leaned back in his chair. "Identical."

"Yes. The man who came back to town wasn't Max. It was Jake. He and Max's boss worked out some scheme so that Jake would pretend to be his brother and finish the undercover operation he started. The funny thing was that no one knew the difference. Not you. Not even Creed. But I could always tell them apart when few others could."

"So the man who has been hanging around for the past week has been Jake? Agent Price sent a civilian in to Creed's operation?"

"No, of course he didn't. Jake is a cop too. Plus, he's had experience working undercover."

He nodded then looked at her. "And he's Robby's father and your ex?"

She nodded. "Yes. I'm sorry, Kent. I should have told you sooner but it wasn't my secret to tell."

"And this newfound affection between the two of you?"

"That was unexpected. I never thought I would see Jake again and, if I did, I figured he would never forgive me for not telling him about Robby. He still might not. I don't know what our future holds but I know when I couldn't reach him, when he wasn't responding to my calls and I was afraid Creed had discovered he was undercover, I couldn't even think straight. I couldn't imagine my life without him in it."

Kent stood and walked around the desk. He put his hands over hers. "I'm sure I wasn't the only one who saw the chemistry between the two of you, Sabrina. It's obvious he cares for you too."

Something in her chest fluttered at the idea and she couldn't stop the smile that spread across her face. "I hope you're right. I don't want to lose him again, Kent."

He walked back to his desk, opened a drawer and pulled out a set of keys which he handed to her. "My uncle-in-law has a cabin out near Deer Lake. I'm sending you the GPS coordinates. Since I know you don't have a car here and you won't want to use a marked cruiser, borrow one of the cars from the impound lot and take Max, uhm Jake, to the cabin. He can use it as a safe house. Now that Creed knows he's a cop, he needs to stay out of sight. Creed's men will be searching for him to finish the job they started."

She shuddered at the thought of his life in danger and how he'd barely escaped them.

"He can hide out there until he's healed, then we'll figure out what to do. I'll be in touch with his—Max's—supervisor and update him."

"Thank you, Kent."

She turned to walk out but he called her name and she stopped at the door to turn back to him.

"Sabrina, be careful you're not followed. It's awfully isolated out there and there won't be any backup if they find him."

She nodded then walked out and made the arrangements for a car to be made available for her. Once that was done, she hurried into the conference room where a paramedic she recognized was bandaging Jake's ribs. "I don't think he has any broken ribs as far as I can tell," he told Sabrina. "But he needs to be in a hospital and have an X-ray to be sure."

"They'll heal," Jake assured him, dismissing that idea. He must have sensed her hesitation because he pushed himself to his feet. "I'll be fine. I don't need a hospital."

"Are you sure?"

He nodded then leaned against her. "I'd be too exposed there. I just need to get somewhere safe where they can't find me then I'll be okay."

She carefully put his arm over her shoulder so he could lean on her. "I have just the place. Let's go while it's still dark outside and before Creed's men realize you came here. They'll be looking for you."

He nodded and accepted her help to walk out to the car. He slid into the passenger seat while she drove.

"Where are we going?" he asked once they were on their way.

"To an isolated cabin on Deer Lake. It belongs to someone in Kent's family. He gave me the keys." She gripped the steering wheel. "I told him, Jake. I told him everything."

He reached for her hand and she took his. "It's okay," he assured her. "We're going to need all the help we can get."

She nodded, knowing that was the truth. Now that Creed knew about him, he would send his men after them both. She was already a target and, now, Jake had become one too.

Now that Jake had been outed by Creed, he needed a place to lay low and recover from the beatings they'd inflicted on him. Sabrina was thankful that Kent had offered this place for him to stay.

She gripped the steering wheel as she drove toward it, her emotions threatening to get the better of her. She'd been so worried about him but also had her doubts about whether or not he'd left on his own. She was ashamed of that now. She should have trusted that he would never leave her and Robby without a word.

She drove for over an hour, stopping only for gas and groceries at a small convenience store, then searched the dark, isolated streets until she found the turnoff for the cabin. She got out and unlocked the gate that blocked the entrance, insisting that Jake stay put when he tried to get out to do it. She pulled the car forward then closed it behind them as she followed the long road that led to a clearing and a small cabin. She glanced around, spotting lights in the distance but not too close. It was isolated which was good. No curious neighbors would be wondering why he was laying low. She unlocked the cabin door then switched on the overhead light, thankful the place was wired for electricity but she would need to build a fire to run out the chill in the air.

She helped him inside then settled him on the couch before making a fire in the fireplace. Now that the adrenaline had worn off, he was moving slowly. She'd insisted he needed to be in a hospital but he'd refused to go, assuring her that he was sore but not badly injured.

"Let me fix you something to eat," she said as she retrieved a bag of groceries from the car. She'd stopped at a small convenience store once they'd cleared town and she'd determined they weren't being followed. They hadn't offered many options but she'd managed to find the necessities. She popped open a can of soup and poured it into a boiler on the stove. As she waited for it to heat up, she grabbed the bandages and got to work making certain his wounds were clean.

He grabbed her hand and squeezed it, causing her to look

up into his eyes. He put his hand around her neck. "I'm fine, Sabrina. I promise."

"I was so worried about you when I didn't hear from you. I just knew Creed had done something to you. I was so afraid I would never see you again." Her voice cracked with emotion and she cleared it away.

He touched her cheek. "I have to admit, all I could think about was getting back to you and Robby. I didn't want to die and leave you alone. And I never wanted you to wonder if I'd just left you again."

She glanced up at him, wondering if he could see the doubts in her face. "How did you know?"

"I didn't. I just kept thinking that's what you might believe. You obviously did."

"Only for a moment, then I realized the truth that you wouldn't do that."

"Even though I did once before?"

She sighed and replaced the bandage on his arm. "That was different, Jake. I pushed you away. I was a mess."

He touched her face again. "And I was foolish. I should have fought harder for you. I should never have let you push me away. I promise you it will never happen again, Sabrina. I don't ever want to be without you again."

He leaned in and kissed her and she melted into his embrace. All their past baggage seemed to vanish in his kiss. It was both exciting and new and familiar and comforting.

"I'd better check on your soup."

She stood and walked to the stove. Her knees were still shaking from that kiss. Her world had been changed in one moment when she'd thought she might not see him again and it opened up something in her. She wanted to be with Jake. She wanted him in her life and she wanted Robby to know him. He was a good man that she'd let slip through her fingers once. She couldn't let that happen again.

She turned off the stove and emptied the soup into a bowl.

She turned around and he was behind her, touching her hair, and every inch of her wanted to fall into his embrace.

He kissed her and she kissed him back.

The world vanished around them during that kiss and she knew only one thing—she didn't want to be without Jake in her life again.

They sat by the fire talking and dozing for hours as the sun rose outside the window. She glanced at her watch. She needed to get back but she didn't want to leave him. "I'll fix you some breakfast then I really should go."

He pulled her back down for one more kiss. "Promise me you'll be safe."

She touched his face. "I will. Promise me you won't leave this cabin for anything."

"I won't even stick my head out the door. I promise."

"Good. I don't want anything to happen to you, Jake. I want you to stick around and spend Christmas with me and Robby."

He stroked her face and smiled. "There's nothing I want more than to be with you both."

She scrambled some eggs and made coffee and Jake managed to make it from the couch to the table to eat. Only, he hardly touched his breakfast.

"What's the matter?"

"I was just thinking about the mission. It's over now. I know that. I can never go back. Creed may not realize I'm not Max, but he knows I'm law enforcement."

She nodded. "That's true. Your cover is blown."

"I feel like I've let you down."

"You haven't."

"I was supposed to come here and finish what my brother started. I couldn't do it. I failed him and I failed you too."

She shook her head. "No, that's not true. You did the best you could."

"I'm not going to be able to bring Creed or his organization down. I didn't even find out who his supplier was."

"Don't worry about that. We'll figure out something else. We still have the flash drive you got. Jan is still working on cracking that."

He shook his head. "You don't understand. As long as he's still out there, as long as he's still in power, he's a threat to you, Sabrina. He sent men to kill you. He's dangerous and I couldn't do anything to stop him from coming after you."

She appreciated his concern for her but she'd been a target before he'd even arrived in town. This wasn't his fault. "This isn't over, Jake. I'm still determined to make him pay for what he did to my brother. I won't stop."

She saw concern spread across his face. "I don't like you being out there and me stuck here unable to do anything to help you."

"You came back to me. That's all the incentive I need to keep going. Now, at least, we can try to charge him for abducting you."

He shook his head. "That won't hold up. Creed is smart. He'll have his men testify that it never happened and I can't prove I was there."

She realized he was right. "At least all the lying is over now and I don't have to pretend you're Max. It's been so hard keeping that secret. I want the world to know how much you mean to me. How much you've always meant to me, Jake."

He touched her face and drew her to him. "You mean a lot to me too, Sabrina. You always have."

She leaned her head against his chest. She'd once loved this man so much but she'd lost that to grief and anger when her brother had died. She'd let those feelings rob them both of years of being together and of him being in Robby's life.

"I'm sorry," she told him.

"About what?"

"I should have told you right away when I discovered I was pregnant. It was wrong of me to keep Robby from you all these years."

He brushed a stray hair from her face. "I confess I was hurt when I found out he was my child but I'm not angry about it. I understand how it happened. I'm just glad to know that Robby helped you get past all that with your brother. I wish it could have been me that helped you through it. I should never have left you, Sabrina. For that, I'm sorry."

She was glad to hear him say that and sad for all the years they'd lost.

A ding from her cell indicated she had a text message. She pulled out her cell phone and glanced at the screen. "It's from my mom. She took Robby to the park and wants me to meet them there." The message included a photo of Robby laughing on the swings.

She showed it to Jake, who smiled. "Looks like he's having a good time."

"He loves to swing."

Jake stared at the image then smiled. "When I saw him the other day laughing and running around those inflatables, it made me realize what I was fighting for."

"I know. Me too. We'll make this the best Christmas he's ever had, won't we?"

He nodded. "Yes, we will. Together."

She kissed him again then grabbed her things. "I'll try to come by later this evening to fix you something to eat."

"You shouldn't. I can take care of myself. Besides, it's too risky. Someone might follow you here."

"I know how to watch for a tail," she assured him. "But I understand your concern. Promise you'll call me if you need anything?"

He nodded. "I will. I promise. But I'll be fine."

She still didn't want to leave but she had to think of Robby. If her mother was wanting her to come, she might need some help with him.

She got back into the car and headed toward town to the park but her mind wasn't far from the kiss she and Jake had shared. She was still reeling from it and from the near miss they'd experienced.

Nothing like nearly dying to make you realize how much you care about someone.

She reached the park and turned in. She could see the playground from the parking lot and it was full of kids running around, laughing, playing, swinging. This place was always busy during the day but Robby loved coming and it worked off some energy for him.

She spotted Robby climbing up the slide and called his name. He turned and waved to her with a big smile.

"Watch, Momma!" he yelled then slid.

She clapped and cheered him on. "Good job, baby," she said as he immediately spun and turned to climb back up and do it again.

Sabrina spotted her mother sitting on a bench on the other side. She had a book in her hand and hadn't noticed Sabrina yet until she approached her. "Hi, Mom."

She looked up then smiled and closed the book. "Sabrina, what are you doing here?"

What was her mother up to? "What do you mean? You asked me to stop by."

"No, I don't think I did."

"Mom, you texted me a photo of Robby on the swings and asked me to stop by the park." She pulled out her phone and showed her the message.

"I—I didn't send that." She dug through her own purse and pulled out her cell phone.

"What do you mean?" She took the phone and scrolled through her mom's messages. The texts she'd received weren't there. "But I—"

Suddenly, dread filled her. She scrolled through her mom's images saved to the camera but didn't see the one she'd received either. Someone else had been taking photos of Robby. Someone else had sent that message asking her to come.

She spun around to put her eyes on Robby. She couldn't see him but tried not to panic. That didn't mean he wasn't inside the play place climbing back up to the slide. She circled the structure but didn't see him.

"Robby!" Her voice screeched his name. People stopped and turned but she still didn't see Robby. She climbed up into the playground structure and checked every slide and ladder and nook and cranny for him. Nothing.

She hopped off, praying he'd gone to the swings but he wasn't there either.

"My little boy, he's gone," she told the adults she spotted. "He's got dark hair and was wearing a red jacket."

Another mother stopped her. "Are you okay?"

"I can't find my son. Robby!" she screamed again as panic ripped through her.

Now her mother was up looking too and calling his name. Several of the parents had joined the search and were also calling his name.

One woman grabbed her shoulder and pointed near the parking lot. "Is that him?"

Sabrina spun around to see a man carrying a little boy in a red jacket. He was sprinting across the grass toward a van waiting in the parking lot right by her car.

Her heart sank and she took off after him. "That's my son!" she shouted to him but the man only ran faster. She was hardly to the grass when he hopped into the van with Robby and slammed the door. The van sped away carrying her baby inside.

She wouldn't let that stop her. She ran to the car only to find two of her tires flat. She took out her cell phone and took photos of the van as it sped out of the park and onto the main street.

When it was out of view, she crumpled to the grass as sobs racked her body.

Robby had been abducted.

Chapter Nine

The sheriff's office arrived quickly and processed the scene but Sabrina was too stunned to participate in asking questions or gathering evidence. She'd given a statement to Deputy Mike Tyner, who was the first investigator on the scene and handed over the photos of the van speeding away but that was all. She could usually pull herself together and do what needed to be done in stressful situations, but this was her child, her baby, that they'd taken from her.

A car stopped and she spotted Jake getting out of the back seat. He was moving slowly but he was here and she was thankful for whomever had given him a ride. He'd promised not to leave the cabin; however, when your child had been abducted things changed.

She stood and ran to him and he circled his arms around her as she pressed her face into his chest. He grunted as if it hurt him to move that quickly but he didn't release her.

"What happened?" he asked after holding her in silence and letting her cry for several moments.

"There were at least two of them. One grabbed Robby and threw him into the van. Another was driving. They sent me this photo and lured me here to watch." She handed the cell phone to him and he glanced at the image then his jaw tensed.

"This says it came from your mom's phone."

"She didn't send it, Jake. I checked her phone. She didn't send it and she didn't have this photo of Robby. They were watching him, ready to snatch him up."

"And they wanted you here to see it happen."

She'd thought the same thing. "They have our baby."

He glanced past her and she turned and followed his gaze to her mother sitting back on the same bench where she'd been, only now she was surrounded by deputies peppering her with questions.

He walked that way and she followed along with him.

"Did you notice anyone paying extra special attention to Robby today or any other day?" Mike asked. He held a notebook in his hand and was jotting down notes.

"No. I didn't see anyone." Mrs. Reagan glanced up and locked gazes with Sabrina. Tears filled her eyes. "I'm so sorry, honey. I should have been paying more attention but I didn't see anyone."

Her first instinct was to lash out. Her mother had been reading and not paying attention to Robby, but she bit her tongue. This wasn't her fault. She knew exactly who was to blame for this.

Deputy Lisa Patterson pulled her and Jake aside. In her hand, she held her mom's cell phone and an evidence bag. "I'm going to take this back to the lab and see if someone can decipher what happened. We'll look for fingerprints although your mom insists she had the phone in her purse the entire time and didn't leave it alone for a moment. Only someone must have sent those messages then deleted them."

"There is another possibility," Jake said. "The phone could have been cloned. It's obvious whoever did this meant for Sabrina to be here to watch the abduction happen. They sent that message then waited for her to arrive. They wanted to torture her with it."

She grimaced. "And we all know who wants me to suffer."

Creed had had her son kidnapped.

"Well, I'm not going to sit around here and wait for him to act. I'm going after him and getting Robby back."

Jake grabbed her arm to stop her. "And do what? Burst up into his factory with nothing more than indignation. Do you really think Robby will be there? We have to be smart about this."

"What are we supposed to do besides just sit here and do nothing?"

"We wait. He did this for a purpose, Sabrina. He wants something from us. He'll contact us and I don't believe he will hurt Robby. He needs him to get to us."

"No. I won't sit around waiting, Jake. I'm going to find my son. We know where Creed's operation is located. I'm going there."

"No, you're not." She turned and saw Kent heading her way. She hadn't seen him earlier so he must have just arrived. "I can't let you do that either, Sabrina. Look, I've got eyes on the warehouse for now and there is no sign of Robby. Jake is right. Creed needs him alive but he knows his operation is compromised. He's probably got him holed up in a motel room or someplace like that and we're checking everything. Believe me, finding Robby is a priority for all of us."

Another car parked and her mom's boyfriend got out and ran up to the marked off area where a deputy stopped him. Sabrina spotted him and waved him through. He hurried over and hugged her mom, who fell apart into his arms.

"Is there any update?" he asked, glancing at Sabrina.

"Not yet," Jake told him. "But it's still early. The sheriff's office is doing everything they can."

He nodded. "Of course they are." He tightened his grip on her mom. "I'll take you home," he told her.

As they walked past, her mom stopped and reached out her hand to Sabrina. "I'm so sorry, honey."

Sabrina turned away. She still couldn't look at her.

"This is not your fault, Bev," Jake told her. "Just give her some time."

They walked off and Sabrina watched them climb into Bob's car then disappear down the road.

"That wasn't very kind," Jake scolded her.

She knew it wasn't and she didn't mean to blame her mom but her emotions at the moment were so raw. "I can't worry about her feelings right now, Jake. I just want my son back."

Kent finished conferring with his deputies then walked back toward her and Jake. "We've interviewed all the families that were here today and no one saw anything unusual. I'm going to release them but we've got everyone's contact numbers plus we've documented all the license plate numbers of the vehicles in the lot. I've also issued a BOLO for the van and we're trying to get tech to see if they can enhance those photos you took and see a tag number. I'll have someone get started on searching road cameras too along this area. Maybe we'll get a hit on something."

"Thank you, Kent," Jake said, shaking his hand. "And thank you for sending Deputy Parkman to get me."

Kent glanced at Sabrina briefly then back at Jake. "I knew you would want to know. I also figured Sabrina would need you here with her."

She was glad she'd told Kent the truth about Jake and Robby. It would have been awkward to try to explain it in the midst of this chaos but now he understood why Jake had to be involved in this. Plus, he was right. She did need Jake with her now more than ever.

"You should go home," Kent suggested. "I'll let you know if there are any developments."

Jake nodded. "I'll take her home and stay with her."

Since Jake had no car with him and the car from the impound had two flat tires, Sabrina decided they could use her mom's car which was still sitting in the parking lot. Bob had taken her home and Sabrina still had the spare key. She climbed into the passenger seat as Jake eased into the driver's. She should have offered to drive given his injuries but she couldn't bring herself to do so.

They were nearly to her mom's house when she realized this wasn't where she needed to be. She'd followed along and let others decide for her, but she had to think of Robby. "I don't want to go home," she told him. "Turn around. Take me to the sheriff's office. I want to be there when something comes through."

"I don't think that's a good idea, Sabrina. Let your team do their jobs. I know you trust them."

Tears filled her eyes and she pushed back the wave threatening her. "Don't ask me to do nothing, Jake. I can't do that, not with Robby out there all alone. He needs me to find him."

He pulled to the curb at her mom's then reached out and took her hand and held it. "And we will. We'll find him. I promise. We'll bring him home where he belongs."

She was grateful to him for his support but her anguish was unbearable. She pulled her hand away as the truth of the situation hit her. He didn't want her there, he didn't want her at the station. He didn't want her involved and she needed to be involved. No one cared as much about bringing Robby home as she did and that included Jake.

He hadn't been in their lives because he'd left her the last time tragedy had struck.

She pulled her hand away from his as anger gripped her. She was tired of being told what to do. "You made me a lot of promises once, Jake, and you didn't follow through with them. How can I ever trust you now with something so important?"

"What are you talking about?"

"Years ago when my brother died, you swore to stand by me. Next thing I knew you were leaving town and not looking back."

"That's not fair, Sabrina. I tried to reach you."

"You proved to me and my son years ago that we couldn't

trust you. What makes you think I can trust you now with my son's life. You already proved to me years ago that when the going gets tough, Jake Harris gets going."

She opened the car door and sprinted out and ran inside. She couldn't face him. And she certainly couldn't trust him to find her son.

She and Robby were on their own.

Jake watched her run into the house. He leaned back in his seat. His instinct was to go after her but nothing she'd said wasn't true. His face burned with shame at the way he'd left her years ago. He'd tried his best but now looking back he knew his best hadn't been good enough. He should have pushed to remain with her. He wouldn't make that mistake again. No amount of pushing him away to wallow in her grief was going to make him leave her, or Robby, ever again.

Still, it couldn't hurt to give her some space.

He turned the car around and headed back for the sheriff's office to check in on the investigation. Like her, he wanted to be there to see where the evidence led. He couldn't imagine what Sabrina was going through. He'd only known his son a short time but knowing Creed had taken him had left a gaping hole in his heart. He couldn't lose him now.

The department was bustling when he entered. It seemed everyone was on alert. He noticed Kent and Sheriff Thompson in the same conference room he'd been treated in earlier. It appeared to have been transformed into some kind of command center. He walked in and spotted Robby's photo, the one from the text message Sabrina had received, posted on a whiteboard along with details of the investigation.

Sheriff Thompson spotted him and walked over. "Agent Harris, it's good to see you up and moving better."

She extended her hand and he shook it. "Thank you. Is there any news?"

The sheriff glanced at the photo of Robby then shook her

head. "Not yet. My team is still working on it. Is there a reason you're back here?"

She gave him a quizzical look and he realized she didn't know yet about his connection to Sabrina or Robby. "I just want to help if I can."

"I'm sure we have this under control," she assured him. She turned to Kent. "Keep me updated. I'll be in my office."

Jake approached Kent as the sheriff exited the conference room. "Sabrina said she'd told you the truth about me, Kent."

He nodded. "She did."

"But the sheriff doesn't know?"

He shook his head. "I've only known a few hours. I was trying to figure out the right way to tell her when I received the call about the abduction. I haven't told anyone."

Jake stared at the photo of Robby on the board. A swell of love and emotion for the child overwhelmed him. "I can't ever go back undercover in Creed's organization but we still need to preserve the investigation in case it ever goes to trial. I don't care who knows Robby is my son but I think for now we should limit the number of people who know I'm Jake and not Max."

"Agreed," Kent stated. "I spoke with Agent Price and he agrees too. However, I have to let Sheriff Thompson know but it won't go farther than that. No one wants to risk Creed going free on a technicality."

A deputy got up and placed a pin on a map. "We've had another sighting," he stated.

Kent walked over to it and Jake followed him. "What is this?"

"We've been receiving tips all afternoon about the van used in the abduction. From the best we can piece together, it headed west out of town." He ran his finger down a line on the county map. Multiple pins indicated locations the van was seen.

"That's the wrong direction from where Creed's factory is located," Jake said.

"I noticed that too. It's possible like you said that he's taking Robby somewhere else to hold him or they could be circling around but that seems risky. The more mobile he is, the greater chance of being pulled over. So far, we lost them headed out of town but we've issued a BOLO to the neighboring towns and counties too. We're also issuing an Amber Alert for Robby. I used the photo that was sent to Sabrina's cell phone for the alert."

"Good thinking." He was glad to see Kent in action. It helped him to know that this office was capable of handling this situation. "We should still check out the factory."

"*We* will," he said, emphasizing the word *we* as a way of warning Jake to back off. "I've already told you I've got someone watching the factory. You should go back to the safe house. Creed is still targeting you."

Jake shook his head. "I'm more worried about finding Robby than I am about Creed coming after me."

"Then go be with Sabrina. She needs you now more than ever."

He was questioning that. "I'm not sure she does." She was strong, much stronger than he'd ever given her credit for. She'd pulled herself up from the dark pit of grief and depression, giving birth, and raised Robby alone for all these years. That was strength.

Kent leaned against the desk and locked eyes with him. "She needs you now more than ever," he said again. "She's suffered enough. She doesn't need you letting her down again."

It was a strange thing for her boss to say. "Isn't that kind of personal."

"You're right that I'm taking this personally. She's part of my team and I care about Sabrina. I've watched her grow and learn and take on Creed's organization practically on her own. Then you showed up. She deserves better than to be left alone again."

"She practically told me to get lost," he argued but Kent wasn't letting him off the hook that easily.

"She's stubborn, that's for certain. And she lashes out when she shouldn't but it's just her defense. She needs you, Jake. She needs you to be there for her more than she's ever needed anyone at the moment. Don't let her down."

Jake realized Kent probably knew Sabrina better than he did. Or, at least, the woman she'd grown into since he'd left her. He was glad to know she had someone looking out for her. It was obvious to Jake that Kent was more than just Sabrina's supervisor, he was also a friend.

"You're right. She does. I'd better get back to her." As he headed back to the car, he realized Kent was right. He'd taken her refusal too personally. He was wounded too by Robby's abduction and trying too hard to make things right with her. He could never change the fact that he'd left her but he could prove to her that he would never do it again.

He drove back to the house. There wasn't much use watching his back as he drove but he still did. Creed wouldn't bother sending his men after them now. He had the upper hand and likely figured they would come to him when he called. And he was right. There was nothing he wouldn't do to get his child home safely. He made it to Beverly's house and parked. The lawn blow-ups were deflated and lying in a heap on the grass. It seemed to fit his mood. They shouldn't be up and happy without Robby around to see them.

He leaned against the steering wheel and did his best to catch his breath before getting out. He entered the house without knocking. Bev was in the kitchen sipping on a mug of something hot. Bob was by her side holding her hand. She still looked distraught and who could blame her. The photographs of Robby were prominently on display above the mantel, a reminder to everyone in the household who and what was missing.

He headed down the hall to the bedroom Sabrina had taken over but the door stood open and the room was unoccupied. When he turned, he spotted the playroom door standing open. He peeked inside and found her sitting on the floor surrounded by a sea of toys, a stuffed animal in her arms as she cried.

She looked up at him with anticipation in her face. "Is there any news?"

He hated to disappoint her. "Not yet but they're working on it. They've traced the van to the outskirts of town."

"Near Creed's factory?"

"No. The other way. Kent believes he's probably got Robby holed up in a hotel room somewhere. They're checking them all."

He slid down and sat beside her. This time, she didn't lash out when he put his arm around her. Instead, she leaned into his arms and sobbed, and Jake held her as she did.

Sabrina paced in front of the whiteboard in the conference room. She'd convinced Jake to bring her back to the sheriff's office but it hadn't been easy. They all wanted to treat her like some victim who needed to hide out in her bedroom. And she had, at least for a little while, but now she knew she had to be proactive if she hoped to find Robby. She couldn't allow Creed to win. She was going to get her son back.

She grabbed all the files she could on the men she'd associated with Creed. One of them had to be involved or know where he'd taken Robby. She pored through those files, picking out names to investigate. She'd arrested most of them at one time or another over the past several years so she knew them and their loyalty to Creed. It wouldn't be easy to break them but she had a new motive now.

She chose several names to bring in for questioning then went into Kent's office to share her findings.

He looked through her notes then sighed. "There's no way I'm giving you permission to go after these men."

"Why not? All of these men are known associates of Paul Creed. They need to be questioned about Robby's disappearance."

"None of these match the description of the man who abducted him from the park."

"But we didn't get a description of the driver."

"Look, I'll send people out to look for them and question them—"

"I should be the one to do it," she interrupted. This was her lead and, although she trusted her coworkers, she had more at stake and needed to ensure the proper questions were asked.

"There's no way I'm sending you out there. You shouldn't even be here. I told Jake to take you home, not back here. This is an open investigation that you don't need to be anywhere near."

She glared at him. "It's my son who's missing."

"Which is exactly why you can't be a part of the investigation. Your judgment is too clouded. I'll send the others to split up and find these men and question them. That'll have to be good enough."

She turned and stormed out of his office. It wasn't right that she was being shut out. She knew Creed and his men better than anyone else in this department.

The cell phone she'd tossed onto her desk dinged with a new message but Sabrina turned her head away instead of glancing at it. Robby's story was all over the TV news and police bands and had garnered so much attention that her phone had been blowing up for the last few hours. She was grateful for friends who cared but the constant bombardment of people who knew her sending her thoughts and prayers during this trying time was more than she could wrap her mind around.

She didn't mean to be ungrateful because she was thankful to have people who cared about her, but she also didn't need the constant reminder that her son was missing. No one knew better than she and her aching arms that Robby was gone. Besides, Jana had set up a tracing alert on her cell in case someone other than her friends from her contacts tried to call.

All she wanted was her son back and she would do whatever it took to make it happen.

She glanced up and spotted Jake heading her way. He was still moving slowly but he was working through the pain to do what he could. He should have been resting but he was just as determined to find Robby and she appreciated that.

"How do you feel?" he asked as he slid into a chair beside her desk.

"How do you think?" She cringed at the sharpness of her tone. She didn't mean to take out her frustrations on him but she couldn't hold in her anger. She wanted her son back. "I'm sorry," she told him.

"You have nothing to be sorry about, Sabrina." He reached out and took her hand in his and she savored the feel of his strength. "I may not be moving so fast at the moment but I have strong shoulders. Feel free to place your burdens on them any time."

She squeezed his hand, grateful for the reassurance and that she wasn't alone in this.

"Have you called your mom?"

She let go of his hand and turned away. Her mom wasn't to blame for this and she knew her misplaced anger was irrational but she hadn't been able to bring herself to forgive her yet. She should have been watching Robby more closely. They both should have been. "No."

"You should. She's hurting, Sabrina."

"So am I." She blew out a frustrated breath. "I can't deal with her right now, Jake. I have to focus on getting him back.

Once Robby is home then I can forgive her for not keeping him safe."

He nodded then leaned back in the chair, seeming to decide not to push the subject.

"Has there been any word?" she asked him. She knew he'd been talking with Commander Stover who headed up the patrol division. They'd established roadblocks in and out of town soon after the kidnapping at the park.

"So far there haven't been any further sightings of the van."

"So then they either got through the roadblocks before patrol set them up or else he's holding Robby somewhere inside the perimeter."

"Kent is checking all the motels in the area but there are dozens of places they could be holding him."

She knew that. "I made a list of known associates of Creed's and gave it to Kent. He's going to have the team go and question them."

"I think that's a good idea."

"I should be the one doing the questioning. I'm the one who knows these men." She was hoping he might back her up on that idea but instead he shook his head.

"It's better you let the others handle it. Those men all know you. You've questioned them before and they never gave up Creed. Maybe some new blood will change that. In the meantime, they've also got eyes on the factory."

She shook her head. She doubted he was there. Creed would make sure Robby was someplace where he wouldn't be found.

Her phone lit up and they both turned to look at it on the desk. She'd silenced it earlier but that hadn't stopped the messages and calls. She couldn't even bring herself to read the texts or listen to the voicemails. She switched it off then placed it inside a drawer. "I can't deal with people right now," she explained to him.

"I understand. Can I get you something? Anything? Coffee? Water?"

She shook her head as the tears threatened her again. "I just want Robby back."

"We're working on it. I promise you I'll bring him home, Sabrina. I promise." He stood then leaned over and kissed her. "I'm going to check in with Jana and see if she's had any headway with discovering if your mom's phone had been cloned."

Sabrina watched him go. She wanted to believe in him and his promises but she was scared to trust him again. She'd put all her hope and faith in him once only to be disappointed and let down. He'd left her when she'd needed him most. Now she and Robby both needed him.

She had to pull herself together if she had any hope of finding Robby. She couldn't allow Creed to win. She wasn't going to allow him to take someone else she loved from her.

After Jake left, she somehow found the strength to get up and walk to the restroom. She washed her face then stared at herself in the mirror. She had to be strong for Robby's sake. She loved him too much to fail him. She couldn't allow grief and despair to pull her under the way it had when her brother had died. She had to be stronger than that for her son's sake. She had to call on the strength he'd given her to do whatever she had to do to find him and bring him home.

"Lord, please bring my baby home."

That simple request sent waves of tears through her. Jake wasn't the only one who'd let her down. It felt like God had abandoned her years ago after her brother's overdose. Then Jake had left her and her father had died. She'd thought at the time that all that loss was more than she could handle. Only losing Robby was on a whole different level and, if God could bring her child back to her, she was willing to give Him a second chance.

She dried her face then walked back into the squad room only to find someone sitting beside her desk. Bob stood when he spotted her. "Do you have a moment to talk?"

She sighed. There was only one reason he would be here and she wasn't ready to face it. "I really can't—"

"I'm not here to scold you," he told her. "I just wanted to check in on the search for Robby."

"No, nothing concrete yet but my team is working on it and they're very competent." She might be struggling with trying to let go of control over the situation but she did trust the people she worked with to do a good job.

He nodded. "Good. I'll let your mother know."

Once he was gone, Sabrina walked into the conference room and stared long and hard at the whiteboard that contained all the evidence they'd collected so far about Robby's abduction. There had to be a clue in there somewhere that they were overlooking. There had to be something that indicated where Creed might be holding him.

A ding sounded and she gave a weary sigh. She'd thought she'd silenced her cell phone. She reached into her pocket to get it but it wasn't there. Only then did she remember she'd slipped her cell phone into a drawer.

That ding sounded again and she realized it was coming from her jacket pocket. She reached inside and pulled out a silver cell phone. It wasn't hers. In fact, she couldn't recall ever seeing it before.

She glanced around, wondering who could have slipped it into her pocket and when. The phone chirped again and she opened it. A message popped up with a photo—an image of Robby. His big blue eyes were full of tears and his face was scrunched with fear.

Tears filled her eyes as her heart raced and she quickly scanned the message.

Want to trade?

She gasped. He was willing to trade something for Robby's life.

Forgetting her concerns, she quickly texted back. Anything.

You for the kid. You come to me and I'll let him go.

She fell into a chair at the conference room table as the demand hit her. Creed wanted her to turn herself in to him. If she did, he would release Robby.

Her hands shook as she quickly responded. Deal.

Voices outside the door startled her, causing her to drop the phone. She quickly shoved it beneath the table with her foot as the door opened and Jake entered.

He put on a brave smile. "Hey, there you are. Kent is sending Deputies Shaw and Patterson to question the names on that list you gave him. He wanted to know if you had any particular questions you wanted them to ask or advice for them."

If Jake saw this phone and text message, he would want to confiscate the phone and try to use it to track Creed's movements. He would never allow her to trade herself for Robby, which was just what she was planning to do. "No, I trust them. They'll do fine."

He shot her a quizzical look. "Okay, if you're sure."

"I am. They're both excellent investigators. They'll uncover the truth. I just need a few minutes to myself, if that's okay."

"I understand." He hesitated by the door then turned back. "I'll be around if you need me."

As anxious as she was to get him out of the room so she could continue bargaining for her child's life, she suddenly realized he would never let her go. He would fight her tooth and nail. He wouldn't understand her need to do whatever she could do to get her son to safety. Plus, he was watching her like a hawk now. How was she going to get away to see Creed without him knowing? She couldn't. Jake would surely stop her before she could trade herself for Robby. Neither would anyone else in this department.

She had to get out of here and get rid of Jake.

Once he was out of sight, she leaned down and picked the silver phone back up. She quickly sent another text to Creed.

Where can we meet?

He sent back directions to meet at the shopping center, promising to release Robby there once she arrived. She was a little surprised that he hadn't told her to come to the factory. Of course, he probably knew the sheriff's office had it under surveillance by now.

On my way.

She slid the cell phone into her pocket then walked out of the conference room. Kent and Jake were huddled up talking to Drake and Lisa about questioning Creed's men and the others in the officer were occupied with their work. No one was paying her any attention.

Good.

She walked down the back hallway then slipped out of the station through the back door. Jake still had the keys to her mom's car but thankfully Sabrina knew she kept a spare in a magnetic case just above her tire. She quickly slipped it out then hopped into the vehicle and started it.

She pulled out of the parking lot of the sheriff's office and realized this would be her last time doing so. Tears filled her eyes at the idea of never seeing Jake again but she pushed those away. She couldn't concentrate on what she was losing, only on saving Robby's life. He would need Jake once she was gone.

She only hoped Jake could forgive her for what she was about to do.

She drove to the shopping area and parked away from other vehicles. She was about to text Creed to let him know she'd arrived when another car pulled up beside her and several men got out. She recognized one of them as Lucas Davis, the man who'd threatened her with a knife in this very parking lot.

She got out too, keeping her hands where they could see them. She didn't want any misunderstandings. "I'm unarmed," she said.

Lucas grabbed her then patted her down before nodding to another man in the car. He got out and opened the door to the back seat of the car. "Get in," he told her.

She hesitated, noticing the back seat was unoccupied. She backed away, suddenly having second thoughts about trusting Creed or his men. He'd assured her Robby would be there and he wasn't. "Where's my son?"

"We're taking you to him. Now get into the car," the man demanded, his tone firmer this time.

Lucas shoved her and she bit back a retort. "He was supposed to be here. Creed promised he would release my son." Only now did it sink in to her how irrational she'd been to believe him and how foolish she'd been to leave without telling Jake.

She glanced around the parking lot. They were far enough away from the other cars that even if she screamed out for help, no one would reach her in time. Besides, she didn't see anyone anyway. Lucas grabbed her arm and, this time, shoved her toward the car.

She climbed into the back seat. Another man was sitting by the door and Lucas slid in on the other side of her. As the door closed and the car sped away, Sabrina knew she'd made a terrible mistake.

Chapter Ten

Jake slipped into the break room, pulled out some change then popped it into the vending machine for a drink. He had some over-the-counter pain relievers in his pocket and he took them out and swallowed several along with the drink. He didn't want to take anything stronger because he didn't want to be slowed down by them but, for now, he needed something to stem the rising pain he was experiencing.

He fell into a chair and rubbed a hand through his hair. He was doing his best to keep up a good facade for Sabrina's sake but it was difficult. Creed was dangerous and having his son in Creed's hands was overwhelming.

He took a deep breath then went in search of Sabrina. Her strength during this crisis amazed him. He'd been afraid that she would lose herself to grief and despair as she had when her brother died, but instead her determination had steadied her. It couldn't last, however. The longer he was gone, the harder it would be for her to maintain her tough demeanor.

Please, God, help us find him.

He checked her desk, and the photo of Robby as a baby stabbed a pain through his heart. It wasn't right. He'd only just found his son. He couldn't lose him now. And he didn't want to lose Sabrina either. No matter what happened, he wasn't letting this tear them apart. Nothing would separate them again.

He stuck his head into the conference room, surprised when she wasn't there. This was the last place he'd seen her.

"Have you seen Sabrina?" he asked of the deputies in the conference room.

They glanced at one another but all shook their heads. "We haven't," one of them said.

He searched several more places, including knocking on the ladies' room door, before panic began to set in. He pulled out his cell phone to call her then remembered she'd turned her cell off and placed it into her drawer. He hurried back to her desk and opened it. Her phone was still there, still turned off. Her gun was in her drawer as well so at least he knew she hadn't gone anywhere.

At least, not anywhere officially.

Dread filled him. It wasn't like her to be out of contact, especially not today, not when she'd been so worried about missing news. He dialed her mother's number and wasn't surprised when Bob answered instead of Beverly.

"Is everything okay there?" Jake asked him.

"Sure, we're okay. I gave Beverly something to help her rest."

"That's a good idea. You haven't heard from Sabrina, have you? I mean, she hasn't called, has she?"

"No, she hasn't. I know her mom would love to speak to her. She's so upset." Bob's tone changed as he must have been wondering why Jake would be asking. "Why? Has something happened?"

"I don't know yet. I'll call you back." He ended the call then hurried outside and burst through the back door, anger and fear settling into him as he noticed her mother's car was missing from the space where he'd parked it earlier.

What have you done, Sabrina?

Anger rolled through him at her recklessness. Why on earth would she up and leave this way without telling anyone where she was going? He didn't know but his gut told him it couldn't be good.

He hurried down the hallway and into Kent's office, hoping against hope that she was there but not at all surprised when she wasn't.

"What's the matter?" Kent asked, seeing his worried expression. "Is something wrong?"

Jake rubbed his face as the reality of the situation set in. "I can't find Sabrina. She's gone."

"What do you mean she's gone?"

"I can't find her anywhere and her car is missing. She's gone, Kent. She left."

Kent picked up the phone and typed in a number. Jake heard it ringing on the other end. "Her cell phone is still in her desk drawer along with her service weapon."

Kent hung up the phone. A worried expression crossed his brow. "Are we thinking that something happened to her?"

Jake didn't see how someone from Creed's organization could have gotten past all the deputies in the department in order to abduct Sabrina. She would have made that difficult for them. "I think it's more likely that she left on her own. She's going to face Creed."

Kent sighed and fell into his chair. "Why would she do that? That's suicide."

"We all know Creed is behind this. She must have decided to go and confront him herself. I should have been watching her more closely."

Kent picked up the phone again and hit a button. "Jana, I want you to scan Sabrina's emails and cell phone. I want to know if someone from Creed's organization managed to send her a message."

Jake hadn't considered that. "Good idea."

"I'm also issuing a BOLO for her and the car."

Jake was thankful for that. Hopefully, they could find Sabrina before she did something she couldn't come back from.

The car ride seemed to last forever but finally the car neared the factory. Lucas grabbed her head and shoved her down before they reached the factory gate, obviously so that whoever was watching, like the police, wouldn't see her. Someone opened the gate and the car pulled forward. Lucas released her and she glanced behind her and saw the gate being closed once they were through.

Panic gripped her. She'd been having second thoughts since the moment she'd climbed into the car trapped between two criminals. What had she been thinking? And why hadn't she told Jake what she was planning to do? Perhaps his talking her out of it wouldn't have been such a terrible thing.

The car stopped and the men got out of the car then held the door for her to exit. She reluctantly did, doing everything to remind herself that she was doing this for Robby. "I want to see my son," she demanded as she got out.

The men didn't respond except to lead her up the steps to the factory doorway. Once inside, she glanced around, expecting to see Paul Creed greet her. Instead, one of the men slid open a door then another shoved her inside. They grabbed her and tied her to a chair.

She struggled against them. "Where's Robby? Where's my son?" she cried.

"Mr. Creed will be in to speak with you later," one of the men stated as he tightened the ropes against her wrist.

They walked out, closing the door and leaving her alone. She had no idea what was going to happen or when. Creed had promised not to harm Robby. He was going to drop him at a shop and call the authorities. That was the deal they'd made for Sabrina turning herself in. Only, she had yet to see Creed since she'd given herself up.

She pushed back tears. She couldn't allow them now. She

only prayed that he would keep his word and Robby would be safe. Hopefully, Jake would find him soon and she knew he would take care of him. That was one of the main reasons she hadn't told him about her plan. Robby needed at least one parent to bring him up. She wished she could be around to see it but she'd done what she had to do.

She was sad that she might never see Jake again and hated the way they'd left things. She'd pushed him away because she had to, not because she wanted to. She'd wanted to tell him how much she'd fallen for him again and that she wanted to have a future with him, but that hadn't been possible. He would have stayed with her and never allowed her to trade herself.

She was lost in her thoughts and worry and had no idea how long she'd been alone in the room before the door opened and Creed entered followed by two of his men.

She braced herself for whatever was about to happen. This couldn't be good.

Creed's grin was maniacal as he stood in front of her. "Hello, Deputy Reagan."

"Where's my son? Is he safe?"

"Don't worry about him. I gave my word that I wouldn't harm him and I won't. My man is picking him up and bringing him here so you can see him and know that I kept my word. I'm a man of my word, unlike that friend of yours Max Harris, who infiltrated my organization and lied to my face every day."

He still didn't know Jake had fooled him. He didn't know the real Max was dead.

"What are you going to do with me?" She'd expected to be dead already but instead they'd tied her up and locked her in this room. And he was going to show Robby to her. What game was Creed playing?

"Oh, don't worry. We are going to kill you. However, my supplier has been putting so much pressure on me to get rid of you that I felt it only prudent to make sure he sees that you've been neutralized. He's on his way here now so you've got until he arrives and sees for himself to say your last good-byes. I have to admit, I won't miss your constantly badgering my employees and my operation."

"You won't get away with this," she told him. "The sheriff's office knows that if I go missing, they'll look at you."

"No. They might believe that at first but there won't be any proof. No one abducted you. You came willingly. We'll float the idea that you got Robby back then took off. You'll be missing and so will your vehicle. Don't worry. We'll set up some drops to make it look like you've been using your bank card along the way before you completely vanish."

"I would never leave my son. Anyone who knows me knows that."

He knelt beside her and smiled. "Of course you wouldn't. You and Robby are both going to disappear."

Her heart sank as she realized what he was saying. "You promised me that Robby would be safe. You gave me your word. You said you would drop him off somewhere safely."

"And I'll keep that promise. He is safe. I never agreed to return him to the sheriff's office. He'll be taken somewhere and given a new life. It's already been arranged."

She pulled at her binds and tried to lunge at him. "That wasn't our deal."

He jumped up and backward, then laughed at her futile attempt to get to him. "I'm changing the deal. Be thankful I'm letting you see him at all. He could already be on his way out of town to a new life with a new family."

He walked out the door and they locked her inside again. Only once he was gone did she let the sobs rock her. Robby was supposed to be safe. Creed had gone back on his word and now her son wouldn't be safe. Her attempt to trade herself for him had failed. Now she was going to die and her son would be left alone and vulnerable.

I'm so sorry, Jake.

She should have listened to him and trusted him. If she had, they might all be safe and together.

Jake stared at a photograph of Sabrina and Robby sitting on the mantel at her mom's house and his heart clenched. *Why did you do it, Sabrina?* Why had she left them with no word at all? He turned away and to the current situation... telling Sabrina's mother what had happened to her daughter.

Beverly's chin quivered as she sat at her kitchen table with Bob, Jake and Kent and listened to Kent explain. "What do you mean she's missing too? Has that man done something to Sabrina too?"

Kent glanced his way and Jake intervened. "No, Beverly. We believe Sabrina left on her own to go confront Creed. We have video surveillance showing she got into your car and drove away on her own. No one was forcing her." He still couldn't believe how she'd slipped away. How he'd allowed her to slip away.

"But why?"

"To find Robby. She's certain Creed took him."

"And you don't know where she is? Why not go there and get her back?"

"We've been watching the factory where Creed set up shop but, so far, we've seen no sign of him or of Sabrina."

Beverly shook her head and Jake saw the despair shining in her face. He understood what she was going through. She'd already lost one child, now a grandchild and her daughter were missing too. "I knew this vendetta against Paul Creed was going to come to no good," she said.

Bob held her hand. "She's smart," he assured Beverly, then he looked Jake's way. "She wouldn't have gone off without a plan, would she? She must have had some idea where to find Creed or Robby."

Jake thought for a moment then agreed with him. "You're

right. I think we would have found her by now if she wasn't. Creed must have found a way to contact her."

"How?" Kent asked. "We've looked through her cell phone and her email. She didn't receive any messages and no department phone calls were routed to her."

"So maybe he contacted her in another way," Bob suggested. "Could it be someone inside your office that passed a message to her?"

Kent frowned and tapped his finger against the table nervously. That wasn't a prospect that any cop liked to think about. Finally, he had to concede it was possible. "I don't like the sound of that but I suppose it's feasible. Creed seems to have his hands in just about everything around town." He glanced at Jake, who saw something else brewing in that statement.

"Kent, has something happened?"

He nodded. "The warrants against Creed and the men who abducted you were denied by the judge. He wants more probable cause before he issues warrants. It might be nothing."

"Or Creed might have gotten to him. Having a judge in his pocket might explain how he's gotten away with his activities for this long."

"Sheriff Thompson is speaking with the DA's office but, for now, we can't arrest him. If he can do that, then he might have used someone in our office to reach Sabrina. I'll go back there now and start working on that angle. If he did contact her, we need to find out how and what he said."

Jake nodded. "I'm going to stake out the factory. I know it's a dead end but I have to do something."

Kent turned back to Beverly as he stood. "I'll call when there's news."

"Thank you, Kent." He turned to leave and Beverly called Jake. She stood and grabbed his arm. "Promise me that you'll find them, Jake. Promise me you'll bring them home."

He nodded then hugged her. "I will." Outside, he found

Kent standing by the sidewalk waiting for him, a look of concern on his face.

"Jake, you shouldn't make promises to her that you can't guarantee to keep."

But Jake wasn't deterred. "I didn't," he assured Kent. "I will find Sabrina and Robby and I'll bring them both home." Nothing would stop him from putting his family back together.

Jake drove out to the industrial area of town but instead of heading to the factory, he planned to turn off earlier and meet up with the surveillance vehicle Kent had sent it to keep an eye on the factory after Robby's abduction at the park but, so far, the deputy on duty hadn't reported anything suspicious.

Jake wasn't sure what he planned on doing, but the answers to where Sabrina and Robby were had to be inside that factory.

His phone rang and he picked it up and glanced at the screen before answering. "Hey, Kent. Any news?"

"The car she was driving was found abandoned at the shopping center. Video cameras show her getting into another car with several men. We're working on identifying them and the car."

His heart sank into his stomach. Believing she'd gone to Creed was one thing but having it confirmed was another. "Did it look like she was being forced?"

Kent sighed. "They might have strong armed her into getting into the car, but she met up with them of her own free will. I've pulled employee records for the department and I'll start going through them. If we have someone in our office feeding Creed information, I want to know about it."

"Keep me updated," Jake told him and he promised to.

He didn't like the idea that Creed had eyes and ears in the sheriff's office but it didn't surprise him. Creed had to have gotten a message to Sabrina some way. He pulled into a clearing in the woods where another vehicle was parked. The deputy got out to meet him as Jake approached.

"Commander Morgan said you were coming by," the deputy, who Jake recognized as Deputy Parkman, explained.

Jake got out and shook the man's hand. "Have you seen anything?"

"There has been some activity, cars coming and going all day, but I haven't noticed anything that might indicate Deputy Reagan or her child is there."

He wasn't surprised. Creed was too smart to keep them in the one place Jake and the rest of the sheriff's department knew he operated out of. "I'm here to relieve you," Jake told the deputy. "Kent wants you to return to the station."

Deputy Parkman handed him a pair of binoculars. "I'll leave it to you."

He climbed back into his car and drove off. As he did, Jake used the binoculars to scan the factory. Much of it was hidden by the fence surrounding it but they were on a hill so they had a better angle. Plus, if he climbed onto the car, he got an even better view of the property. Some kind of activity was happening there. He spotted several trucks lined up along the outside loading docks and, as Deputy Parkman had stated, cars were continually coming and going.

He jotted down names of the men he recognized along with their activities. For the ones he didn't know, he wrote down descriptions. He even tried snapping pictures but they were just too far away to come out clearly.

He didn't really care about the drug activity at the moment. That was far down on the list of things he cared about, but it might be useful if it could help him in finding Sabrina and Robby.

He huddled in for the long haul. His phone was on vibrate in his pocket so he wouldn't miss a call. He'd never expected his heart could be so fragile until he'd learned he was a father and seen the glint in his child's face. He'd loved him from the first moment and everything in his life had changed in that instant. He'd gotten over his anger at Sabrina for keeping Robby's birth from him. It did nothing to help them move forward and he could understand the events that had led up to it. Again, if he hadn't left her, he would have known. Plus, he'd seen the dark place she'd been in after her brother's death.

Only, now he didn't know how he was supposed to live his life without his son, or Sabrina, a part of it.

A car turned off the main road and approached the factory. He watched as it stopped at the gate for entrance. He pulled out the binoculars and scanned it, seeing multiple people inside, including what looked like a car seat in the back surrounded by two men.

He jumped from the car and hurried closer through the brush for a better look before they disappeared through the gate. He lifted the binoculars and zoomed in. Dark hair was evident as the middle occupant in the car seat and, when one of the men turned to speak, he caught a glimpse of the child's face.

It was Robby.

His gut clenched as the car entered through the gate and it closed behind them. He slipped the binoculars' strap over his head then jumped up, grabbing ahold of a branch and climbing up into the tree for a bird's-eye view. He spotted the car when it stopped in front of the main entrance and the doors opened. Jake held his breath, praying he wasn't about to see what he thought he was about to see. Several men exited the vehicle then the little boy. The men each grabbed an arm and rushed him up the steps to the factory door.

He started to rise, clutching his gun then stopped. There was little he could do at the moment alone but, now that he knew Robby was here, he was determined to go in after him.

He pulled out his cell phone, ready to call Kent and update him on what was happening. He wasn't sure what their next move was but he wasn't leaving this place without his son. And he still needed to find Sabrina.

Before he could place the call, the doors opened again and Sabrina came out with Robby in her arms. She appeared to be sobbing softly and pressing Robby against her as she headed back to the car. She wasn't alone. The two men who had walked Robby inside were now following her, guns in hand, as she opened the back door of the car and strapped Robby back inside. Jake zoomed in on the vehicle as she kissed Robby's cheek then closed the door.

Jake held his breath and waited to see what was happening. What deal had she made to get Robby back and how could Creed allow her to just walk out?

Only she didn't get into the car. Instead, one of Creed's men climbed into the driver's seat. The other guy grabbed her arm and pulled her away from it.

She was letting this guy leave with Robby but she was staying behind. It made no sense to him. He couldn't believe what his eyes were seeing. Every instinct inside of him was telling him this was a mistake. It had to be a terrible mistake.

The goon grabbed her arm and pulled her back toward the doors as the car sped out of the parking lot with Robby inside.

Jake leaped from the tree, hightailing it back to his vehicle. He didn't understand what was happening but no deal where Robby was left alone with one of Creed's men was good. Whatever deal she'd made with him wouldn't be honored. She had to be aware of that.

He had to make a decision and fast.

He ran to his car and jumped in, starting it and pulling out. He knew where Sabrina was now but the farther away that car went, the less chance he had of finding Robby again. He now knew where she was but he couldn't help her at the moment.

He could, however, rescue his son.

Jake headed for the road, spotting the vehicle as it sped past him. He pulled out and followed the car. He didn't know where this guy was heading with Robby but he needed to intercept him. And, when he did, he would need backup to go back for Sabrina.

He pulled out his cell phone and dialed Kent, who answered right away. "Hey, what's up?"

"I just saw Sabrina trade herself for Robby."

"She did what?"

"They brought Robby to the factory. I watched her walk out and put Robby into a car with one of Creed's men."

"So she's been there this whole time?"

"I'm not sure. It's difficult to see past the gates but I definitely saw her buckle him into a car seat, then the car drive away without her. I'm following behind it now. I have no idea where he's going but this may be my one opportunity to get Robby back."

"Where are you?" Jake gave him directions. "I'm sending patrols and I'm right behind them. Don't do anything until we intercept you."

"Hurry," he said, unwilling to make any promises. He would rather wait on backup but if he thought for a moment that Robby's life was in danger, he would act. He wasn't going to risk losing Robby again. But he also had to be careful to make certain his son wasn't injured or taken captive again by the driver. His gut wanted to ram the car and run him off the road but that would only put Robby's life at risk even further.

"Just follow behind him without letting him see you," Kent instructed. "As long as he's driving, Robby should be fine. I've got cruisers on the way to you. We'll be discreet until we know where he's going and what he plans to do with Robby."

Jake agreed that was best. He was itching to get back to the factory and rescue Sabrina but she would want him to put Robby first so that's what he was going to do. Besides, he had eyes on his son. He didn't know what was happening with her at the moment.

He followed the car for several miles, doing his best to remain invisible. The driver didn't seem to notice he was being followed. He remained on the line with Kent until the driver turned into a motel parking lot on the outskirts of town.

"He's at the Western View Inn. Looks like he's parking."

Jake parked too then got out and watched the scene unfold. He hid himself behind cars as he quietly approached them. Thankfully for him, the driver didn't get out right away or he wouldn't have had time to make it to him. He reached the side of the car and dared to peek through the passenger's side window. The driver was looking down at his cell phone while Robby was still in his car seat and appeared to be unharmed. Good.

The driver opened the door and got out and Jake saw the opportunity. He gripped his gun then popped up as the driver's side door closed but before he could open the back door. He trained his gun at the kidnapper. "Don't move," he told him.

The guy seemed startled and reached for the handle.

"I said don't move," he shouted and the man took a step backward and held up his hands.

Jake circled the back of the car, his gun still trained on him. "Now back away from the door."

The man did as he was told but his eyes were back and forth thinking of a way out of this. Suddenly, sheriff's office cruisers filled the parking lot. Two deputies hopped out and grabbed the man from behind, cuffing his hands.

"We've got him," Deputy Parkman assured Jake and only then did Jake relax and put his gun away.

He opened the back door, unbuckled Robby from his car seat. Red streaks lined his face, evidence he'd been crying. He sniffled and coughed as Jake released him then pulled him to him. Robby placed his head on Jake's shoulder and Jake rubbed his back.

"It's okay, Robby. You're safe now. No one is going to hurt you again."

He hurried him away from the car, not wanting Robby anywhere near even a single man of Creed's. An ambulance had arrived and parked on the outskirts of the scene so Jake headed there but, when he tried to hand him off to the waiting paramedic, Robby clung to him.

"No, don't leave me," he cried.

Jake's heart broke at the fear in his little boy's plea. He rubbed his hair and reassured him. "I'm not going anywhere, Robby. I'm right here with you."

He longed to be part of the activity going on at the motel but staying with Robby was more important at the moment. His son needed him and he wasn't moving until he calmed down.

He held Robby while the paramedic examined him. "He doesn't appear to have been harmed," he assured Jake. "Wherever they had him, they took care of him."

Jake breathed a sigh of relief. That was something at least. *Thank You, Lord, for bringing Robby back safely.*

Kent appeared at the ambulance. "Has the suspect said anything?" Jake asked him. He could see the man he'd followed was now in the back seat of a patrol vehicle.

"His name is Allen Clifford. He has an extensive rap sheet for drug possession and robbery. He knows he's been caught red-handed in a kidnapping scheme so he's spilling everything. He was supposed to drop Robby off in room seventeen to a woman who was going to place him into foster care. He claims it's part of a scheme to get money from the foster care system for each kid."

Jake's stomach turned at the thought that, if he'd allowed this man to go through with his mission, his son might be lost to the system by another evil scheme of Creed's to make money.

"We're sending in a team now to the hotel room to apprehend whoever is in there. How is Robby?"

"He's scared but he's not hurt. And he misses his mom."

Kent nodded. "We don't have the manpower to be in both places at once. We'll go take care of that once we're finished here."

Given his injuries, he'd already exceeded his physical limits and his body was refusing to comply with his desire to join in on the raid. Instead, he remained outside with Robby while Kent's team breached the room and took a woman inside into custody. He only hoped she hadn't been alerted to their presence and phoned Creed or someone else to warn them.

If they knew Robby had been rescued, they might have no reason to keep Sabrina alive.

Deputy Parkman approached the ambulance. "I can stay with Robby if you'd like," he offered. He reached out for Robby and, to Jake's surprise, Robby reached out to him. "We're old friends, aren't we, Robby?" He shrugged at Jake's quizzical look. "Sabrina's brought him to the station a few times. If you'd like, I can make sure he gets back to his grandmother. I know Kent spoke with her and let her know he was safe."

Jake appreciated the offer but he hardly knew the deputy and he wasn't taking any further chances with Robby's safety. Only, he couldn't take him with him either and he needed to get back to Sabrina. He needed to trust someone in her department but given that there might be a mole working against them, his options were limited on that front.

"Thanks for the offer, Parkman, but let me talk to Kent about it first." Kent was really the only one in Sabrina's department that Jake trusted.

He waited until Kent returned from the raid then talked his options over with him. "I trust Parkman," Kent told him. "But I'll go by and check in on him myself once we're done here if that will make you feel better."

"It would." That had to be good enough for Jake. Time was running out for Sabrina. He leaned down to Robby. "Deputy Parkman is going to take you to see Grandma, okay?"

Robby shook his head. "No. I want Momma."

"I know. You go get your grandma while I go get your momma." He reached out his hand to shake. "Deal?"

Robby giggled then shook his hand. "Deal."

Parkman ran and pulled the car seat from the car then buckled it into his cruiser before returning for Robby.

"Don't worry about him," Parkman said. "I'll make sure he gets home."

Jake handed him off and was glad to see Robby didn't fuss. "Your momma and I will see you soon," he promised Robby. And he meant to keep that promise no matter what it took.

Once he knew Robby was safe, Jake turned back to the scene. He was just in time to see a middle-aged woman being led in cuffs to the back of a police cruiser. Jake bypassed her and headed to room seventeen. He glanced inside as Kent oversaw the room being processed.

He turned when he saw Jake. "Robby okay?"

"Yes. He wasn't harmed. Deputy Parkman is taking him back to Beverly's house."

"Parkman is a good guy. It's going to be okay."

He shot Kent a glare to remind him of what he knew about his suspicions that someone in the department was working for Creed. "What's happening here?"

"The woman we just arrested is named Gilda Mitchell. She's a state social worker from Alabama. Apparently, the plan was that she would take Robby and claim he was found abandoned. In return, she gets a kickback for placing him into the foster care system and he's placed with a family more interested in making money than caring for kids."

It was the worst part of the system. People always tried to game it and his son was nearly a pawn in it.

"How did Creed get involved in that scheme?"

Kent shrugged. "Too early to say. I'm sure he knows people involved. The organization pays him for the child and he's rid of him without actually having to harm him. Paul Creed is definitely a bad guy but it takes a certain kind of evil to directly harm a child."

"Did his man have any information about Sabrina?"

"Not much. He's only a driver. Apparently, Creed promised to let her see Robby so they took him to the factory for that meet-up."

Jake rubbed his face as the evil of the world rattled him but he did his best to shake it off. He had to because he still had one more person he loved to rescue. He was ready to get Creed and his men out of the world for evil deeds and in jail. And he was ready to go find Sabrina and bring his family back together once and for all.

Chapter Eleven

Jake paced in front of the cars at the motel. He needed to get back to Sabrina before something terrible happened to her. Every moment he wasn't there, her life was in danger.

"Calm down," Kent barked at him. "You can't go in alone. You could place both your lives at risk."

"I can't keep standing here and doing nothing either," Jake told him. "Now that I know Robby is safe, I need to go find his mother."

He couldn't allow himself to think about the danger she was in. They'd discovered the plan for Robby but he doubted Sabrina's life would be spared. Creed had made it clear that he and his supplier wanted her dead and out of their way. He glanced at his watch and realized he'd already been gone for so long.

He couldn't wait any longer. "I'm outta here."

"Where do you think you're going?" Kent demanded as he walked off.

"You know where. I can't let anything happen to her."

"You can't go, not without a plan of action. We only have a small tactical team and they're regrouping after breaching the hotel. We need to finish up here first."

Kent and his team were still processing the hotel scene and he knew how long it took for forensics teams to finish. He couldn't wait. "It might be too late by then. I'm sorry, I have to go."

"I can't let you do this, Jake."

He stopped at his car door and looked back at him. Kent didn't seem to understand that nothing was going to stop him. "You can't really stop me. I don't work for you, Kent. I'm going to find Sabrina and bring her home no matter what you say."

He climbed into his car and took off before they could argue any longer. He didn't have to wait for the sheriff's office to come up with a plan. He needed to put eyes on her, needed to reach out to her and tell her how much he loved her. He couldn't risk waiting any longer.

He knew waiting would be prudent. They needed a plan to breach the factory and the sheriff's office could come up with that once but Jake was going in first, alone, to find her. His gut was telling him there was no time to wait. It had already been over an hour since she'd traded herself for Robby.

Time was not on their side.

He pulled off the road before he reached the factory and parked in the same clearing he had earlier. He got out, checked his weapon, then moved through the brush and grass until he spotted the factory. He took out his binoculars and scanned the area for the best place to enter covertly, picking out a portion of the fence he could climb over without being seen. Once over, he could hide in the brush, then make his way along the side of the building to the door. It was his best chance of sneaking in unseen.

Headlights approached and Jake crouched down. He took out his binoculars and watched as a car approached then stopped in front of the factory. The doors opened and two of Creed's men Jake didn't know by name stepped out, only they didn't appear alarmed by this car. It must hold someone they were expecting.

Jake jogged down the embankment to the fence and readied himself to climb over it once these men went back inside. He didn't want to risk getting captured before he could enact his plan to get inside and find Sabrina.

The engine shut off and a man got out of the car. He glanced around the lot then headed into the factory.

Jake zeroed in on his face then stumbled backward in shock as he recognized the man.

What was he doing at Creed's organization and why were Creed's men not questioning his presence?

He moved up the steps and was led inside. Creed's men didn't even have their guns drawn as they escorted him into the building.

They slammed the door behind him and Jake pulled out his cell phone. He was still going in after Sabrina, but the sheriff's office needed to be alerted in case they didn't make it out.

Kent answered immediately. "Jake, please tell me you've changed your mind. I can have a team to the factory in less than an hour."

"I can't do that," Jake replied. "I'm going in after Sabrina but I thought you'd like to know I figured out who has been leaking information to Creed."

Sabrina wiped tears from her eyes as she huddled against the wall. Her hands were still tied but they hadn't rebound her feet after they'd let her see Robby. Creed had at least honored that. Only placing her child into that car and watching someone else drive away with him had broken her. She didn't know what was going to happen to Robby but she prayed he would be safe.

God, please keep him safe. Don't hold my foolishness against him. She was sorry she'd been so stubborn and angry at God. She understood now that her anger had been misdirected. She should have allowed God, and the people in her life, to comfort her in her times of grief, not push them away. That hadn't solved anything for her. In fact, it had only created more problems.

"I'm sorry," she cried out. The idea that she was going to give God one more chance to prove Himself to her was laughable to her now and proof at how far she'd distanced herself from Him. He didn't owe her another chance, but she prayed He would give it to her and knew He would.

She was in this mess because she hadn't trusted God or the people in her life. She'd targeted Creed out of revenge and pettiness over her brother's death. She'd set herself on a mission and now her child was lost because of it.

God had brought Jake back into her life at least so Robby had one parent out there searching for him.

Find him, Jake. Please find our baby boy!

If only she had trusted him instead of having to do everything on her own. That no longer mattered and she hoped Jake would know that if it came down to a choice between saving her or Robby that she hoped he would choose Robby.

She had to trust now that he wouldn't stop until he brought Robby home. She knew that. She took a deep breath then released it as a sob as she realized the truth—she'd fallen in love with Jake again. She wished she'd told him that before she'd left. Now he might never understand why she'd done what she'd done or that she'd longed for a future with him.

The door opened and Sabrina wiped her face on her sleeve as Creed walked inside. He wasn't alone either. This time, in addition to his men, he had a visitor with him. She couldn't see his face immediately but she recognized he was different from the other men she'd seen before from his gray hair. Must be his supplier come to make certain she was taken care of once and for all.

"And this is Deputy Sabrina Reagan, the deputy who has

been harassing my men and interfering with our operation. Now that we have her, she won't give us any more hassles."

She didn't look up at the men who meant to do her evil. She didn't need to look them in the face knowing what they planned to do with her.

"I'm familiar with Deputy Reagan," the man stated.

Sabrina's heart stopped as she recognized that voice. She looked up, stunned at the face that stared back at her. She knew Creed's supplier well…and so did her mother. Creed's supplier, the man who wanted her dead, was Bob Crawford, her mother's boyfriend.

Confusion washed over her at the recognition. "Bob? What—what are you doing here?"

She couldn't wrap her head around it. He'd always been so nice to her but all the while he'd been running drugs and having Creed do his legwork? He was the man behind Paul Creed's operation? She felt ill thinking about how gentle and caring he'd been with Robby. How could she have let this monster around her son?

"It's nice to see you again, Sabrina."

Anger exploded inside of her. He'd been in her house, around her mother and son. He'd pretended to be a decent human being. She couldn't find the words so she simply lunged at him.

They all jumped back before Bob laughed. "Now, now, don't take this so personally."

Suddenly, her voice returned. "Don't take this personally? You've been dating my mother, you're trying to murder me and you've sent my son off somewhere. How can I not take that personally?"

"You've made your own bed, Sabrina. If you hadn't kept coming after these men transporting my product, your family would have been fine."

Anger burned her cheeks. "My brother wasn't fine after using your product."

He knew all about her brother, Robby, and how his death had affected them all yet he was still trying to feign innocence and place the blame on her. "If he hadn't died, maybe I wouldn't have been coming after your organization so intently."

She didn't see an ounce of empathy or regret in his expression. "Your brother made his own choices. You can't blame me for that."

"I can and do. I blame you all."

"Don't worry about your mother. She'll be understandably upset about your disappearance but I'll be there to make sure she's taken care of…and to, of course, reinforce a reasonable explanation about how you took off with Robby. I'm thinking that perhaps your agent Harris—Jake—broke your heart again and you couldn't bear it so you packed up Robby and left town. She'll turn to me for comfort and I'll be there for her." He knelt in front of her. "I want you to believe me when I say this, Sabrina. I truly do care for your mother."

Sabrina pulled at her binds again and tried to lunge. "Stay away from her. You're a monster."

He laughed then stood and turned to Creed. "Go ahead and have your men take care of her, but do it outside of town. I have a truck heading out on a long haul. Place her inside it and they can dump her body once they're out of the state."

"Will do," Creed said.

Bob turned back to Sabrina and she glared at him again. "How can you look my mother in the face and pretend to care what happened to her family?"

"I care deeply about your mother, Sabrina. I didn't want this. This was all your doing."

"Jake will never give up looking for us. Never."

He looked confused then seemed to understand. "Why not? From what I hear, he's already left you once when you pushed him away. He'll do so again or else he'll pay the price too. Nobody gets in the way of my business." He turned to

Creed and his voice hardened. "Clean this up or else. Then, we'll do business."

He sounded like a different person and she suspected that was his normal tone. He put on a face while he was with them but this was his real persona—a drug-dealing murderer. And her mom wouldn't know the difference until it was too late.

"I always knew there was something about you that I didn't like," Sabrina told him as he was walking out.

Bob turned to her one last time, smiling. "Shame on you, Deputy, for not trusting your instincts."

Crawford walked out and Creed turned to his men. "Grab her and take her outside. Let's end this once and for all."

His men came over and grabbed her arms, pulling her to a stand. She dug in her heels and went limp. "I won't go. You can't do this," she cried.

Creed stomped over and smacked her hard. Pain seared through her and the men lost their grips as she crumpled to the floor.

She clutched her cheek and glared up at him, her face stinging from the hit. She wouldn't let him see her fall apart. She might die, but he wouldn't get the added bonus of seeing her beg for her life.

"Get her," Creed told his men who grabbed her again and pulled her up. "Toss her into the trunk of the car while I go find out where this truck is located. I'll text you the information."

One of the men grabbed her from behind and held her while the other gagged her so she couldn't scream for help. It didn't matter. Who would hear her all the way out here? No one was coming to help her. She was on her own.

They dragged her to the doors then down the steps toward the parking lot.

The one with the keys hit the key fob and the trunk popped open on a car parked a few feet away. This was it. They were going to place her into that trunk then kill her and dump her body somewhere out of state.

Bob Crawford would get away with murdering her, all the while pretending to care for her mother.

She'd failed Jake and Robby and now she'd failed her mom too.

Jake crouched beneath a set of steps as the factory door opened and two men walked out, shoving Sabrina in front of them. He recognized them as Dax and Ethan, the same guys who would have killed him if he hadn't gotten away from them. He gripped his gun and assessed the situation. Sabrina's cheek was red and she looked to have been crying and that angered him. If they'd harmed her, they would have to answer to him.

He scanned the area. The parking lot was clear of people. Everyone else, including Creed's newly discovered partner, Bob Crawford, must still be inside. He hadn't noticed them exiting the building. Of course, if he was involved then he must be overseeing the operation.

Ethan and Dax pushed Sabrina toward a waiting car and opened the trunk. He couldn't wait any longer to act. Once they had her inside, they would kill her…just as they'd planned to do with him.

He was too far away from his own vehicle to get to it in time to catch up with them and follow them. He wished he were. He would much rather take the risk of running them off the road than having to confront them at such a central location. Creed and his other men could emerge from the factory at any moment.

He had no choice. He had to act now.

Sabrina looked terrified as Dax grabbed her arm and pulled her toward the open trunk. She jerked away from him but he pulled her back and shoved her down. Jake acted while they were watching her and darted toward the car. He slammed the butt of his gun against Ethan's head. Dax spotted him and slammed the trunk, reaching for his gun as Ethan collapsed on the asphalt.

"I wouldn't," Jake told him as he reached for his gun.

Dax reluctantly moved his hand away and held it up. He stole a glance at the factory and, for a moment, Jake worried someone might be behind him. He changed positions so that he could see both the factory entrance and the man.

Jake reached in and grabbed Dax's gun from its holster. "Get on the ground," he instructed and Dax did as he was told. Jake searched him for the keys and found them. He popped open the trunk, barely missing a kick from Sabrina as he did.

She gasped when she saw him and took his arm, quickly climbing out. Jake cut her hands free and removed the gag then pulled her to him.

"You came for me," she gasped.

"Of course I did. I wasn't going to let Creed hurt you."

"Robby! They took Robby."

He touched her cheek to calm her. "He's fine. He's with your mother."

"But how?"

"I was here when you loaded him into that car. I followed it to a motel where they were going to hand him off to a social worker from out of state. I got him out."

She nearly collapsed in his arms with relief. Tears slid down her cheeks. "Thank you for making sure he's okay."

"I would never let anything happen to him. I promised you that."

She nodded. "You did."

He leaned his forehead against hers, so overwhelmed by the feeling that she was with him. They still needed to get away from these men but, at the moment, he was thankful she was alive. "How could you trade yourself to Creed like that? How could you do it?"

"I had to do something to protect Robby. I didn't want anything to happen to him."

"You had to know Creed wouldn't keep his end of the bargain."

Her eyes widened. "It wasn't Creed who put the hit on me, Jake. It was Bob Crawford. He's been spending all this time with my mom at her house and he ordered me to be killed and Robby to be taken away. He's the supplier behind Creed."

He nodded. "I know. I saw him when he walked into the factory. I could hardly believe my own eyes."

"I never suspected him, not once."

"He'll get what's coming to him but, first, we need to get out of here."

He spotted a pack of zip ties in the back of the trunk and used them to bind Dax's hands then forced him into the trunk. As he slammed it, he handed the gun to Sabrina then pushed her toward the gate where he'd climbed over.

"Let's get out of here before someone else comes out." He took a moment to send Kent a message letting him know he'd found Sabrina. Kent had promised his team would arrive in an hour and it had already been over thirty minutes. "Reinforcements should be on the way."

They darted across the parking lot and reached the gate. Jake interlocked his hands together and she placed her foot into them, lifting her to the top. She quickly climbed over.

He heard commotion and turned to see a man descending the factory steps and running to Ethan, who was still on the ground unconscious. He called for help and Jake knew their time was limited before they were discovered.

He scrambled up the fence but not in time. The man spotted him and called out. "Hey, you! Stop!"

Jake hit the ground on the other side and, by the time he did, several more men he didn't recognize were exiting the building. He spotted both Creed and Bob and knew they'd been discovered.

"Let's go," he said, pushing Sabrina to run up the embankment to where his car was parked.

She hurried up the hill and he was right behind her, pushing her to go faster.

It wasn't fast enough. Several shots rang out and hit the tree as he ran by. He stopped and crouched behind it. They'd already gotten weapons that could reach at this distance. He spotted someone with a rifle. He might be able to shoot this far but his aim wouldn't be good. He also spotted armed men heading for the fence and climbing over. They were coming after them.

"How far is your car?" Sabrina asked.

"That way," he said. "It's not too far. We can hide in the trees. They've only got one rifle and his aim won't be good at this distance."

He urged her on and the shooter fired as they moved. He kept going. Stopping wasn't an option. They had to get to his car.

They made a dash through the clearing and spotted his car. His heart leaped at the sight.

Sabrina swung open the door and climbed inside while Jake followed. He turned the key then backed up and turned around before speeding away.

"We did it," Sabrina said giving a relieved laugh. She leaned over and hugged him. "You saved me."

He was about to congratulate himself when shots rang out and one whizzed past her face and through the windshield, cracking it.

Sabrina screamed and another shot rang out, sending the car out of control. Jake fought to keep it on the dirt path but another bullet nipped at his shoulder and the pain was blinding.

"Jake, watch out," Sabrina screamed just before the car went off the path and rammed into a tree.

They were both thrown and Jake slammed into the steering wheel. Pain doubled him over and the gun slipped from his hand.

He did his best to catch his breath and get his bearings but his breath caught when he spotted Sabrina on the floorboard. There was blood on her head and she was unconscious.

Movement in the rearview mirror told him Creed's men were closing in. He leaned over to try to retrieve his weapon but it was just out of reach and all the blood seemed to rush to his head. He struggled to move as darkness played at his vision.

If he lost consciousness now, they were both dead, but he couldn't stop the darkness that pulled him under.

Chapter Twelve

Sabrina groaned as the pain in her head brought her back to consciousness. Everything hurt to move but she had to, the memory of the attack flooding back to her. She opened her eyes and saw Jake slumped over the steering wheel. A splotch of blood was on his shirt at the shoulder indicating he'd been shot.

She reached for his hand and felt for a pulse. He was still breathing. *Thank You, Jesus.* He was still alive.

Movement outside the car told her it wouldn't be for long. Creed's men were out there while she and Jake were trapped inside this vehicle. She'd seen the front end smash against the tree and, even now, could hear hissing as the engine's fluids released. They weren't going anywhere in the car.

She felt in her pocket for the gun Jake had handed her but it wasn't there. She searched the floorboard but couldn't find it but she spotted Jake's gun under his leg. She reached over and grabbed it as footsteps neared the car. They were coming.

From her position, she could see each window and saw when two figures approached the car, one on each side. She saw they each were armed. She didn't even wait for them to reach for the door. She fired through the window, hitting the one on her side of the car then the other. She heard them both hit the ground and scrambled off the floor. She peeked through the window. They were both on the ground. She opened the passenger door and got out and ran to the one on the ground beside her side of the car. She kicked away his gun then checked for a pulse. He was dead. She cautiously ran to the other and didn't even have to check him for a pulse. It was obvious from the hole in his head that he wasn't getting back up. She was a good shot.

She opened the driver's door and tapped Jake's cheek. "Wake up," she told him. "Wake up. We have to get out of here."

As she'd suspected, the car's front end was a mess. They weren't driving out of here in this car, which meant they needed to get somewhere to hide before the rest of Creed's men arrived.

Killing two of his men wouldn't help to endear her to him.

She tapped his cheek again and he finally roused. "Wake up, Jake."

He groaned. "What happened?"

"We wrecked the car. Come on. We have to get out of here."

She pulled him from the seat and he struggled for a moment to steady his legs.

"Can you walk?"

"Give me a second," he responded.

She heard voices floating on the air. "I'm not sure we have seconds."

She grabbed him under his arm to help steady him then led him away from the car and into the brush. They were moving slowly but at least they were moving. Creed's men would start searching for them once they discovered the car.

Sabrina couldn't get her bearings. She'd been in these woods many times but she was turned around either out of fear or from the crash. Her ears were ringing and she felt a little dizzy but she wouldn't let that stop her. They had to keep moving if they were going to survive this.

And they had to survive for their son's sake.

Jake steadied as they walked and soon they were dashing. She spotted the roof of something that looked like a building through the brush. "I need to stop here for a minute." She leaned him against a tree then walked to the brush.

She spotted the old sawmill and realized where they were. They could take refuge inside there until they could figure out a way to find help and make certain that Jake's shoulder wound wasn't life-threatening.

She walked back to him. "We're near the old sawmill. We can take shelter there for a few minutes."

He leaned on her as they made their way through the brush to a dry creek where they crossed over. She pushed open the door and went inside then helped Jake to sit down. On the other side of the room, she spotted a chair and ropes on the ground.

"What do you think that's from?"

He grimaced. "That was for me. This is where Jacoby and his men held me after we left the high school."

He unbuttoned his overshirt then took it off and pulled up the sleeve of his T-shirt so she could examine his wound. The bullet had only grazed him but it was bleeding heavily and running from Creed's men wasn't helping that.

"Here, use this as a bandage," he said, holding out his top shirt.

She took it from him and tore it into several pieces she could use to bandage his shoulder and stop the bleeding.

"We have to find a way to call for help," she told him and Jake agreed.

He dug through his pockets then groaned. "My cell phone must have fallen out of my pocket when I was climbing over the fence. If we can make our way to the highway maybe we can flag down a car. That's what I did when I escaped from Jacoby's men."

"Then that's what we'll have to do."

"Kent knows I'm here. He promised to send backup so help is at least on the way."

That was good news. So they just had to survive until the cavalry arrived.

"They'll be looking at the factory for us so it might take them some time to figure out what happened."

He shook his head. "Parkman knows about the clearing where I parked. Hopefully, he'll check it out and see the car. They'll know we're running through the woods."

She hoped they made it in time but, in case they didn't...

She leaned in and kissed him. He was startled at first but then he relaxed and kissed her back. "I love you, Jake."

He stroked her cheek. "I love you too, but don't give up on us yet."

"I'm not but I wanted you to know. When I thought I was going to die, all I could think about, besides Robby, was you and the fact that I never told you how much you mean to me."

He shook his head. "Why did you do it, Sabrina? Why did you give yourself to Creed?"

"I did what I thought was right to save Robby."

"Did you really think Creed was good for his word?"

She shook her head, feeling her face warming with shame. "I wasn't thinking. All I knew was that I couldn't lose him. Are you certain he's safe?"

He nodded and held her close. "I promised him I would bring you home. I plan on keeping that promise."

He kissed her and she sank into his arms. This was something she thought she might never experience again and she wanted it to last. She wanted a future with Jake. Five years ago, she hadn't been able to look past her own pain and grief to see how life could be good again but now she knew, with him and with God's guidance, they could be a family.

Suddenly the doors swung open and they were surrounded. Sabrina grabbed the gun she'd dropped on the ground then scrambled to her feet with Jake behind her. She didn't aim it at them as Creed, Bob and two other men had them cornered. Instead, she tucked it into her back waistband out of sight.

Creed grinned at them. "You thought you could come in and take her?" he asked Jake. "You thought wrong. Neither of you will get away with this."

"The sheriff's office is on their way here now," Sabrina told him. "Leave now before you're arrested."

Bob laughed. "The cops are busy out looking for Robby. Trust me, Creed. They're preoccupied."

"Is that what you think?" Jake asked him. "They're not looking for Robby any longer. He's safe and sound back at Beverly's house."

Bob scoffed. "That's not true."

"We found your man, Allen Clifford, Creed, heading to the Western View Inn to hand him over to that lady from out of state." He squeezed Sabrina's shoulders. "Robby is safe and you'll never get your hands on him again."

Bob pulled out his cell phone, pressed a button then placed the phone to his ear. The tension in the air was palpable as he tried to verify Jake's story. Sabrina felt the tension in Jake and said a silent prayer that what Jake had told her was true, that Robby was safe. She knew he wouldn't lie to her but she also needed reassurance that her child was no longer in danger.

She shot arrows at Bob. He'd sneaked into their lives and, for whatever reason, had become enthralled with them. Had his plan all along been to keep eyes on her or had he actually cared for her mother as he'd told her?

She glanced at Bob and saw his face pale. He ended the call then threw his phone against the wall.

Creed stepped toward him. "Then it's true?"

Bob nodded. "They have your man in custody along with

the social worker. And, yes, the boy is back with his grand-mother. I just spoke with her."

Sabrina's heart leaped with joy. She'd trusted Jake's word but to hear it confirmed was elation. Robby was safe. Even if she and Jake didn't make it through this, at least he would be okay.

Suddenly, she felt something at her back and realized Jake was going for the gun. She stiffened as he did, realizing he meant to fight them. She wasn't against fighting back but one gun wasn't going to get them out of this mess.

While Creed was focused on Bob, Jake pulled his gun and stepped in front of Sabrina. He held it against Creed's head.

Suddenly, everyone's attention was on them.

Creed laughed. "You're not going to kill me, Jake."

"You threatened and harassed the woman I love and you abducted my son to use as a distraction while you tried to kill his mother. I don't think I'll have a difficult time killing you, Creed."

"Max would never have—"

"Max couldn't stand you, Creed. He wanted nothing more than to bring you down. He despised every moment he spent with you. Besides, I'm not him. He might not have killed you but he might have if he'd lived through what I have these past few days."

He grabbed Creed's arm then backed up toward the door. "Now, we're going to walk out of here and no one is going to come after us or this is going to end badly for your leader here," he warned them all.

Sabrina ran to the door and opened it while Jake led Creed out, keeping the gun trained on him. The others were watching them closely, ready to strike but they didn't move, obviously waiting to see what happened.

She hurried through the door with Jake behind her. Only, seconds after she stepped through, another of Creed's men who'd remained outside grabbed her and clamped his hand over her mouth.

Sabrina tried to scream and Jake heard her. He spun around, the gun pulling away from Creed, who took advantage of the situation and tried to grab it from his hand. The others raced from the building, another one of them running over and helping restrain her. They dragged her away as Jake and Creed struggled for the gun. She was helpless to intervene and Bob didn't seem to care enough to do so.

As the men held her, he approached her, his usually kind face morphed into a snarl. He was angry that his plan had been disrupted and she couldn't help herself. She smiled at his discontent. To know that Jake had thwarted his plans gave her a moment of satisfaction.

"I've spent years building up my business, Sabrina, and I'm not going to let you and a fake undercover agent show up and ruin it."

"When did you know about Jake?" she asked him. "Did my mother tell you?"

"Not right away. She kept that secret until after Robby had been taken. By then, Creed already knew his friend Max was a cop. It didn't matter what his name was."

She stole a glance at Jake, who was still struggling with the gun. "Aren't you going to stop them?"

He shrugged. "I'll let Creed deal with him while I deal with you." He threw back his hand then punched her, sending her to the ground. Pain radiated through her and she was temporarily stunned, unable to move through the pain.

Suddenly, a cry rang out. She startled and looked over to where Jake and Creed were huddled together still fighting for control. Jake fell holding his leg and she saw blood pooling around his fingers and a knife protruding from his thigh. Creed laughed but Jake quickly used his other leg to sweep over Creed, sending him to the ground. They both scrambled for the gun that had fallen. Jake reached it first and fired. Creed crumpled to the ground.

That was enough for Bob. He grabbed Sabrina by the hair and pulled her up. "I'll kill her," he said, but he'd hardly gotten the words out when lights and sirens lit up the area and multiple Mercy County Sheriff's Office SUVs surrounded them.

Bob tossed her to the ground then took off running with several deputies taking off after him.

Sabrina jumped to her feet and ran to where Jake was lying on the ground. She pressed her hand against his leg. The shoulder wound hadn't been bad but this one looked worse.

"We need help," she cried and Kent hurried over.

"Call for an ambulance," he shouted. "We have a man down."

"I'm okay," Jake said, trying to sit up. "I don't think it's very deep." He touched Sabrina's face and she leaned into his hands as tears welled up in her eyes. "It's over," he told her. "It's over and we're safe."

She kissed him and was so thankful that he'd come for her. "What about Bob?" she asked Kent.

"My men will catch him. He can't get far. There's already a warrant out for his arrest. We issued it after Jake alerted us he was there along with ones for Creed and his men. The judge finally came through. Turns out he was just being overly cautious. I have a team readying to search Bob's house and business."

"Trucking might have been his legitimate business, but he used it to transport drugs," Jake said.

"My mother will be heartbroken. She thought he truly loved her."

Jake held her hand. "Your mom is strong. She'll be happy to have you and Robby back with her."

"What about Creed?" Sabrina asked then realized she knew

the answer as she spotted him lifeless several feet away. He was dead. He couldn't harm her, or anyone, ever again.

Jake was right. This nightmare was truly over.

Sabrina watched as her mom pulled another tray of Christmas cookies from the oven and placed them on the table to cool. She was putting on a good face for Robby's sake and he was having a good time helping her decorate cookies for Santa, but Sabrina knew her heart was broken over Bob and his involvement with Creed.

They both turned as the small kitchen TV showed news footage of Bob, along with Mick Jacoby, Ethan, Dax and many others from the organization, being arrested by the sheriff's office and led away in handcuffs two days prior. Her mother's face paled at the reminder and she quickly picked up the remote and clicked off the television. The arrests were all over the news and Creed's organization, as well as Bob's trucking business, had been dismantled once and for all. Drugs may still find their way into Mercy County but, if justice prevailed in these cases, these men wouldn't profit from it. And the cases against them seemed strong. Jana had finally been able to decrypt that flash drive Jake had stolen, which linked Bob to Creed's organization. That was more evidence the DEA could use to dismantle his operation and flush out his connections to other drug organizations.

Sabrina put her hand on her mom's arm. "Are you sure you're up for this?"

She nodded and patted Sabrina's hand. "I need to stay busy."

"Whenever you're ready to talk about it, I'm here," she said and her mom hugged her, then quickly composed herself and turned back to the cookies, picking up a tin of icing. "Robby and I are going to decorate cookies then make some hot chocolate and watch a Christmas cartoon, aren't we, Robby?"

He cheered and licked the spoon for the icing.

Sabrina was happy to see him settling back so well after all he'd been through. She kissed the top of his head and rubbed his hair. She'd nearly lost him and had worried about residual effects but, so far, he seemed fine. They hadn't harmed him and, for that, she was thankful.

"I'll be in the garage putting the you-know-what together," she whispered to her mom, who gave her a conspiratorial wink.

She walked outside to her mom's car and opened the trunk where earlier in the day she'd picked up a box containing a new bike for Robby's Christmas present. She only needed to assemble it to have it ready for him when he awoke Christmas morning.

A car stopped at the curb as she was struggling to get a grip on the oversize box. She turned and saw Jake get out of the car and approach her. His injuries from their fight for survival were still evident—the sling on his arm, the limp in his step from the knife wound to his leg, and the bruises and cuts on his face from the car wreck and beatings. It was a wonder to her that he was still standing.

"Need some help with that?" he asked.

She nodded. "Thanks. It's a little awkward for me but can you handle it?"

He lifted the box from the trunk with little difficulty. She closed the trunk and motioned to the garage. "Carry it to the garage."

He walked up the driveway and set it down on the garage floor. "A new bike? I'm sure Robby will love it."

"He's been wanting one for a while now. He thinks his tricycle is for babies and wants a big kid bike. Of course he'll still have training wheels for a while."

"Do you need some help assembling it?"

She smiled. "That would be nice but I was going to wait until he'd gone to bed to start. I don't want him running to the back door and seeing pieces scattered around."

"Makes sense. Where is he now?"

"Mom has him occupied decorating Christmas cookies."

He nodded. "That's nice."

This would be the first Christmas that father and son would be together and she realized how special that was. "Do you want to see him?"

He nodded. "Of course, I do. I never want to leave him again." He reached for her hand and she took his. "I never want to leave either of you again."

She closed the distance between them and kissed him. "And you never have to, Jake."

"I went shopping this afternoon and got Robby some presents. They're in the car. But I have something for you too." He reached into his pocket and pulled out a ring and held it out to her.

Her heart raced as he reached for her hand. She stared up into his eyes and saw everything she wanted out of life.

"Sabrina Reagan, will you make me the happiest man alive and be my wife?"

Tears of happiness filled her eyes. She'd loved Jake for so many years and knew she would love him for the rest of her life. The decision was an easy one but she still hesitated to say yes. "I want to marry you, Jake. Only, are you sure you can forgive me for not telling you about Robby?"

He waved away those concerns. "I want a future with you and my son and that means moving forward not looking backward. Besides, I'm the one who needs your forgiveness. I should never have left you five years ago. I regret it so much and every day since. Max told me I was a fool for letting you go but I couldn't stand by and watch you destroy yourself. I'm so sorry. I promise you here and now that I will never leave you again. Never. Don't ever doubt that."

His assurances were just the balm she needed to get past her worries. She would never doubt him again and never push him away. "I won't."

He smiled as he slipped the ring on her finger then pulled her to him for a long kiss to seal their future together.

"Does this mean you're moving back to Mercy?" she asked him. They hadn't discussed it and she was willing to go wherever he wanted, but she needn't have worried.

"Absolutely," he assured her. "Where else would I live? This is where my family is."

She was certain Kent would offer him a position at the sheriff's office but they could work all that out later. All that mattered now was that they were together and would always be.

She clasped his hand in hers. "Let's go inside and give our son the news that we're going to be a family." They walked hand in hand into the house to give Robby the best Christmas possible.

* * * * *

Colorado Christmas Survival
Cate Nolan

MILLS & BOON

Cate Nolan lives in New York City, but she escapes to the ocean any chance she gets. Once school is done for the day, Cate loves to leave her real life behind and play with the characters in her imagination. She's got that suspense-writer gene that sees danger and a story in everyday occurrences. Cate particularly loves to write stories of faith enabling ordinary people to overcome extraordinary danger. You can find her at www.catenolanauthor.com.

Books by Cate Nolan

Love Inspired Suspense

Christmas in Hiding
Texas Witness Threat
Colorado Mountain Kidnapping
Colorado Christmas Survival

Visit the Author Profile page at millsandboon.com.au.

Behold, a virgin shall be with child, and shall bring
forth a son, and they shall call his name Emmanuel,
which being interpreted is, God with us.
—*Matthew* 1:23

To Dana R. Lynn, Rhonda Starnes,
Belle Calhoune and Tina Radcliffe.

Writer friends are a precious gift,
and I am blessed by your friendship and support
over these many years. Thank you.

Chapter One

"Knock, knock."

Hope Prescott looked up from her computer, smiled and called to her daughter, who was curled up on her office chair, face buried in a book. "Hey, Emi. Look who's here."

Emi kept her eyes glued to the page until Hope prompted her again. "Earth to Emi. You have a visitor."

Emi glanced up and her whole face transformed. "Uncle Steve!" The book went flying as she leaped from the cozy corner chair.

"Hey there, sweet girl." Steve scooped the seven-year-old blonde bookworm into his arms as if she weighed nothing. He turned to Hope. "Why are you still here? I told you to take the afternoon off."

"And I told you I had a marketing campaign that needed finishing touches."

"It can wait until after Christmas. Go. The rest of the gang left hours ago."

Hope rolled her eyes. "If you make me leave, I'll only take it home with me."

"Not this time." Steve pulled an envelope from his back pocket and handed it to Emi. The little girl opened the envelope and gasped.

"Christmas Village! You got us tickets?"

Hope ground her teeth and glared at her boss. He might be her best friend in the world, but he had no right getting her child's hopes up over something impossible. "No room at the inn," she muttered.

Steve laughed and whispered into Emi's ear.

Hope's heart sank at the way her daughter's eyes lit up. She would have given anything to bring some Christmas joy into Emi's life, but by the time her daughter had discovered the best Christmas celebration in all of Colorado, everyone else in the state had snatched up the tickets along with every room in the small mountain town.

"Uncle Steve's friend has a ski chalet we can stay in. It's ours for..." Emi looked at Steve, who whispered in her ear again. Her eyes grew round. "Two weeks! We get two weeks at Christmas Village!"

Hope opened her mouth to protest, but Steve shook his head. "I won't hear another word about it. Emi deserves a special Christmas and who better to provide it than her favorite uncle?"

"Does that mean you're coming with us?"

A shadow passed over his dear face, confirming the feeling that had been nagging at Hope lately. Steve was keeping something from her.

Whatever it was, he shrugged it off. "Not this time. You need to get going before the storm blows in. Leave the computer here. Pack up your stuff. I want you on your way in—" he glanced down at his watch "—fifteen minutes."

There was no missing the underlying tension in his voice this time. Why was he so anxious for her to be gone? "Steve, what's wrong?"

He gave Emi a kiss, then set her down and stepped into the doorway. "We'll talk about it when you get back. No worries. Just go give your daughter the Christmas she needs. And if you really have to work, you can play along with Twelve Days 'til Christmas."

Hope stared at him as he disappeared into the hallway. Playing on their social media platform was not work. Her job was getting other people to play.

As Steve's footsteps receded down the hallway, Hope begrudgingly powered down her computer. He was right. She needed to set aside her work and focus on her daughter. Emi's childhood had been derailed by her father's death, and as much as Hope didn't want to think about her deceased husband and his betrayal, she couldn't deny the hole it had left in her daughter's life. So, she would shirk her workaholic ways and concentrate on Emi and Christm—

A piercing alarm shattered the air, cutting off her thoughts. Her phone dinged, and she grabbed it.

Intruder Alert: Exit Code 8

Hope's heart raced. Code 8 meant extreme danger and they were supposed to use the secret exits Steve had designed. But where was he? If they were alone in the building, she couldn't leave without him. Except she was supposed to. That was what they'd practiced.

She dashed across the room and peered down the hall. There was no sign of Steve, but in the distance she could hear the sound of running footsteps followed by a gunshot, and then silence. She slammed the door and engaged the safety latch.

"Mommy?"

The look of terror etched on her daughter's face galvanized Hope. Steve had been paranoid about a workplace attack. He'd made them practice escapes until the steps were drilled into their minds. She'd never expected to need to use them, but she knew what to do.

"Get our coats and backpacks." Her heart pounding, Hope

pressed the panic button under her desk, which would ring at the sheriff's office. That was the fastest way to get help, though she hoped law enforcement had gotten the same alert she had. She shrugged on her coat, took the backpacks from Emi and grasped her hand before heading into a back passage that would open into the parking lot.

As she and Emi raced down the empty passageway, Hope's thoughts strayed to Steve and she whispered prayers for his safety. She listened for sirens and prayed law enforcement would get here fast, but as more gunshots echoed in the hallway, terror seized her heart and she feared it wouldn't be soon enough.

Hope punched in a special code that would deactivate the alarm on the door and eased it open. Snow was falling steadily as she poked her head out and looked around the quiet garden. All was peaceful and still back here, but her car was parked on the other side of the building—the side where all the shooting was coming from.

What should she do? She could try running away to wait for rescue, but Steve had built his tech complex in the middle of nowhere. With the storm blowing in, they risked death by exposure. She glanced down at Emi, who was huddling inside her coat—her bright pink coat. If anyone came looking for them, she'd stand out like a neon sign. Whipping off her own coat, Hope wrapped it around her daughter. She really had no choice but to try to get to her car.

"We have to be very quiet, baby," she whispered. "We're going to slide along the side of the building so no one looking out will see us."

Emi nodded, but her body was trembling. Hope couldn't tell if it was from cold or fear, but her heart broke for her baby girl. Worrying wouldn't get them to safety though. Holding on tight to Emi's hand, she began to sidle along the building. There were no windows on this back wall, so they were able to move quickly, but when they reached the corner, and Hope paused to take stock, she could hear voices. A shaft of light spread out from an open door.

"I don't see anyone out here. Maybe he was telling the truth that she left."

"Her car's still in the lot."

"Well, then where did she go?"

"If you hadn't hit him so hard, maybe we could have asked him."

Hope stifled a gasp as she listened to the argument. What had they done to Steve?

"Boss said to teach him a lesson."

The door slammed shut, and the voices faded away as Hope glanced down at Emi. If her daughter weren't here, she'd risk going back in to look for Steve, but her first concern had to be Emi's safety.

This side of the building housed the company cafeteria, and the walls were floor-to-ceiling glass. They were meant to be a relaxing way of bringing the outside in, part of the natural aesthetic Steve had created for his company. Most days, Hope appreciated the chance to bask in the sun while she had her lunch, but today all that glass was a hindrance to her escape.

"We're going to have to crawl along this wall—like inchworms," she teased, trying to make Emi relax. "I'll go first and you follow right behind my heels, okay?"

Emi shivered and silently fell to her knees. Hope dropped down in front of her and began to inch her way along the wall. The lunchroom had never felt as big as it did while she made slow progress through the drifts that were still piled up from last week's storm. When they finally reached the end, Hope peered around the edge and her heart sank.

Steve's motorcycle was parked in his spot by the front door, and an unfamiliar truck, presumably belonging to the gunman, was idling in the walkway. Her car sat alone in the lot, spotlighted by the glow of the lights.

Where was the sheriff? Why hadn't anyone responded yet?

Another round of gunfire echoed from inside the building and terror spurred Hope onward. "We have to run as fast as you can, Emi. I'll open the door and you jump in and get your seat belt on yourself, okay?"

Again, Emi gave a silent nod.

Hope fumbled in her pocket for her key fob. "One, two, three, run," she whispered, and the two of them dashed across the parking lot. Fearful that the sound might be overheard, she waited until they were crouched behind the car to push the button on her fob. As soon as the car beeped and the door was unlatched, she helped Emi in and closed the door securely. If only she could assure her daughter's safety that easily.

By the time Hope had opened the front door and settled in her own seat with the key in the ignition, she could hear shouts from the front of the building.

She quickly turned the key and shifted into gear as gunfire erupted behind her. "Stay down low, Emi," Hope warned as she lead-footed the accelerator.

The car shot forward, tires spinning on snow that had begun to accumulate in the lot. She fishtailed as she shot around the corner, but the back tires caught and she was able to straighten out and speed down the long snowy road that led out to the highway.

"Mommy, I'm scared."

I am, too. Hope didn't say the words aloud, but her white-knuckled grip on the steering wheel betrayed her terror as she drove up the entrance ramp to Highway 160.

The Colorado highway could be a snowy death trap, so she didn't dare take her eyes off the road or her hands off the wheel, but she needed to reassure her daughter. "It will be okay, Emi. We trust Jesus to protect us."

Hope smiled despite her fear as she heard Emi begin to murmur prayers. Echoing her daughter, she whispered the words beneath her breath, alternating them with "Jesus, take the wheel" as she stared through her rearview mirror into the swirling world of white—and saw headlights appear behind them.

There was a chance it was nothing, just fellow travelers in a storm. But she'd seen no other vehicles in either direction since leaving the parking lot. Anyone with sense was safe at home. She tried to focus on prayer, but fear settled in her heart.

The headlights grew brighter, and her fingers clenched the steering wheel. The truck was traveling too fast for the road conditions.

She glanced back, panicked as the vehicle behind closed the distance between them, but with road conditions deteriorating, she couldn't go any faster. She cast another look in her mirror, and terror washed over her at the sight of a gun protruding from the passenger window. "Emi, head down!"

The back windshield exploded.

"Mommy!" Emi screamed.

Another gunshot and Hope swallowed her own scream. The truck drew closer until she felt it slam her back bumper. She pressed her accelerator to the floor, but it did no good as the truck sped up and rammed her from behind.

He was trying to drive her off the road! As she struggled for control of the car, Hope crouched over the wheel, trying to see ahead on the curving road. Her wipers couldn't keep up with the heavy snow, but as they cleared a swath, there was no missing the blinding headlights of an approaching eighteen-wheeler.

The vehicle behind revved and shot forward. Hope prayed and swung the wheel with all her might as the hard hit sent her skidding across the highway directly into the path of the oncoming headlights.

Jesus, I trust in you. Please help us.

Ian Fraser rubbed his brow, fighting the eye fatigue that came with trying to see through driving snow. He should have stopped at the last rest stop and waited out the storm, but something had urged him to keep going. Maybe it was knowing the local veterans' center was counting on his truckful of Christmas trees for their annual fundraiser. Maybe it was wanting to be safe at the ranch in this ferocious storm. Or maybe he was just hungry. Whatever the reason, he'd kept going, and there was no use regretting it now. He had enough regrets in his life. No need to add new ones.

Keeping one hand steady on the wheel, he stretched, trying to ease the kink in his neck, but the sudden glare of headlights ahead caught his full attention.

And gunshots. Who was foolish enough to be firing guns in this weather? They could set off an avalanche that would close down the whole highway.

Ian pumped the brakes to slow his rig, but the car in the other lane was flying toward him at an alarming speed. The driver appeared to turn, but Ian watched as the car spun helplessly out of control right into his path. He grasped the wheel tightly and swung his own rig to the left, barely missing contact with the car and the truck that had been traveling behind it.

Ian slowed his truck to a halt and quickly hopped down. There was no way that driver had been able to avoid crashing and he could only hope they'd managed to find a soft drift.

Wind whipped stinging bites of snow into his face as he trudged through the rapidly accumulating snow.

"Hello," he called. "Anyone there?"

The gusts scattered his words, so he cupped his hands to his mouth and tried again. There was still no response, but that didn't satisfy his concerns. If the people were injured, they might be unable to answer.

Doubling over in his fight against the wind, Ian scoured the sides of the road, looking for where the car had gone over the side. Praise the Lord, it had been here rather than farther up the pass where the mountainside dropped off beside the road.

After a few minutes of searching, he found where the car had plowed headfirst into a deep drift. The doors stood open, and two men in balaclavas were searching around the outside.

"You all right over there?" Ian called.

The men looked up, and Ian thought he must be imagining the irritation on their faces.

"Just looking to help out whoever crashed here," one of them called back.

They seemed to confer a moment before one headed in his direction. "Looks like there was a woman and a child in the car. They must have been ejected. We're searching down below. Can you set up flares on the road?"

"Sure thing," Ian answered. "Did you call for help or should I?"

"My buddy called it in."

Ian turned to get the flares from his truck, but instinct that had served him well through multiple tours in Afghanistan made him turn back just in time to ward off a blow to the back of his head. The gun glanced off his temple instead. That same instinct sent him to his knees pretending to be struck. He stilled his breathing and waited, ready to spring if the man attacked again, but he seemed to be satisfied and headed off downhill, calling to his friend to hurry.

Ian lay in the snow, waiting until he was sure the man was out of sight before he rose to his knees. His temple ached, but he knew God had been looking out for him. Another few inches and he'd be dead. What had he stumbled into?

Suddenly he wondered about the car he'd seen go off the road. Had that been an accident? Or had these men had something to do with it? And who were the missing occupants of the car?

He was all about helping people in need, but Ian was outnumbered and outgunned here. The best thing he could do was get back to his truck and make that call to highway patrol.

Not wanting to draw their attention, Ian crawled his way

through the snow until he reached the side of the road. He rose cautiously, but there was no sign of the men, so he hurried across to where he'd left his truck. As he reached the cab, he noticed a piece of pink fuzz caught in the driver's side door. He glanced back quickly to see if either of the men had followed him, but there was still no sign of them. They were too busy searching for people who, he suspected, were hiding in his truck. He pocketed the fuzz, opened the door and quickly climbed up, pulling the door shut behind him.

The moment he settled in his seat, Ian knew his suspicions were correct. The woman and child had taken refuge in his truck. He sensed their presence, and the summery scent of lavender tickled his nose in confirmation.

He started the ignition and shifted the truck into gear. "I know you're there. Give me one good reason I should trust you over them."

Chapter Two

"The blood frozen to your temple might be a good one."

Ian reached up and touched the side of his head. When his hand came away sticky, he simply nodded and put the truck in gear. "Where are you headed?"

There was silence for a long moment before he heard her soft reply. "Anywhere you're going is fine, as long as it's away from them."

Ian turned his attention to the road and started driving. All thoughts of waiting out the storm had vanished the moment he'd spied that pink fuzz, but the driving conditions were steadily deteriorating. Snow was piling up faster than plows could keep up. He had chains on his tires, as required by state law, so he was less worried about spinning out than he was about visibility. If they took it slowly, all should be well.

But would they be able to take it slowly? Ian glanced in his side-view mirror. Would the men continue searching the area where her car had gone off the road, or would they soon be on his tail? Driving Highway 160 required concentration in the best of times, but this stretch ahead was particularly perilous.

He should radio for help, but first he needed to know what he was dealing with. At the moment, he had nothing more to go on than two huddled figures and a piece of pink fluff. He'd heard from the men with guns. Now he needed to hear from his stowaways.

"You can come out now."

Silence from the back seat only amplified the howling of the wind and the rhythmic slap of his tire chains against the road.

Ian blew out a soft breath and tried again. "I'm sure you're scared, but you're safe with me. My name is Ian. I'm a rancher. I saw you go off the road and just tried to help." He touched the tender side of his head and chuckled softly. "And got a pretty nice headache as a result."

"I'm sorry."

The voice sounded genuinely remorseful, which made Ian feel a little better about his choice to drive off with strangers in his truck. He was trusting his instincts here, that anyone who had been running from those men must be in trouble.

"Okay, whenever you're ready. But this storm is only getting worse, and it would be a big help if I knew what we're up against."

"Thank you."

Ian strained to catch her words over the raging storm. "I could hear better if you would come up here and talk with me. There's no sign of your pursuers," he added as reassurance.

"They'll be back."

The defeated tone of her voice nearly undid him. "Then come tell me about them so I'm prepared."

He could hear some shifting around followed by whispers before the curtain parted and a woman emerged between the seats. Ian reached out a hand to steady her against the roll of the truck, but she flinched away and slid into the passenger seat.

He risked a quick glance, just long enough to observe her huddled inside a heavy winter coat. A faux-fur-trimmed hood obscured most of her face, but as she turned to face him, he noted stray whisps of blond hair framing delicate features. He felt her studying him in return, so he waited, allowing her time to feel at ease.

"Whenever you're ready, tell me what happened."

She tilted her head toward the back seat, and gave a subtle shake. Ian only caught the motion out of the corner of his eye, but he understood her meaning. Whatever she needed to say, she didn't want the person back there to hear. Because it was a child or for some other reason? He reached over and turned on the radio, flipping through stations until he found one that was playing popular Christmas music. He flipped another switch to raise the volume on the back speakers while he lowered the sound in the front.

"Thank you." She paused before continuing. "If you're really a rancher, why are you driving a truck full of trees in a blizzard?"

Ian chuckled. "I guess that does seem odd." Maybe if he offered some information about himself, she'd be more at ease. "My parents own a ranch that's been in the family for generations. My brother, my sister and I each have our own acreage to do what we want with. When I got out of the army, I decided to try my hand at growing Christmas trees. This truckful is headed toward a veterans' center for a fundraiser."

"That's really generous."

He smiled again, but this time it was more forced. "I do what I can to help. Now, have I answered enough questions? Are you ready to tell me the story?" He felt her hesitation. "I can't keep you safe if I don't know who they are and what they want."

"That's just the problem. I don't know who they are."

Ian stared into the swirling snow and considered her answer. It was interesting for what she'd left out. "But you know what they want?"

"Not really."

From his years as an Army Ranger, Ian had plenty of experience in knowing when to wait and when to coax for information. This seemed a time to wait. He focused on the road ahead, but he was acutely aware of the tension radiating off the woman sitting in his passenger seat. She was nervously fingering her gloves, and he sensed she was trying to decide what she should say.

He also caught her frequent glances toward the side-view mirror.

A glare of headlights from a snowplow in the oncoming lane made Ian shield his eyes to see better, but she reacted more dramatically, sliding down in the seat until she was below the dashboard level. Whoever those men were, they clearly had her terrified.

She wedged herself into the corner against the door and folded her arms across her chest in a gesture that came across as more defensive than defiant.

"I don't know who they are, but they invaded my workplace late this afternoon. I would assume it has something to do with that break-in. But my daughter and I got away, and they've been chasing us ever since. I don't understand that part. If there was something they wanted, wouldn't you think it would be back there?"

Ian wasn't sure what he'd been expecting, but it wasn't that. He needed more details, but at least it was a start. If she was being truthful, he'd learned two important facts. She was innocent, and the men pursuing her were extremely dangerous. No surprise there.

"Have you reported it?"

"No, but a safety alert went out, so the sheriff's office should have gotten that, and I hit the panic button on my desk before we fled."

"What kind of company do you work for that has such fancy security?"

"It's a tech company, but we design apps and social media

platforms, nothing that should have triggered something like this."

Ian thought back to the two men who had attacked him. That did seem sort of extreme for something having to do with social media unless it was corporate espionage. But why attack…? "What's your name?"

She hesitated just long enough to warrant suspicion, but he got that she was scared. "I already told you my name. Ian Fraser. Do you want me to call the sheriff?"

"Please."

"Then I'll need a location and some more details. And your name."

She gave him the address.

"Whoa. They've been chasing you that far?"

She nodded, and a whimper escaped her lips. He was beginning to understand the depth of her fear. "Was there anyone else there?"

"I don't think so. Steve, he's my boss, he was in my office just before they burst in. He said everyone else had left."

"Why were you there?"

She hiccuped, and he realized she was trying to hold back sobs. "You sound like Steve. He asked me the same thing right before he…"

Her voice trailed off, so Ian prompted. "Right before he what?"

"Right before he gave Emi a Christmas present and said he was sending us on vacation for two weeks."

"Emi is your daughter?"

She glanced at the back seat again before answering. "Yes."

"Why was your boss sending you on vacation?"

She turned her body so she was facing Ian directly now. "It was a Christmas present for Emi. He's been looking out for her ever since…ever since…"

Her voice faltered, so Ian gave her a moment before asking, "Ever since what?"

She cleared her throat and again spoke softly. "Ever since my husband died."

This was like playing a game of twenty questions, but instead of getting closer to the solution, each response opened up more questions.

Even across the cab, Ian felt the shudders that suddenly wracked her body. Remembering how she'd flinched when he'd tried to steady her, Ian took his cue. She was too skittish for him to extend a comforting hand, so he tried to calm her with his voice.

"Take your time. Do you need a tissue? There should be a box under the seat."

He waited while she located the tissues and wiped her tears. She looked in the back seat. "Emi?"

There was no response, and she visibly relaxed, but her voice was lower when she continued.

"I think she's asleep."

She took another moment to get her emotions under control, and Ian used the time to carefully study the road behind him. Still no sign of any other vehicle. Actually, there was a surprising lack of traffic, even allowing for the road conditions. With the storm worsening, they'd probably close off the pass at the foot of the mountain.

"Steve came to give Emi her present," she continued. "He told us to leave, and then he headed back to his office." She took a deep breath. "I heard shouts and then gunshots, and then someone running in the hallway."

She shivered at the memory, but her voice assumed a matter-of-fact tone that he took as a means of getting herself through the retelling as she detailed their escape. Ian still couldn't believe that this brave woman had managed to escape gunmen on a treacherous highway in a blizzard.

"I've got enough to call it in now," he assured her. "But I still need your name."

She didn't respond immediately, but Ian understood her

hesitation. She didn't know him as anyone more than the driver of the truck she'd hidden inside of in a desperate move to escape men trying to kill her. In her position, he'd be hesitant too.

He wished there was something he could do to reassure her that she was safe with him, but only kindness and time would accomplish that. "There's water in the box where you found the tissues if you'd like something to drink," he offered. "Sorry I don't have something hot."

"Thank you," she murmured. "Hope. That's my name."

Ian decided against pressing for a last name. "Thanks for trusting me, Hope."

There was usually reliable cell service along this stretch due to the tower at the top of Wolf Creek Pass, so he opted to call 911 rather than use the truck's CB radio. He identified himself, established their location and relayed what he knew.

The operator took the information and his contact details. She promised that law enforcement was dispatched to the crime scene, but there wasn't much she could offer him in terms of support on the road. Multiple-vehicle accidents had traffic backed up in both directions across the pass, and emergency responders had their hands full. She promised to let him know as soon as help was available, but Ian caught the tension in her voice and the unspoken reality. They were on their own, trapped on a mountain pass with potential killers.

It wasn't good news. Hope could tell from the slump of Ian's shoulders as he listened to the operator. She hadn't really expected anything different. People had warned her against traveling across Wolf Creek Pass, but she'd never planned to do it in a storm, much less with men chasing her.

She opened the water bottle, listening for the crack of the seal and mourning the circumstances that made her be suspicious of a man who was clearly trying to help. Without her, he would be delivering his trees and heading home. Instead, he was risking his life to protect a woman and child he knew nothing about. She owed him a measure of trust for that.

Ian disconnected the call and glanced over at her. "She said the sheriff was dispatched, but I got the sense he was already there. She took my contact information and said she'd let us know."

"Thank you."

"But we're going to have to wait on getting help out here. Apparently there are accidents on both sides of the pass."

"Beware the wolf."

He threw her a look.

"Beware the wolf. That's what all the signs say. The ones warning you to take it slow over Wolf Creek Pass."

Ian nodded. "I've driven it many times. You're right. You do have to take it slow. Not like we have much choice in this weather."

Hope stared at the near whiteout conditions and whispered a prayer of gratitude that the man was able to keep a sense of humor even under such dire conditions. "I'm sorry you got caught up in this. I shouldn't have hidden in your truck."

"Why did you?"

She shrugged as she thought about it. "I didn't know what else to do. When they ran us off the road, I knew it was only by the grace of God that you managed to avoid hitting us. I also knew they wouldn't give up since they'd followed me that far. I was going to try to cross the highway and take shelter under the trees until help could come." She shivered at the memory. "But then the wind blew your door open." She paused and sighed.

"I'd been praying for rescue. Your truck...it felt like an answer to my prayers. At that moment, I wasn't thinking that doing it would put you in danger."

She could see a smile curl his lips as he began to speak.

"I'm not sure anyone has ever considered me an answer to their prayers before."

Some instinct made her tease him back. "I said your truck."

Ian threw back his head and laughed. "Touché."

"There's no need for regrets. It was the right decision," he continued quietly when the laughter had drifted off. "You and Emi could have frozen to death waiting on rescue."

Unspoken, the words *if the gunmen hadn't gotten you first* hung between them.

"We have a long, slow drive down the mountain. You can rest if you want."

Hope turned toward the window. Huddled inside her jacket she pretended, but she knew she wouldn't sleep, and she knew she wasn't fooling him. Too many thoughts spun through her head in a dizzying whirl.

As much as she wanted to forget what she'd seen, she had to try to remember the details.

She owed that much and more to Steve. He'd been her best friend since sophomore year of college. It was almost a cliché. He and Keith had been the computer geeks she'd met when her laptop died in the midst of a research paper deadline. They'd fixed her computer and saved her 4.0 GPA. In return she'd kept them supplied with cookies. Years later, when Keith had betrayed her and she'd been a widowed single mother, Steve had rescued her again, giving her this job and drawing her back into life.

She'd repaid him with more than cookies that time. The app he'd designed was incredibly clever, but he'd had no clue what to do with it. Her marketing expertise provided the solution, and before long, Twelve Days 'til Christmas was climbing the charts across all platforms. She was still stunned at the success of the campaign that had left them all financially independent. It had been the perfect collaboration of Steve's technological brilliance and her marketing savvy. They'd been riding an incredible high.

Until today.

Tears rolled down her cheek unchecked. "I need to call the hospital and check on my friend."

"You can try, but they probably won't release info if you're not next of kin."

Hope sighed as she looked up the number and called the county hospital. She was essentially the closest thing he had to kin other than his admin, Helen.

As Ian had predicted, the hospital refused to even tell her if Steve was a patient. Next she tried Helen, but that call went straight to voicemail.

She didn't know what to do now, where to turn. She couldn't continue to rely on the kindness of a stranger. Once they made it off the mountain, she would be on her own, responsible for protecting Emi against men who what…wanted her dead?

"Do you think you would recognize their truck?"

Ian's voice had an edge to it that jolted Hope from her misery.

"Take a look at the side mirror, and see what you think."

Hope reached for the crumpled tissue she'd dropped in her lap and rubbed the tears from her eyes. "The mirror is covered with snow."

Ian pressed a button to lower the window, and she used her jacket sleeve to clear the snow and ice. Her heart sank as a familiar silhouette materialized. For a brief moment, she wanted to close the window, let the snow build up again and pretend she'd never seen the truck. Fatigue crashed through her as she turned to Ian instead.

"It's them. They've caught up."

Chapter Three

Defeat was back in Hope's voice. After hearing the details of what she'd endured, Ian understood why, and on a personal level, he wanted—*needed*—to help. Something deep within his protective nature was triggered by the sight of that truck bearing down on them. It hardened his resolve to do whatever was necessary to keep this woman and child safe. "Not yet they haven't," he promised. "We're not giving up so easily."

Hope turned from the window. Her shoulders were slumped, and she seemed to want to disappear inside her jacket. Obviously, she didn't share his confidence. Understandable. She was exhausted and probably hungry, and she had to be absolutely terrified.

"They have guns, a fast truck and apparently a strong motive to catch me...or kill me."

Ian winked at her. "You have me."

Hope choked on a laugh. Not exactly the reaction he'd intended, but if it helped defuse her anxiety, all the better. "I'm not joking. I know it sounds egotistical, but I'm a trained Army Ranger, and I know these mountain roads."

"What are we going to do?"

Ian didn't respond immediately. The actual answer was

that he wouldn't know until the men made their move, but he doubted that would instill confidence.

"The first thing we need to do is make sure everyone is secure. You should go in the back with Emi."

"But—"

"It will be easier for me to focus if I know you're not a visible target. There are seat restraints, and you'll find extra blankets and pillows in the cabinet that you can use as protective cushioning. Make sure you're both belted in. This might get rough."

Hope rose without a word, though he could see she was biting down hard on her lip. The truck lurched as a sudden gust of wind caught the Christmas trees lashed in the back. This time she was the one who grasped his arm to steady herself, and Ian felt her soft touch straight to his heart.

"It'll be okay," he said gently.

She nodded bravely and stepped into the back.

"Mommy?"

Emi's frightened voice cracked his heart.

"It's okay, love," She echoed his promise. "This is Ian, and he's going to keep us safe."

Ian's heart swelled at the ring of trust in Hope's voice. She was probably forcing it for the sake of her daughter, but he still took the responsibility of her trust seriously.

He cast a glance out the window. Snow was coating his mirror, but he could see well enough to realize the gap between the trucks was down to a car length now. He needed Hope to get settled fast.

"Hi, Emi. Your mom is going to build you a pillow fort because the road is getting bumpy really fast." He put emphasis on the word *fast*. He didn't want to alarm Emi, but Hope needed to know they were running out of time. "Closing in, Hope."

"Gotcha."

He heard the cabinet door slam, and within minutes, she confirmed their status. "We're belted in."

Ian nodded acknowledgment and then forced himself to shut out the soothing sound of Hope's voice as she comforted her daughter. Likewise, he shoved aside his anger at the men who were trying to harm them. He needed a clear mind and full concentration on the road ahead and the men in the truck.

Snow was piling up in drifts along the side of the highway, nearly to the top of the mile markers, but Ian had driven this route enough to know every landmark, every twist and turn. He was banking on two things—their pursuers lacking his familiarity and their being focused more on his truck and the people within than on the road itself.

A sudden jolt interrupted his thoughts. Were they serious? They were going to try to run him off the road with a truck a quarter his size?

Ian rolled down his window to clear the snow off his mirror, and suddenly their plan made sense. A shotgun was protruding from the passenger window of the truck.

He wasn't particularly worried about them hitting Emi or Hope because there was no window in the back of the cab, but taking him out would cause a crash that would likely kill them too.

His vow of protection suddenly took on more urgency.

"Hang on."

Two could play this game. Ian floored the accelerator, murmuring a prayer that the chains would let him keep traction on the snow-covered road. As the truck picked up speed, he swung hard to the left, cutting off the other truck and sending it skidding across the road. He eased off the gas and gently swung back into his lane.

"Everybody okay back there?"

"So far."

"I'm going to try to put some distance between us, but I'm sure they're not giving up." Ian kept a wary eye on his mirrors as he focused on the road. His truck was now almost to the most treacherous section of the pass, so he had to downshift and feather his brakes—not so easy on a snowy road. He hoped he'd put the killers out of commission long enough that he could make it to a flat stretch, but he wasn't counting on it.

Five minutes of driving proved him right. The one thing he had going for him was the lack of traffic in either direction, but that meant that the headlights currently reflected in his mirror belonged to the enemy. This was not the place he wanted to encounter them. Two quick switchbacks made traveling this road concerning in good conditions, dangerous in bad weather and potentially deadly with someone trying to force you off the side.

He had a plan in mind and, though it wasn't ideal, it should work. He didn't want to worry Hope, but he needed to warn her.

"Company is gaining on us again, but I know how to handle them. Just up ahead, we'll be coming to the first of two runaway truck ramps."

"That sounds… terrifying."

Ian grimaced. "Not as bad as the alternative. This descent is very steep, and there's a hairpin turn ahead. Sometimes trucks lose their brakes or are heading down too fast to make the turns. The ramps are a way of slowing down rather than crashing."

"How's that going to help us?"

"The signs are covered in snow right now, but I know where the first ramp is. I'm going to build up speed heading into it, but I'll wait until the last minute to make the turn up the ramp. Hopefully, they'll speed on by."

"We'll be praying, right Emi?"

Ian listened to the sweet sound of their voices joined in prayer and calm settled over him.

It was a risky plan that required careful timing for everything to go right. He had to avoid letting the other truck catch him too soon, increasing speed enough to fool them but not enough to risk overshooting the ramp.

All in near whiteout conditions on the side of a mountain.

Ian joined his voice to theirs. "Lord, help us."

Minutes dragged by as he carefully watched the road. The other truck was gaining on him, slowly pulling within firing range. Ian alternated between watching them in his mirror and keeping alert for the ramp.

The first gunshot felt like it ripped through him, though there was no indication the truck had been hit. A second shot pinged off the back of his cab. *Please Lord, let this ramp appear.*

At last, as they came around a curve, he recognized the landmarks. On his right, walls of sheer rock rose straight up from the road, but on the left, the land sloped down. Time to accelerate. There would be one more curve. He had to lead them into it before veering sharply right and up the ramp. Eyes intent on the road, Ian recognized the arch of the snow-covered sign overhanging the road.

He accelerated again and watched in the side mirror to be sure his pursuers were following. When they increased speed as well, he angled the truck toward the ramp and hit the gas hard at the same moment he doused his lights. The truck headed up the ramp in darkness, and Ian held his breath until he saw the lights of the other truck fade around the corner and out of sight.

He quickly eased off the gas, downshifted and let the ramp do its job. Slowly, the large truck lost momentum, until it came to a standstill three-fourths of the way up the ramp. Ian bowed his head in a prayer of thanksgiving.

"That was—"

"Terrifying. I know. I'm sorry."

"Amazing," Hope replied.

Ian huffed grimly. "Well, if you enjoyed that, I'm sure there's more to come."

* * *

Hope knew he was right. Once the men realized the truck was no longer ahead of them, they'd circle back. Her body started to tremble. What did they want with her?

"Mommy, you're shaking."

"I am. You know how scared I get when we go on the roller coaster? This is a little like that, isn't it? Imagine riding a roller coaster in the snow!"

While Emi contemplated the fun in that, Hope spoke to Ian. "Now what? Are we stuck here?" What had seemed like an ingenious plan suddenly left her feeling like they were sitting ducks.

"Under normal circumstances, we'd contact highway patrol and pay to get towed out, but we can't wait for that. I'm going to try to back down."

Heart in her throat, Hope felt like she was holding her breath for a lifetime as he ever so slowly eased the big rig back down the ramp. She didn't think she imagined Ian's weary exhale when they finally leveled out on the highway and were facing forward. "Any sign of our friends?"

"Not yet."

Ian's tense reply matched her own feelings, so she bit back her next question. He sensed it and answered anyway. "I'd prefer to turn around and head back, but that won't stop them from finding us again. We have to keep moving forward. It's not a good solution, but it's the best we have."

Hope recognized the same resignation in his voice that she'd felt when she chose to climb in a stranger's truck. When you were trapped with killers on a long stretch of mountainous highway in a blizzard, your options were severely limited.

"The most treacherous turn is in about two miles. If we can avoid them until that, there's a turnoff to a campground not much farther along. We can hide out there."

"And if we can't?"

"Let's just pray that we can."

There was a lot of room for something to go wrong in Ian's plan, but he was right. They could only pray it went right.

For a mile or so it did. Hope thought she might go mad from the tension and the inability to see what was happening. She agreed with Ian that she needed to be back here with Emi, out of the line of fire, but that meant she had no way of knowing what was happening. She didn't like not being in control of her own life. Since her husband's death four years earlier, she'd been responsible for every life decision for herself and Emi. Now, at the most critical moment she'd ever faced, it was clear how very little control she really did have. She had to give it up to God…but that was much easier said than done. Especially with men shooting at you.

Hope didn't have to be in the front seat to see the sudden glare of headlights, nor did she need to hear Ian's frustrated groan to know who was driving the truck heading straight at them.

Shots rang out, and the front windshield exploded.

Hope tried to muffle her scream, but it was too late. Emi launched herself into her mother's arms and clung tight.

"Ian?" Hope waited desperately to hear his voice, to be assured he hadn't been hit. She couldn't live with herself if he came to harm because of her.

"All in one piece," he responded. "The same can't be said for the windshield."

Hope peered through the gap between the seats and gasped at the shattered glass. The windshield looked like a massive spiderweb.

"Hope, I'm going to need your help. I have to break through a section of the glass, or I won't be able to keep driving. There's a toolbox wedged behind my seat. I need the hammer and a blanket. I can't stop here, so you'll have to come hold the wheel steady while I smash through the glass."

He had to be joking. Her hands were shaking so hard, there was no chance she could hold a bicycle steady, let alone the wheel of a truck full of Christmas trees. But if he could do all this for her... Hope took a deep breath and steeled herself to do what was necessary. After retrieving the hammer and blanket, she braced herself against the back of his seat.

"You can do this," he encouraged her. "Just slide into the seat as I stand up. Both hands on the wheel and hold tight. It's no different than steering your car."

He eased around her, and while she clung to the wheel, holding on with all her might, he used the blanket to cover the windshield and pounded the glass with the hammer. She flinched at the sound of glass splintering, but then it was over, and Ian was congratulating her on a job well done.

He shoved the blanket full of glass into the well under the dash and then guided her up, still holding the wheel as he slipped back into his seat. Hope slid over into the passenger seat, feeling like a giant rag doll, completely spent but waiting to see what happened next.

"It's snowing inside the truck!"

Emi's excitement was amusing, but it didn't take more than a moment to realize Ian couldn't continue to drive like this. Wind was gusting snow through the broken glass, reducing visibility almost as badly as the webbed glass had. "We have to get off the road, don't we?"

Ian nodded. "I was hoping that would work, but the storm is too powerful. Our last chance is the second runaway truck ramp." Tension thrummed in his voice. "This one won't be as easy as the other. Think of it more as a rocket launch compared to your last roller coaster."

Hope's stomach dropped.

"It's going to be harder for me to get up the ramp with visibility so low. Can you see out your corner of the windshield?"

Hope realized that the shatter hadn't spread to the right of the passenger side. She pulled herself up to the window and peered through her section of glass. Snow was starting to build up now that the wipers couldn't work, but she could still see the road. "What am I looking for?"

"Make sure we're not too close to the rocks. See if you can tell if I'm centered in the lane."

While Ian tried to swat the snow out of his face, Hope squinted into the dim path cut by their headlights. "It will be easier to see if I lower my window." She pressed the switch, and as the window slowly rolled down, she saw exactly what he meant by rocks. Right outside her window was a wall of rock so close she could reach out and touch it. "You need to move more to the left or we're going to scrape into the rocks."

Hope watched with bated breath as the truck slowly eased away from the wall. The flatbed section fishtailed just enough that she felt the jolt as the trees brushed along the rocks.

Now that she had space, she leaned her head out the window. "I can see the ramp up ahead. If you keep going straight, you'll hit it right on center."

"Make sure you're belted in," Ian warned. "This ramp is steep."

Hope pulled her head in just as she noticed headlights reflecting off her mirror. She reached to secure her belt. "They're back," she murmured.

"I see." Ian shook his head as if to clear his thoughts. "Let's focus one step at a time. If I try to head down this road, unable to see, we'll go off the cliff at the curve. This ramp is our only chance. We'll worry about them once we've stopped."

Hope swallowed hard. It took everything she had not to melt into total panic, but he was right. Keeping a cool head and taking the challenges one at a time was the only way through this. But she'd be praying the whole time.

"Don't put your head out again. We can't risk them taking a shot at you. Whatever guidance you can give through your corner of the windshield will be help enough."

Once again, Hope bent toward the glass. Ahead, the ramp rose before them. So much snow covered the lane that it was difficult to see where the road ended. Only when the gusts blew could she see the black-and-gold-striped posts edging the side. Hopefully, Ian had similar ones he could see out his side window. The truck hit the base of the ramp, but it didn't take long to realize they didn't have enough momentum to make it. Against all logic, Ian pressed down on the accelerator, hoping to get even a little farther up and away from the truck bearing down on them again.

A gunshot sounded, and his side mirror shattered into pieces. Emi's whimper cut to Hope's heart, but it was too late to move back to her now. If they had even a prayer of surviving, Ian needed her up here guiding him.

A barrage of gunfire erupted, and suddenly the truck shifted.

"I think they got a tire," Ian muttered. He held tight to the wheel, but Hope could feel the change in traction. The truck started to slide and tilted heavily toward the left. Now it was Hope who wanted to whimper. *Please Lord, have mercy.*

"We have to get out, Hope."

She nodded. It was obvious they were no longer safe in the cab. "How?"

The truck gave another lurch and gravity took hold.

"Hang on, we're going over."

Hope's heart stuttered in terror as she gripped the roof hold. "Emi," she cried. "Hold tight to the harness."

"Mommy, I'm so scared."

"It'll be okay, baby. As soon as the truck settles, we'll climb out." She forced a reassuring tone, but her mind was racing a mile a minute thinking of the terrifying danger ahead.

Wind howled down the ramp. The truck sounded like it was coming apart at the seams, and with a final shudder, the cab twisted, landing on the passenger side. The gunfire had ceased momentarily, but that was almost more frightening. What were the men doing?

Ian groaned, and Hope realized he had landed hard with

his arm twisted under him. Before she could ask him about it, he was struggling to unharness his seat belt.

"Are you okay?" he queried.

"Yes. Emi?"

There was no answer, so Hope unsnapped her belt and dove between the seats. Emi was curled in a ball in the corner, tears streaming down her face. "Are you hurt, baby?"

Emi shook her head, but she couldn't get any words out.

While she'd been checking on her daughter, Ian had been trying to force the driver's door open. As soon as he got it unstuck, he gave it a shove upright.

Immediately the door was riddled with bullets.

Hope screamed. At this point, she didn't care who heard. The men were sitting out there just waiting to shoot them as they emerged from the truck.

Ian crawled into the backseat with them. "Be very quiet," he whispered. "I think they've gone along the road so they're parallel to us. We're going to go out through the windshield and climb around the side of the cab away from them."

He raised the lid on the bench Emi had been sitting on and pulled out some tarps. "We'll wrap these around us as protection from the glass, and then surf down the side. Can you do that?"

Roller coasters, surfing. Hope was beside herself, but she would try anything that gave her a chance at escaping the killers. She nodded and reached for one of the tarps. "I'm taking Emi with me." She grabbed their backpacks and strapped them to her chest.

Ian ripped the harness loose from the bench and quickly used it to attach Emi to Hope's back. Then he wrapped the tarp tightly around them and guided them back to the front seat. "I'm going to lift you through the window."

"But your arm—"

"Don't worry about my arm. Just slide down the truck, keep low and wait for me. I'll be right behind you."

Hope held the tarp tightly closed as Ian pushed her through the glass. She could hear the moan he tried to muffle. The man was in serious pain, but there was nothing she could do to help him until they were free.

Gunshots still sounded around them, but she ignored the sound and focused on her assignment. Once they had cleared the windshield, she flattened herself and surfed down the cab of the truck. She landed softly in a drift of snow and whispered to Emi to stay quiet. Moments later, Ian landed beside them.

More gunshots followed, and suddenly the acrid smell of diesel filled the air.

"They've hit the fuel tank," Ian whispered urgently. "We've got to get as far away as we can before it blows."

He ushered them to the far side of the truck and over a cement barrier. "Run for the trees," he urged.

If it was a matter of sheer will, Hope would have raced up the hill, but the snow was knee-deep, and it felt like they were wading through cement.

She could smell the fire now and knew it wouldn't be long before the truck blew. Ian came beside her and wrapped his arm around her, urging her on but also shielding her with his body. They were mere steps from the trees when the truck exploded. Ian covered her as they dove into a snowbank, while all around them, burning pieces of the truck showered down.

When Hope dared to lift her head and look back, she knew she would never forget the heartbreaking sight of the truck full of burning Christmas trees lighting up the sky.

Ian pulled himself up beside her, but he didn't waste time bemoaning his truck or the lost cargo. "We have to keep moving. If we can get deep enough into the woods while the truck burns, we'll be able to get away."

Hope looked up at him in disbelief. Getting away meant heading deep into the mountains in a blizzard, far from help.

Dear Lord, have mercy.

Chapter Four

They hid within the tree line, just out of sight, and watched the truck burn. "Your truck. All your trees." Hope looked up at Ian, tears welling in her eyes at the thought of all he'd lost because of her. "I'm so sorry."

Sadness flickered across his face, but he shrugged it away. "You and Emi are safe. That's all that matters. Speaking of..." He knelt beside Emi and made a face. "Who looks like a snowman?"

Emi hid her face behind Hope's legs, but she whispered. "You do. I'm a snow girl."

"Well, snow girl, we'd better start moving before the heat from the fire turns us into puddles. Ready to explore the forest?"

Emi reached for Hope's hand and clung to it. "Is it dark in the forest? I don't like the dark."

Ian nodded. "The dark can be scary. But it can be exciting too. Like an adventure. Let's pretend we have cat eyes and can see in the dark." He leaned back and squinted at her. "Do you want to walk or ride on my shoulders?"

Emi leaned into Hope. "I want to stay with Mommy," she whispered.

"Deal. But you let me know if you get tired, okay?"

Emi nodded, and Hope's heart gave a quick stutter as she whispered a prayer of thanks. Hiding in Ian's truck had been risky, and they were still in dire straits, but God had handed her a blessing in Ian. If anyone could get them out of this alive, it was him.

Ian stood and brushed the snow off his coat. "We should get moving."

"Is there no one we can call for rescue?" Her voice sounded desperate, but she was beyond caring. Desperate was exactly how she felt.

"When I spoke to the dispatcher, she said all the roads were shut down. I'll try again, but..." He cast a look back at the burning truck. "I want to be sure we've lost those men first. There's a campground on the other side of this mountain. I've got a compass on my phone, so we'll be able to find it even in the storm." He studied her briefly before continuing. "The terrain is rough. It's going to be challenging."

She understood that he was trying to warn her without scaring Emi. "We'll do whatever we have to."

"I've noticed that about you."

He smiled as he said it, and Hope had the sudden thought that the fire wasn't the only thing capable of melting snow. Ian had a warmth about him that...that she shouldn't be focusing on. They needed to get moving.

Ian looped their backpacks over his uninjured shoulder, and in that moment, Hope realized he had nothing of his own with him. Guilt swamped her. She'd been counting her blessings, but he had lost everything because she'd chosen to hide in his truck. He hadn't kicked them out. Instead, he'd risked his life for them and continued to do so. God bless him. There was nothing she could do about it now, but somehow, when this was over, she would find a way to make it up to him.

She grasped Emi's mittened hand a little tighter and followed Ian deeper into the woods. Within minutes, she realized he hadn't been overstating in calling this trek rough. Snow covering the ground made it difficult to judge their footing, and in many places they literally had to hold hands and form a link as they moved from tree to tree trying to keep their balance in a snowstorm that would have challenged even the most agile of cats. When Ian paused for a breather, she knew it was for her and Emi more than for him, but she was too tired to be embarrassed.

"Wait here," he murmured. "Catch your breath while I circle around. I don't think there's any chance we've been followed, but we're going to have to cross the road, so I want to be certain before we risk exposure."

The snow was coming down so hard that Ian was invisible mere moments after he left them. Panic surged through Hope. Would he find his way back to them? And what would they do, stranded alone in the forest, if he didn't?

Emi tugged at her arm. "I'm hungry."

Hope's stomach growled in agreement, and the two of them laughed quietly. "I have some granola bars in my backpack, but Ian says we're going to a camp. Can you wait a little longer?"

Emi nodded, and Hope's heart filled to bursting with love for her little girl. She was such a champ. It had been the two of them against the world ever since Keith died, and she'd never been prouder of her daughter.

As they waited alone in the cold, her thoughts returned to the question that had been plaguing her mind ever since they fled. What had happened back there? Was it really just another case of workplace violence? Was it possible that she, Steve and Emi were just numbers to add to a growing list of statistics? But if so, why had the men continued to chase her? Nothing about this made any sense.

Hope shivered. Where was Ian? She had absolutely no idea how much time had passed since he left. Time had ceased to have meaning hours ago. Minutes were measured in distance covered, not hands on a clock. She shivered again. He'd been gone long enough that her toes were freezing inside her fur-lined boots.

Emi was huddled against her, but if Hope was this cold, how could her daughter possibly be warm enough?

"I think we should do a snow dance." Hope certainly wasn't in the mood for dancing, and they had to be quiet, but she needed something that would get their blood flowing and warm them up because escaping those men meant nothing if they froze to death.

"What's a snow dance?"

"Well, it starts out like this." Hope led Emi behind a wide evergreen. She raised her arms and fluttered them as she did some impromptu ballet steps. "You pretend to be a snow-flake, but then the wind howls and the snow blows in all di-rections." She twirled herself in a circle and waved her arms wildly while she stamped her feet and flung her head back. "Can you do that?"

Emi got very still before gently unfurling her arms as Hope had done. She danced silently among the snowflakes, and Hope was lost in the beauty of the moment. Her baby girl had always loved to dance. Hope grasped her hands and soon they were swinging and twirling, heads thrown back in pure joy, embracing the ferocity of the storm—until a cracking branch stopped them in their tracks.

What had she been thinking? Hope chastised herself. There were wild animals out here, not to mention men who maybe wanted her dead, and she was dancing with her daughter in the snow. Reacting quickly, she pulled Emi down behind a snow-covered boulder. The cracking sounds increased, ac-companied by mild snorting. Hope eased up so she could see over the rock and froze.

Emi poked her head up beside her mother's. "Is that a rein-deer, Mommy?"

Hope was caught between awestruck and terrified. "It's an elk. See the huge antlers?"

"It's big."

Hope couldn't argue with that.

"Will it hurt us?"

Honestly, the elk looked far more peace-loving than the gunmen who'd been on her trail. "Not if we stay quiet and don't scare him. He looks like he's trying to make a bed to wait out the storm."

"But what about Mr. Ian? How will he find us if we're hiding?"

"He has a compass." Not that it would help if they moved away from the elk. They needed to stay within sight of the spot where he'd abandoned them. Gone to make sure they were safe, Hope corrected herself. It only felt like they were abandoned in the forest at the mercy of gunmen and elk.

"He already found you."

Hope's mouth opened in a scream, but Ian's gloved hand gently covered it. "Shh, shh. I'm sorry I scared you."

The elk rustled around in its bed and turned toward them.

"Stay low," Ian murmured. "We're going to crawl in the snow until we're at least a hundred feet from him. Hope, you face forward and go first. Emi, follow your mother. I'll bring up the rear, crawling backward so I can keep an eye on him."

Hope's heart thudded in her throat. Her feet were numb, her fingers frozen, and her mind felt on the verge of surrendering to hopelessness.

Ian rested a hand on her shoulder. "It's overwhelming. But you've got this. We can make it to the cabins."

"And then what?" Hope knew she sounded petulant, so she made the effort to pull herself together. If anyone had a right to complain, it was Ian, and he was trying to reassure her. "Sorry, ignore that."

Hope slowly and silently turned away from the elk and began to crawl through the drifts of snow. Her coat snagged on branches, and her legs were dead weight, but she lowered her head and powered through.

Behind her, she could hear Ian encouraging Emi. Minutes crept by as they slowly eased away from the elk. Finally, Hope heard the words she'd longed for.

"We can stop now."

Ian knew he had to give them a few minutes to rest, but he also knew they had to push on. He'd tried calling for help again, but the answer was the same. The mountain road was shut down. Even the plows couldn't get through. They were on their own until the storm passed. Since it was showing no sign of letting up, their only hope of surviving in the wilderness was to make it to the campsite before they encountered any more predators—either animal or human.

With all his heart, Ian wished there was another solution. Their choices were severely limited by terrain that was treacherous even in summertime. Now, with the landscape covered in snow, they were risking a deadly fall with every step. And they had to do it with a child.

"Hope, it's safest if Emi lets each of us hold a hand again. We'll have the other free to help us cling to the rocks, but we can't risk her slipping."

He didn't miss the tremor caused by his words, but Hope bent over to talk to her daughter, and when she stood back up, Emi tentatively reached out her hand to his. The simple gesture punched him in the heart. Painful memories of the child he'd lost assaulted him, but he shoved them aside to focus on the task at hand.

"I promise I won't let go," he whispered as he took Emi's mittened hand in his.

They trudged along for a time before the ground suddenly began to slope downward.

Ian stopped and glanced back at Hope. "I know you're frozen and tired, but we have to take this part slowly. The ground is uneven and the drop-off is very steep. We basically have to find handholds of rock to ease our way down.

I'll lead the way, but each step I'll wait until you feel secure before moving, okay?"

Her head bobbed consent, so Ian turned his attention forward. Slowly, slipping and clinging to rocky outcroppings, they made their way down the face of the mountain. The journey seemed to take forever as they struggled to keep their balance with wind gusting around them. The wind was an advantage, as it helped pin them against the rocks rather than blowing them off the side, but Ian knew that could change with a single gust.

The other advantage of this dangerous situation was it kept his focus on the task at hand rather than allowing him to think too much about the destruction left behind. He prayed the snow was heavy enough to prevent his truck from igniting a forest fire and compounding the disaster.

He'd have to replace the lost Christmas trees. The veterans' center counted on the proceeds from their holiday sale to provide much-needed help to the local vets who struggled from the effects of war.

But all of those things had to be left in God's hands. Right now, he had only one assignment—get Hope and Emi safely to the cabins so they could be rescued when the storm ended.

It felt like hours had passed by the time they finally approached a stream that bordered the camp. The running water hadn't frozen, but he found a spot that was narrow enough to cross safely.

He stopped at the edge of the water. "Emi, we're almost there, but we have to cross the water here. If Mommy says it's okay, will you let me carry you across? It would be safer that way."

Emi could barely hold her head up by that point, but she turned questioning eyes to her mother. Hope wasn't in much better shape; still, she managed to nod.

"When you're ready, lift your arms so I'll know."

Emi only hesitated a moment before lifting her arms to him. Ian bent to pick her up. The throbbing pain in his arm melted away as she snuggled into his arms and wrapped her arms around him, but it was replaced with a deep ache in his heart. Ian closed his eyes, momentarily overwhelmed by the sense of loss. His own child had died along with his wife in childbirth, but if his son had lived, he would have been nearly Emi's age. Pain threatened to drive him to his knees, and Ian knew he would be useless if he allowed his thoughts to wander back in time.

He ruthlessly shoved the memories and his regrets aside. "Be careful," he called to Hope as he plunged into the creek. "There are rocks under the surface that make it slippery. If you want to wait, I can come back for you after I get Emi across."

He shook his head in bemusement as he offered, because he already knew she would make her own way through. Hope's stubborn refusal to give in to any kind of weakness was evident in even their short acquaintance. He was grateful for that trait — it had kept her alive against all odds so far.

Once Hope had reached the creek bank safely, they pushed on, able to walk side by side now that the land was flat and they only had to wade through the snow. Emi seemed content in his arms, so Ian continued to carry her. "Please don't expect much, from this cabin," he warned Hope. "It's a summer campsite mostly for tents and RVs, but there are a few rustic cabins—emphasis on the rustic."

"If it's dry and out of the wind, you'll hear no complaints from me."

Ian doubted he'd hear complaints regardless of the cabin's condition. He hoped it would be at least somewhat of a comfort after this ordeal—a safe place to sit the storm out and wait for rescue. But he had his doubts.

They broke through the woods into the clearing. Away from the shelter of the trees, the snow had accumulated more. Ian's muscles felt like rubber, so he didn't know how Hope was still standing. "Almost there," he reassured her.

She didn't answer but tipped her head slightly, indicating she'd heard.

"Walk behind me and let me plow through the snow. You can follow in my footsteps." Hope's silence betrayed her fatigue as she fell in behind him.

When they reached the steps up to the door, Ian started to put Emi down before realizing the little girl was asleep in his arms. His breath hitched as he handed her over to Hope.

He climbed the steps and reached for the door, praying it was unlocked.

It was. Finally, something was going their way. The aged wood was warped enough that it required several hard slams of his shoulder to get the door to open. The final hard blow sent him stumbling through the doorway into the dark cabin. Hope waited by the bottom of the stairs while Ian took out his phone and used the flashlight to scan the room. It was, thankfully, clean, and there was no evidence any wildlife had taken up residence.

Ian waded his way back down the steps and lifted Emi into his arms. Hope followed him up and through the doorway. She managed to shove the door shut before collapsing on the nearest chair. Ian left his flashlight propped on the table while he gently deposited Emi on the sofa and covered her with warm blankets.

He turned and surveyed the room. "It's not home sweet home, but it will do."

Hope blinked her eyes as she struggled to stay awake.

Ian grabbed a fleece throw off the bed, crossed the room and tucked it around her. "Go ahead and rest. I'll check the cabin and see else what I can find to keep us warm..."

Ian let his words drift off. Hope was already asleep.

Wind howled around the cabin, rattling the windows and seeping through the cracks just as doubts seeped into his

brain, taunting Ian with the responsibility he had assumed.
He knew resting here was risky, but he had no choice. Hope
had reached her physical limit and there was no other shelter in the area. Yet, despite his encouraging words to her, he
wasn't confident this cabin was a refuge. If the men who'd
run him off the road discovered they'd escaped the truck inferno, they would resume their hunt. And, if they knew the
area, this campsite was an obvious place to start.

Chapter Five

Wind-driven ice pellets stung Ian's face as he made his way around the campground. Each passing moment that revealed no sign of tracks eased the weight on his shoulders.

When he was as certain as he could possibly be, he made his way back. Standing in the shelter of the building, he tried calling the sheriff again, but the only reply was a recording that all circuits were busy. They'd have to make do here until the storm eased.

He quietly let himself in the door, and stood in the entrance brushing snow from his shoulders. It was too cold in the cabin to take off his jacket, but he pulled off his knit cap and shook it out. Hope and Emi were still sleeping soundly, so he made his way to the kitchenette. He rifled through the single cabinet and found a supply of tea bags and hot chocolate. Further digging revealed a Sterno stove that must have been left over from summer camping. Happy that he could surprise them with a warm drink when they awoke, Ian set it up and then stepped outside to fill a pot with fresh snow. He took a moment to scan the campground before heading back inside. All was calm—except for the howling wind and driving snow. Their pursuers had probably chosen to seek shelter for the night.

As he set the pot over the small flame, his thoughts retraced the events of the day. Hope claimed to have no idea who was after her. Could he believe that? Ten years in the military had honed his instincts, but they seemed to fail him regularly when women were involved. His failure with his wife was proof of that. He shook off the dark thoughts. Another woman's life depended on him now. Another child's too. He couldn't let his memories and regrets distract him from keeping them alive.

While he waited for the water to heat, he dug up some mugs and a tin of old crackers to add to Hope's protein bars. It wouldn't be a feast, but they were out of the storm and that was something to celebrate.

Ian yawned. He would have been happy to take a nap like Hope and Emi, but he refused to let down his guard no matter how safe they seemed. He sat on the floor, resting his head back against the sofa, and sent off a text to his sister. Within minutes she replied with a barrage of questions demanding more information.

Ian smiled reading through them. It was a rhetorical question in his family whether his parents had destined her for detective work by giving her the middle name Nancy. As a young boy, he'd dubbed her Nancy Drew, but rather than be annoyed as he'd secretly hoped, she'd adopted Nancy as her hero. A career as an FBI agent had been a logical choice. It was a long shot, but hopefully Nancy could help him figure this out…

Whimpers interrupted his reminiscences, and Ian rolled onto his knees so he was at the same level as Emi. The little girl was caught in a nightmare. Hardly surprising given what she had endured today. Instinctively, he reached out and gently stroked her back, murmuring soothing words. "It's okay, Emi. You're safe. No one will hurt you."

When she had finally settled back into a peaceful sleep, he turned around, only to find Hope wide awake and staring at him.

He moved across the room and sat on the rug beside her. "I hope that was okay?"

She didn't speak right away. She just nodded as she studied him. "You're very good with her."

Ian heard the unspoken question behind her words. "My sister is an FBI agent, but when she was a child, she used to have nightmares. She read too many mysteries and was always dreaming of bad men chasing after her." He tripped his fingers along the fringe of the rug. "When I heard Emi's whimpers, I didn't think. I just reacted the way I'd always calmed Nancy. I'm sorry if I overstepped."

Hope's smile was beautiful. "You calmed my frightened child as you did your sister. The same child whose life you saved multiple times today. There is absolutely nothing to apologize for."

Her soft voice was a benediction to his soul. He hadn't always been there for Nancy, any more than he had been for his wife, and that pain was buried deep within. It wasn't something he wanted to share with a virtual stranger, but he appreciated her kind words nonetheless.

Ian pulled himself up and walked over to the Sterno stove, where the pot of water now bubbled gently. "Tea or hot chocolate?"

The look of adoration in Hope's eyes made him laugh. He could get used to someone looking at him like that—like some conquering hero. He pushed the thought aside. All he'd done was offer her a hot drink. He was nobody's hero.

Hope wasn't sure how much time had passed while she was sipping her tea when she first noticed the flash of headlights. Across the room, Ian was instantly on alert. He cast her an apologetic look. "I hate to wake Emi, but we have to be prepared to move out."

"They could just be some other travelers seeking shelter in a storm."

They both knew that likelihood was small.

Ian moved to stand beside the window, shifting the curtain only enough to have a side view of the area in front of their cabin.

Hope quicky gathered the few things she'd removed from her backpack. She pulled her coat closed and then managed to zip Emi into her jacket and slip on a hat and gloves without fully waking her. If there was any chance of letting her baby girl sleep, she intended to take it.

"What do you see?"

"Looks like their truck, but so far no one has gotten out, so I can't be sure. They have the headlights focused on the cabins on the far side."

Hope heard the engine gun and the sound of wheels spinning in the snow.

"And now they're swinging this way. Duck."

Ian flattened his body against the wall. Hope dropped to the floor and held motionless as the headlight beams flooded the room and swept past. The engine cut off, but somehow the silence was more frightening. Had they seen something? She held on to threads of dwindling hope that they were just travelers seeking refuge.

Ian's indrawn breath severed the last clinging strands of that hope.

"Time to go. Two men have emerged." He paused and glanced toward a sleepy Emi. "They're armed," he added quietly.

Hope's heart sank at his words. Almost immediately, car doors slammed, and she heard a harsh voice issuing commands. She uttered a prayer that the heavy drifting snow had filled their footprints. If not, their hideout would be obvious.

"Should we head out the back?" she whispered, the words barely audible to Ian.

He shook his head and held up a finger that she took as a sign for silence. Tension vibrated through her body as she watched Ian observing the men. She had to trust him. And pray.

Long minutes stretched out. There was no sound from outside other than the howling of the wind, and Ian didn't move from the window. Hope trembled with anxiety, knowing their lives could very well depend on what happened in the next few minutes.

Finally, Ian backed away from the window and silently crawled toward her until he was close enough to whisper in her ear. The warmth of his breath couldn't prevent the chill his words sent through her.

"It's them. One man has gone to the far end to search those cabins. The second man started at the middle cabin and seems to be headed this way."

Hope suppressed a shiver and tried to think rationally. "So we should go out the back?"

Ian shook his head, and she could feel his hair brush her cheek.

"I have something different in mind. I want you and Emi to hide in that corner out of sight. I'm going to wait by the door and listen for his progress. When he enters the cabin, I'll get him from behind."

"But wouldn't it be better just to get away…or hide until they leave?"

"If he enters this cabin, he'll see evidence we were here and immediately alert his partner. They'll be on our trail in no time." He glanced at Emi. "And there's little doubt they'll be faster than we are. This will buy us time to make our getaway."

Hope let her eyes quickly scan the room and saw he was

right. The remnants of their meal, the Sterno can and dishes, would all give away their presence.

"Once I have him restrained, we can make a run for it. The back door is close to the woods. If we go out that way while the other man is still searching, we should be able to make it back into the woods before he realizes this guy is missing. By the time he finds him, we'll have gotten a good start."

Dozens of doubts and thoughts of all the ways this could go wrong formed a knot in Hope's chest, but she knew he was right. Their choices were limited to bad and worse. She nodded her acceptance. "How much time do we have?"

"I'll check. My fingers will give you an estimate of how many minutes."

Ian swiftly crawled back to the window and eased the curtain aside. Hope slid Emi into her arms and shushed her little girl's whimper as she crouched and carried her to the corner. She cuddled Emi close as she held her breath waiting for Ian's signal.

Three fingers went up.

Terror ripped through Hope's heart. She knew Ian's plan was the best option they had, but she felt so exposed and vulnerable. How was she supposed to protect her daughter from such evil when she didn't even know why they were in danger?

The sound of boots stomping on the steps cut into her thoughts, and she froze. A hand twisted the latch, and the sound echoed loudly in the silence between her breaths.

The latch held, the door stayed closed, and moments later, Hope heard him stomp back down the steps. Relief poured through her veins in a rush of warmth. She looked to Ian, but quickly noted that rather than relaxing, he was moving into position beside the back door—the one that was supposed to be their escape route. He signaled her to stay hidden.

Hope glanced down at Emi, ready to warn her to stay silent, and her heart cracked at the fear etched on her daughter's face. Instinctively, she pulled her closer and stroked her fingertips along Emi's cheek in a comforting rhythm. "Don't worry," she whispered. "Ian has this all planned."

Emi nodded bravely, and Hope's heart constricted. She turned Emi so her face was cuddled into Hope's jacket, hoping to hide whatever was about to happen from Emi's eyes.

Outside a voice called out in the distance. Hope couldn't make out the words, but she could clearly hear the reply from right outside their back door. "No sign of them, but I'm not giving up yet."

He had barely finished shouting his reply before she heard his hand on the back door latch. Her eyes widened as she realized this one was unlatched. Had Ian done that on purpose?

Hope watched frozen as the door slowly began to open. A head appeared and he scanned the room before stepping fully inside. She saw the moment his gaze settled on the Sterno stove and pot. He quickly lifted his eyes and searched the room.

Hope's heart pounded as his gaze latched onto hers.

Behind the intruder, she could see Ian silently urging her to keep the man's attention.

"Hope?"

Hope frowned at the man's questioning tone. If he'd been chasing her all this time, how did he not recognize her?

"Who's asking?" Hope fought to keep her voice level and devoid of the fear that had her quaking in her boots.

"Are you Hope Prescott?" The man's voice rose dangerously.

"Who are you?"

He raised his weapon and pointed it at Hope. "I'm the one asking questions here, not you. Answer me."

Ian decided the time for waiting was over. He put a finger over his lips for Hope to stay silent and waited until the man began to speak.

"This is your last—"

Ian stepped forward and struck the side of the man's neck, sending him to the floor in an unconscious heap. He quickly used a dish towel as a gag and told Hope to grab the rope he had pulled from the cabinet earlier. Once he had the man completely restrained, he pulled off his belt and used it to secure him to the table. Then he ran to the window to make sure no one had heard the disturbance. By then the man was coming to, but with the gag in his mouth, there was nothing he could do to prevent their escape.

"Let's go," Ian said quietly. "There's no way he can escape. There's a truck down by the last cabin. We can use that. By the time his friend realizes what happened, we'll be long gone and the snow should cover our tracks."

Ian picked up his pack and walked to the open door. He peered out, and when the coast was clear, he beckoned to Hope and Emi. Once they were out the door, he shut it silently behind them, lifted Emi into his arms and made a run for the tree line. When they were safely out of sight, he set Emi down beside Hope. "Wait here."

He snapped off a broken pine branch and ran back, dragging the broom behind him to erase their footprints. When he reached the steps, he lifted the broom and ran toward the end cabin, leaving exaggerated prints behind. After he had passed two cabins, he lowered the branch behind him again and ran into the woods, leaving no footprints behind as he circled back to Emi and Hope.

"I'm guessing there's no truck for us to use," Hope muttered ruefully.

Ian shook his head. "Sorry. That was a ruse to buy us additional time. We're strictly on foot."

"Figured as much. But where are we going?"

"For now, just safely away from here. Once I know we haven't been followed, we can try the sheriff again or call my sister if he doesn't respond." Ian tried to put on a good face. "It's not the best solution, but…"

"It's the best available one," Hope finished for him. "Lead on."

Ian lifted Emi once again. The little girl no longer hesitated when he held her but instead burrowed against his chest. That should have made him smile, but instead it saddened him that she understood the danger too well to protest. The weight of her in his arms brought other pain to his heart, but he shoved that away.

Grasping Hope's hand, he pulled her along beside him and gestured to a coil of rope he'd tied around his waist earlier. "I looped this rope around my waist so you would have something to hold on to and a way to get my attention. I know you'd probably prefer to walk side by side, but this way I can shield you from the wind and you can walk in my footsteps. Okay?"

Like her daughter, Hope was too weary to object. She just nodded.

Ian looped the other end of the rope around her wrist and tucked it into her gloved hand. "Ready?"

She nodded again.

Ian cast a glance over his shoulder to make sure they were not being followed. He was optimistic that his strategic maneuvers would succeed in getting them safely away, because he'd noticed one important fact about his opponent—he was not dressed for hiking through the wilderness. Hopefully neither was his partner.

Ian forged his way through the heavy snow, keeping his head down and shielding Emi with his body. He wished he could do more for Hope, but he could tell that keeping her daughter safe meant more to her than her own comfort.

For an hour they kept moving forward into the swirling snow. Not once in that time did Hope tug on his rope, and his admiration for her grew with each difficult step. Finally, deciding that enough time had passed to be sure they hadn't been followed, he led them into the shelter of a cluster of trees.

One look at Hope, and Ian knew they had to stop. He took stock of their surroundings and decided they were safe enough here. "Let's stop and rest. We need to eat and drink."

Hope barely acknowledged his words, so he urged her to sit against a tree. She stumbled, nearly face-planting against the tree, but Ian grasped her just in time. He guided her until she was seated and then set Emi down beside her. He slung off the backpack and worked the frozen zipper until he got it open enough to pull out the Mylar blanket, some beef jerky and a semifrozen water bottle that he'd grabbed from the cabin.

He helped Hope to wrap the blanket around them, and then handed her the jerky. "You might break a tooth trying to bite this, so try to let it soften in your mouth. Even if you just suck on it, you'll get an energy boost."

Her lack of response was frightening. "Hope?"

She raised her head and looked at him with eyes that were glazing over. Guilt was quickly followed by fear in his gut. He'd pushed her too far. He unscrewed the cap from the water bottle and pushed it into her hand. "Drink some water."

She numbly did as he directed.

Emi huddled against her mother under the blanket, but Ian was less worried about her. He knew he'd kept her warm with his body heat, and she hadn't been exerting herself the way her mother had.

Ian watched as Hope dutifully swallowed the cold water and shivered. Drinking ice water was not wise in this environment, but it was better than dehydrating. While she sucked on the jerky, Ian pulled out his phone and tried to reach the sheriff's office once again. This time he couldn't even get a signal. They must be too far into the mountains now.

"Hope, look at me."

She lifted her head again.

"I want you and Emi to stay here. I'm going to walk out on the ridge to see if I can get a signal to call for help."

Despair filled her eyes, and in that moment, Ian would have done anything to be able to promise rescue. He squatted down in front of her. "I'll be right back."

He took a moment to note their coordinates on his phone before heading off through the trees. He was half-frozen himself, but he had to find a way to get help. Fighting a sense of failure as strong as any of these roaring winds, Ian trudged through the deep snow. He'd been pushing so hard to escape the killers, but those men weren't the only threat.

If he didn't find help or shelter, they would die out here. And it would be his fault.

Chapter Six

She was so sleepy.

All Hope wanted to do was snuggle under the blanket with Emi and go to sleep. Did that mean she was dying? She shivered and tried to pull Emi closer to keep them warmer, but her hands and arms didn't want to cooperate. Wasn't lack of coordination a sign of hypothermia? Her brain was working too slowly to be sure.

Where was Ian? Were they going to die out here alone in the wilderness? Would everyone think they had just disappeared? Would anyone find their bodies, or...?

Hope's mind was processing well enough to cut off the thoughts before they got too gruesome. She pulled the Mylar blanket tighter to keep out the wind that cut through them like blades of ice.

"Emi. Are you awake?" Her daughter's head moved up and down against her side. "Are you very cold?" Again Emi nodded. "I'm going to pull you onto my lap so you can be warmer against me."

Hope didn't know why she hadn't thought of that sooner. If she pulled Emi into her lap she could protect her daughter at least from the cold snow beneath them and from the wind that was the worst. At least her maternal instincts were still strong.

Snow continued to fall, and she tried to shake it off her shoulders or Ian wouldn't be able to tell them from any of the snow drifts around them.

Ian. Somewhere out in all this blowing white nightmare, Ian was trudging through the snow looking for help. He had to be as cold as she was, and his life was in danger because she had chosen his truck as a refuge. Her body shuddered, and this time it was guilt as much as cold that caused the tremors. If something happened to him, it would be her fault.

"Hope?"

Her heart swelled with relief at the sight of his snow-covered frame. "Over here. We're the white mountain on your right."

Ian laughed, and a pleasant warmth flooded her body at the sound.

"The silver blanket helped me distinguish you." The humor fled his voice with his next words. "I had no luck finding a signal. We're going to have to make a shelter here until the storm stops."

She must be hallucinating. This hulk-shaped being said they were camping out here. That was impossible. She started to laugh.

"Hope."

Ian crouched in front of her, concern etched on his face. It *was* him. And he *was* serious. Her laughter froze just like the rest of her. "How are you going to build a shelter out here? There's nothing but—" she looked around "—snow."

"I'm going to build us a snow cave."

Hope shuddered. "That sounds cold."

He smiled gently. "It will be better than this. But it will take me some time to build it. Are you okay for now?"

Hope nodded to reassure him, but as she did, she realized she was better. The blanket was trapping her body heat and her mind was clearing. With that clarity came concern for him. "Can I help? I've warmed up enough, I think."

"No, this is a one-person job. And honestly, I'll work more efficiently if I know you and Emi are safe."

Hope looked up at him hoping he would read the question in her eyes, the one she didn't want Emi to hear. *Are we safe?*

Ian gave a short nod. He pulled a pair of binoculars from his pack. "I borrowed these from the cabin. I searched the area as best I could through the dark and snow. I saw no sign of anyone following us, but you can keep watch if you want to help. Honestly, I think the greatest danger we face at the moment is from this storm. It shows no sign of letting up, so I need to start working on the shelter. The snow will work as a shield, but it also provides camouflage in case anyone does come looking for us. I just have to find a good-sized drift to tunnel into."

Hope studied the white landscape. "You've got plenty to choose from."

She watched anxiously as Ian got to work. Initially he seemed to wander, aimlessly poking his arm into various drifts, but once he settled on one, her anxiety transformed into amazement as she watched him tunnel his way into the huge drift. He paused periodically to check for stability and pack the snow.

Emi had fallen asleep snuggled against Hope inside the blanket, but now she stirred and stretched. She opened her eyes and looked around, clearly disoriented by the snow hitting her face. "Where are we, Mommy?"

Hope lifted an arm that was working in better coordination with her brain now and brushed the snow from Emi's cheek. "We're still in the forest, but look, Ian is building us our own snow cave."

Emi squiggled her way up, twisting until she could see, and a huge smile burst on her face. If for nothing else he had done in the past twenty-four hours, Hope's heart was near bursting with gratitude to Ian for the cave that had inspired that smile.

"What are we going to do in it?"

Hope laughed despite the desperate conditions. How could she make *We're going to wait for rescue* sound intriguing to a seven-year-old? "We're going to snuggle inside it and tell stories until our rescue team comes."

"Will we have a campfire?"

Hope scrunched her face up. "Think about that."

Emi started to giggle. "The snow would melt." She thought a little more. "Can we have a fire when we get to Christmas Village?"

Just like that, Hope's joy deflated. Explaining waiting in a snow cave was one thing. How was she supposed to explain that they were running for their lives and Christmas Village did not fit into that picture? She defaulted to the age-old line. "We'll have to wait and see." It was true, wasn't it? Maybe, if they prayed really hard, the sheriff would catch the villains who were chasing them.

Hope nearly laughed at herself then. Who was making up stories now? But the idea of people pursuing them so tirelessly preyed on her mind. She still had no idea why or what they wanted. And that man who had called her name but didn't seem to know her—who was he?

Emi squirming in her lap disrupted Hope's thoughts and she looked up to see Ian approaching them. He made a sweeping bow before them and spoke to Emi, "Your Highness, your snow castle awaits."

Emi scrambled to her feet and jumped off Hope's lap—and nearly disappeared into a snowdrift that was taller than she was. Ian scooped her up and carried her to the entrance. He set her down in the doorway he'd carved before returning to extend an arm to Hope.

She tried to push her own way up, but her legs were either still numb from the cold or had fallen asleep because as she stood, she stumbled and fell into his arms. For just a moment, she stood there, allowing him to hold her while she waited for her legs to regain their feeling. She tried to take another step, but she stumbled again.

Ian scooped her into his arms and carried her to the cave. Emi waited in the opening, clapping gleefully. "Mr. Ian carried you just like he carried me, Mommy."

Hope blushed and ducked her head. "He did because Mommy's legs went numb from someone who has been sleeping on them." She hoped the teasing words would be enough for now, because most of her mind was fighting off memories of her husband carrying her over the threshold on their honeymoon. Tears gathered in her eyes, but she angrily swiped them away. She had shed enough tears for the man who'd destroyed her dreams and ruined her life.

"If you can, it would be best to crawl inside," Ian warned. "I made the roof as stable as I could, but it's best if we don't push against it."

Happy to keep her head down, Hope crawled her way into the cave. It was small, but comfortable enough, and she was amazed at the difference it made to be out of the wind.

"How did you learn to do this?" she asked as Ian followed Emi into the center.

"I had Army training, but I also belong to a veterans' group. We go hiking in the wilderness in all seasons, so we've trained in survival techniques."

As he was talking, Ian took the Mylar blanket he'd brought in with them and spread it on the snow against the back wall. Once he had it flat, he looked up and grinned. "That and all the years of building snow forts with my brother and sister." He gestured to the floor. "It would be best if you sat on that. I have another one you can pull around you."

Hope studied this man who was a seemingly endless font of surprises. "What about you?"

He shrugged. "I'll be fine. Make yourselves comfortable. I'm going to go take another look around outside."

* * *

After assuring himself that there was still no indication they'd been followed, Ian crawled back into the cave and immediately busied himself digging food he'd taken from the cabin out of the backpack. He'd left a note for the owners that he would replace it as soon as possible. The cave would keep them warm, but they had to be sparing in the food they ate. If they ran out of water, he could start a fire and melt snow, but he had no way of replacing their food supply.

He handed Hope a protein bar, but she immediately broke off half and handed it back to him.

"Eat. You need energy as much as we do. More, because you're doing all the work."

"I'm trained to go days without food if necessary."

She kept her hand extended. "Please. I can't eat if you won't."

Understanding that he wasn't the only one with a sense of pride and duty, Ian accepted the bar. From what he could tell of Hope, he knew that she was someone used to standing up for herself. What was her story? Where was Emi's father? None of it was his business, and yet he wondered.

"I don't suppose in any of this vaunted training, they've taught you how to predict how long a storm like this might last?"

Hope grinned as she spoke, and Ian appreciated her attempt to lighten the tension.

"Nope, but the last weather report I saw said the storm should move on by morning."

Morning seemed a long way off when you were running low on food and stranded in the wilderness. Ian checked again for a signal. He couldn't call the sheriff, but he could try to get another text through to his sister. Sometimes that worked when there wasn't enough of a signal to call.

Had to evacuate cabin. Made a snow cave. Need rescue ASAP.

He added in their coordinates and hit Send.

"God willing, my sister will get the message and arrange our rescue. Now, what shall we do to entertain Miss Emi?"

"Mommy said we can tell stories like if this was a real campout."

Hope laughed and shook her head in wonder. "What do you know about real campouts?"

"They have them all the time in my books."

A shadow crossed Hope's face at her daughter's words, and Ian wondered what she was thinking about. Was she remembering the scene back at her office? They needed to talk about that more. What had seemed like possibly an unfortunate incident of workplace violence took on a new light when you considered how relentless these men had been in their pursuit. If he wanted to talk to Hope, he needed to distract Emi. Unfortunately, the backpack didn't seem to contain anything that would interest a seven-year-old girl. What would entertain a child of that age? He had absolutely no experience to draw on.

Ian shrugged away the desolate thoughts that tried to intrude. He gazed around the small cave, and inspiration struck. "Emi, I'm guessing you like to read, right?"

Her face lit up and he knew the answer. She nodded. "Mommy calls me a bookworm."

"I wish we had a book for you to read here, but I was thinking of something else you might like to do."

She cocked her head and waited.

"Do you know what people did before they had books?"

Emi bobbed her head eagerly. "We learned about that at school. They played telephone."

Ian looked to Hope for explanation, but she just shrugged. "Can you explain, sweetie?" she asked.

"In the olden days they told stories, but when they told them over and over they changed. Just like when you play telephone and you tell someone a story and they tell the next person, but by the time it gets to the last person it's so different that you all laugh."

Ian did laugh and smiled at Hope. "I think your daughter just summed up prehistory."

"Are we going to play telephone?"

Her innocent question had Ian thinking of whispering in Hope's ears, and he felt a flush rise in his cheeks. He had to clear his throat before he could answer. "No, that wasn't what I was thinking. Since you read so much, I'm sure you know about the cavemen, right?"

"Oh, yes."

Ian was tempted to ask for her take on them, but he reminded himself he was creating a distraction because he needed to talk to Hope. "Have you heard about how they told stories by drawing pictures on the walls of their caves?"

Her face lit up with interest, and Ian vowed to show her drawings from the Chauvet and Lascaux caves once they were safe. For now, he'd have to inspire her imagination.

"The cavemen used sticks and different kinds of dyes to tell stories by drawing pictures on the cave walls. They did such a great job of it that their drawings lasted for thousands of years and people go on trips into the caves to see them."

"Can we go there, Mommy?"

Hope smiled and hugged her daughter. "Maybe. But not tonight."

Emi looked back at Ian. "So, what are we going to do?"

"I thought you might like to make drawings on our cave walls. We don't have colored dyes, but you could use my pencil and carve them into the ice."

"What would I draw?"

"That's up to you. You think of a story." Ian was making this up as he went, but he seemed to have hit on something that engaged Emi, so he ran with it. "Want me to do one first?"

She bobbed her head. "Yes, please."

Ian thought hard for a moment, and then picked up the

pencil he'd dug out of his pack. He walked over to the wall closest to the door and began to sketch a stick figure on the snow. Emi hung back at first, but with Hope's prompting, she came over to watch. He'd noticed that about her. She had a natural reserve that only lifted when she was safely within arm's reach of Hope. Was she just shy? Or had something in her young life given her cause to be cautious?

Ian glanced at Emi and added a hat and pigtails just like she had. Then he started to sketch his dog. He wasn't much of an artist, but few kids could reject a dog.

"Is that me?" Emi asked softly, and he didn't miss the note of longing in her voice. He smiled down at her. "It is, and this is Rocco. He was my dog when I was your age."

"That's a funny name for a dog."

"He was a funny dog." He held out the pencil to her. "Do you want to make up stories about the adventures of Emi and Rocco?"

She glanced at Hope, who nodded. "Okay. Thank you, Mr. Ian."

Once Emi was lost in her world of drawings, Ian crossed the cave to sit beside Hope.

"Thank you for entertaining her."

"You're welcome. But I confess I had an ulterior motive. We need to talk."

"About what happened?"

He tilted his head toward hers so he could whisper his thoughts. "Yes. We need to rethink the attack back at your office. Random workplace shooters don't generally follow the employees deep into a blizzard and continue their pursuit through the night."

Hope nodded. "I know. I've been thinking about that."

"Did you come up with any new ideas?"

"Not really. I've been rethinking those moments before Steve left my office and headed down the hallway. I told you he'd come to give us her present, tickets to Christmas Village, but I had this nagging sense something was wrong. I asked him about it, but he said we'd talk after Christmas."

"That's something. I don't want to make you relive it, but I think we have to reexamine every part of it. You never know what else you might remember." He paused to allow Hope to gather her composure. "When you got the alert, what did you do?"

"I ran to close the door, but..." She hesitated. "I couldn't resist looking. I wanted to help Steve. I couldn't just abandon him."

"Did you see anything?"

"No, the hallway was still empty, but I heard shouts and gunfire."

She closed her eyes, so Ian waited in silence. It appeared she was trying to replay the scene and he didn't want to interrupt any part of it.

She finally opened her eyes and looked up at him. "I didn't see anyone, so I slammed the door and followed our procedure to evacuate." She gave an involuntary shudder. "But I know they were definitely after me. As Emi and I were escaping to the parking lot, we heard them talking. They said that Steve told them I'd left." She choked on a sob. "Then one told the other that maybe if they hadn't hurt him, Steve, they could've found out more about where I was or where I might have gone."

Ian tried to stay calm, although every nerve in his body was thrumming with anger. "There was nothing they said or nothing unique about their voices that could give them away?"

Hope shrugged. "Not that I noticed."

Ian ground his teeth in frustration. "It makes no sense, unless... You don't have any enemies, do you?"

Hope smiled briefly. "Not that I know of. I mean, my life is pretty simple. Work, Emi's school, food shopping. Not very exciting."

Ian wanted to ask about Emi's father, but he couldn't find

a tactful way to bring him up. "I hate to say this because I don't want to scare you, but I think it's safe to assume they won't give up."

Beside him, Hope's entire body wilted. "I know. I pretty much figured the same. But what do I do to avoid them if I don't know who they are or what they want?"

Ian was about to answer, to try to give some vague assurance, when his phone buzzed. He glanced down at the message. "It's from my sister." He frowned as he read. "She says the front stalled over us, and the snow is still falling at a fast rate even down in the valley. She'll come to rescue us as soon as she can get through."

Hope made a valiant attempt at a smile. "At least if she can't get through yet, we can hope the bad guys can't either."

Ian didn't want to dash her fragile hopes, but the bad guys weren't his only concern. The cave had them warm enough that they wouldn't freeze to death, but they were running out of food. Even if he held back on eating, it was just a matter of time before there was nothing left.

Chapter Seven

"Emi's not the only one who loves stories," Hope murmured as she and Ian sat alone in the darkness. Emi had finally tired of drawing and had snuggled up asleep in the blanket beside her mother. Hope was cold and hungry, and in need of distraction. Getting to know her handsome rescuer seemed like a good idea.

"You want to make cave drawings?"

Hope laughed. "No, I want to learn about you. Tell me about your life out here. What it's like to run a Christmas tree farm."

Ian was quiet for a moment. "It's a lot of hard work, but I like the physicality of it. After the war, I needed to find a purpose, a way of keeping my mind and body busy. Working a long day makes it easier to sleep at night."

Hope sensed some brutal truth underlying that answer, but she didn't push. She knew of the toll war had taken on veterans, and she remembered Ian's voice when he'd spoken of delivering trees for the fundraiser. "I'm sorry my trouble made you lose your trees. I hope you'll let me pay to replace them."

"Not necessary. There are plenty more back at the ranch

where those came from, and I seriously doubt anyone is out Christmas tree shopping in this weather. Think no more of it."

And don't ask any more questions about it either. That was the message Hope took away, so she changed the topic.

"Do you have children? Back at the ranch, I mean."

"Why do you ask?" His voice was dry, and he had to clear his throat to get the words out.

A sense of unease left Hope unsure how to answer. She hadn't meant any harm by asking, but there was a quality to his response that made her realize this was an uncomfortable topic as well.

"I'm sorry. You're so good with Emi. It seems natural. I just thought…" Her voice trailed off.

"She's a scared child."

"Yes, and you kept her physically safe," Hope replied, feeling on safer ground. "But it was more than that. You respected her feelings. I think she recognized that and it made her feel emotionally safe too."

Ian cleared his throat again. "We're trained in how to treat children."

She accepted his brusque explanation, sure once again that she was treading on sensitive personal space. She owed him the same respect for his feelings that he'd shown Emi.

"Well, thank you."

Ian's voice was hoarse. "No problem."

She felt him shift and stand before he spoke again. "I'm going to go stand watch."

"Please don't." Hope stood, too, and reached for his arm. She missed in the dark and stumbled forward. Ian's arms came up to catch her, and she felt the tension in his body. She held very still. "I'm sorry. I shouldn't have pried."

They stood in silence, inches apart, something new and raw filling the air between them. "I was married once. My wife and child died in childbirth."

He turned and headed out of the cave, leaving Hope's heart breaking for the pain she'd heard in his voice.

Ian crawled back out of the cave entrance to give himself a bit of breathing room. He gratefully accepted the slap of frigid air. Hope's innocent question had touched a little too close for comfort. He regretted brushing her off, but he wasn't about to divulge his heartbreak to a woman he'd known for less than a day, no matter how intense the experience had been. There was something about life-and-death struggles that bonded you quickly, but that didn't entitle her to his entire sad story.

It was only Hope's vulnerability that was tugging at his heart, he assured himself. There was something so vulnerable about this duo that he couldn't quite put his finger on, but he suspected it went deeper than what had happened yesterday.

When he'd taken them into his truck, he'd assumed responsibility for their safety. He would do whatever it took to get them to the sheriff. Then he would go back to his ranch, pick up a new load of trees to replace the ones damaged in the fire and go on about his life—however lonely it might seem.

And it was going to be lonely. He could be honest with himself about that much. In less than twenty-four hours, Hope and Emi had winnowed their way into his life and his heart, resurrecting the thoughts he usually kept deeply hidden, reminding him of all he'd lost.

Ian stood and walked out into the cold. With the wind howling in his face, he breathed in deeply and closed his eyes against the onslaught of ice and snow. The pain felt right, normal. Together with regret and a swamping sense of guilt, it defined his days. He needed that pain now to remind himself that sweet Emi and her mother weren't just a reminder of all he had lost. They offered a glimpse of a life he no longer deserved.

Chapter Eight

Hope woke to the sound of jingling bells and her daughter's excited voice.

"It's nine days 'til Christmas, Mommy." Emi squirmed against her. "Remember? Today we find a Christmas tree." She shoved her device in front of Hope's face. "But the app's not working."

Hope rubbed her eyes and looked from Emi's blank screen to the rounded white walls, waiting for something to make sense in her foggy brain.

At least she understood the problem with Emi's device. "We don't have internet out here."

She'd been working on marketing the platform for Twelve Days 'til Christmas for the better part of the last year, and the success of it had driven Steve's company's profits into the stratosphere.

Steve. Her heart sank as memories of the past day came rushing at her. The invasion, being run off the road—several times—escaping the camp and trudging through endless miles of wilderness until finally ending up here. She and Emi were in a cave made of snow in the middle of a forest in the dead of winter. And somehow, they hadn't frozen to death. That was thanks to Ian. But what had happened to Steve?

She opened her phone hoping for news, but there was still no service.

And where was Ian?

After her rude intrusion into his life story last night, he'd gone outside to stand watch. Of course, he hadn't said that was the reason, but she'd seen something shift in his eyes when she asked about children. On top of all the danger she'd brought into his life, now it seemed she'd also caused him pain. And that was the last thing she wanted to do.

He must have come back in once she and Emi were asleep because the other blanket had been used. She had a strong sense that while he might have used it to keep warm, he likely hadn't slept a wink. She was already getting to know he had an overdeveloped protective instinct, for which she was extremely grateful.

"Mommy, do you hear those bells?"

Hope pushed her thoughts aside and listened while she dug out the last piece of protein bar and handed it to her daughter. "I do hear the bells. Ian said his sister was going to come with horses, so maybe she's here." Was it possible they were finally going to be rescued?

Hope pushed her hair out of her face and finger-combed the long blond tresses. She hated to even think what she must look like, but she had no way of fixing her appearance. Giving up, she reached for the last water bottle and handed it to Emi. She sure hoped that the bells meant horses, because they were down to the last bottle of water and were out of food.

The sound could mean danger too, of course, but Hope felt no fear. Logically, someone coming to cause them harm was unlikely to herald their arrival with jingling bells. She knew, though, that her feeling of security was due more to Ian's protection than logic. Still, she held Emi back from running out to see if there were truly horses until Ian poked his head in the cave entrance and called out for her.

"Emi, are you awake? I think you're going to want to see this."

Emi tugged at her hand. "Come, Mommy. Let's go."

Hope fell to her knees and crawled after her daughter. Emi's squeal of delight made her crawl faster. When she emerged, weak sunlight was filtering through snow that still drifted lightly to the ground, but her attention was drawn immediately to Emi, who stood in shock, hands cupped over her mouth.

Hope turned to follow the direction of Emi's gaze, and her own mouth fell open in surprise. Reindeer? Was she imagining things? She looked over at Ian, who was watching Emi's reaction with pure delight. When he finally looked her way, she just slowly shook her head and smiled. "Thank you."

Hope and Emi watched in awe as the reindeer pulled a sleigh over the snow-covered slope. "I thought you said she was bringing horses."

"I did, but I guess the drifts were too much for the horses. Reindeer have webbed feet that let them walk on top of the snow."

"Like ducks."

Ian laughed. "Very big ducks, Emi. You already know I grow Christmas trees on our ranch, but my sister raises reindeer too. They're her special project."

"Your sister the FBI agent?"

Ian smirked. "I spend a lot of time filling in for her on reindeer duty. But she loves them like they're her children."

There was that word again. *Children.* But Ian said it without flinching this time, so Hope let it go.

"This is amazing. I've never seen a reindeer outside of a movie."

The sleigh pulled up beside them, and a woman jumped down to greet them. She threw her arms around Ian and hugged him tight. "You had us worried, bud."

"Emi, Hope, this is my baby sister, Ellen, otherwise known as Nancy Drew."

Nancy rolled her eyes. "Did he tell you that story?"

Ian shrugged. "No, just that you loved reading mysteries."

Hope watched the interplay between brother and sister, and a tightness banded her chest. She was an only child, and since her husband had died, Emi would be too. Hearing Ian talk about his family had warmed her heart, and now seeing their evident bond reminded her of the hopes she'd once had to build a big family of her own.

"Hope?"

She shook herself. This was neither the time nor the place for dark memories. "Yes?"

"I was just saying we should get going right away. Nance says there is no good news about the incident at your office, which means…" He glanced toward Emi. Her daughter was totally entranced by the reindeer and probably wouldn't hear his words, but she appreciated his tact. She didn't need him to finish the sentence. The attackers were still on the loose.

"I just have to grab my pack."

"I'll get it. I want to grab the blankets too. Why don't you bring Emi over to meet the reindeer with Nancy while I get our stuff?"

"You really call her that?"

He laughed. "It started out as a joke, but it became her nickname. She never really liked her real name after that. I think Emi will like her. She's a bookworm too—when she's not catching bad guys or caring for reindeer."

Emi stood by Nancy's side, which told Hope exactly how excited she was by the animals. Normally with strangers she hid behind Hope, but something about Ian and his sister seemed to cut through her reserve.

Nancy waved her over as Ian headed back into the cave.

"Thank you so much for coming out in the storm…" Hope

smiled. "I don't know what to call you," she admitted. "It doesn't seem right to use a family nickname."

Nancy grinned back. "These days the only people who call me Ellen are my bosses. Even my coworkers call me Nancy. Not sure I'd remember to answer if you called me anything else."

Nancy guided them toward the reindeer, but Hope and Emi stayed a healthy distance back as she approached them and stroked the big head. "Hope, Emi, I'd like you to meet my best friends."

"What are their names?" Emi asked softly.

"This is Sundancer. And over here is Conner. Splasher and Glitzen stayed back at the ranch."

Emi grinned. "Those sound almost like—"

"Shh," Nancy teased. "They already think they're too cool pulling my sleigh. Let's not give them any ideas."

Emi giggled and Hope's heart danced. Maybe Emi would remember this as a grand adventure involving reindeer rather than being traumatized by the experience.

She couldn't ignore the fact that they were still in danger, though, and Nancy had clearly not forgotten either. Hope noticed how the FBI agent's gaze was constantly roaming the hillside even as she chatted with them. She was on full alert, which meant Hope needed to be too.

"Should I get Emi settled so we can move out?"

Nancy nodded solemnly. "I don't like the isolation out here now that the storm has petered out."

She showed Hope how to climb into the sleigh and then lifted Emi up. "You two take the back seat. Ian and I will ride up front to keep watch."

She strode across the snow to meet Ian and help him with the bags.

"You didn't say she was cute."

The words drifted on the air, catching Hope's ear.

"Emi? She's seven and adorable," Ian replied.

Nancy punched his arm. "Yeah, she is, but I meant the mother."

Hope couldn't help but stare, wanting to see his reaction. He tilted his head and looked down. "Let's not go there, okay?"

There was nothing teasing in that reply, and Hope's heart gave a little lurch. Ian had a story, and she knew his hadn't had any happier an ending than hers.

Nancy dumped the two backpacks in the back seat and handed the blankets to Hope while Ian circled the sleigh and climbed in the other side. She picked up the reins and flicked them gently. As the reindeer took off, flying across the snow, with Emi squealing in glee, Nancy pointed to the bag beneath Ian's seat. "Mom sent some thermoses full of coffee and hot cocoa. I think there are some doughnuts in there too. She thought you might be hungry."

Ian glanced back at Hope who nodded. He poured a steaming mugful of cocoa and carefully passed it back to her. "This one's for Emi, but it's hot, so be careful."

Hope took the mug and held it so Emi could blow on it. The cocoa cooled quickly in the freezing air, so she snuggled her daughter into the blanket and handed her the mug. When Ian passed her a napkin holding fresh-baked cinnamon doughnuts, she inhaled and murmured, "I think I already love your mother."

Ian handed her a mug of coffee. "This should cinch it. My mother makes the best coffee ever."

Hope thought hot anything would have been a blessing, but when she sipped the hot, sweet coffee, she closed her eyes in bliss.

She settled back into the blanket beside Emi and slowly sipped her coffee while the reindeer pranced through the snow. She'd lost all sense of time and place while fleeing in the storm, but now the wind had eased, and scraps of blue sky peeked between the clouds as the storm blew eastward. She sighed. There was still danger, and so many questions needing answers, but for the moment she was content to count her blessings—Ian and his family being at the top of the list.

That sense of peace didn't last long. The sound of engines caught her ear first, and then she noticed how rigidly Ian and Nancy were sitting. They were both scanning the forested mountainside and were on full alert. Hope saw Nancy gesture toward the floor, and Ian bent and picked up a rifle. That was when Hope noticed Nancy already had one resting on her lap.

"What should we do?" she asked quietly.

Ian deferred to Nancy, who spoke urgently. "Get down on the floor. Hide the Mylar blankets under you because the silver will make you a target. There are lap rugs on the floor. Pull them over you. Better to get you hidden before they see you."

Her no-nonsense instructions sent adrenaline rushing through Hope's body. Her limbs went tingly, and she felt the same lack of coordination the cold had caused. Pulling herself together, she took the empty cocoa cup from Emi and helped the little girl settle in the well behind the front seat. Hope climbed down beside her and pulled the blankets over them like an awning. And then she began to pray.

Ian glanced at his sister. Truth be told, there was no one he'd rather have beside him in this moment than Nancy. Her instincts were excellent and her marksmanship was even better. He hoped their combined skills were enough because they were open targets out here in the middle of nowhere.

The sound of the snowmobiles got louder.

"Could just be people out for fun after the storm," he suggested.

"Could be."

Her clipped tone matched his doubts.

"There. See that flash on the south mountain?" Nancy murmured. "The sun just glanced off a rifle barrel."

Ian trained his eyes in the direction she'd indicated. He

could make out two snowmobiles. The lead one had a rifle aimed in their direction. "Do you think they're in range yet?" He was trained military, but his sister knew these mountains, and he trusted her judgment.

"Close, but they're still moving, so it will be hard to hit the target from there."

The target. *Them.*

"How do you want to handle it?" Ian asked.

"If we were on flatter ground, I'd give the boys their head and let them run for it. Pretty sure they can't outrun a snowmobile, but they're fast."

Ian would have smiled were the situation not so serious. Nancy's pride in her reindeer was legendary in their family. "But we're not on flat ground. So?"

"Your call. How much of a risk do you feel like taking?"

Ian didn't have to think long. The lives of the precious child and her mother hiding behind their seat were not something he was willing to risk. "None."

Nancy flashed him a glance, and Ian knew he would have some explaining to do later. He was not known for his cautious nature, but he was not willing to risk the life of an innocent child.

"Then we make for rough ground," Nancy decided. "It will be tough on the humans and the sled, but my boys can handle rocky slopes better than a snowmobile can. The snow should cushion the worst of it."

"Hope?"

"Do whatever you have to. We'll manage."

Nancy nodded her approval. "I'll try to narrate what we're doing so you aren't surprised. My plan is to get down this rocky slope and head across the stream. If they know what they're doing, they'll skip the snowmobiles across, but once we're on the other side, I can let the boys have their heads."

"Emi, do you know how fast reindeer can run?" Ian asked.

"No," came a tremulous voice from beneath the blanket. "Can't they fly?"

Nancy choked on a laugh. "That would sure be a help if they could. My reindeer aren't the kind that can fly. But they run very fast. It will almost feel like flying."

Ian appreciated his sister's steady humor, but the fact was, reindeer couldn't outrun a snowmobile. Any advantage they had from their surefootedness was lost because they were carting the sleigh. No two ways about it—they were in trouble again.

Since Nancy had to keep a close eye on the terrain ahead, Ian turned in his seat to watch their pursuers. A rifle shot exploded in the air as the reindeer raced across the snow, eliminating any question about intent. Fortunately, the shot went wide and drove harmlessly into the snow a safe distance back.

"We okay?" Nancy whispered.

"So far. The lead driver is gaining, but his aim is off so far. I'm going to take a shot to warn them back. Hope, keep Emi down. I'm going to be shooting over your head." Ian locked the rifle into position and aimed. He counted down quietly so Nancy would know when to expect the shot. "Three, two, one."

He fired at the lead snowmobile. The driver zigzagged. Ian hadn't expected to hit them, since they were still too far out of range, but perhaps they'd be less aggressive if they knew they would draw return fire.

"Hold on," Nancy warned him as she called to Hope. "Rocky ride approaching."

Ian swiveled to look forward just in time to see Nancy swerve the reindeer into a stand of pine trees. The distance between the trees was barely wider than the sleigh, making the task somewhat like threading a needle, but Nancy's hands stayed steady on the reins, and she barely flinched as the branches brushed the sides of the sleigh. "Nice work."

Nancy only huffed out a breath in reply as she continued

to thread her way between the trees. "Good thing I didn't bring the big sleigh."

"This was a good move. I can get a better aim at them now because they can't zigzag in the trees." Ian turned to kneel on the floor of the sleigh and level the rifle across the seat back.

He waited until both snowmobiles had entered the trees before firing again. This time his bullet bounced off the windshield, and the driver momentarily lost control.

"Good news, bad news. I hit him. But that means they're in range. Can you slump down below the seat and still drive the sleigh?"

"Enough to make me less of a target. You?"

"I'll sit to the side and only pop up to shoot."

Ian eased up so he could see, and a bullet whizzed by his head. This wasn't looking good. The narrow confines helped the enemy as well as them because the trees helped frame the shot better than a wide-open field of snow. "How much longer in the forest?"

"About a hundred feet," Nancy answered. "Then we exit into a stream. That should at least give them a moment's pause."

Another shot hit the rear runner, and the force of it vibrated through the sleigh. Ian heard a muffled cry from the back seat, and his heart ached. No child should have to endure this. That had been one of the hardest parts of being a soldier for him—seeing the impact of war on children. He was not going to let these men get Emi if it was the last thing he did.

It wouldn't be smart to raise his head again, so Ian leaned over the side of the sleigh and took two quick shots. A cry told him at least one shot had hit its mark.

"Good job," Nancy praised. "Now hold your fire. We're going into the water."

Ian crouched down in the seat and grabbed hold of the side rail as he braced himself. The reindeer dashed right into the running water, but the sleigh jolted as it hit the rocks. A layer of snow had built up on them, but the fiercely flowing water kept it from accumulating enough to make an easy ride. He wondered how the snowmobilers would handle the transition from ground to water.

"I don't understand how they found us," he said quietly to Nancy.

She was concentrating on pulling the sleigh out of the stream and onto a stretch of deep open snow. "I don't think they followed me," she replied as she gave the reindeer their heads to race across the shimmering snow. "They approached from the opposite direction. Most likely they waited for the snow to end, grabbed some snowmobiles and headed out in the direction you'd gone. Did you track straight or weave?"

Ian muttered under his breath as he took another shot. "I tried to follow my compass, but we couldn't see a thing in the wind and driving snow, so mainly I just kept going. I knew they weren't dressed for the weather, so I figured they couldn't follow us too far."

Nancy chuckled as she carefully glanced over her shoulder. "I guess that explains their current predicament."

Ian looked back and laughed in a combination of relief and amusement. "First rule of snowmobiling. Don't stop in soft powder." As he watched, the snowmobiles were slowly sinking into the snow as the men stood and pointed their rifles.

"Heads down."

Rifle fire cracked through the air as Nancy urged the reindeer ahead. "Gee-haw."

The air around them exploded with repeated shots that fell short as they drew out of range.

Ian released a sigh of relief once they were safely away. Nancy slowed the sleigh so Hope and Emi could climb out of the well and settle back onto the seat. "Everybody okay?"

Ian watched Hope nod, but he could see how badly her body was trembling. "It'll be okay now. We'll be at the ranch soon."

Nancy gave him a sidelong glance, and Ian shrugged. They

both knew he was offering a false promise. These men had proved one thing very clearly. They didn't give up easily, and they'd be back on their trail before long. The question remained—why?

Chapter Nine

"Those are our parents standing on the porch waving at you," Ian chuckled as the sleigh pulled up to a beautiful log-cabin-style ranch house. White lights twinkled along the roofline and green garlands were draped across the porch. Best of all, smoke curled from a chimney. For the first time, Hope felt her lips curve in a genuine smile.

The house represented a home and warmth, good people, family...and peace.

And she was bringing danger to their doorstep.

Hope leaned forward to speak to Ian. "I can't stay here."

"Of course you can. My parents will be thrilled to meet you and Emi. Nancy told them we were coming."

Hope shook her head vehemently. "I can't risk their lives. You know what these men are like, what they'll do to get to me. I just need a ride to the sheriff."

Ian frowned and looked at Nancy. "You tell her."

Nancy pulled back on the reins and the sleigh came to a rest. "There's no use arguing with my mother. But it's okay. Both Ian and my father are former military. I'm with the FBI. My other brother isn't here because he's deployed, but you don't need to worry. We've got you covered."

Hope sputtered in frustration. "I wasn't questioning your ability. It's just, I've already asked too much of you. I don't want to drag the rest of your family into a mess I don't even understand. I don't want to cause any more trouble."

Nancy laughed. "You don't know our mother. She will not take no for an answer."

Hope was out of time to convince them because Ian's mother was already hustling down the steps, welcoming words on her lips.

"Told you," Nancy teased. "Don't mind her," she added, glancing at Emi. "She's just dying for some grandbabies of her own."

Hope felt Ian stiffen. Was it the baby mention or Nancy's not-so-subtle implication?

"I heard that, Nancy." Mrs. Fraser wagged her finger playfully. "You just shush. This little lamb has had a terrible fright," she continued as Ian helped Hope and Emi down from the sleigh. She crouched beside Emi. "We need to get you all warmed up. How does a bubble bath sound?"

Emi looked to Hope, who could only shrug. She knew how to accept when she'd lost a battle. At least temporarily. "Honestly anything with hot water sounds good to me right now. Thank you, Mrs. Fraser."

"Oh dear, no. We're not so formal here. You just call me Sarah. Now come on in. Poppa has a fire burning in the hearth, so once you get washed up, we can settle in and have lunch by the fireplace."

Hope mustered a smile that she hoped was warmer than she felt. "Thank you, Sarah. You're too kind. I don't..."

But Ian's mother was already hustling Emi into the warmth of the house. She shrugged and turned to grab their backpacks before following. From the other side of the sleigh, she could hear Nancy's voice.

"She sure is different from Shelby."

Hope had no idea who Shelby was, but the comment clearly

upset Ian. She couldn't hear his reply, but the look on Nancy's face told her it was not all in fun.

Feeling guilty for overhearing something that was clearly not meant for her, Hope grabbed the packs and hurried up the front steps. She caught up just in time to see Emi's reaction as she stepped into the house. Her daughter was speechless with wonder, and Hope had to admit, it was a pretty amazing sight. They'd walked into a Christmas wonderland.

A huge tree decorated in white lights and handmade ornaments dominated one side of the large room. Fairy lights twinkled in evergreen boughs that hung from the rafters. Soft Christmas music played in the background and the scent of pine filled the air, mixing with the aroma of baking, but it was the roaring fire in the stone fireplace on the opposite wall that beckoned Hope.

"It's like Christmas Village but inside," Emi whispered in awe as she spun in a slow circle trying to take it all in. Hope felt a bit like a kid herself. Everywhere she looked there was something else to notice, but the effect wasn't overwhelming at all. It was welcoming and felt like what she thought coming home at Christmas should feel like—warm and inviting. Unexpected tears pricked her eyes, and she quickly blinked them back.

This wonderful room only reinforced her conviction that they couldn't stay here. They couldn't bring danger to this family or home. She would clean up and let Emi recover and eat, but then Ian would have to take her to the sheriff or she'd call him to come get her.

An hour later, warm from the bath and cozy in some fleece-lined clothing Sarah had brought her, Hope was struggling to maintain her resolve. Everyone in Ian's family was just so nice, so welcoming. When she entered the kitchen, she had to stop and smile. Her normally shy daughter was chattering away as she stood on a step stool helping Ian's mother arrange cornbread on a platter for lunch. What was it about this family that brought out the best in her daughter?

Another burst of longing hit Hope, and she quickly ducked her head. The acceptance and love in this room represented everything she had ever wanted. Everything she thought she'd have when she married Keith. Everything that had proved to be nothing but an illusion built on her pipe dreams and starry eyes.

Was that what she was doing now? Imagining what she wanted to find?

"Hope, you're just in time to help bring the food to the table."

And just like that, her negative thoughts evaporated as she was caught up in the happy bustle of a loving family.

When everyone was gathered around the table near the hearth, they joined hands and bowed their heads as Ian's father led them in a prayer of thanksgiving for the meal they were blessed to share. After a rousing chorus of amens, the food was passed and happy chatter resumed. Hope found herself feeling like she was caught in some twilight zone. Outside lay danger, men she didn't know shooting at her and pursuing her with a determination that defied her understanding.

But in here, the spirit of Christmas reigned with peace, love and joy, laughter and good conversation. She leaned down to offer Emi another helping of cornbread and beef stew and was shocked out of her happy mood at the sight of her child's sad face.

"What's wrong, love?" she whispered as she slid her arm around her daughter's narrow shoulders.

Emi sniffled, and Hope's heart squeezed, fearing the days of terror had caught up with her. "You can tell me."

Emi looked up, eyes shining pools of unshed tears. "We missed two days of the countdown. We'll never win now."

Hope bit back a smile. This she could deal with. "You know

the point of Twelve Days 'til Christmas was never about winning. That's the number-one rule. It's all about the fun."

"I know, but I *was* having fun. *And* I was winning stickers."

Hope couldn't help but smile then. Adding Christmas stickers had been one of her contributions. If she'd learned anything as a mother, it was don't come between a girl and her stickers.

"What is Twelve Days 'til Christmas?"

Hope looked up and was startled to see everyone at the table focused on them. Ian's mother had asked the question, so Hope directed her answer to her. "It's the social media platform my company created. You can play it on an app or on any computer or device. Basically, it's a countdown to Christmas with different activities to do each day. We created a safe online space that gives people a small-town community feeling. Just like towns have a calendar of events, we focus on different activities each day. The kickoff was the Christmas tree lighting on our town green—all virtual of course, but people got to share photos and videos of their families counting down and singing along."

Suddenly self-conscious with how she'd gotten carried away, Hope smiled bashfully. "I'm just a little over-the-top enthusiastic about it." She shrugged. "It's been pretty successful."

"So, Miss Emi, what were the days you missed?" Poppa asked.

Emi's pout lifted a bit as she replied. "I missed the snowball fight and we don't have a tree."

"But Emi, you got to sleep in a snow cave and do cave drawings," Ian suggested. "Doesn't that count?"

"Only if we'd had a snowball fight."

"Now she tells me," Ian teased.

"You could play with reindeer," Nancy offered. "Would that help?"

Emi brightened. "That could count for reindeer-games day,

right, Mommy? But that's not for five more days." Her face fell again.

The idea that they could still be on the run from these dangerous men in five more days sucked away Hope's Christmas spirit, but she rallied for Emi's sake. "Strictly speaking, the activity doesn't have to be on the exact day. But you could use them for sleigh-rides day if you want. You did go on a sleigh ride with them."

Emi grinned at Nancy. "I bet no one else had reindeer for their sleigh ride. Can we post pictures?"

Hope's festive mood immediately crashed. "We'll take pictures," she promised. "But I don't think we should post them until the sheriff catches the bad men."

Emi's upper lip trembled, and Hope feared a complete meltdown was coming. Her little girl was usually well-behaved, but Hope would challenge anyone who expected better of Emi after all she'd been through. She was frankly glad to see Emi complaining. It was a sign of her resilience.

"So, which one was today—the snowball fight or the tree?" Sarah asked, and Hope smiled her gratitude.

Emi didn't have to think twice. "Today is cut down and decorate a Christmas tree."

"We can certainly do that," Sarah responded enthusiastically.

"But you already have a Christmas tree," Emi said sadly.

"This is a Christmas tree ranch—we have lots of trees, don't we, Ian? And I have an idea for a special tree. Maybe we could dig one up and put it in a bucket by the side of the porch. We can decorate it with treats for the birds and squirrels. And then you can watch from the window when they come eat it. How does that sound?"

Emi clapped her hands in glee. "When can we go? Can we go now?"

Hope was thrilled by Emi's joy until she noticed the matching looks of concern on Ian's and Nancy's faces.

As they started to clear the table, Hope overheard Ian trying to dissuade his mother, but she was having none of it. "It will just have to be your job to keep her safe."

Ian loved his mother dearly, and respected her always, but there were times like now that he wished she could back down and respect his expertise. She always saw the best in everyone and had a hard time accepting evil in the world. He loved that about her, but after what he'd endured with Hope and Emi the past few days, taking this kind of risk felt foolhardy, even if it was hard to resist the chance to make Emi smile.

It will just have to be your job to keep her safe. How did his own mother not understand how harsh those words were to him? He'd been unable to save his wife and son despite all the best medical care. Yet she tossed off the admonition like it was a matter of choice.

Emi's laughter pulled him from his deteriorating thoughts, and even in his harsh mood, he had to admit he found her charm engaging. Nancy had brought the sleigh around to indulge Emi so they could ride over to the Christmas tree sector of the farm, but Emi was currently giggling her way through a reindeer photo shoot. Her unadulterated joy was enough to momentarily lighten Ian's heart.

"Look, Mommy, he likes me." Emi had nuzzled her face against the reindeer's.

Ian stepped forward. "Why don't you give me your phone?" he suggested to Hope. "I'll snap a mother-daughter photo—one on each side of Splasher. You can save it for reindeer games day."

He took a few candid shots, some of them quite silly, and then he aimed for capturing a tender moment between mother and daughter. From behind the safety of the camera, he could indulge himself and study Hope as she was only with Emi—a vision of loveliness and maternal perfection.

The thought jolted him. He hadn't meant to be comparing

her to his late wife, but he realized that every time he watched her snuggle with Emi or laugh with her, a dart of resentment pricked him. This was what he'd lost.

It will just have to be your job to keep her safe.

Yes, it was, and he was taking no unavoidable chances.

Photo shoot over, Ian bundled them all into the sleigh. His mother and father had chosen to follow in the warm truck, so Ian sat in back with Hope and Emi while Nancy drove.

Emi was chattering on about the reindeer and Christmas trees so fast that his head was spinning. She'd sure come out of her shell in the past few hours.

"So, tell me about this reindeer-games day," he prompted Hope. "What does it mean for the thousands of people who haven't just been rescued by reindeer?"

Hope laughed lightly, and Ian found himself transfixed. Emi wasn't the only one who was showing her true personality.

"The platform has dozens of suggestions from pin-the-red-nose-on-the-reindeer, to a reindeer-race contest which basically is a traditional three-legged race, but wearing antler hats. We've got reindeer-shaped-food recipes and sing-alongs with reindeer-themed songs. You'd be surprised how many of those there are. There are virtual links to so many possibilities—online reindeer games that our coders developed, virtual reality trips to a reindeer rescue and videos to learn about reindeer and virtually adopt one."

Ian listened in awe as her voice grew more animated with every word. "You did all of this?"

Hope blushed adorably. "Oh, no. I had lots of help. I developed the concept, but our coders did all the work."

Ian just shook his head in amazement. "It's very creative. No wonder Emi is so excited. But how does Christmas Village tie in?"

"It doesn't. Not really. Emi saw an ad for it on television and couldn't stop talking about how many days of the activities she could fill in there. Unfortunately, by the time she discovered it, every ticket was sold out."

"I'm sensing there's a *but*…"

Hope ducked her head, and he watched her take a deep breath. Some of the glimmer had worn off her voice when she spoke again. "The day of the attack, Steve surprised her with tickets. Somehow, he had gotten a pair and found us lodging. That's why he was in my office just before the attackers came in—to give us the tickets and make me leave early."

Ian noticed the shadow cross her face. "What?"

She shrugged. "Maybe it's nothing, but like I told you in the cave, I picked up on something being off. He was really eager to get me out of the office."

All fun fell away, and Ian went on alert. "You think he knew something was going to happen?"

"Maybe? No." She shook her head. "That wouldn't make sense. How would he know we were going to be attacked?"

Ian didn't respond right away. He wasn't sure what to do with the information, but he wasn't going to ignore a possible clue. "I don't want to discuss it in front of Emi," he murmured, "but we should talk to Nancy when we get back. This is her area of expertise. Not mine."

The sleigh pulled up behind the entrance to the tree lot, and Ian drew in a sharp breath. This was even worse than he'd feared. The end of the storm must have drawn out all the tree shoppers. Families eager to cut down their perfect tree swarmed the entranceway armed with axes and saws. Ian studied every adult face, not willing to overlook any possible threat.

He turned to Hope. "I should have done this before, but we need to exchange phone numbers—just in case we get separated," he added, trying to make it sound a little less ominous.

Once they had done that, Nancy hustled Emi and Hope around to the back where local volunteers were doling out steaming mugs of cocoa.

"This is like something straight out of Twelve Days 'til Christmas," Hope pronounced, her voice full of delight. Her joy was infectious, and Ian found himself smiling even as he trailed behind keeping watch.

"All of this is Ian's pet project," Nancy replied. "He recruits all these volunteers to make this sale a huge success for the veterans' center's programs."

As Ian listened to Nancy sing his praises, he was reminded of all the trees that had burned with the truck. Insurance would cover the truck, and he could never regret stepping in to rescue Hope and Emi, but the trees were undeniably a big loss. He should be happy about the crowds today, because they'd help make up some of the replacement cost. And he would be happy—but he wouldn't let down his guard.

"Ian, we're heading back to the live-tree section," Nancy called.

Ian nodded. "Right behind you." He was probably being overly cautious. There was no reason for the gunmen who had chased them to expect Hope to be at a Christmas tree sale. And yet, concern lingered. They'd been uncanny in their ability to track her so far.

Ian hurried to keep up as Emi skipped on ahead and Hope and Nancy quickened their pace to keep up.

"Stay with us, Em," Hope called, but Emi was delightedly running from tree to tree, sniffing the snow-laden pine branches.

"It smells like Christmas, Mommy."

Hope bent down to sniff the branch, and Ian watched in amusement as she purposely buried her nose in the snowy branch. When she lifted her head, she smiled at Emi.

"You're right," she agreed.

Emi started giggling, and Hope deadpanned. "What's wrong?"

Emi laughed even harder and pointed at her nose.

Hope turned to Ian, a mischievous grin on her face. "Do you see something wrong with my face?"

Ian struck a thoughtful pose and pretended to study her. "Hmm. I think your face is quite…" *Lovely*, his heart suggested. *Perfect.* "Quite cold," he finished lamely.

Emi giggled harder.

"But you know," he continued, "I think Emi's face is missing something." He scooped a handful of snow off the branch and made a fluffy snowball. "You wanted a snowball fight, didn't you?" With exaggerated steps he headed toward Emi, who ran and hid behind her mother.

Ian handed off the snowball to Hope, who turned and plopped it on Emi's nose, inducing a fit of laughter. Then she scooped another handful and advanced on Ian.

"Emi's not the only one missing something."

Before Ian had time to realize what was happening, she'd lobbed it right into his face.

Sputtering with surprise and delight, Ian bent down and grabbed another handful, which he didn't even bother to shape before tossing it at Hope.

When she looked up at him with joy shining in her eyes, something flipped in his heart. Her lashes were sparkling with the powdery snow. Her cheeks glowed red from the exertion, and she looked so relaxed and happy that she stole his breath away.

Without conscious thought, Ian stepped toward her and gently brushed the snow from her face with his gloved fingertips. His fingers stilled, and he was entranced, only vaguely hearing Nancy call Emi to check out a special tree.

Her insistent voice finally penetrated his haze, and he hastily stepped back, tripping over a tree in the process. As he fell backward, landing flat on his back in the snow, he could see Hope laughing merrily, but he also saw a glimmer of something dangerous in her eyes, something he'd vowed never to allow again.

He jumped up and vigorously brushed the snow from his coat. "We'd better go catch up with Nance. I don't want them getting too far ahead of us."

Hope's face shuttered, and despite the sting, Ian assured himself that it was for the best.

Hope hurried forward to catch up with her daughter and Nancy, while Ian followed behind at a safe distance, chastising himself for getting caught up in fun and letting down his guard. He carefully scanned the back lot and went on alert when he spied a person behind the trees. But seconds later a woman and child called out to the man, and he smiled and pointed to a tree.

Just another family shopping for trees, Ian decided, but it served as a reminder that he couldn't allow himself to get caught up in Hope's little family. He'd lost the right to have his own family when his wife and son died. His only role was to protect Hope and Emi. And he'd keep reminding himself of that as often as necessary.

"Emi, Emi, where are you?"

The fear in Hope's voice sent Ian running ahead until he caught up to her. "What happened?"

"We were looking at trees," Hope responded, panic rising in her voice. She ran behind a tree to look at something. "I called to her to come back, but suddenly she wasn't there."

Fear clogged Ian's throat. While he'd been musing about families, Emi had gone missing. "Where's Nancy?"

"She went running through the trees to look for her."

Ian considered what to do. "The best plan would be for you to stay here in case Emi just got lost and comes back. But I don't want to leave you alone. Nancy should have stayed with you, but come, we'll look together."

"No. You're right. I'll wait here. I'll be fine."

Ian knew he couldn't take the time to argue with her. Every passing second meant Emi could be farther and farther away—either lost or taken.

"Call me immediately if she comes back or if anything scares you."

"Just find my daughter. Nothing scares me as much as losing her."

Chapter Ten

Ian raced through the trees, Hope's words urging him on. Images of Emi laughing with the reindeer raced through his mind. He could not let anything happen to this little girl.

"Mr. Ian!"

For a moment Ian thought he was hallucinating, but when he swung around, he saw Emi sitting on the ground with tears streaming down her face.

"Emi, what happened?"

She hung her head. "Don't be mad."

Ian deliberately lowered his voice. "I'm not mad at all. Your mama and Nancy and I were so worried. Why did you run off?"

She looked up at him, wide blue eyes still shimmering, but now with joy. "I saw a bunny. I tried to get closer, but he ran away. I followed him, but he ran more, and then…then I got lost."

Ian swallowed back all the fears, all the guilt, and just picked her up in his arms. "How about we call your mommy and tell her I'm bringing you back?"

Ian pulled out his phone and dialed. When he heard Hope's worried voice, he said, "I have someone here who wants to talk to her mommy." He felt her gush of relief as he handed the phone to Emi.

"I'm sorry, Mommy. I chased a bunny, but he got away and I got lost, but Mr. Ian found me."

Ian couldn't make out Hope's words, but as he watched Emi's reaction, he was struck again at how great a mother Hope was.

After a few minutes, Emi passed the phone back to him. "Mommy wants to talk to you."

Ian took the phone and cradled it by his ear to hear as he trudged through the snow with Emi in his arms. "Hope, hey. Emi's safe with me. We're heading back now."

There was no answer, so Ian pulled back to look at the phone. It showed the seconds continuing to tick on the call. "Hope?"

"Ian, help!"

Hope's scream through the phone triggered the most paralyzing fear Ian had ever known.

"Hope, what's happening?"

Only the sounds of a struggle came through the phone. Ian looked down at the young child in his arms and faced an impossible choice. With every cell in his body, he wanted to run after Hope and rescue her, but he was responsible for her child. Ian could feel Emi's trembling body, and in that instance, he knew he would do anything to help this frightened girl who had endured way more than any child should in the past few days.

"I need you to hold tight, okay? I'm going to bring you to Nancy and then help your mommy."

Emi nodded against his shoulder and snuggled into his arms in a way that left Ian breathless. He fought back against the longing to feel his own child's arms around him, and concentrated instead on calling Nancy. *Pick up*, he mentally begged, but the phone rang through to voicemail. He could only pray she was rescuing Hope.

As he reached the edge of the sale yard, Ian spied his mother volunteering on the hot cocoa line and called to her. She looked up and must have registered the panic on his face, because she instantly set the ladle down and bustled toward him.

"Emi got lost and needs to be watched with an eagle eye. I have to go find Hope."

His mother took Emi from her arms and didn't ask questions. She just touched his arm and whispered, "I'll pray."

Her mother's touch centered him, and Ian nodded his thanks. "Have you seen Nancy?"

"Last I saw, she and Hope were searching for this one back by the taller trees."

Hope struggled against the man whose arms held her tightly. His gloved hand covered her mouth, and he hissed in her ear, "If you ever want to see that pretty little girl of yours again, you'll stop fighting and come quietly."

Hope stopped struggling at his words. Emi was safe with Ian, but that also meant there was no one to help her, since she and Nancy had separated. She would have to rescue herself. That required a clear head rather than panic. Step one: let him think he'd scared her. She forced her entire body to calm so he'd believe she was cooperating.

"That's better," he muttered.

"What do you want with me?" Hope tried to ask, but his hand was too tight against her mouth, and nothing but garbled sounds emerged.

She fought back against the mind-numbing fear and focused on the man and the way he was holding her. He had one arm wrapped around her neck with his hand over her mouth. The other hand was clutching her left arm as he dragged her backward. That left her right hand free, and because she had taken off her gloves to answer her phone, it wasn't encumbered.

She formulated her plan and then mentally counted backward from three. *Two. One.* She took a deep breath in through her nose, and then made her entire body go limp in his arms. The sudden shift threw him off balance, and she reached up with her free hand to claw at the inside of his wrist where his jacket met his glove.

He groaned in pain, and his hand slipped away from her mouth long enough for her to let out a piercing scream.

"That was a stupid move," the man grunted as he grappled to regain control, but Hope wasn't giving up so easily. She twisted in his grip and raised her hand to his head. She grabbed at his knit cap trying to grasp his hair.

He yanked her arm hard and his hat came off in her hand, exposing a tattoo that snaked up the side of his neck and into his hairline. While her body fought to escape, Hope made her mind focus on memorizing the design of intertwined letters and lines.

He twirled her around and for one terrifying moment, their eyes met. Hope shivered at the darkness that stared back at her. She forced herself to hold his gaze as she put all her force into her leg and kneed him.

He fell back with a howl. Hope turned to flee, and her heart lifted at the sight of Ian emerging through the trees. She wanted to run straight into his arms, but the man had run off through the trees, so instead she called, "Help me! We can't let him get away."

Knowing Ian would follow, she turned and chased the man who moments before had tried to kidnap her. The snow was deeper here, and though that made running more difficult, it was easy to follow his footprints.

Ian easily caught up. He ran beside her long enough to check that she was okay, and then he sprinted ahead. Hope wasn't used to running long distances and between the abduction attempt and the stress of the past few days, she felt her energy fading quickly. She slowed to a light jog and then to a walk, praying that Ian could capture him.

The sound of a car engine starting up dashed that hope, and she struggled to summon the energy to keep going. When she finally broke through the last of the Christmas tree rows, she saw Ian trudging back up the road as a truck disappeared in the distance.

When he saw her, he ran forward and quickly closed the distance between them. He opened his arms, and Hope walked straight into them, collapsing against the strength of him as his arms wrapped around her. *Safe.* She was safe.

All the trauma caught up with her, and she started shivering uncontrollably.

"You're okay, I've got you. You're safe," Ian murmured as he tightened his comforting embrace.

For a few moments, Hope just let herself rest against him, drawing strength from him, trying to ease the anxiety that had her entire body trembling. Eventually, she eased back so she could look up at him. "Emi?"

She tried to form the words to ask where her baby was, but his face was so close, and the expression in his eyes so kind and comforting. She focused on them, trying to erase the fear she'd felt staring into the unfathomable darkness of her abductor's eyes.

Ian reached up to brush some snow from her hair, and his gentle touch was too much. She had to close her eyes against a rush of emotion.

"Emi is with my mother. Let me know when you can walk," he murmured. "I don't know where Nancy is or I'd call her to help."

Hope hung her head. "I tried to find her. I know you said to wait," she added in a rush. "But I was so scared, and it seemed foolish to do nothing when we could cover more ground if I was looking too." She looked up at him again. "I was wrong not to listen to you."

Ian laughed softly. "How hard was that to say?"

Hope pulled back out of his arms and joined in his laughter. "Not as hard as it would have been if you hadn't just rescued me."

"Oh, I don't get any credit for that," Ian said. "From what I could see, you had it all taken care of before I even got here."

Hope felt the admiration in his voice and her heart lightened. "I tried to be smart, not scared." Her fear was receding under his steady presence.

"Smart is always good," he replied. "But healthy fear is important too."

She nodded. "I promise to follow your directions from now on."

His laugh was hearty this time. "That sounds like something the teacher might force you to write fifty times on the board as punishment." His voice grew serious. "It's not something I want to be right about, but if anything, this proved these men know no boundaries and aren't giving up."

Hope shuddered. "What am I going to do?"

He tilted her chin with a gentle fingertip until she met his gaze again. "First thing is to accept you're not alone. I will not leave you until this is completely over, and you and Emi can have your life again."

Hope nodded, thankful for his assurance, but a chasm opened in her heart at his final words. Once this was over, he'd be gone from her life. That thought disturbed her much more than it should.

Ian wrapped his arm around her shoulders. "Let's go find Nancy and Emi. And you can tell me what just happened."

Hope absorbed the comfort of his embrace as she tried to find the words to explain how she'd been caught unawares.

"Nancy and I separated, and I was checking behind the trees. I saw some other people in the distance, but all of a sudden there was an arm around my neck pulling me back behind the trees." She shivered at the memory. "He told me if I ever wanted to see my little girl again, that I had to go with him."

Ian hugged her a little tighter. "I'm sorry. That must have been terrifying."

Hope grinned up at him. "He'd never understand, obviously, but those were fighting words to a mother. He unleashed mama bear. I pretended to go along, but only until I could outsmart him. You appeared right after I broke away."

Hope fell silent. She didn't want to admit to Ian what had made her miss the threat until it was too late. She'd seen a couple, and that had triggered memories of a time when she was young and happy. Once, she had been part of a couple like that, shopping for their first tree right after she'd found out she was pregnant with Emi. Her heart had been so full of hope, so filled to bursting with joy that she was building the family she'd always wanted.

Her parents had been older and occupied with their careers. They'd never said so, but she'd always suspected she was a surprise. A welcome one, but a gift they weren't quite sure what to do with. They'd passed away within a year of each other shortly before she'd married Keith. In the past year, she'd sometimes wondered if maybe she'd been so quick to marry him to recapture the family she had lost.

After Ian called to say he'd found Emi, she'd lost herself in thoughts about how everything had fallen apart. Then the man grabbed her.

"Hope? Earth to Hope?"

She bolted alert and laughed. "That's what I'm always saying to Emi." Her face fell as she remembered the last time she'd said it… Steve had just walked into her office. "I need to call the hospital again and check on Steve."

If Ian was surprised by her abrupt change of topic, he didn't show it.

"Okay, but I think there's someone who's waiting to see you."

Hope looked up, surprised to see they were already back

at the yard. Emi was waving at her, and nothing had ever looked so wonderful. She pulled away from Ian and ran toward her little girl and scooped her up in a hug. "I am never letting you out of my sight again," she whispered as Emi returned the hug.

Chapter Eleven

Emi led Hope to where Ian's mother was waiting by a truck filled with the potted trees. Sarah reached up to give Hope a warm hug.

"Don't tell Ian I said so, but he was right. We're going to take these trees back to my crafting barn and work on them inside."

Hope laughed. "I just told him he was right that Nancy and I should have stayed together."

His mother chuckled. "All the more reason for me not to say it. His head will get too big." She turned to Emi. "What do you say, are you ready to help me make these trees into a feast for the birds and squirrels?"

Emi looked at her shyly. "Can Mommy help?"

"Of course. The more the merrier. And when we're done, we'll go back to the kitchen and bake those cookies you missed out on. How does that sound?"

Emi beamed and looked to her mother for approval. Honestly, Hope thought it sounded exhausting. All she wanted to do was curl up next to a fire and sleep. She stifled a yawn and tried to inject some enthusiasm into her voice. "Sounds like a great plan."

As they climbed into the truck, she looked around for Nancy and Ian. They were standing by the sleigh, and it looked like Nancy was on the receiving end of all the rebukes Ian had spared her. She needed to apologize. It had been her idea after all.

"Don't mind them," Sarah commented in a stage whisper. "They've been having spats like that since they could talk."

Ian and Nancy turned and waved. "I heard that," Ian called.

"Then stop yelling at your sister and come help us get these trees back to the barn."

"Yes, ma'am."

Nancy gave her brother a quick hug before she climbed up in the sleigh and headed back to the reindeer barn. Ian strode over and climbed into the back of the truck.

When they arrived at the barn, Hope was amazed yet again. The door rolled back to reveal what looked like Sarah's personal craft store.

"Wow! I've never seen anything like this," she exclaimed.

"My mother is a one-woman craft army," Ian explained. "All those wreaths and bouquets and decorations you saw for sale at the tree lot—she made all of those to support the veterans' center."

"Stop your nonsense," Sarah tsked, coming up behind them. "We have work to do."

She quickly set Emi and Hope to work making edible ornaments out of birdseed. Once the cakes were formed, Emi got to work using an assortment of cookie cutters, but Hope needed to stand and stretch.

She headed to a remote corner of the barn and tried once again to reach the hospital. She explained that she was Steve's closest living relation—true even if their relationship was friendship. Unfortunately, the nurse on duty was a stickler for rules and wouldn't even confirm that Steve was there. But since the operator had put her through to a floor, Hope decided he must be. She breathed a sigh. If he was in the hospital, that meant that he was at least alive. Ian had promised to bring her to the sheriff tomorrow, so she would beg to stop by the hospital and check for herself.

Nancy had returned from the reindeer barn and was standing guard near the door with Ian. Hope hurried in their direction, but as she drew close, she could overhear snippets of their conversation.

"Stop blaming yourself, Ian."

"They almost got her," Ian replied. "She could have been kidnapped."

"But she wasn't." Nancy crossed her arms as she faced her brother. "You said yourself that she did a fine job of fighting him off. And you got there as quickly as you could."

"Not fast enough to catch him," Ian replied as he paced across the room.

"No, because you were off rescuing her daughter."

"Who should never have been allowed to wander away in the first place."

Nancy walked up to him and put a hand on each shoulder. "Listen to yourself, Ian. Something else is driving this reaction. You have nothing to feel guilty about."

He shook her off and turned away, but Nancy followed, unaware of Hope's approach.

"She's a child. She wandered off chasing a rabbit. Children do that kind of thing. Do you know how many calls law enforcement gets for things like this? It's nerve-wracking for the parents, but it's okay. She was fine."

"Nancy is right." Hope walked into the scene feeling very much like she she'd interrupted something she didn't really understand but needed to correct. "All of this is on me. If I hadn't stowed away in your truck, you and your family wouldn't even have been involved. But now I've brought all of this on you. If anyone is at fault here, it's me. I let Emi wander away, and if I had been more alert, that man never would have had a chance to grab me."

"Nope, nothing like Shelby," Nancy muttered, and somehow Hope felt that was a compliment.

"I'm sorry you took the blame too, Nancy. This is all on me." She turned and glared at Ian. "Your sister did nothing wrong and neither did you." Then, deciding it was time to defuse the tension, Hope turned to both of them. "I'm very sorry I involved you, but you need to know we may never be able to drag Emi out of here. She's hooked."

Nancy laughed. "You've probably realized by now that my mother's life goal was to be Mrs. Claus. She'll be happy to welcome Elf Emi into the fold."

Hope laughed and was surprised to realize how much steadier she felt. "Your family is amazing."

Nancy shrugged. "We've got our good days. But we're just like everyone else—human." She stopped and stared at Ian, "And fallible."

Then Nancy got serious. "This afternoon happened, and we have to learn from it and do better. So, let's talk." She waved Hope over to a sofa and chairs that created a seating area in an alcove by the barn door.

Ian had been silent since Hope's speech, but in what seemed a gesture of reconciliation, he spoke. "There's coffee or tea if you'd like something to drink."

Hope's calm had fled with Nancy's invitation to talk, so she decided a cup of something hot to hold would be a good idea. "Thank you. Coffee would be great. I could use the caffeine boost. I'm not much of an Elf Hope, I'm afraid."

Nancy laughed. "Hang around my mother long enough and you won't have a choice."

As Hope waited for Ian to bring over the coffee, she couldn't help but wish she would have a chance to spend time with his mom. Nancy might think her family was like everyone else, but as an outsider who'd never had anything like this, Hope knew they were truly special.

Ian handed her a mug of steaming coffee and set cream

and sugar on the end table before settling onto the sofa across from her.

"No coffee for Nancy?"

Nancy laughed again. "He's not punishing me. I don't drink it unless I'm on duty." She cleared her throat, and in a voice low enough for just the three of them to hear, began to speak. "After this, we have to acknowledge that the attack at your office was most likely an attempt to kidnap you. Can you think of any idea why?"

Hope was truly shaken hearing Nancy utter the words. Even though she'd come to the same conclusion, it was particularly rattling to hear it confirmed by someone in law enforcement. "I've wracked my brain, but I have no clue."

Nancy persisted. "Is there anything in your life that you can think of that would be a reason people would want something from you?"

Hope thought hard. "Not really. As I told Ian, I live a pretty simple life. When my husband died, Emi and I moved here to take the job with Steve's company. Basically, I work, I take Emi to school, I sleep. Wash and repeat. Add in buy groceries once a week. There's absolutely nothing special about me or my life."

Ian begged to differ. After knowing Hope for slightly less than two days, he already knew there was a lot about her that was special. She was an outstanding mother, a dedicated and creative worker, beautiful, kind, courageous... He caught himself before he got too carried away.

Hope had covered everything about her current life, but there was a glaring question that needed to be asked. He and Nancy had spoken about it earlier. Ian couldn't figure out how to broach the topic of her husband, so he surreptitiously nodded the okay to Nancy.

She picked up on it right away. "Hope, this is delicate, and I know it's extremely personal, but I have to ask. What about your husband? How did he die? Could that have anything to do with this?"

Ian's heart ached as he watched Hope's whole body shrink in on itself, a transformation that deeply troubled him.

"My husband was having an affair. He died in Los Angeles, in a car accident with the woman he'd gone to see."

Her words were robotic, as if she were repeating well-rehearsed lines that relayed the facts and required no emotion. Silence hung heavy in the cold barn air. Ian had no idea what to say to that. He was drowning in all the hurt that swam in her eyes.

Nancy's voice, when she picked up, was gentler than he'd ever heard it. "The woman, did she have family? Could it be someone bent on revenge?"

Hope looked up, horror replacing the despair in her eyes. "I don't know." She hung her head, and her voice was barely audible. "To be honest, I was in such shock at the news that I never even inquired if she had family."

"Do you know her name?"

Watching Hope process that question, Ian suspected that the name haunted her.

"Susan."

She said it so quietly that Ian had to struggle to hear the name, but the pain behind it rang clear.

"I know it's a long shot, but if you can give me a last name, I'll have my people look into it," Nancy assured them. "Moving on, what about work? Any problems there?"

"No."

Ian noted that Hope appeared on steadier ground talking about work.

"Steve has been very successful. The company is doing well. And the program I told you about at lunch, it has been extremely profitable."

"Would anyone have issues with that?"

"Why would anyone have a problem with us being success-ful?" Hope looked genuinely confused by the notion.

Nancy's eyes widened. "Because people can be that way. Any disgruntled employees? Someone who got fired?"

Hope shook her head vehemently. "Not a chance. Steve is one of those bosses who believes in rewarding his employees for their efforts. Everyone got a really nice bonus when the app crossed a million downloads and then an even nicer one when it hit ten million."

"Ten million?" Nancy questioned. "That's a lot of down-loads."

Ian swallowed a laugh at his sister's understatement.

"I'll bring it to our tech guys and see if they have any thoughts," she added.

"If there's anything to do with the finances of the com-pany, I don't know why they'd want me. I'm just the design and marketing person. I have nothing to do with money. You'd need to talk to Steve about that. But we can't do that. I called the hospital. They won't tell me anything, but I got the im-pression he *is* there." She thought a bit more. "Maybe our ac-countant can help."

"I'll check with the hospital and reach out to the head of accounting. But tell me about your relationship with Steve," Nancy prompted.

Hope released a deep sigh, and Ian could see the toll this conversation was taking on her. She looked on the verge of collapse. He loved his sister, and knew she was an excellent agent, but Hope needed a break, so he spoke up.

"It looks like Mom and Emi are finishing up. Why don't we head back to the house, get Hope something to eat, dis-tract Emi, and then we can talk more."

Nancy looked like she wanted to protest but thought bet-ter of it. "Okay."

Once they were back at the house, his mother took charge

as Ian had hoped. She edged Nancy aside and prepared a cup of hot tea and a scone for Hope.

When Hope was settled by the fireplace, and Emi and his mother were up to their elbows in flour and sugar and out of hearing range, Nancy dove right back in with questions that came fast and furious.

Ian, who was sitting beside Hope on the sofa, interrupted. "This is my sister the hard-nosed Fed. Don't let her overwhelm you."

Hope laid a hand on his arm. "It's fine. I can take the hard questions if answering them will help solve this problem and stop the danger."

Ian relented. He knew they were both right, and frankly he wasn't sure where this strong need to protect Hope came from. He could tell himself it was just because he'd witnessed all she'd survived these last few days, but that wouldn't be honest. Deep inside he knew it was something more, something he was feeling that he couldn't allow to develop.

He abruptly stood and paced to the window. As he listened to Hope's soft voice, he couldn't help but be aware of every nuance in her words.

"I told Ian a condensed version of this. Steve and I met in college. My computer crashed when I was in the middle of an important project. I was on the verge of hysterics, but someone told me there were these two guys who were wizards at anything related to computers. I found them and threw myself on their mercy."

She paused and took a sip of her tea, but he sensed she needed the moment to compose herself more than she needed the beverage.

"Steve was one of those guys." She bit her lip and swallowed hard. "My future husband was the other. We clicked and became a trio of sorts. Steve always had a different girlfriend, but the three of us were tight as thieves. When we graduated, they went on to form a business, Keith and I married and life went on pretty much the same. For a time."

Her pause this time was longer and seemed heavier.

"I should have realized something was off when Keith started traveling more. Afterward, I berated myself for a long time, wondering what I could have done differently, wondering if the outcome would have been different if I'd noticed his dissatisfaction sooner."

She visibly shook herself. "I'm sorry. I shouldn't have shared that. My failures as a wife have nothing to do with this." She swiped at a tear. "I really have no idea why anyone would be after me."

Ian ground his fists in his pocket as he listened to the pain that poured out of every word. He understood all too well what it felt like to be left behind. To have so many questions and no way to get answers. To have to go on living when the doubt and grief swamped you.

"So, this is the rest of my sad story, in case you can find any meaning in it," Hope continued. "After Keith died, I was in a pretty bad place—adrift. I had a young child, no money, no ideas, and frankly I was drowning. Steve threw me a lifeline. He relocated the company here to Colorado and offered me the marketing job. That had been my major in college and I'd helped them out when they were getting started—until Emi was born. By then the company was doing well enough that we could afford for me to stay home."

Nancy cleared her throat. "I apologize if this is intrusive, but know I'm asking with our goal in mind."

Hope gave a single nod and waited.

"If the business was doing so well, why were you destitute when your husband died?"

Hope buried her face in her hands for a moment before sitting up and stiffening her back. It was all Ian could do not to envelop her in a hug, but he had no right.

When Hope spoke again, there was a bitterness he hadn't

heard before. "Apparently my husband had developed a taste for the good things in life. He'd wiped out our accounts. I suppose supporting your family while entertaining another woman can do that to you, regardless of your business success."

"Did he have ownership in the company?"

"Initially, when they founded the business, yes. But I found out that Steve bought out most of his shares. We've never spoken of it, but I think Steve knew more than he let on, and I think he felt guilty about how it left me." She wrapped her arms across her chest and hugged them close. "It was never his fault. I didn't blame him."

Nancy sat back, and Ian read the frustration on her face. "I'll do some digging, see what I can find out." She looked at her phone and sighed. "I spoke to the sheriff while you were moving up here from the barn."

"Did he know anything about what happened?"

"No, different sheriff. Our ranch is in a different county than your office. I explained what happened out at the lot today and connected it to the other events. He said he would check in with law enforcement investigating the events at your office, but in the meantime, he'd send a deputy out to investigate the tree lot. I'm afraid he's going to want to talk to you. I just got a text that he's down by the road, so I'll meet him."

Ian knew Nancy had been right to call the sheriff, but right now he didn't appreciate her bringing more difficulty to Hope. Then his sister surprised him.

Nancy walked over to the sofa and sat in the spot Ian had vacated. She grasped both of Hope's hands in hers and said the words that had been burning in Ian's heart.

"Don't ever consider yourself a failure. He was the one who broke his vows. Don't waste any time worrying about it." She hung her head a moment. "I get that it's hard when you have unanswered questions." Nancy's voice cracked. "But you have made a new life for yourself and your beautiful little girl. Celebrate that. Ian and I will do everything in our power to help you reclaim it. Right, little brother?"

Ian wanted to go hug his sister tight, but he knew she'd resent it, so he joked instead. "In this family we have learned to always follow Nancy's directions."

Chapter Twelve

The visit to the sheriff's office the next morning frustrated Hope. She'd endured another humiliating round of the same questions the deputy had asked the previous evening, and received nothing in return. No news about the attack, and the only information she had about Steve came from Nancy's sources. He was in a medically induced coma. His close friend, Helen, was with him—no surprise there. Helen was his admin and could talk her way into anything—but no other visitors were allowed.

Hope struggled with that as they drove back to the ranch. More than almost anything, she wanted to be the one by his side. But she had to stay with Emi, because the attack yesterday proved they were still in danger from an unknown source.

"Did you know that reindeers' eyes change color?"

Emi's cheerful voice broke into Hope's thoughts. "What, sweetie?"

Emi held up the book she was reading. "Nancy gave me this book about reindeer. It says their eyes are gold in the summer but turn blue in the winter."

"That's interesting," Hope replied. "What else did you learn?"

"That they have hairy noses and their hooves are like snow shovels."

Emi turned back to her book, reading and occasionally sharing reindeer trivia. Hope stared out the window at the passing scenery and mined her memories for anything that would explain the trouble they were in.

Eventually the rhythm of the car lulled Emi to sleep. Hope carefully removed the book from her lap. Since Ian was driving and Nancy was doing work, Hope opened her phone to check her own work email.

Immediately, a text message popped up. A scream rose in her throat, but she swallowed the sound as she felt Emi shift beside her.

"What's wrong?" Ian asked.

"I just got a text message. It's a photo. Here." She handed the phone to Nancy, not willing to risk Emi overhearing her describe it. The photo showed them at the tree lot. There was a sniper's crosshairs superimposed on Emi's head. Below the image was a demand.

Pay up or you'll pay a higher price.

Hope started to shake uncontrollably. "What does this mean? How am I supposed to pay if I don't know who or what this is?"

Ian focused on the demand. "We have to presume this is connected to the attack at your workplace. It must involve Steve. Are you sure you don't know anything?"

"I don't." Frustration laced with fear in her voice. "And we can't ask him if he's in a coma."

"Is there anyone else you could ask?"

"Helen. She's his dear friend as well as his admin. If anyone knows anything, she would."

Nancy handed her phone back and Hope called, but it went straight to voicemail. She left a message begging Helen to reply immediately. "I'll email her and explain in case she tries to contact me when we aren't in range."

Hope opened her work email and was immediately overwhelmed with hundreds of company emails. Most were from coworkers checking on her and expressing condolences. Guilt swamped her. She'd been so busy trying to stay alive that she hadn't even thought about her coworkers' reactions.

She clicked on her important-email tab, and her heart thudded as she saw one from Steve. She opened it and scanned through, but her hands were trembling so badly she could barely hold the phone. She handed it to Nancy again. "You read it."

Nancy started to read aloud.

"Hope, if you are reading this, I'm probably in trouble. Our company has been threatened. I have it under control, but this is my backup plan. I'm composing this email so you'll have all the facts, but each day I'll reschedule it. You'll only receive it if I have been unable to access my email for 24 hours. Not to be excessively dramatic, but if you are reading this, something (most likely very bad) has happened to me.

Two months ago, when Twelve Days 'til Christmas was climbing the charts and being hailed as the marketing coup and top app of the season, I received an anonymous threat. It was a ransomware demand. I didn't take it seriously, so what followed falls squarely on my shoulders.

I was not worried.

I should have been.

Last week, I received the most serious demand yet. If I do not pay the asking price (which has now quadrupled from the original outrageous demand), they will hold their own grand finale and reveal that they have stolen all the data from our subscribers and will put it up for sale on the dark web."

Nancy stopped reading and shot Ian a look.

"Is that it?" Hope prompted.

"No." She read on.

"Call me arrogant (and you will because you know me so well), but I was not willing to surrender our hard-earned money to these criminals. I decided to dig into the app and find out how they found an entry point and if they had stolen our data.

I found a malicious code that makes the app crash. When it does, you have to input your information again to regain access. The link they give within the app is a portal—to their mother ship.

By now you're probably calling me every name in the Greek alphabet and not in a good way. I know I should have sought help, but who better to reverse engineer this than the man who created it in the first place?

Sadly, I must admit that if you're reading this, I've failed. That pains me because it means I have been unable to stop these villains in their plan to release all the private information of our Christmas family. My platform, that was supposed to be a source of comfort and security, is on the verge of becoming every family's cybersecurity nightmare.

I'm sorry."

Silence settled in the car as Nancy finished reading.

Outside a few snowflakes sifted through the air, but inside the tension was thick.

Ian was the first to speak. "First we have to determine if this was actually written by Steve."

Hope swallowed past the lump in her throat. "It sounds like him. *Portal. Mother ship.* Steve geeks out over sci-fi. His first college project was a design that let you travel into the spaceship with the aliens and go on adventures. It was sort of a mashup of all his favorite movies."

Ian laughed. "Steve sounds like an interesting guy."

"He's the best."

Hope caught the look Ian and Nancy exchanged. "No." She shook her head. "Not that way. There was never anything romantic between us. He's my best friend. We connect in some inexplicable platonic way.

"Anyway, this sounds completely like Steve, down to the admission of arrogance. He is very arrogant about his tech ability. He's amazingly creative and just sees things in a way others don't. We need to go see him."

"As you said, he's in a coma," Ian objected.

"People in comas hear things. Maybe if he hears my voice he'll respond."

Ian expressed his unease. "They said no other visitors, and given the text you received, I don't think we can risk it. Helen is there. Let's do a video chat with her when we're back at the ranch. My mother can occupy Emi."

Reluctantly, Hope agreed and sent a text praying Helen would see it and consent to a meeting.

Once they were back at the ranch, Ian had Nancy set up the meeting on a secure server. When they were all gathered, and Helen logged on, he asked Hope to do the introductions and take the lead as they got right to business.

"Helen, can you check your emails?" Hope asked, after she had updated her on the situation. "Steve scheduled an email to me that would be sent if he couldn't access his email. Maybe he sent you one, too."

Helen looked confused and doubtful but she opened her phone. She rolled her eyes. "There are hundreds of them."

"Search for the most recent one from Steve."

A moment passed, then Helen gasped. "You're right."

Ian watched impatiently as Helen read through the email. He wanted to tell her to read it out loud, but from the delicate flush on her cheeks he suspected there were private parts to it that she might not care to share.

When she finally finished, she spoke to Hope in a broken voice. "I can't read it aloud. I'll forward it so you can."

After Hope scanned the email, she spoke to Helen in a tender voice. "Are you sure you're okay with me reading this?"

Helen's eyes glimmered with a mix of tears and something Ian couldn't quite identify. But she nodded. "I don't know if anything he wrote will help, but we have to see. We have to find who did this to him and stop them from hurting families who trusted us. Share whatever you need."

Steel, Ian decided. That's what he'd seen in her eyes. The same solid determination that he'd found in Hope.

Hope read:

"My dearest Helen,
If you are reading this, most likely I am no longer alive."

Hope looked up and smiled bravely at Helen. "You'll get the chance to tell him he's wrong."

Helen choked on a laugh. "That might just kill him."

Ian had a sudden uncomfortable sense of being an outsider. There was nothing surprising in that. These three had worked closely together for years on something that clearly was very personally important to them.

Hope spoke again. "I'm skimming over this. The first part is basically what he wrote in my email, but this is different.

'It was terribly unfair of me to allow you to work these long nights without telling you why we were doing it. I should have explained and taken better advantage of your expertise. I sent a copy of the codes to Hope, but she won't know what they mean.'"

Hope made a disgruntled sound, and Ian thought he heard her muttering under her breath.

She looked at Helen. "What is he talking about? He didn't

give me anything. There are no codes in my email." She paused and glanced at Ian. "It gets personal after that, his appreciation of Helen. No need to share it."

Helen shook her head. "Go to the last paragraph."

Hope read.

"I've instructed Victor to pay them before Christmas Eve to stop the release of information. My company, this app are worth nothing compared to the lives that will be ruined."

Silence descended over them, and in it they could hear the faint beep of the machines breathing life into Steve.

"No," Hope whispered. "We can't pay. We can't give in."

Tears streamed down Helen's face. "I understand why you want to fight, Hope. This was your baby as much as Steve's. You poured all of yourself into making it a success. But we can't put the company before the people." Her voice cracked. "Steve wouldn't want that."

Hope waved her off. "That's not it. It's not about me. It's about all the families who trusted us."

She looked at Ian and then at Nancy. "Do you really believe if we pay this ransom that will be the end of it? Will they really just say, *Thanks, we'll trash all the data we stole?*"

Nancy slowly shook her head.

Hope closed her eyes a moment, then faced Ian. "I know you didn't sign on for this, but I have to fight it. I have to stop them."

Nancy laughed. "You don't know my brother. Those are fighting words you just gave him." She looked with love at her brother. "Ian never could stand a bully."

Helen spoke up, and Ian noted that she looked calmer, determined. "What do we do?"

Everyone turned to Nancy.

"I can start," she offered. "I know who to call. There's a Joint Ransomware Task Force. I'll call my friend in IC3—

that's our internet crime compliance center. They're the initial contact for anyone who has been a victim of a ransomware attack."

"Helen." Hope's voice softened. "I think you should stay there with Steve." Helen started to protest halfheartedly, but Hope stopped her. "He's in critical condition. Talk to him, see if you can get through to him. We need him, and to be honest, we need his brain working to defeat these guys."

Helen gave a sad smile. "I won't leave his side."

"What am I doing, boss?" Ian teased.

Hope smiled shyly. "Sorry, I just feel really strongly about this."

"And I'll do whatever I can to help."

After Nancy ended the conference, Hope headed back into the main part of the house. She was happy with their decision, but the sniper's target on Emi's photo preyed on her mind, and she needed time with her little girl.

She stepped into the kitchen and found herself in a Christmas bakeshop. Emi and Sarah had been making cookies, so cinnamon and vanilla scented the air. Emi came rushing toward her covered in butter, flour and sugar. Hope had never in her life been so happy to see anyone. She fell to her knees, and Emi rushed into her arms, giving her a huge hug that felt like love and smelled like everything Christmas.

Hope wrapped her arms around her daughter, and while she hugged Emi tight, she absorbed her surroundings. Ian's mom was wearing her red apron and a smile. The fire in the great room snapped and crackled while soft Christmas music played over the sound system, and the tree was lit with presents piled beneath it. Love filled the air.

This what she had been trying to capture in the community of their app. This sense of family and holiday joy, everything that had been missing from her own life.

It was what Steve had been trying to infuse into a virtual

community. Their app was meant to celebrate the holidays with family in every sense—whether biological or found, in real time or virtual. It would be fun for families together, and a haven for those without. It brought love and joy and peace—all the things that Christmas was supposed to be. That's what she was fighting for, and she would do everything in her power to save it from some grinch-like villain.

"Mommy!" Emi squirmed in her embrace. "You didn't tell me you posted my picture with Splasher."

"Hmm, what?"

Emi ran and grabbed her device, waving it at Hope. "I thought we were saving it for reindeer-games day."

Hope glanced at the photo, and her mind froze.

"Emi, I think your mommy needs to talk to Ian and Nancy. Why don't you come help me make a plate of cookies for them?"

Hope roused herself enough to nod her thanks to Sarah. She kept the device and went in search of Ian, because the stakes had just been raised. The photo from the tree lot had been bad enough. But this photo—this was the one Ian took on her phone. And somebody had posted it to her account on the platform.

Ian took one look at Hope's ashen face and jumped to his feet. "What's wrong?"

She held out Emi's device, and he looked at the photo he'd taken of Hope and Emi with the reindeer. "You posted it? Maybe not the wisest—"

"I didn't post it. Emi just showed it to me. Someone hacked my phone."

Hope looked on the verge of collapse, so Ian guided her to the sofa.

Nancy joined them. "Hope, we need to talk about something. Ian and I had just been considering moving to a safe house because of the sniper photo from earlier. This reinforces it. I know you're going to object to my suggestion, but please think carefully about what is best for Emi."

Hope stared at her calmly, but Ian could feel the tremors wracking her body. He rested his hand on her arm to steady her.

"We have a friend. His name is Adam. He's a very good man with a wife and little girl. We think you should send Emi to stay with them until this is resolved."

Hope pulled away from Ian and jumped to her feet. "I can't do that! I can't send my daughter away with a stranger."

"I know he's a stranger to you, but he's a good friend of ours. We wouldn't suggest this unless we felt it was absolutely the best way to keep Emi safe."

"But you're strangers too. I'm sorry, I know that sounds awful after all you've done for me, but she's my baby girl."

Ian came and wrapped his arms around her. "It's because she's your very precious baby girl that we want to protect her from the evil person behind this."

"Why can't I go with her?"

Ian swallowed hard. "Because somehow this is all tied to you." He let that sink in before continuing. "Adam has the most secure house I've ever been in. Emi will be safe with his family, and you will be able to focus on helping us take down the enemy without worrying about them hurting her."

Tears filled Hope's eyes as she stared at them in disbelief.

"Talk to his wife Isabelle, at least," Nancy suggested. "I think you'll feel better about this if you do."

Numb with grief, Hope took the phone. She couldn't believe she was even considering sending her baby away. But as she glanced at the photo on her own phone and remembered the sniper image, she knew she'd make the hard choice, even if it broke her heart.

Chapter Thirteen

They decided on Christmas Village for the handoff, hoping that the crowds of tourists would provide anonymity for the switch. The irony of the setting was painfully apparent to Hope as she wandered the streets with Emi before stopping in front of a storefront to chat with Adam. She finally got to visit Christmas Village, only to be separated from her mother.

Ian and Nancy had been right though. The conversation with Isabelle had calmed many of Hope's fears. Meeting Adam now, she immediately knew he would stop at nothing to protect her daughter. Emi was nervous, but Hope pasted on a fake smile and told her it was a great adventure to meet a new friend. Perhaps too wise for her years, Emi put up no fight.

They pulled the switch in a busy restaurant, and once Adam left with her daughter, Hope couldn't hold back her tears any longer. Ian reached across the table and clasped her hands. She knew he only meant to comfort her, and their hands in each other's felt so right that she held on to his strength and let it fill her.

When she thought she could speak without her voice crack-ing, she lifted her head and looked across at him. Her voice could barely be heard above the clamor of the restaurant, and he leaned in to hear.

"When I was a child, and I read the Narnia books, I always wondered how a mother could send her children away to live with a complete stranger." She shuddered. "Then I grew up and learned about Operation Pied Piper. I understood it on an intellectual level, but it still horrified me." She bowed her head a moment, then looked up at him, her eyes a sheen of tears. "Today, I understand in my heart."

"A mother's sacrifice to save her children. You're very brave, Hope."

She shook her head. "Not brave at all. Just confused and desperate."

"For what it's worth, my mother thinks you made the right choice. And I might be prejudiced, but I think she's one of the all-time greatest mothers, so you should take it as a compliment."

"She thinks that, really?"

Ian smiled. "She feels awful that you were dealt such a bad hand, but she very much admires the way you've handled it."

"It's not like I've had much choice."

"Maybe she's just used to how badly I manage." Ian winked, trying to make her smile.

"The great Ian Fraser is not perfect?" Hope's attempt to rally fell flat.

"Great, huh? I could get used to that."

Hope listened to his joking words, but they rang hollow. Something in the conversation felt off. She couldn't identify what, but something had shifted in his expression when he was talking about a mother's sacrifice. "A penny for your thoughts?"

Ian shook his head, though Hope sensed it was more to clear it than to refuse her.

"Just thinking that enough time has passed. We should get to the house and start searching for this clue," Ian urged.

That had been their other reason for choosing Christmas Village. Thinking of Steve's last-minute gift of the tickets and ski chalet, and his urgent attempt to make her accept, had given Hope the idea that they might find the codes there. It was the only thing she could think of.

They headed out of the restaurant. Soft snowflakes were falling. Combined with the twinkling white lights on every building, they created an air of enchantment. Anger suddenly surged through Hope.

"Penny for *your* thoughts now," Ian teased.

She looked up at him and saw he had picked up on the anger that blazed in her heart.

"I'm just so…so… *Mad* doesn't even come close. Look at this place. Emi was deliriously happy when we got here, but she never even got a chance to enjoy it because these people—whoever they are—have some diabolical plan. What scrooges!"

Ian laughed. "Meet Lioness Hope. The mama who would probably bring down a king if he hurt her little girl."

"Or die trying," Hope replied without thinking.

They both fell silent, the realization that that was entirely possible hitting home with thunderous force.

They got in the car and traveled the short distance to the ski chalet Steve had borrowed for them. Hope's anger resurged as they approached the beautiful log-cabin-style home fully decorated for Christmas. When they entered and found the same holiday wonderland effect inside, tears once again slid down Hope's cheeks.

"Steve had the house decorated for Emi." She swiped away the tears. "He knows her so well. She would have adored spending two weeks here." She smiled wistfully. "She'd have imagined she was living inside her favorite book, only in Colorado rather than Wisconsin."

Ian came up beside her and drew her into a hug. "I'm sorry. Emi doesn't deserve any of this mess, and neither do you."

Once again Hope drew strength from his support. Her resolve strengthened. She would do whatever it took to overcome this, to take these men down and restore her daughter's life to normal.

She moved away and headed into the room to where a stack of presents sat beneath a towering, fully decorated Christmas tree. "Oh, Steve." She sighed and glanced back at Ian hovering in the doorway. "Come on in and let's get started. This might take a while."

"But they're your presents."

"No time for sentimentality. We have to find whatever it is that will explain why they're after me."

She was already on her knees, tearing open the first package, but she froze and let out a soft cry as she unwrapped a book. "What did I tell you? Just look at how the cover is such a close match to this chalet." The tears that seemed ever present since she'd sent Emi off with Adam welled yet again. "Steve has been a better father figure to Emi than her father ever was." Impatiently, she swiped a hand across her face and jumped up. "Will you keep looking? I need to call Helen and check on how Steve is doing." She grabbed the phone from her pocket and smiled sadly at Ian as she hit the call button. "Dive in. Pretend you're a kid on Christmas morning. I'll just rewrap them whenever I get to give them to Emi."

By the time Hope competed her phone call and returned to Ian, he was sitting in a pile of wrapping paper with presents piled around him. A small pile of yet-to-be-opened gifts still sat beneath the tree. "Nothing yet?"

He shrugged. "Plenty of stuff to keep Emi in books and crafts for the next decade, but I don't see anything that looks remotely like a code. What's the report on Steve?"

Hope knew her face was glowing every bit as brightly as the Christmas tree as she answered. "Great news. They started bringing him out of the coma this morning. Helen says so far things are looking good. The doctors are pleased."

"Excellent news. I don't suppose he's coherent enough yet to explain all this?"

Hope shook her head. "Helen said it's a matter of layers. They do it slowly. He's still on a ventilator."

"Then back to work. Maybe we can have good news for him when he's finally fully conscious."

As Hope settled down beside him, he explained his system. "I don't know if it was intentional, but I noticed there are different wrapping papers, so I started opening the ones that were the same as Emi's book. They all seem to be for her. I left you the ones in the other paper, presuming they were personal to you."

"Thanks."

"Steve sure is generous," Ian commented as they continued to dig through the pile of presents.

"He is. He's absolutely brilliant, and he has a heart of gold. That's what confuses me so much about this. All the employees love him and he has no enemies that I know of."

"His industry is highly competitive. You never know who might be looking to take him down out of spite."

Hope shivered at the thought. "Why do people have to be so evil?"

Ian smiled gently. "No wonder my mother likes you so much. You have a gentle heart."

"I'll take that as a compliment—" Hope stopped abruptly as she noticed one more present tucked deep into the branches at the bottom of the tree. "Ian, look. The wrapping on that one doesn't match any of the others."

Every trace of fatigue fell away as Hope crawled under the tree to retrieve the present. She knew Ian's interest was piqued when he knelt beside her on the floor. Her fingers were trembling from excitement, making her fumble as she tried to unwrap the box. She flexed them and carefully undid the paper.

"Pretty amazing patience," Ian murmured. "I'd be tearing into it."

Hope glanced up at him, his face so close to hers that she felt herself sucked into the blue depths of his eyes. Suddenly she was very warm despite the chill in the house. She forced her gaze back to the package, and a thought occurred to her. "What if I'm destroying evidence by opening it?"

She sat back on her heels. "Maybe I shouldn't open it at all. What do you think?"

"It's not impossible," Ian answered slowly as he thought through the implications. "But we can't know without opening it. Steve said he sent it to you. He obviously had a reason. Just open it carefully."

Hope's fingers itched to rip the paper from the box, but she sighed deeply. He was right. Slowly she slid a finger under the tape, loosened it and eased the edges of the paper apart. She opened the box, and gently lifted the present from the box. "It's just a Christmas ornament." She sagged back, looking from the present to Ian. "I don't understand. What about a Christmas ornament could be so important that they would track me? Could we have misunderstood?"

"No." Ian picked up the ornament and rolled it around in his hand. "I think this might actually be what he meant."

Hope shook her head. "He gives Emi an ornament for the tree every year. He's been doing it since she was born. That's probably why it's wrapped differently."

"No. Look. See this seam of glue? I don't think that's original. It looks like someone forced it open and then resealed it. You wouldn't notice it unless you were specifically looking, and someone just seeing it hanging on the tree would never suspect anything." Ian handed her the ornament. "It's kind of ingenious, really. He sent it as a clue, but if nothing had happened to him, and he'd been able to stop the attack, you would never have even known there was something there."

"Presuming there is," Hope added.

"Only one way to find out. There should be a knife in the

kitchen. Let's try to open it. I promise, if it's nothing, I'll fix it before Emi sees it."

Hope followed him into the kitchen and set the beautiful ornament on the table. It was a heavy ball shape decorated with a Currier and Ives scene labeled Christmas Past. As she studied the print, Hope mentally tipped her hat to Steve. He'd found an ornament that captured all the joy they'd been trying to create with their Twelve Days 'til Christmas platform.

She turned to Ian, who was waiting with a paring knife. "Let's do this, Doc."

Ian chuckled as he held the ornament steady with one hand and carefully slid the knife along the seam, rotating the ball as he went. When he finished, he set the knife aside and gently twisted the top and bottom in opposite directions. It split easily into two halves, and Hope gasped. Nestled inside the bottom half was a flash drive wrapped in plastic.

She threw her arms up in the air and did a little happy dance. "We did it! We found it."

Impulsively, she flung her arms around Ian and hugged him. "Thank you. Thank you for keeping at it with me." When she stepped back, she was still bubbling with happiness. "Now all we have to do is bring this to Nancy's team and see what they can figure out."

Ian stepped aside and gathered the pieces up. "We'd better get going then. It's going to be dark before long. I'll call Adam and alert him while you get ready."

Hope glanced out the window at the sky and was shocked to see how much of the day had faded away. The mountains glowed with the reflection of the setting sun, and a soft pink haze filled the pale sky as dusk settled. She wasn't eager to head to her safe house without Emi, but nothing about staying here would fill the emptiness in her heart.

Deciding it was better to leave the presents behind for now, Hope stuck the flash drive in an inside pocket of her parka and headed back to the front of the house. She pulled up short at the front door as movement outside caught her attention. "Ian," she whispered. "Please tell me I'm imagining that there are men out there by our car."

Ian came up behind her, and resting his hands on her shoulders, he peered out the window. She felt the frustration roll through his body.

"Won't lie," he muttered. "There are men out there, but now they are under our car."

"Do you think they're installing a tracking device?"

"At best."

"And at worst?" She felt his hands tense on her shoulders before he answered.

"They're planting explosives."

Hope couldn't stop the tremors that rolled through her body. "What do we do?"

"You have the flash drive?"

She nodded against his shoulder. "I just zipped it into the inside pocket of my coat."

"Okay. When I was searching before, I noticed snowmobiles outside. Have you ever driven one?"

"A few times. I'm no expert, but I can drive in a straight line."

Ian glanced out the window again. The men were still under the car. "Let's make our escape out the back while they're busy. Make sure you're completely bundled. I'll grab some helmets."

Quietly and efficiently, they gathered their belongings and hurried to the back exit. Ian found the snowmobile keys hanging by the back door. He grabbed them and they silently headed into the yard. The house backed onto an open field of snow that spread out across the valley toward the base of the mountains.

"If we hurry, they'll have no way to follow," Ian murmured as he made sure she was properly set up on her machine and checked the fuel gauge before he settled onto his own.

Hope hit the kill switch, inserted the key into the ignition and turned it to the on position. She released the choke and waited for Ian. At his signal, they simultaneously pulled on their cords. Hope didn't know if Ian was praying, but she certainly was.

The engines revved and caught, and Hope switched to a prayer of profound gratitude.

Ian gestured for her to lead the way. Hope swallowed her fear and let the machine shoot forward. They'd only made it about a hundred yards before shouts heralded men emerging from the side of the building. She glanced over her shoulder only once, but it was enough to see rifles aimed in her direction. Remembering how the men had zigzagged several days ago to avoid Ian's shots, she did the same.

Powder kicked up beside her as the shots landed alarmingly close. "Ian," she shouted, worried that he was behind her and more of a target.

"Right here," he shouted back, his words barely audible over the whine of the snowmobiles. Riding in elaborate figure eights, Ian attempted to draw their fire away from Hope, but it seemed that only one of them had a target on their back. And that was her.

Gradually, they drew out of range, and Ian's whole body sagged in relief. He gestured to Hope, and pulled up beside her. "I think we've lost them," he called.

"I hope so," she replied. "I'd hate to be driving the whole way with them shooting at me."

He nodded. "We'll slow the pace now that we've lost them. I want to stay low and take it easy. With this new snowfall, there's the risk of avalanche if we go too high or too hard."

Hope's expression suddenly had a *Now he tells me* quality to it, and Ian had to fight back a laugh. She had to be one of the most courageous and resilient women he'd ever encountered. "Try to appreciate the beauty around you," he said with a wink.

Hope smiled and gazed at the snow-covered mountains. "God's handiwork is amazing."

Yes, it is, Ian thought as they moved forward, but he wasn't thinking of the mountains and sky. Appreciating Hope's beautiful heart came easily, but despite how much he tried to ignore it, he couldn't deny that her stunning physical beauty took his breath away. But that wasn't what he should be focusing on, now...or ever.

For a while they cut across the lower side of the mountain, and Ian let his tension unspool as they zipped along the tree line. The stars were starting to emerge in the deepening twilight, but the moon had yet to rise over the mountain. The still night air brought peace to his soul.

But peace didn't last long.

The unmistakable whine of approaching snowmobiles echoed across the mountains. Ian saw Hope's body go rigid. He should have known better than to let down his guard. This enemy didn't know the meaning of defeat. Every single time he thought he'd outsmarted them, they reappeared. If they weren't so dangerous, he'd admire their perseverance.

He glanced over his shoulder, but he couldn't see anyone behind them. He looked to Hope, who was pointing upward. Turning his head, Ian saw two snowmobiles steadily climbing the mountain above him, and his heart sank. If they triggered an avalanche, he and Hope would be directly in its deadly path.

The thought had barely entered his mind, when he saw one of the figures swing his arm and fling something.

Ian watched the arc of the object and rage filled him as he realized they must have hurled whatever device they'd earlier been planting on the car. He held his breath, hoping it would sputter and die. Instead, a deafening explosion echoed across the mountain as the device detonated.

Ian prayed hard, but he knew there was little chance they hadn't intentionally triggered an avalanche. Where would the snow crack, and which way would the avalanche head? As the low rumble started, and the shelf of snow started to fall away, Ian knew the answer was not in their favor. "Hope," he bellowed. "Head to the right side. As fast as you can!"

Chapter Fourteen

Panic thrummed along Hope's nerves. Everywhere around her the mountain was exploding in a river of snow. *Dear Lord, help us.*

"Hope."

Ian's voice was a lifeline she could barely hear over the roar of the avalanche.

"Head to the side!" He was yelling and pointing, but all she could see was a massive wave of white cascading toward her.

"Turn hard right. Your only chance is to get to the side."

By this time, Hope wasn't even sure where the side was, but she yanked hard on her snowmobile, sending it shooting off to the right moments before the first wave of snow crashed down on them. She squeezed the accelerator as hard as she could, and the machine rode the snow as she pushed through to the edge. She turned back to ask Ian if this was far enough, but he wasn't there.

Terror poured through her. "Ian," she screamed at the top of her lungs. "Ian! Where are you? *Ian!*"

She could hear nothing over the thunderous roar of wave upon wave of snow.

Fear threatened to paralyze her, but she knew Ian's only

chance at survival could very well depend on her. She had to find him. Hope pushed the snowmobile harder and raced down the slope parallel to the path of the avalanche.

Her heart caught at the sight of his snowmobile upended against a tree, but there was no sign of Ian nearby. As the snow rushed past, she braked and jumped off, forgetting she was still attached until the cord pulled loose and her engine cut off. Furiously, she dug through the snow looking for any sign Ian had been buried beneath the machine. She screamed his name until she was hoarse as she scoured the snow for a hint of his hunter green jacket or blue helmet, but all around her was nothing but an endless sea of white.

"Ian." Her voice faded to a whisper as despair overcame her. He'd been caught up in the avalanche because of her. He'd put her safety first. And he wouldn't have even been here were it not for her. Grief and guilt threatened to swamp her as surely as the snow had buried him. She couldn't give up. She owed him too much. But what could she do? Everything she'd heard about avalanches emphasized how little time you had to rescue someone, but night was falling rapidly and she couldn't even find where to look.

She fell to her knees in the snow. "Lord help me," she begged. "Give me the courage, lead me to your faithful servant, Ian."

She stood and brushed off the snow. Yes, it was dark, but the nearly full moon was rising, casting a glow over the snow-covered mountain. Determined to find Ian, she picked her way along the edge of the avalanche's path, calling his name, stopping to listen for a reply or search for any sign of him. Now that the avalanche had finished its downhill rush, an eerie silence was left behind. Over and over, she called his name into the void.

"Hope."

Her heart lifted. Was it him? She called again, but only silence echoed back. Had he really called her name, or was she hallucinating in the cold?

"Ian," she called again and again as she trudged through the snow, conscious that with every passing moment, the chance of rescue grew slimmer.

"Hope."

The muffled voice carried on the wind, and Hope spun in circles trying to see anything in the moonlight. "Ian, where are you? I can hear you but I can't see you."

"Hope, help."

His voice was fading and panic shot through her. "Don't give up. I'm here. I'll help you."

"Over here. Quick."

Hope squinted into the shadows cast by the mountain. There, just to the left of a tree she saw an arm moving feebly. "Ian, I see you. I'm coming."

Heart pounding, she pushed through the piles of snow and rock that had come to a rest at the foot of the mountain. When she finally reached him, she fell to her knees and wanted to do nothing more than kiss him.

Shocked at her own reaction, she shook herself. The man was buried up to his neck in snow and needed serious help, not romance. Setting aside her foolishness, she started pawing at the snow around his chest. She remembered seeing a video of someone being rescued. The focus had been on first clearing the snow from his head, but then relieving the pressure around his chest so he could breathe.

"How did you survive that?" she asked. "I thought... I..." She stopped herself. He didn't need her fear or her guilt. "Can you breathe okay now?"

Ian nodded and took deep breaths of the cold, crisp air. Now that his second arm was free, he could help her loosen the snow encasing him.

"I think if you can stand and loop your arms through mine, I can use the leverage to push free."

Hope scrambled to her feet. "Like this?" she asked as she crossed behind him and fell to her knees again. She wrapped her arms under his and clasped them across his chest, then leaned back against her heels, pulling with all her might.

The first try loosened him a little, but she couldn't pull him free.

"My legs feel like they're encased in cement."

"Should I try to dig around them more?"

"No, let's just try this another time."

She resumed her position and rocked back hard on her heels. Slowly his body began to slide free.

"One more time, I think," Ian said.

Hope heard the strain in his voice. "Give yourself a moment to rest."

"Can't," he rasped. "Snow keeps filling back in."

"Okay, this is it," Hope promised. "We'll do this together. Teamwork."

She locked her arms around his chest and pulled with everything she had. Sheer determination, fueled by thoughts of the debt she owed him, gave her a superhuman strength. She pulled and pulled, feeling the resistance lessen. "Now, on three. One, two, three."

She closed her eyes to concentrate, putting everything into the final lift, and pulled.

As if being released from a giant suction cup, Ian's body slid free, but the momentum carried them over on their backs. Hope took a deep breath and opened her eyes only to find Ian's face mere inches from hers, his deep blue eyes staring gratefully down at her.

Their gazes locked, and for a long breathless moment no one said a word.

Slowly he lowered his head until his lips caressed hers, and then he kissed her with all the heightened emotion of a man who had just escaped death's grasp.

* * *

Cold wind blowing up the mountain brought Ian crashing back to reality. He pulled back, horrified that he'd let emotion overwhelm his sanity. Poor Hope must think he'd lost his mind.

"I'm so sorry," he whispered, searching for the courage to face her. But when he gazed into her eyes, he saw reflected back at him the same mix of awe and regret that he was feeling. "I don't know what came over me."

Hope smiled tremulously. "A brush with death, no doubt."

He agreed, because that made it easier on both of them, but the lingering taste of her kiss made him doubt the explanation was that easy. He pushed the thoughts away. Better that he focus on how to get out of here.

"I'm guessing my snowmobile is a loss."

Hope gulped, and he suddenly remembered hearing her screaming his name. He imagined relief that he wasn't dead might explain away her kiss too.

"It's crashed against a tree."

"Is yours still functioning?"

"I think so. I left it higher up the mountain when I was looking for you. I'll go get it."

"You don't need to go alone. I can come with you." Or did she want an excuse to get away from him?

"I'm just worried about your strength. You should rest."

He shook his head. "Not necessary. I'll probably crash later. No pun intended. But for now, I'm running on pure adrenaline."

They hiked back up the mountain, careful not to dislodge any more snow. As they passed the twisted wreckage of the snowmobile he'd been riding, Ian whispered a prayer of gratitude.

"The minute I knew I couldn't get to the side in time, I jumped off the machine. I've heard that the best thing you can do if caught in an avalanche is to try to swim with it, so that's what I did. I pretended I'd caught an ocean wave and swam as I tumbled downhill."

Hope shuddered. "I can't even imagine how terrifying it was."

He grasped her hand. "Probably pretty similar to how you felt when you saw the snowmobile and couldn't find me."

Hope hung her head a minute before she stopped and looked up straight into his eyes. "I've never been so terrified in all my life. And that includes being driven off the road, stranded in a snow cave and chased by gunmen."

"Hey," he said softly. "The snow cave was pretty cool."

Hope smiled so widely that Ian felt the warmth clear to the tips of his toes.

"You're right. It was like nothing I've ever experienced before. Now I can add surviving an avalanche to that list."

A long moment built between them as the sheer magnitude of what they'd survived crashed over them.

"Thank you," Ian murmured. "Thank you for not giving up, for finding me."

She rested a gloved hand on his cheek. "And thank you for everything you've done for Emi and for me."

He grinned. "Anytime. But before we get too carried away, let's make sure your snowmobile is still functioning."

They resumed climbing, keeping a wary eye out for any sign of their attackers, though Ian was pretty sure the avalanche had blocked them from getting down the mountain. Hopefully, they'd seen him hit and presumed they were both dead. He shivered, thinking how very close to that reality he'd come. Hope had saved him.

When they finally reached Hope's snowmobile, Ian was relieved to see it hadn't sunk too deeply.

"Is it okay? Or do we need another snow cave?"

"It will be okay. I'm going to dig around the skis. Can you stomp down the snow ahead of us to create a firm pack?

That will allow us to get free and build some momentum so we don't get stuck again, since this time it will be carrying both our weight."

"I can do that."

They got to work, and before long, Ian had the snowmobile unstuck. "Because I'm so much bigger than you, I think you should sit as far forward as you can. I'll sit behind you and reach around you to drive. I think you'll be warmer that way, but I don't want to make you uncomfortable, so let me know if you are."

"Aye, aye, Captain."

Hope climbed onto the snowmobile and hunched over the handles.

"They call that the Squirrel," Ian teased. "Because of the way you have to hold your hands."

"They can call it whatever they want," Hope replied. "As long as it gets me to the house and a warm fire."

"You still have the flash drive?"

Hope patted her coat pocket. "Safe and dry."

"Then let's head to the house." Ian climbed up on the extended seat behind her and wrapped his arms around Hope as he reached for the handles. "Ready?"

Hope nodded, and Ian set the machine in motion. He had to rock it back and forth a few times to fully break loose, but then they were off and racing back down the mountain toward the safe house and warmth.

The moon had risen, lighting their way. Snow sparkled and stars studded the dark sky. Ian allowed himself to relax and soak in the beauty of it. His head was so close to Hope's that he could whisper in her ear. "More of God's handiwork."

Even through all the layers of clothing between them, Ian felt her body sigh and relax back against his chest. They'd survived a close call with death today, but for now, with his arms wrapped protectively around her, he could just thank God that they were whole.

The night was cold, but the wind had died down, and despite everything they'd endured, it was the perfect night for a peaceful moonlit ride.

Ian decided he would cherish the peace while he could, knowing that renewed danger was as inevitable as the sunrise.

Chapter Fifteen

Warm. She was finally warm.

Hope snuggled under the blanket as she rested beside the fire and fought off sleep. It would be so easy to close her eyes and just drift off.

Ian had gone outside with Nancy to wait for her team. There'd been a last-minute switch of safe houses—Adam's idea. After Ian had notified him that they'd located the drive, Adam had decided he wanted a house with a built-in cyber shield to better protect them from being hacked.

Time was running out. Hope had lost track of what day of the countdown they were on, but she knew the deadline was drawing near. They couldn't afford any errors now.

Maybe it was a good idea for her to sleep while she waited, just so she'd be sharper when they arrived. The fire was so cozy, and she'd been so cold for so long. She closed her eyes, promising herself it would be just for a little while.

Hope had no idea how much time had passed when the sound of voices roused her from a deep sleep. She blinked and yawned and was stretching under her blanket when Ian entered the room followed by a group of men and a woman she'd never seen before.

Ian came and leaned over. "Had a good sleep, I hope."

She couldn't help but smile up at him. "It was lovely. I'm just sorry you didn't have a chance to rest."

"I'm used to going long days without sleep."

"Army life?"

He nodded. "And calving season."

"I sometimes forget you're a rancher and not always my personal bodyguard," she said with a wink as she pushed back the blankets and swung her legs around. She tipped her head toward the door where the group had gathered. "What happens now?"

"Nancy will introduce you to her team, and I'll let them take it from there."

Hope stood and ran a hand through her sleep-tousled hair before following Ian across the room.

Nancy and her team stopped talking as Hope and Ian approached.

"Hope, let me introduce you to the people who are going to help us resolve this. Ned and Erin are Adam's friends, but also longtime hiking buddies of mine. They're computer whiz kids whose specialty is codebreaking. Jacob and Russ are my colleagues. They are on the cybercrime task force and have a lot of experience dealing with ransomware attacks."

Hope's heart filled at the sight of these professionals who had all gathered here to help her fight back against the ruthless men who'd hurt Steve and threatened her and Emi so many times. "I can't thank you enough. I—"

Ned cut her off with a wave of his hand and a smile. "Please, no thanks are necessary, Hope. We appreciate all the risks you've taken to get the drive for us. Nancy already filled us in on everything she knows. If we have any questions we'll let you know. Now, let's get some coffee and get to work. We've got criminals to take down."

Hope smiled her appreciation. "Nancy put the flash drive in the war room Adam created upstairs. If you want to get to work, I'll bring up the coffee as soon as it's ready. It will give me something to do other than stress."

"Sounds like a plan to me," Erin agreed.

The team trooped upstairs, and Hope got to work. Ian just stood at the counter watching. Hope could see that he was barely keeping upright, and his eyelids kept drifting closed. Once the coffee was brewing, she walked around the counter and took him by the arm. "Come on," she urged. "I happen to know where there's a really comfy sofa near a warm fire."

Ian attempted a protest, but the adrenaline crash he'd predicted took over. He was fast asleep as soon as his head hit the pillows. Hope pulled a blanket up over him and kissed his forehead. "Sleep well, my hero."

She studied him for a few minutes, puzzling over the paradox that was this man. Her hero, her protector, but also a man reluctant to let down his guard, to open up. *What secrets does that heart of yours hold, Ian?*

The coffeemaker dinged, pulling her from her thoughts before she could allow them to suck her into memories of the kiss they'd shared. A kiss she should never have allowed—or enjoyed so much.

Shoving the memory away, she focused on preparing the tray, filling it with creamer, sugar, and an array of treats she'd found in the cabinet. When all was ready, she carried it up the stairs and knocked on the door of what had been the master bedroom before Adam repurposed it.

Nancy opened the door and took the tray from her. When Hope would have turned away, Nancy beckoned her in. "Come in. I have a surprise for you."

Hope entered the room, amazed at the number of computers and the variety of different images being projected on screens. She had no idea how Adam had pulled this off so quickly, but she was learning not to underestimate the man.

Turning away from the baffling computer work, she followed Nancy to the far corner, where a smaller laptop was set up.

"I thought you might like to talk to Emi," Nancy offered. "Ned set up a secure line. As soon as you're ready, Isabelle will sign on."

Hope's hands flew to her mouth. "Seriously? It's safe?"

"You've got my thousand percent guarantee," Ned called over, his eyes never once leaving the stream of numbers and symbols that whirred across his screen.

Hope settled herself into the chair, and within minutes Emi's beloved face appeared. "Hi, Mommy. I miss you this much," she said and stretched her arms out to demonstrate. "But I'm having so much fun. Mia is my new friend, and she has a dog and her mommy is expecting a baby brother, and we did painting and coloring. Mia loves to draw pictures and she is teaching me how to draw horses so I can draw Nancy's reindeer, and tonight we're going to make a gingerbread house."

She finally had to pause for breath, and Hope jumped in. "So, you're happy there?"

"I am. Mia is the bestest friend I ever had." Her voice dipped for just a minute. "I want to come home and see you and Uncle Steve and Ian, but this is fun, so it's okay if it takes a while before you can come get me."

Hope almost laughed out loud. Here she'd been worried about Emi missing her and being miserable, and instead her daughter was having the time of her life in a place where she was safe.

"Mrs. Isabelle says I need to say goodbye because I'm going to help Mia set the table for lunch. Bye, Mommy. I love you."

Isabelle's face took the place of Emi's on the screen. "I guess you can tell for yourself that she's doing well."

"I can. Thank you so much for caring for her. That sounds like quite the energetic duo you have there."

"Oh, they're amazing together," Isabelle replied. "And we're all learning *so* many reindeer facts. Did you know that their eyes are golden in the summer, but turn deep blue in the winter?"

Hope laughed. "So I've heard."

Isabelle joined in the laughter, and her face was filled with such warmth and love that Hope found herself wrapped up in it. "I know you have to get back to them, but thank you again. I hope one day we can meet under happier circumstances."

"Count on it," Isabelle promised. "I have every confidence in my husband and his team."

The screen went dark, and Hope sat for a moment, offering a silent prayer of thanksgiving for all the generous and caring people God had sent to help her.

When she rose, she looked over at Nancy. "I think you created a monster teaching her all those reindeer facts."

Nancy laughed. "She can help out with my reindeer anytime."

Hope's mood dimmed a little at the thought of what would happen when all this was over. Would she and Emi just go back to their lonely life together? A life she'd been totally content with before.

Until she'd met Ian.

Brushing the thought aside, she turned to the team. "My daughter just reminded me that it's lunchtime. Anyone hungry?"

Shaking heads and distracted murmurs of "no thanks" didn't really surprise her. They were all deep into the work they were doing. If only there was some way she could help.

Ian was still soundly asleep when Hope went downstairs, so she selected a book from the library shelf, poured herself a mugful of coffee and settled in a chair by the fire. With her fears for Emi dissipated, she allowed herself to relax. Her daughter wasn't the only bookworm in the family.

* * *

Ian woke, disoriented and sore. Every bone in his body ached like he'd been through the wringer. He closed his eyes and let the memories wash over him. He'd survived an avalanche. Little wonder he felt like his body had been pulverized.

With that memory came the one of what had happened in the aftermath, a kiss that had transported him out of a world of fear and pain and into one shining with possibility. Except it could never be.

He opened his eyes and could see Hope curled in a chair by the fire. She'd obviously fallen asleep while reading. The book lay abandoned on her lap and she'd nestled so that her head rested against the high back. For a moment, he indulged himself in fruitless daydreams of a life he didn't deserve.

Hope was so beautiful, inside and out. More than anything he'd ever wanted, Ian found himself yearning for a future together with her. A life with Hope and Emi would be filled with everything that was bright and loving and happy, a dream come true.

But on the wings of that dream, all his failures came rushing at him. He'd proved beyond doubt that he didn't have what it took to be a husband. Hope had already suffered at the hands of one deceitful spouse. She deserved someone so much better than him.

As if his focus had stirred her, Hope shifted slightly, opened her eyes and smiled at him.

"You're thinking again," she teased.

Ian sighed. "How do you know that?"

She yawned, stretched and straightened in the chair. "You get this serious expression. Your brows pinch together, and you look like you're sucking lemons."

"You've only known me a few days."

She laughed softly. "You've spent a lot of time thinking hard. Understandable with all we've gone through, but you really need happier thoughts."

Ian didn't respond right away, and in the silence they could hear the team members walking around up in the war room.

"You'd rather be up there with them, wouldn't you?" Hope asked.

"Hmm?"

"You'd rather be busy plotting the resolution of this mess than babysitting a morose mother who misses her little girl."

Ian smiled at her. "I miss your little girl too. I haven't learned anything new about reindeer in the past twenty hours."

Hope smiled sadly.

"Come on, that almost got a laugh," Ian teased.

"And you avoided answering."

Ian shrugged. "Once maybe, but no, not now."

"What changed that?"

"Not what. *I* changed."

"I'm sorry," Hope said softly. "I don't mean to pry. You don't have to share anything if you don't want to."

But Ian found that he did want to. "That's kind of you after we basically put your entire life under a microscope."

Hope dipped her head. "I won't deny that was hard, but it was necessary. So it's okay. I absolve you of any guilt you might be feeling about digging into my life."

Ian hesitated a moment, knowing he was about to reveal a part of himself to her that he'd never shared with another person. He wasn't completely sure he understood why he felt compelled to share it. Perhaps just a self-destructive impulse, because something about Hope was opening doors to parts of him that had been locked tight for a long time. Maybe because he needed to close them against irrational dreams that dared to try and break through.

He hung his head knowing he was about to disillusion her. He wished it was unnecessary, but he'd heard the words she whispered when she thought he was asleep. Better she realize now that he was nobody's hero before she began dreaming her own impossible dreams.

"Back at the restaurant, you asked what I was thinking." He took a long, deep breath and exhaled slowly. "I was thinking about my wife."

"You must miss her."

Her voice was soft, kind. Ian fell silent, thinking how to respond. "It's not that."

He looked over at Hope, and their eyes locked. There was a misplaced look of empathy in the way she gazed at him. Nancy had given her the wrong impression. Shelby wasn't the problem. He was the one who had failed her. Hope needed to understand why he wasn't worthy of a relationship.

"We started dating in high school. Some friends wanted a double date, so we agreed, since we knew each other from math class. We hit it off and dated for the rest of high school and college. I wasn't thinking serious or long-term, and I didn't think she was either.

"I'd decided to join the army right out of college, following in my dad's footsteps. Shelby wasn't very happy about that. But I wouldn't change my mind.

"That's when she started to push about getting married before I left." He paused. "I don't want you thinking I'm saying that to make her sound bad. It was a thing with her group of friends at the time. They all wanted to get married before they graduated. I guess I got caught up in the idea of it too—the knowledge that someone would be waiting for me to come home."

He took a deep breath and exhaled. "That was really self-ish of me. Shelby wanted more. She needed someone to come home to, also. And I wasn't there. The more time I served, the more committed I became. War does things to you. It messes with your head. Even when I was home on leave, I wasn't the husband she needed."

Hope was sitting quietly, listening. There was no judgment on her face, but he knew that would change.

"She was desperate to have a baby. For years, I believed she

thought that if we had a family, I'd resign and come home."
He shrugged. "Maybe I would have. I was excited when she
got pregnant. But then she miscarried. For a time, we were
closer. I was home for a bit. But then, just after she found out
she was pregnant again, I was called up. I was deployed when
she lost that baby. There were two more miscarriages, and I
begged her to give up. We could adopt. We could just be the
two of us. But she wanted to try again."

Ian's voice was cracking, and he stayed silent until he
could speak without emotion dragging him down. "I was
gone again, by the time she found out she was pregnant. We'd
had harsh words before I left. She begged me to stay, said she
needed me."

"But you were in the army. You didn't have a choice."

He shrugged. "That's true. But what haunts me is that I
wanted to go. I was more at home with my squad by then than
I was with Shelby. I knew that it made me a terrible husband."

He let out a heavy sigh. "In hindsight, and with help, I
came to understand that it was one of the effects of war. My
thinking had become skewed by the life I was living. But that
didn't help Shelby." He buried his head in his hands.

Hope rose from her chair and came to sit on the floor in
front of Ian. She felt the pain pouring out of him and needed
to be close, to offer comfort the way he had comforted her.
She pulled his hands from his face and held them tightly.
"What happened?"

"There were complications. She died and so did my son."

"Oh, Ian." Whatever she had been expecting it was not this.

"I was so angry."

The look in his eyes when he raised them to meet hers
broke her heart. "Of course you were. That was a horrible
thing to have happen."

He looked down at her, and the agony was raw on his face.

"No." He shook his head. "I was angry at her." His voice fell to a whisper. "At myself."

Hope went still. This was it. She understood that what he was holding inside himself over this was the dark pain she glimpsed every so often when he thought no one was looking.

"I found out that the doctor had told her not to get pregnant again. He told her it could cost her life and her baby's." He swallowed hard before continuing. "She risked it anyway. Because she wanted to be a mother more than anything in the world." He had to pause for another deep breath. "I think I knew on some level that she risked it because she needed a child, she needed someone to need her in a way I didn't, couldn't. She needed someone to be there with her. And I wasn't."

"Ian—" Hope tried to protest, but he started talking again, his voice hoarse.

"When you started talking in the restaurant about how it felt to have to let Emi go, something broke loose in my brain, and I finally understood. Shelby had been sacrificing so much. Each time she lost a child, she lost a bit of herself. And I was too caught up in my own life to realize it. All these years I've been angry at her for the choice she made going against the doctor's advice. I thought she was trying to manipulate me, knowing we were drifting apart. But it wasn't that at all. I failed her. And I can never make it up."

Hope didn't even know what to say. She could only hold on to his hands and pray for the words. She didn't have the power to heal him. Only God could do that.

"Have you prayed about this?"

Ian seemed startled by her question. "What would I have prayed for? It was too late to bring her back."

"For healing. For you to learn to forgive—Shelby and yourself."

Ian stood, and Hope felt the connection between them breaking. "I've prayed for her and for our little boy." His voice cracked. "I've prayed to God to take away my anger at her." He gave a harsh laugh. "I guess He heard that prayer. All this time, the one I should have been angry with was myself."

Grief formed a lump in Hope's chest. She could barely speak. "If that was the lesson you took away from what I said today, then I'm sorry, but you misunderstood." She stood and faced him. "I know a little bit about what it's like to be in Shelby's shoes. My husband didn't want me in his life either."

Ian looked up, startled. "No. I didn't mean it like that. I never cheated on her."

He hung his head and kept talking. "I'm sorry. I didn't mean to remind you. You asked what I was thinking earlier. I shared this because I wanted you to know that your courage today affected me deeply. It made me see things differently. You changed my feelings about what happened."

Hope waited, sensing that he wasn't done. "I'll still carry the anger and guilt, but those feelings won't be directed at her."

"Is that why Nancy doesn't like her? Because you blame yourself?"

"What?"

"I've heard Nancy compare me to Shelby a couple of times." She rolled her eyes. "It was never a compliment to Shelby."

Ian shook his head. "You're right. Nancy wasn't a fan of Shelby, but it's not because of me, even though she never wanted me to marry her. They were best friends once, then something happened. I don't know what it was, but they were rivals after that. All through high school."

Before Hope could reply, a resounding "Yes!" echoed from upstairs. Hope looked at Ian.

"Let's go," he said, and they ran for the stairs.

Chapter Sixteen

Nancy was high-fiving her team as Hope and Ian burst through the door. "We did it!" she exclaimed. "Steve's drive held enough samples of code that we were able to match the fingerprint to a known hacker."

Hope blinked in confusion. "They left a fingerprint on the drive?"

Ned answered. "Yes and no. Not a fingerprint in the literal sense that we could test for a match, though that would have been nice too. This is more specific to coding. The best way I can think of to explain it is if you asked two people to write about the same thing. Supposing they were sufficiently literate, you'd still get two very different texts. It's the sentence syntax, the word choice. That sort of thing. The stylistic expression. Coding is a little like that. The basic code is the same, but the way each person puts it together reflects their style. Steve got us started. He'd gathered samples to point us in the right direction. I'm guessing he wasn't far from cracking it when he was attacked."

"So that might explain the attack at the office?" Ian prompted. "If the person suspected it. But how would they know?"

As Ned spoke, and Hope recalled Ian's comments about

Nancy and Shelby being rivals, something clicked in her brain. "I think Steve knew who it was and was just trying to prove it," she replied.

"What do you mean?" Jacob asked as he swung around to face her. "This person isn't widely known. He's the leader of a cyber gang that has been sabotaging small-town banks and mom-and-pop companies. The gang has flown under the radar because they haven't been going for the major corporations or governments that would draw national media and law enforcement attention."

Hope spoke up. "*She* was honing her craft."

"What?"

"I know who is behind this."

All eyes were on her now, so Hope began to explain.

"Ian said something to me a few minutes ago. It triggered a connection. Back in college, Steve had another partner besides my deceased husband—a woman he was dating. My roommate for the beginning of sophomore year. She had transferred in and was given a suite with me. She and Steve met the first weekend and hit it off instantly. She was more than a computer geek. She was brilliant, probably the smartest person I've ever known." Hope paused, fighting back a swell of emotion.

"There were rumors of a scandal at her last school, but she seemed really nice and the four of us were a thing for a while. She and Steve had a class together, and they were working on some supersecret project. He caught her cheating. I don't know all the details because I didn't understand any of it at the time—something about accessing other people's files. She got kicked out of school. Steve was heartbroken. He told me later that he'd been the one to turn her in.

"He got over her, and we all moved on. I haven't thought of her in a decade or more. But when Ian and I were talking before, something reminded me of her... Adrianna. This, more than arrogance, explains why Steve was trying to undo what she'd done. I'm sure he realized right away who it was. I imagine it was a personal challenge to him to defeat her. To let good win."

She fell silent, then added quietly, "It probably also explains why she's been coming after me. She would know that the way to hurt Steve was through me. She was jealous of our friendship."

"Why now though?" Erin asked.

Hope shrugged. "I can't say for sure, but I'd guess because of the success of Twelve Days 'til Christmas. And the fact that it was something Steve and I did together."

She could see doubt lingering on a few faces. "If you have a secure line, I could call the hospital. They were bringing Steve out of his coma yesterday. Maybe he's alert by now and can confirm."

Ned handed her a phone, and Hope immediately dialed Helen's number. Her nerves were thrumming as she waited for Steve to confirm what she knew in her heart. The phone rang through to voicemail, so she tried again. *Pick up. Pick up.*

"Hello?" Helen's hesitant voice came over the line.

"Helen, it's Hope. Is Steve awake yet? Can he talk?"

"Hope, where are you? Is everything okay?"

"I'll explain the ins and outs later. I just need to know if he can talk."

Helen's voice was heavy. "He's still on a respirator. It's been a slow process. He can't talk."

Hope's heart sank, but she wasn't giving up. "Does he respond at all?"

"He squeezed my hand." Helen's voice lightened with those words, and Hope could almost feel her smile.

"I have something really important I need you to do. Talk to him. Tell him I'm on the phone."

Hope listened while Helen spoke gently.

"His eyes opened!"

Hope let out a huge sigh. "Ask him this. Is it Adrianna?"

"What?"

"He'll know what it means. Watch carefully for his reaction."

Hope waited. So much would hinge on Steve's response.

"Hope? His eyes grew wide and he squeezed my hand. He tried to nod."

Chills raced along Hope's arm and radiated out through her body. She closed her eyes and drew a breath. "Thank you. Tell him…" Her voice broke. "Tell him I'll take care of it. I have a team. He just needs to concentrate on getting well so he can see Emi for Christmas and give her the repaired ornament himself." She listened while Helen repeated her message verbatim.

"He smiled, Hope. He smiled."

Tears flooded Hope's eyes as she said her goodbyes and handed the phone back to Ned.

"Take a minute," he said gently. "We've got this now. We'll take her down."

Hope sniffed and nodded. When she turned around, Ian was smiling softly at her.

"Come on." He rested an arm around her shoulder and led her from the room. "I think they're going to be busy for a while. Let's go cook dinner."

All of the tension from their earlier conversation vanished as they opened cabinets, scoured the fridge and tried to settle on a meal plan. "Adam really thought of everything, didn't he?" Hope commented as she peered into the freezer compartment. "Although the amount of food is a little disconcerting. Does he really expect it to take so long to fix this?"

Ian laughed. "Nope, that's just Adam. Prepared for any emergency."

"Well, I, for one, am very grateful. Problem is Emi's tastes run to finger foods and pizza." Her voice dropped. "It's been a long while since I fed a group. I don't even know what to do with any of this."

"No worries. I've got it."

"What, you're a soldier, a rancher, a Christmas tree guy and…a chef?"

Ian whipped a towel over his shoulder and picked up a knife. "Prepare to be dazzled."

Hope burst out laughing. "I prefer to be fed."

"All in good time, my dear. Alas, I find myself in need of a sous-chef. Are you available?"

"Ah, he speaks French as well. *Mais oui, monsieur.*"

Ian laid out an array of vegetables and handed her a paring knife. "If you'll peel these, I'll tend to the roast."

Hope set happily to work feeling more content than she had in a long while. Yes, they were still under threat, but she had confidence in the team Adam had assembled. Her daughter was safe and happy, and she was in a cozy kitchen cooking with a man…with a man who, if she were being honest, she wished could be part of her future.

But even if she could have gotten past the fear and doubt in her own heart, their conversation earlier made it clear Ian was still buried in the guilt and grief of his past. She'd barely survived marriage with a man who didn't love her enough. She owed it to both her daughter and herself to never settle for that again.

Ian loaded the last of the dishes into the dishwasher and picked up a cloth to wipe down the counter while Hope poured tea. The evening stretched ahead of them, and he needed a way to fill it that would keep him from wanting to kiss her. He'd been fighting the memories of their impulsive kiss on the mountain slope all day, but they were never going to fade as long as she was with him, smiling, teasing and chatting happily.

He'd developed a deep admiration watching the way she coped with adversity, forging ahead no matter what obstacles appeared. And seeing her with his family, blending in, befriending his mother and sister—it was like the universe had designed an entirely new way to torment him. But this cozy domesticity elevated the torture to a whole new level. This was all he had ever wanted of life: someone who could be a partner, a friend, a—

"Ian, you're going to rub the finish right off that counter." Hope rested her hand over his. "What is it? What's bothering you?"

He looked down into her eyes and saw the same glimmer he knew must be reflected in his own. A wish for something that couldn't be.

Pulling away, he tossed the rag in the sink. "Just impatient, I guess. Wondering how long it will take them to execute their plan."

Hope picked up her tea mug. "I saw a chess set in the library. Do you play?"

"I do actually."

"Good. Then you can teach me," she called as she headed out of the kitchen. She stopped in the doorway and grinned back at him. "Fair warning, I've never been able to get the hang of it."

Ian shook his head and followed behind her. "That's what Nancy's husband said just before he whomped me."

Hope stopped short. "Nancy is married?"

Ian glanced up the staircase before following Hope into the library. He lowered his voice. "She was. Her husband was killed in combat a little over a year ago."

Tears sprung to Hope's eyes. "That makes me feel even worse for involving her in this."

"Don't," Ian reassured her. "Working, keeping her mind occupied, it's how she has dealt with her grief. She'd let you know if she couldn't handle it." Even as he said the words, Ian wondered if they were really true. He had a nagging feeling that Nancy hadn't dealt with her loss any better than he had his. Both had submerged their grief in work.

Which was what he needed to do now. Focus on Hope and the job they had to do. He settled himself in front of the chessboard and grinned at her. "Ready?"

An hour later, the chessboard lay abandoned and Hope was curled on the sofa. "I told you. I just don't have a head for it." She laughed. "I think I've spent too many hours playing board games with Emi."

"How's she doing with all this? Nancy said you spoke to her earlier."

"I did." She shook her head in bemusement. "She's having the time of her life and says Mia is her 'bestest' friend. My shy little girl is making friends all over the place. Isabelle may have a bone to pick with Nancy though. Apparently they're being inundated with reindeer trivia."

Ian threw back his head, laughing. "She's quite the little charmer." *Just like her mother.*

Hope stretched and propped a pillow beneath her head. "So how do you know Adam and Isabelle?"

"Adam and I are both veterans. We met in a local wilderness therapy group."

"That sounds intriguing. Tell me more."

Ian stared into the blazing fire for a long moment before answering. "I told you that war does something to you," he said abstractedly. "It's not like you think when you sign up— all guns and glory." He buried his face and massaged his brow. "You see a lot of things you'll never be able to unsee, get called to take risks that strike fear in your heart. But you do it all anyway because you know your country is counting on you."

He looked up and saw that Hope was sitting up, fully concentrating on him and what he was saying.

"You're on, 24/7. So, when you come home…it can be hard to adjust, find a purpose." He stood, uncomfortable with expressing his thoughts, needing to move. "It wasn't as bad for me as for some. Adam had a tough time of it." He looked over at her and smiled. "He's doing great now though. Wilderness therapy taught us to reconnect with ourselves through nature. Then he met Isabelle and Mia." He hesitated, thinking of how much Adam's situation had been like his own. He met Isabelle when she was also being pursued by men with an intent to kill. Ian swallowed hard before continuing. "Making a family with them has been the best thing ever for him."

"That veterans' center in town, the one the Christmas trees were for, that's important to you, right?"

Ian glanced at her and saw the wheels churning in her head. "Very."

She jumped up and started pacing. Her face was twisted in the cutest expression, and Ian couldn't decide if he should be excited or wary of what was causing it.

"Who's going to wear a hole in the rug?"

The question jolted Hope from her thoughts. "What? Oh!" She started to laugh. "Sorry, I get excited when the ideas start popping."

"I can see that. Want to share?"

She bit her lip. "I've been wracking my brain trying to think of some way to repay you for what you've done for Emi and me."

"There's no need—"

She put a finger over her lips to shush him. "Not for you, maybe. But it's something I need to do. And I think I have an idea how." She cast a glance at the discarded chess pieces. "I may not be much good at chess, but there is one thing I'm really good at, and that's not me being boastful."

Ian looked away, unable to bear the beauty shining forth from her spirit. "And what would that be?" he asked hoarsely.

"I'm really good at marketing things, at creating campaigns to raise awareness." She walked toward where he was standing by the fireplace and lifted his hands in hers. "I'd like to repay you by helping raise awareness—and money, of course—for your veterans' center, for the wilderness therapy. Not just at Christmas, but all year long, to help people like you and Adam, who give so very much to help others."

She gazed up at him, waiting for his answer.

There really was only one answer he could give. With the firelight glinting off her blond hair, and her eyes gleaming with such generosity and kindness, Ian gave in to what he'd been fighting so helplessly and he kissed her again.

Chapter Seventeen

Believing in Ian, wanting to help him…and losing herself in his kiss…were very different things. The part of Hope that had been lonely for so long, the brave version of herself who was trying to build a new life, that part wanted her to surrender, to allow her brain to accept what her heart knew. She was falling in love with this incredible man.

But her brain knew what her heart failed to recognize, that this man was wounded in a way she couldn't heal, that he had too many issues he needed to resolve, and she couldn't risk her daughter's happiness on a fragile hope that he could come to love her too.

But she couldn't bear to hurt him. Not after all he'd done for her.

Slowly, she drew back, resting her hand on his cheek and gazing into his eyes—eyes that flared with conflicted feelings that told her she was right.

She closed her eyes a moment to compose herself, then drew a breath and spoke. "I care for you, Ian. More than I should. And I'm so very grateful for everything you've done for me, for my daughter."

She lowered her gaze, knowing she couldn't hide what

burned in her heart, what must be reflected in her eyes, and forced out the words she didn't want to say. "This is wrong. We can't mistake gratitude for something more, can't make promises we won't keep. Can't pretend we could share a…"

Her voice broke before she could add the word *future*, and she turned and rushed from the room. Humiliation flooded her. In trying to be kind, she'd said much more than she'd intended. In telling him what they couldn't have, she'd revealed what she yearned for.

Needing to focus on what she *was* here for, Hope hurried up to the war room, hoping she'd find they'd made some progress, that this could all be over soon, and she and Emi could go home.

Hope fixed a smile on her face when Nancy answered her knock at the door. "Any luck up here with the genius squad?" she asked, her voice deliberately light.

Nancy ushered Hope back into the hallway and pulled the door closed behind her. "Don't want to risk disturbing them. They're making some progress, but it's slow work, because you have to do it without alerting the enemy."

Hope shivered. Nancy's language put the name of the room in perspective and reminded her there was much more at stake than her aching heart. They were fighting a war against evil behind those doors. "What exactly are they trying to do?"

"It's a complicated process. First they have to reverse hack and steal back the data she took from all the people who play on your platform. Then we take her site down, and finally, once she's powerless, we close the trapdoor in Twelve Days 'til Christmas so it's completely safe."

Hope's emotions boomeranged between awe and a sense of futility. She wanted to be in the room watching, helping, but Steve had been right. She understood nothing about this part. Her expertise had been in making everyone want to be part of their cyber family. "I feel so useless. All of you are going to these lengths to resolve my problem, while I sit here twiddling my thumbs."

"Don't underestimate your contribution, Hope," Nancy said gently. "You made a valuable connection. *You* told us about Adrianna. And don't worry about them. They're taking down a hacker who could grow into someone who someday could pose a risk to national security. It's what they do all day, every day—just not always with a ticking clock and such urgency."

This *was* like a ticking clock, and Hope suddenly realized she had no idea how close to the deadline they actually were. "I've completely lost track of time."

"Six days 'til Christmas."

Hope sighed sadly. "It's Christmas-movie day. Emi and I were supposed to watch *Miracle on 34th Street* tonight."

Nancy laid a hand on Hope's arm. "When this is over— and it will be—you and Emi can have a lifetime of watching movies together."

Hope caught herself. "You're right. I'm sorry." She sighed again. "I think it's all just catching up with me because I have nothing to do."

"That brother of mine isn't entertaining you?"

Hope's blush gave her away and Nancy smirked.

"Oh, no," Hope assured her. "It's not like that."

"Too bad," Nancy answered. "He needs someone like you. No, scratch that," she said as she opened the war room door. "He doesn't need someone like you—he needs you. Think about it," she said as she shut the door.

For the next two days, Hope couldn't think of anything else.

She knew Nancy was wrong. She and Ian had too many unhealed wounds to be able to make anything work between them. But still the thoughts tantalized. *What if?*

So, she prayed and made food, and brought coffee when needed, caught some sleep when she could, and two days passed at a snail's pace while she tried her best to avoid Ian. The ease, the bond they'd shared, had been severed with a kiss. He was too mired in the past, and she was too scared to be hurt again.

But she missed him.

Ian thought he was losing his mind. How could you miss someone so badly when you'd known them less than a week and were living in the same house?

But time and distance were both relative, and though he and Hope were technically living within the same square footage, he'd barely seen her, even in passing, since his ill-timed kiss.

He busied himself chopping wood for the fireplace, read the books he didn't usually have time for, poked his head into the war room to see if he could help and he stewed wondering how he'd managed to mess things up so badly that they couldn't even be friends.

But truth was, he didn't want Hope for friendship alone. He wanted her for a lifetime, if only he was worthy. She deserved so much more than a man who carried a burden of guilt.

"Ian, Hope! Come in here. We did it!"

Ian didn't think he'd ever heard Nancy sound so euphoric. He went running up the stairs only to collide with Hope on the landing. She smiled shyly, and his heart cracked. He smiled back, and pushed aside the tension of the past two days. "Let's go see what they've done."

The mood in the war room could only be described as cautiously victorious. Ned had fireworks exploding on his monitor. Erin was on the phone speaking quietly but smiling broadly. Jacob and Russ were standing by a screen, their bodies more relaxed than he'd seen them in days. The tension had eased for the team too.

As Hope and Ian entered, Erin disconnected her call and Ned came forward to speak with them. "It's done. We've taken back all the data, and her server is destroyed." He grinned. "Christmas is saved!"

Hope was beaming. "Have you told Steve yet?"

"No. He's been helping us a little, answering questions via Helen, but he still can't fully communicate. We thought you should be the one to tell him."

"What about Adrianna?" Ian hated to spoil their fun, but he couldn't forget that their problems in the past week had been in the real world, not just their virtual community. "What's to keep her from going after Steve or Hope as revenge?"

"We've had a team back at headquarters monitoring her since we began the final takedown," Nancy answered. "My boss was worried she might try to leave the country, so we have surveillance in place. They just notified me that she's on the move. We have eyes in the sky and cars tailing her. They're playing hopscotch so as not to tip her off."

"Can you share a screen so we can see?" Ian pushed.

"Let me see." Nancy picked up her phone and relayed the request back to her home office. She waited for a reply, then opened the link that came through. The front monitor flickered, and the scene came to life.

"What are we supposed to be seeing?" Hope asked as she walked up beside Nancy.

"See that red sports car? It's the fifth car in the right lane."

Hope groaned. "Of course. That's Adrianna. Always had to have the flashiest of everything."

"We have several aircraft in the air monitoring her car so she doesn't pick up on the tail."

"Oh, she'll pick up on it," Hope muttered.

"You don't trust us?"

"I know her. She's wily."

For a time, Hope stood, her eyes glued to the screen, but as time wore on, and Adrianna continued her drive, stopping for coffee, stopping at a fast-food restaurant, then a nail salon, Hope grew restless. "Is it safe to check into the platform now that you've taken down her server? No one has been monitoring the community for days now."

Ned glanced over his shoulder. "Yes. There's a computer

on the far desk that we've been using to check in on it. You can use that."

Hope grabbed a mug of lukewarm coffee off the table and headed toward the desk. She shouldn't complain about this state of limbo compared to the danger they'd been in, but she was so ready for this to all be over. She glanced across the room at Ian, who looked up and then quickly away. She needed to be away from him, so her heart could begin to put itself back together again.

Forcing her attention away from Ian, she settled at the computer and logged into her account on the platform. Immediately photos started to load, a kaleidoscope of images that had been accumulating in the days she'd been offline. She relaxed back in the chair and allowed a feeling of satisfaction to settle over her. All of these people, her community, had been partying on, unaware of the threat that hung over them. It was a sober reminder of how fragile security on the web really was. But they were safe now. Their data was secure. The mastermind behind it had been defeated, if not captured yet. Glancing over at the men and women she had come to know and respect, Hope felt a profound sense of gratitude that there were people like them whose entire lives were dedicated to keeping the innocent safe.

But as she scrolled through her virtual community, she couldn't shake the feeling that it had been tainted. The sparkling trees and merrily lit homes had lost their luster. In her heart she knew it wasn't entirely due to Adrianna and her evil scheme. It was that she'd had a taste of the real thing, the sense of family and home that she'd come to love with Ian's family. And she wanted more of that.

But her community was for people, like herself, who didn't have that in their lives. She shouldn't dismiss the good her platform had done just because it was a pale facsimile of the real thing.

She scrolled through more photos, and gradually her heart

began to lighten. These people were having fun. They might not all be with real family and friends, but that had been the point in designing this—to create a safe space where people could come together even when far apart and find a version of family and community to fill the gaps in their lives.

The murmuring voices across the room grew more animated, so Hope glanced up at the screen. Adrianna's car was alone on the road now, speeding along some mountain highway. Snow was starting to fall, and Hope shivered. There was part of her that never wanted to see snow again. She turned back to the screen, clicked on her profile page and waited for her photo stream to load. It had been a while since she'd posted anything. And it would be a while longer before she felt comfortable. Even knowing the site was secure, she was hesitant...

Her breath caught in her throat as her eyes took in the photo on the screen. Emi, with another little girl that could only be Mia, was stretched out on the white ground making snow angels. And parked, so that just the side was visible, was a red sports car.

The message cloud was flickering, so with trembling fingers she clicked it and a greeting appeared.

You didn't really think you'd gotten off that easily did you, Hope?

Your people may have taken down my server, but I have your daughter.

Who's the one who really pays the highest price?

Merry Christmas xoxo

Hope screamed, and the mug fell from her hands, shattering on the floor.

Chapter Eighteen

Ian was the first to reach Hope. "What is it?"

She was trembling uncontrollably and couldn't get the words out, so she just pointed at the screen.

Ian glanced at the monitor and his heart sank. "Nancy, Ned, you need to come look at this."

Nancy started across, but Ned's shout drew all their attention back. Ian and Hope looked across at the big screen just in time to see the red car shoot off the mountain road and over the cliff before exploding into a massive fireball.

Hope gave a soft whimper and fainted dead away. Ian leaped and caught her just before she hit the ground.

The room around them was a cacophony of voices, ringing phones and frantic replays, but Ian's attention was solely on Hope. He couldn't begin to consider his own grief at the moment as he thought of what Hope must have been feeling in that moment before she lost consciousness.

He carried her across the room and laid her on the sofa, then knelt beside her to check her pulse. Her eyes flickered, but he didn't have the heart to try to wake her. She would have to face this soon enough.

Nancy rushed over to his side. "What happened? Why did she faint?"

Ian swallowed hard. "Emi." He couldn't bring himself to say the words. "Go look at the computer she was using."

She dashed across the room, and Ian knew from her muffled gasp the minute she put it together. She grabbed her phone and ran out of the room.

Ian sat on the floor beside Hope. He'd never felt so hopeless, so useless. What did you say to the woman you loved who had just watched her child die in a fiery explosion? He remembered Hope asking if he'd prayed about Shelby, so now he bowed his head and prayed with all his heart—for Hope, for Emi and, even though he struggled with it, for forgiveness for Adrianna, who had caused all this pain.

Hope's soft whimpers yanked him from his prayers and he turned to see her curling in on herself. He rose and sat beside her on the sofa, pulling her into his arms, trying to absorb her anguish. She clung to him as the whimpers turned to sobs, and he held her close as she drenched his sweater with her tears. He rocked her gently, the way he imagined she had once rocked Emi, and tears sprung to his own eyes. His heart was broken, so he couldn't even fathom the depth of her grief.

Ian didn't know how much time had passed while they sat like that before Nancy burst through the door, her face wreathed in smiles.

"Hope, it's okay. Look at me. It's okay. Emi is fine. She wasn't in the car."

Ian felt the waves of emotion roll through Hope's body as she pulled away from him. She stared at Nancy through swollen eyes, but as the words penetrated, joy danced across her face.

"You wouldn't lie to me, Nancy?"

"No, I promise. Look! I reached Isabelle. She assured me no one took that photo today and the girls are fine." She paused. "I figured you wouldn't want Emi to see you so upset, so she sent me this video instead."

Hope pushed herself up on her elbows. Ian moved aside to make room for her as she swung her legs around and sat upright, but she linked his arm and held him close as Nancy put the phone in her other hand.

Emi's face filled the screen, laughing as she waved and called, "Hi, Mommy. This is Mia. We've been baking cookies all morning with Mrs. Isabelle. I made a special one for you."

Emi held up a red heart with a Santa hat, and Hope choked back a sob. With disbelieving eyes, she looked up at Nancy. "You're sure? You're absolutely sure?"

The smile Nancy gave in return lit her entire face. "As sure as I am that Emi loves reindeer."

Hope turned in Ian's arms, looked up at him and burst into tears all over again. "She's alive. My baby girl is alive."

Ian felt his own tears spilling over as he held her close. He raised his eyes and whispered, "Thank you, Lord."

He was grateful that Nancy left them alone, even if she did wink at him as she sauntered away. He had so many questions, and he knew Hope would too once her mind calmed, but for now, he just held her and let relief wash over them both.

Hope had never felt such joy in all her life. But as she finally lessened her grip on Ian, and slowly weaned herself from his embrace, questions began to flood her mind. "I need some answers," she told him.

Ian smiled gently at her as she eased away. "I figured you might. Should we go ask them?" He angled his head to the front of the room where Nancy and Ned were watching the video replay yet again, and Jacob and Russ were manning the computers. Erin was back on the phone.

Hope stood and started across the room, shaky at first, but she grew steadier with each step. Nancy turned and smiled at her. "You have questions, I presume."

"I need answers," she repeated.

"I have analysts looking at the photo. It's fake, no question. They're trying to trace how and when she posted it, but it's going to take a little time since she was using a new device which presumably was incinerated in the crash."

"She was in the car?"

"Adrianna? Yes."

"So..." Hope wasn't quite sure how to ask this. "Was it a deliberate crash?"

"We have a reconstruction team on the way to the accident site. Local authorities have it cordoned off, but our guys will figure out what happened."

Erin joined them. "When she came out of that last tunnel, she was traveling at a high rate of speed. It's possible she lost control. The weather conditions would have made the road slick."

Hope nodded solemnly. "What about the men who were working for her? The ones who tried to kidnap me?"

Erin had the answer to that, too. "They've been rounded up. Once we had Adrianna's name and the image of the tattoo you described to the sheriff, it wasn't hard to find her henchmen. They're no longer a threat to you."

"Then I have just one more question. Can I go home now? I need to see my daughter."

Nancy smiled at Ned. "You want to answer that?"

"Adam will be delivering Emi to the chalet at Christmas Village this afternoon. If you and Ian leave now, and go by car this time—" he grinned "—you'll beat them there by a few hours."

Hope lowered her face into her shaking hands. She couldn't believe this whole sorry story was finally over. "What about the Twelve Days finale?"

He shrugged. "That's up to you. I'm sure no one would blame you if you wanted to call it off."

"No." Hope straightened and spoke with resolve. "That

would be handing Adrianna a posthumous victory. I may have to change the location and even what we're doing, but I'll talk to Steve. We will figure something out."

"You could live stream it from the ranch, right Nancy?"

Nancy looked startled at Ian's suggestion, but quickly agreed. "Sure. Mom would be in her glory. We could set up out by the reindeer barn if that works for you."

"Thank you," Hope replied warmly. "I'll check with Steve." She looked at Ian. "And your mom. But for now, I just want to get going. If you're really coming with me, we have some presents to rewrap."

He winked. "What are you waiting for?"

"A car?"

Nancy laughed. "You can take my truck. I'll hitch a ride back with Ned."

Hope turned to the other team members and found herself suddenly choked up. "I don't even know where to begin, how to thank you. You've saved my daughter's life and mine, and you saved millions of people from an identity risk they never even knew about. Words fail me."

Russ spoke up. "No thanks necessary. I'd say that it's just part of the job, but I know I speak for all of us that this was more than just the job. We were truly happy to help, Hope. Just give Emi a hug from all of us."

Hope worked her way around the circle of team members hugging each in turn. "You know that fable about the lion and the mouse? Well, I feel like the tiny mouse and you are all undoubtedly lions in your work. It feels silly to say, but if there is ever anything I can do for any of you, just say the word."

She turned to Ian. "I'm ready."

They headed to the door, and Hope found herself overcome with emotion. In these past few days this team had become like family to her. "I love you all. Thank you again."

And then she hurried down the stairs before she burst into tears again.

Hope was quiet as Ian drove toward the highway. If it was this hard to say goodbye to a team she'd known for three days, how was she ever going to bear saying goodbye to Ian?

"Penny for your thoughts?" His voice broke through her reverie, but she wasn't about to share what she'd been thinking.

"As I recall that didn't work too well with you," Hope responded softly.

They both fell silent then, remembering how it had gone when he did share his deepest thoughts. Hope wished she could find the words to break through to him, but as much as she had clung to him, relied on him, cried all over him, nothing had really changed. He was still hung up in his past, needing to make amends for something he hadn't been able to control.

Chapter Nineteen

Even in daylight, Christmas Village sparkled, and Hope's heart brightened with pleasure that Emi would finally be able to revel in it. The expectation of her daughter's joy eased the pang in her own heart that had only grown deeper with each mile that passed. The ride had been unbearably awkward. Neither of them was able to speak of the tenderness Ian had shown her or the way she'd sobbed out her heartbreak in his arms. It was as if they mutually understood it had been an extraordinary situation that had no bearing on their inability to make their way past their individual pain. A relationship begun on such rocky ground held no promise, yet her heart ached, wishing for what she couldn't have.

She'd spent most of the drive staring out the window at the passing scenery, reliving each moment of the past week in her mind. A gentle snow had begun to fall, but the flakes were soft and fluffy and posed no threat. Maybe in time she'd be able to enjoy snow without the fear of freezing to death.

Ian cleared his throat as he pulled into the driveway of the chalet. The FBI had removed his vehicle and taken it in so forensics could do their work. He shut off the ignition and turned to Hope. "I know you were kidding back there about needing my help to wrap presents, and I do need to get back to the ranch, but if you want me to come in and help you get set up…"

His voice trailed off as she shook her head.

Much as it pained her, a clean break would be better. "I think I need some time alone to get my head together before Adam arrives with Emi."

He nodded. "Whatever you think is best. Let me know about setting up the live stream if you decide to do it."

Hope thought her heart might crack wide open if she sat there another moment. "I will. I'll talk to Steve about it." She opened the truck door, but before she stepped out, she turned back to him. "If I couldn't find the words to thank Nancy and her team, I don't know where I'll ever find the words to thank you." She managed a smile. "But I did work up a proposal to promote your veterans' center. I'll see that you get it. Thank you."

And goodbye.

Hope didn't say the last two words aloud, but she knew he heard them anyway.

She hopped down from the truck and ran for the front door without looking back, because she knew if she did, she wouldn't be able to stop herself from running and begging him to stay.

She opened the door to the chalet and was slapped with memories of being here with Ian. Images of him seated under the tree, tearing open the wrapping paper flashed through her mind.

He'd been on this journey with her every step of the way from the moment she'd hidden in his truck. She wouldn't have survived without him.

Guilt swamped her. She shouldn't have sent him away so abruptly. But what else could she have done? With her hand still on the doorknob, she recalled standing there with him and seeing the men installing explosives under the truck. He'd saved her from death then, just like he had so many times. She owed him her life.

Why couldn't she risk her heart?

Should she call him back?

Sadly, she pushed the door closed. No. He'd shown all too clearly that he was still wedded to his wife in memory if not in life.

Acknowledging that it was time for a new chapter in her life, Hope turned and walked into the room. She had a lot to do to ready the house for her daughter. The daughter who was alive despite her worst fears. Tucking her sadness about Ian into a corner of her heart, she shed her coat, deliberately leaving her phone in her pocket so she wouldn't be tempted to call him, and set to work rebuilding Christmas. Thanks to Steve, there was a veritable mountain of presents to rewrap. She lit the fire, put on some Christmas music and got started.

She'd barely made a dent in the rewrapping when she heard a noise at the door. Had Adam arrived early with Emi?

Had Ian come back for her?

The door opened, and Hope's heart lodged in her throat as a woman strode into the room.

"Hello, Hope. I'd say it's good to see you after all these years, but I doubt you feel the same."

Hope tried to speak, but it was as if a vise had closed around her neck. "Adrianna," she managed to croak. "I thought you—"

Adrianna's laugh chilled her to the bone. "Thought I was dead? That was such a magnificent crash, wasn't it? I was sorry I couldn't wait around to see your friends arrive to investigate."

"But…" Hope's heart thundered in her chest. "Your car. How?"

There was that laugh again. Hope shivered as Adrianna flicked a hand at her.

"You never did watch enough movies. It was just that old

brick-on-the-accelerator trick. I don't know if they'll ever figure it out. The car is pretty well toasted."

Hope struggled to focus on Adrianna's voice as reality hit with terrifying force. She was alone in this house with a woman who wanted her dead, and there was no Ian to rescue her this time.

Adam would be arriving with Emi, but the last thing she wanted was for her daughter to arrive to this. Her phone was in her coat pocket on the chair. She couldn't even try to call for help.

"Tsk, tsk. You're thinking too hard, Hope." Adrianna walked across the room and picked up one of the unwrapped presents. "Is this for Emi? You never did introduce me to your baby girl."

Hearing her daughter's name spoken from such evil lips terrified Hope. Knowing she had to find a way to take charge before Adam arrived with Emi, Hope found her voice. "Why would I have? You were never a part of my life after you left school."

"Was forced to leave, you mean."

The venom dripping from Adrianna's voice left no doubt in Hope's mind that this was all payback. "How long have you been planning this?"

"Since the day Steve had his little chat with the dean. He sounded so convincing. So innocent. As if he'd never had a part in any of it."

"You know he didn't. Steve doesn't play dirty." Hope had thought to distract Adrianna so she could make a run for the door, but her words had the opposite effect.

"You always did choose men of…honor." Adrianna sneered as she said the last word with such disdain that her smooth veneer cracked. "Speaking of men of honor, one of them will be paying the ultimate price today."

Hope's thoughts immediately flew to Ian, but Adrianna's next words corrected that thought.

"Too bad. Adam has such a nice family." She shrugged. "That's what he gets for playing hero and interfering in my plan."

For the first time Hope understood why guilt haunted Ian. She wasn't really to blame for whatever Adrianna was planning to do to Adam, but if she didn't find a way to stop it, she'd never forgive herself.

"What are you talking about?" Hope needed information so she could figure out a plan.

"Just a little explosion. A roadside accident." She smiled. "Don't worry. He won't feel a thing. It's your pain I want."

"Adam has done nothing to you."

Adrianna shrugged carelessly. "But he's driving your daughter. Your precious little girl. Steve's goddaughter."

Rage such as she'd never known filled Hope. "Leave my daughter out of this." She lunged at Adrianna.

"Not so fast, dear Hope."

Adrianna lifted her arm, and Hope felt the barrel of a gun press into her side.

"Don't push me too far or you won't live to see the grand finale."

Keeping the gun pointed at Hope, Adrianna picked up the remote and powered on the television, then navigated to a streaming channel. She whipped the scarf from around her neck and signaled to Hope to sit in the chair.

"If you cooperate, we'll watch it together," she promised as she bound Hope's arms behind her back and tied them around the back of the chair.

"Watch what?" Hope ground out the words, though her terrified heart already knew the answer.

Adrianna ignored her. "Steve will have to watch the replay— Oh wait, the hospital will be just as toasted as my car was." She gave another cavalier shrug. "I guess we'll have to enjoy it just the two of us. Too bad I forgot the popcorn."

* * *

The snow was picking up, and the easy drive from earlier wasn't as pleasant now. Ian was glad he had Nancy's truck as the wind kicked up and visibility lowered. He punched the button for the heater. It was cold inside too, without Hope's presence to warm his heart.

As he threaded his way through the crowded streets of Christmas Village, Ian replayed their conversations in his mind. Ever since he'd kissed her, his heart had been conflicted. He was weighted by grief and guilt over his failure to save his wife and child, but was it a life sentence? Hope and Emi had opened his heart in ways he'd never expected, made him feel things he didn't know he was capable of.

Hope had frozen him out after he'd kissed her, but what had he expected? That he could confess his failure as a husband and then have a woman whose husband had cheated on her open her arms and risk it happening all over again?

Snow beat against the windshield, but it was nothing compared to his whirling thoughts. Holding Hope in his arms, when she'd thought her world had ended, had shaken something loose in him, reminded him of how very fragile life could be, of what a gift it was. So now he wondered. What if this wasn't how it had to be? What if he could convince Hope that he had changed because of her, that he could acknowledge his mistakes and learn from them rather than wallow in the past?

He laughed sadly. That didn't sound very convincing even to his ears, but could he really just drive away without even trying? Did he really need to abandon a chance for happiness when it would cost hers also? Or was it possible that God was giving him another chance to redeem himself?

Ian wasn't certain of any answer but one—if he didn't go back, if he didn't at least try, he would never know the answers to any of those questions, and for the rest of his life he would regret losing a chance with Hope.

Before his brain could overrule his heart, he swung into a U-turn and headed back to the chalet.

There was a car in the driveway, but Ian didn't think it belonged to Adam. He'd never seen his friend drive anything this sporty. Concern gave way to fear as he tried to call Adam and got an "all circuits busy" response.

Ian drove past the house, pulled over down the street and headed back on foot. If there was trouble inside, which seemed increasingly likely, he didn't want to alert anyone. The front door stood slightly ajar, as if it hadn't been shut tightly and the wind had blown it open. He eased his way up the steps and silently stepped to the side of the door. He could hear the murmur of Hope's voice, and his heart eased, until he heard the clearly spoken response.

"Steve will have to watch the replay." There was a pause and then: "Oh wait, the hospital will be just as toasted as my car was." A longer pause and slight chuckle gave way to "I guess we'll have to enjoy it just the two of us."

The blood started pounding so hard in Ian's ears that he missed anything she said after *us*. That had to be Adrianna. Somehow his sister's team was wrong. She hadn't died in that crash. She was here to get Hope.

Ian strove for the mental calm he'd learned in the military. He focused his breathing and worked to formulate a plan. Much as he wanted to burst in and rescue Hope, he needed to know what was going on. Thinking first avoided casualties later.

He crept closer to the door and tried to see where Adrianna was. The sight of Hope bound to a chair struck terror in his heart, but at least that meant they weren't planning to go anywhere.

Adrianna was pacing, waving the remote at the television. He ducked just as she started to turn back.

"Adrianna, please," Hope begged. "Think about this. Emi is an innocent child. She has never brought harm to anyone. Your grievance is with me, with Steve. Please don't harm her or Adam."

The raw agony in Hope's plea tore through Ian's heart. He crouched beside the door, and as he tried to strategize, Adrianna's laughter reached him.

"I know," she replied to Hope. "That's why you are going to watch her die. See that outcropping? Keep your eyes focused on that. When Adam's car reaches it, and the bomb detonates, your life will be ruined...like mine was."

Ian's mind struggled to wrap itself around the pure evil that would murder an innocent. Suddenly the "all circuits busy" response made sense. Adrianna must have somehow jammed the signal. They'd underestimated the woman. Clearly the server they'd taken down hadn't been her only resource.

Ian waited until it sounded like Adrianna was facing away again, and he edged forward so he could peer in the opening. He could see the image on the screen, and fury gripped him. He knew exactly where she'd set that bomb, and there was no way Adam would be able to avoid it.

Ian fell to his knees and offered a prayer for guidance. Only God could help him combat such darkness. He knew in his heart what he had to do, but now he needed the courage to execute the difficult choice. He slowly backed away from the door, praying Adrianna wouldn't sense his movement.

Leaving Hope behind was the hardest struggle he'd ever faced, and it almost destroyed him, but as Ian thought about her reaction earlier when she'd thought Emi was dead, he knew it was the only choice. Hope would never forgive him if he chose her over Emi. If he let Emi die to save her life.

When he was a safe distance from the chalet, Ian broke into a run. He hopped in the truck and tried again to reach Adam, but the same "all circuits busy" message came up. His next call was to Nancy.

He breathed a sigh of relief when she came on the line.

"Hey brother. I thought you'd be happy spending time with Hope—"

Ian cut her off. "Adrianna is not dead. She currently has Hope tied to a chair in the chalet and she, or someone who works for her, has planted a bomb on the road Adam is driving."

"I'm putting you on speaker. The team is still here." Nancy's voice reflected the gravity of the situation.

Ian quickly explained what he'd just witnessed. His voice broke as he described leaving Hope. "I can't reach Adam. The circuits are jammed. But I know a shortcut through the mountains. I'm going to try to get there first, detonate it before he arrives. You need to get people to the hospital and clear it. Send another team to the chalet, but don't go in unless she's in imminent danger. Best I can tell, Adrianna plans to make her watch the blast and—" he could barely get the words out "—watch Emi die."

Ian already had the truck in motion by the time Nancy replied. "We'll do exactly that, and we'll keep trying to reach Adam. Keep in touch, Ian. Godspeed. I'm praying for you."

In his mind, Ian mapped the back route to the outcropping. If he pushed the truck as hard as he could, just maybe he could beat Adam to the narrow pass at the outcropping. Snow was falling harder, but he hoped that was to his advantage this time. Adam would drive more slowly given his precious cargo and the treacherous conditions. He glanced at the dashboard clock. Time was running out.

Chapter Twenty

Hope's eyes were burning from staring at the screen, but she couldn't tear her gaze away. She'd been tied to this chair for close to an hour now, and she'd been unable to come up with any way to stop Adrianna's madness and save her daughter's life. Why had she sent Ian away? If the two of them had been here together, they might have been able to overpower her.

Adrianna had made herself a cup of coffee and paced the room as she drank it, further frazzling Hope's nerves. She'd tried reasoning with her, bargaining with her, pleading for old time's sake, but nothing could get through to her.

Hope gave yet another tug on the silk scarf that bound her, and her heart leaped. This time she felt the material give.

Adrianna swung the gun loosely. "I don't know why you're even bothering to try to get away. It's too late for you to stop it now anyway. Based on his departure time, I'd say Adam should be arriving in about ten minutes now, give or take a little extra time for the weather."

"How can you be so heartless?" Hope cried in desperation. "You are someone's daughter. How would your mother feel if she were the one tied to this chair watching you in danger?"

Adrianna shook her head and gave a chuckle. "Poor example, Hope. My mother, as you may recall, was barely aware of my existence. Having a baby didn't fit into her life plan, so I was exiled to an elderly aunt. But nice try. I'm sure your daughter has been well loved in her short life."

Hope didn't know what to say. She prayed, as she had over and over for these past sixty minutes. And she tugged at the silk again. Because Adrianna was wrong. If she could get loose, she could call Adam and stop him.

She gave a final tug, and the scarf shredded. She waited for Adrianna's attention to turn to the screen again. Hope had noticed that it was the only thing that kept her focused. As Adrianna sipped her coffee and stepped closer to the screen. Hope leaped from her chair and ran for her phone.

Adrianna didn't seem to care. "It won't do any good, you know. I jammed the circuits. You won't get through."

Hope had to try anyway, hoping it was a lie, but a recording announcing "All circuits are busy. Please try your call later," echoed in her ear. She tried the state troopers next but got the same message.

"Ah, here they come now."

Hope didn't want to look, but she couldn't stop herself. She gazed up at the screen and watched the truck she recognized as Adam's slowly enter a deep bend before the narrow pass that would lead to the outcropping. Her heart was in her throat, and tears poured down her cheeks as she prayed over and over again for God to save her little girl.

"What the blazes?" Adrianna exploded in anger. "Who is that? What is he doing?"

Hope squinted at the screen, and the heart she didn't think could bear any more pain shattered all over again. "That's Ian," she whispered as she recognized Nancy's truck.

Ian, her hero, the man she had grown to love in such a short time, was driving his truck right at the outcropping. Somehow he'd discovered Adrianna's plan, and he was sacrificing his life to save Emi's. But it was too late. She couldn't watch.

Hope sank to the floor, her face buried in her hands as she heard the explosion blast through the speakers. She huddled into a ball and sobbed.

"This is the FBI," came a voice over a megaphone. "You are surrounded. Come out with your hands in the air."

Numb, Hope lifted her head. They were too late to save anyone, but if they at least caught Adrianna, she could never cause anyone else such devastation.

Adrianna was so mesmerized by the explosion on the screen that she didn't even seem to register the commands from outside. Trying not to draw her attention, Hope crawled for the door. One glance at the television had told her everything she didn't want to know. She couldn't bear to look at the blazing inferno that was consuming those she loved. All she could hope for was to escape this house so law enforcement could close in on Adrianna.

At the door, she knelt and raised her arms but put a finger to her lips hoping someone understood what she was doing. Once she reached the steps, she got to her feet, kept her hands in the air and ran toward safety.

Sobbing, she explained what had happened and where Adrianna was. A female agent escorted her to a car and offered to let her wait inside, but Hope shook her head. "I have to see her captured." Tears were streaming down her face as she whispered, "She killed the people I most love. I have to see her apprehended."

After what seemed an eternal wait as Hope shivered in the frigid air huddled within a blanket the agent had given her, Adrianna emerged from the house, hands cuffed behind her, escorted by multiple agents.

As they passed by Hope, Adrianna stopped short.

"So many stupid men. So many would-be heroes. What is it about you that inspires such wasted effort?" Adrianna spit the words at her.

Hope forced herself to look at the woman who had destroyed her life. "It isn't anything about me. It's who they are."

She could almost feel sorry for Adrianna that she didn't understand there were people in the world who were heroic by nature, who answered a call for help because they knew no other way to live. Men and woman who were not perfect, but who lived their lives as their Savior taught, people who were truly good at their very core. Men like Ian.

Once they took Adrianna away, Hope slid into the FBI car. She didn't know what she was waiting for, didn't care as time passed in a blur. She had nothing left.

After a while, a vehicle drew up behind her car, sirens blaring and lights flashing. It screeched to a halt, and the door flew open. Hope barely registered the noise until her door opened and she looked up into Nancy's face.

She burst into tears all over again. "I'm so sorry. It's all my fault. If it wasn't for me, Ian would still be alive." Her body convulsed in sobs and shivers.

Nancy nudged her across the seat and climbed in beside her. "What are you talking about?"

"Ian." Hope could barely speak his name. "He tried to save Emi, but they're both dead."

Nancy put a hand on each arm and twisted Hope toward her. "Didn't anyone tell you? They're not dead, Hope. Ian's not dead. Neither is Emi." She made a face. "My truck is toast, but Ian wasn't inside. He pushed it off the ledge into the pass to trigger the bomb. Adam was able to stop in time. He and Emi are fine." She shook Hope. "Do you hear me? They're alive."

Hope stared at Nancy in disbelief. She knew Nancy wouldn't lie to her, but having heard the explosion and seen the inferno, she was having a hard time wrapping her mind around it.

Nancy pulled her phone from her pocket and sent off a message. "Our tech people are working on restoring service, so fingers crossed this goes through."

Moments later, her phone rang. Nancy opened it, listened and handed the phone to Hope. "It's for you."

Hope accepted the phone gingerly, as if afraid it would explode in her hand. She lifted it to her head. "Hello?"

"Hope, it's me. I love you. Emi's safe. Adam is fine. We did it."

Hope broke into sobs. Her body heaved as it tried to accept his words.

"Hope? Are you there? Do you forgive me?"

Hope breathed deeply. "You're wrong, Ian. *We* didn't do it. *You* did. There's nothing to forgive. And… I love you too," She added in a whisper.

After speaking long enough to assure herself that this was real, and that both Ian and Emi would be coming home to her, Hope got out of the car and handed the phone to Nancy, who had discreetly given her privacy.

"Your brother is pretty amazing." She felt the smile break though her fears.

"I know you love him and all, but please don't tell him that too often. He'll grow unbearable."

Nancy was grinning while she spoke, so Hope laughed, and as the cold air hit her lungs she felt gloriously alive. "I have to warn you, I plan on spoiling him pretty shamelessly."

Chapter Twenty-One

"Mommy, come." Emi tugged at Hope's arm. "I want you to meet my friend Mia."

Hope allowed herself to be pulled along. She was excited too, looking forward to meeting Mia's mom. Though she and Isabelle had spoken several times since Emi returned, they'd yet to meet in person.

The past forty-eight hours had been filled with work as everyone switched their efforts from solving the ransomware attack to preparing the grand finale of Twelve Days 'til Christmas.

Already they'd live streamed from the tree lot and were currently presenting a video on reindeer rescue in preparation for the final two events: harnessing the reindeer to their sleigh for a busy night ahead and Ian's dad doing the traditional Christmas Eve Bible reading beside the fire.

As exciting as it all was though, Hope was ready for it to be over. She and Ian hadn't had a moment alone since Emi had returned, and she was getting more nervous by the minute. Had the words he'd blurted in a moment of euphoria really meant anything?

"Mommy!"

Hope smiled down at Emi. "Yes, dear?"

"You were daydreaming. This is my new friend, Mia, and her mama, Mrs. Isabelle."

Hope knew she was blushing as she looked up at Isabelle, who gave her a wink that hinted she knew exactly who Hope had been daydreaming about.

Hope crouched down to say hello to Mia and thank her for welcoming Emi to her home. Then, as the girls skipped off to watch the reindeer harnessing, she stood and turned to hug Isabelle. "Thank you for coming. Emi's been over the moon to introduce Mia to the reindeer, but I wanted to tell you in person how very much I appreciate you caring for my daughter."

Isabelle smiled and brushed off the thanks. "It wasn't so long ago that I was in your position, accepting help from strangers to protect a child. I was happy to help. It's what friends do, right?" She looked up at Adam, who gazed adoringly back at her before hugging her close.

"Right," he confirmed.

Isabelle glanced over Hope's shoulder and smiled. "We'll get together soon for a playdate and coffee, but why don't Adam and I go gather the reindeer girls and bring them inside? It's almost time for the reading, and I think there's someone here who's waiting for you."

Hope spun around and came face-to-face with Ian. "Hey." She smiled.

"Hey yourself."

As Adam and Isabelle left to get the girls, Ian reached for her hand. "I've missed you. Walk with me back to the house?"

Hope's heart filled as she nodded and clasped his hand in hers.

The ranch family was gathering on the porch and heading into the great room as Hope and Ian arrived. Chairs had been set up in circular rows around the fireplace, and friends and family quickly filled them. Emi and Mia found a place of honor at Poppa's feet, so Ian and Hope hung back, leaning against the wall.

"I know it's a busy night, but I was hoping to spend some time alone with you," he said softly. "Would you meet me after Emi is tucked in bed?"

Hope beamed at him. "She's going to be excited. It might be pretty late."

Ian bent and kissed her lightly. "I'll wait."

At the front of the room, his mother began to softly sing. "Silent night, holy night."

All around the room voices joined in.

Ian kept her hand tucked in his, and Hope let the joy of Christmas wash over her. "All is calm, all is bright."

Poppa's deep bass rang out. "Now all this was done, that it might be fulfilled which was spoken of the Lord by the prophet, saying, Behold, a virgin shall be with child, and shall bring forth a son, and they shall call his name Emmanuel... God with us."

As the service ended, and the tech staff posted a message of love from Steve to end the celebration, the crowd surged toward the table where treats had been spread.

Ian tugged Hope away into a quiet corner. "Penny for your thoughts?"

She stared at the floor and gathered her nerve. "I was thinking that in churches all around the world tonight, people will gather to celebrate the birth of a child who came to bring us forgiveness." She laced her fingers through his and gazed up at him. "Don't you think that if He could be born only to sacrifice and die for us, we can learn from that and forgive one another...and ourselves?"

She held his gaze as his fingers tightened around hers.

"I think we believe in a merciful God, a God of second chances..." He paused as his voice cracked. "A God who could bring two wounded souls together to find forgiveness and healing...and love."

* * *

Hours later, when the excitement had finally faded away, when Emi had finally stopped talking about reindeer and fallen asleep, when the house was quiet, Hope made her way down the stairs, praying that Ian was still waiting.

As she came around the turn in the stairs, she saw his tall, muscular frame standing by the window, silhouetted by the lights of the Christmas tree.

She sneaked up behind him and rested her head against his shoulder. "Waiting for someone?"

"Only the love of my life."

He turned, and Hope thought he would kiss her, but he reached for her coat, which lay on the arm of the chair. "You're going to need this."

"We're going somewhere?"

"For a walk in the snow."

She laughed. "I feel like we've done a lot of that."

"This is different. It's Christmas snow." He helped her into her jacket and wrapped a scarf around her neck. After donning his own coat, he led her out the front door.

As they stepped off the porch, Hope lifted her face to the snow. It was gentle, nothing at all like the blizzard that had brought them together.

"Where are we going?"

"It's a surprise." He winked, and her heart melted.

Ian led her around the back of the house and through a stretch of woods. She could see a glow in the distance. Puzzled, she cast a glance at him, but he was giving nothing away.

As they neared the edge of the forest, Ian stopped her. He unwrapped the scarf from her neck and turned it into a blindfold.

"Ian, I can't see."

"That's the point." He laughed. "Do you trust me?"

"With my life," she answered solemnly.

"Then come." He held her hand and led her slowly forward.

Unable to see, Hope focused on her other senses. She felt the tickle of the snow against her forehead, heard the crackling of a fire and smelled the sweet smoke mingling with the scent of evergreens in the fresh cold air. And she felt the security of Ian's hand holding hers.

Finally, he stopped. Standing close beside her, he slowly undid the knot in her scarf. As the wool fell away, Hope gasped. Before her stood a beautiful snow cave alight with Christmas lanterns.

"I built it just for us," Ian whispered as he led her toward the entrance. "For our own private Christmas. It won't last forever," he said, taking her into his arms, "but my love for you will. I want us to build a life together, Hope, a future to share."

Love flooded Hope's heart. She rested in his embrace as she gazed into his beloved face. "I haven't yet had a chance to thank you properly."

He started to speak, but she rested a finger over his lips. "I will thank God every day for the rest of my life for the gift of you, and I am thankful beyond words for everything you have done, have sacrificed for me."

She reached up on tiptoes and rested a hand on either side of his face. "But make no mistake about it, this is not about gratitude." She kissed him lightly. "This is because I love you with all my heart, and more than anything I want to build that life with you…forever." She leaned into his embrace and kissed him with all the love that was overflowing her heart.

* * * * *

Romantic Suspense

Danger. Passion. Drama.

Available Next Month

Colton's Last Resort Amber Leigh Williams
Arctic Pursuit Anna J. Stewart

....

Mistaken Identities Tara Taylor Quinn
Kind Her Katherine Garbera

....

LOVE INSPIRED
Hunted On The Trail Dana Mentink
Tracking The Missing Sami A. Abrams
Larger Print

....

LOVE INSPIRED
Texas Kidnapping Target Laura Scott
Alaskan Wilderness Peril Beth Carpenter

....

LOVE INSPIRED
Ambush On The Ranch Tina Wheeler
Cold Case Disappearance Shirley Jump

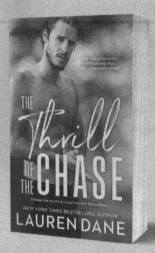
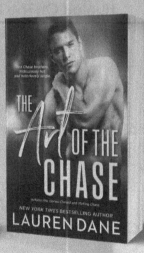

Subscribe and fall in love with a Mills & Boon series today!

You'll be among the first to read stories delivered to your door monthly and enjoy great savings.

WE
SIMPLY
LOVE
ROMANCE

MILLS & BOON